CRACKDOWN

Also by Christopher G. Moore

Novels in the Vincent Calvino crime fiction series

Spirit House o *Asia Hand* o *Zero Hour in Phnom Penh*
Comfort Zone o *The Big Weird* o *Cold Hit*
Minor Wife o *Pattaya 24/7* o *The Risk of Infidelity Index*
Paying Back Jack o *The Corruptionist* o *9 Gold Bullets*
Missing in Rangoon o *The Marriage Tree*

Other novels

A Killing Smile o *A Bewitching Smile* o *A Haunting Smile*
His Lordship's Arsenal o *Tokyo Joe* o *Red Sky Falling*
God of Darkness o *Chairs* o *Waiting for the Lady*
Gambling on Magic o *The Wisdom of Beer*

Non-fiction

Heart Talk o *The Vincent Calvino Reader's Guide*
The Cultural Detective o *Faking It in Bangkok*
Fear and Loathing in Bangkok o *The Age of Dis-Consent*

Anthologies

Bangkok Noir o *Phnom Penh Noir*
The Orwell Brigade

CRACKDOWN

A VINCENT CALVINO NOVEL

CHRISTOPHER G. MOORE

Heaven Lake Press

Distributed in Thailand by:
Asia Document Bureau Ltd.
P.O. Box 1029
Nana Post Office
Bangkok 10112 Thailand
Fax: (662) 260-4578
Web site: http://www.heavenlakepress.com
email: editorial@heavenlakepress.com

First published in Thailand
by Heaven Lake Press, an imprint
of Asia Document Bureau Ltd.
Printed in Thailand

Heaven Lake Press paperback edition 2015

Copyright © 2015 Christopher G. Moore

Illustrations: Colin Cotterill © 2014
Jacket design: K. Jiamsomboon
Author's photograph: Ralf Tooten © 2012

Publisher's note: This is a work of fiction. Names, characters, places and incidents either are the product of the author's imagination or are used fictitiously, and any resemblance to actual persons, living or dead, events, or locales is entirely coincidental.

ISBN 978-616-7503-32-5

For Steven B. Samuels

"Fiction is the lie through which we tell the truth."
—Albert Camus

ONE

"I never knew a man who had better motives for all the trouble he caused."—Graham Greene, *The Quiet American*

THE THAIS HAD an old saying about trouble and people. Keeping company with thugs leads to trouble, the saying went, but keeping company with the wise leads to good things. Over the course of his many years in Thailand, Vincent Calvino had learned there was a small problem with the saying: the locals couldn't explain what separated the thugs from the wise. That little puzzle was left for individual Thais to solve on their own.

Another proverb suggested they simply accept their elders' judgment on such matters, but Calvino, as a foreigner, didn't have a built-in vault of elders to draw on. When he was approached for private investigation work, Calvino had to decide on his own which side of the fence the potential client fell on. Sometimes he got it right; other times, tragically wrong. When things went pear-shaped, it always hit him that the truth had been in front of him all the time, only he hadn't seen it. He'd been stumbling toward a lamplight that turned out to be the kind where thugs gathered like dragonflies. When that happened, he always resolved to update his skills on lamplight analysis and thuggery detection.

Thugs, in Calvino's experience, shared certain qualities: self-righteousness, absence of doubt, greed, paranoia, love of guns and a history of using violence. Each lived like a frog within the security of his own individual coconut shell. But at least once in a while, the wise frog would look over the rim of his coconut shell in every direction. When he did, he would see that his comfy home sat on a forest floor littered with coconuts. The wise spoke of the futility of a frog defending any one shell. But their wise counsel always got lost in the noise of a world of trouble, a world left up to karma.

There was an even more defining characteristic of thugs, one Calvino had put his finger on early in the game. They always believed they could beat the odds, beat the house. They were doomed because no one ever beat the house, not really. Even with a gun.

The wise believed in the power of persuasion and reason. The wise smiled at the idea of someone trying indefinitely to coerce people through fear. Look at a world map, they would say, and color in the places where that belief was always being tested. The map is ablaze with the color of fear. Thugs hide out in every timeline, infect the corridors of power, whisper in the ear of those in the financial centers and approve the bonuses in big corporations.

Calvino knew that, like everyone, he had both elements in his character, and the struggle between the two invisible forces would inevitably play out, leaving him to defend the winner. Each new day was a choice between fear and reason. And many times the choice was blurred, confusing and difficult. No victory was ever decisive.

These were highly dangerous times for a troubled stranger to arrive at Calvino's door. All the lamp-lit places danced with freshly hatched dragonflies. The stranger's trouble always started with a woman. And a cynic would reply, "Doesn't it always?"

The subject of women came up any time two foreign men drank together in Bangkok. After Oliver Ballard had carried his luggage through the door of Calvino's condo, it was only a matter of time before they exchanged records of their victories and defeats, like a couple of soldiers of a bygone era. A battle-hardened veteran, Ballard had come to Thailand certain his luck would change, but his reminiscences soon turned to ambushes, wounds and bravery under fire.

Ballard, white cotton shirt sleeves rolled up above the wrists, belted tan slacks, barefoot, rattled the ice in his glass with his right hand as he rocked on his heels. He was a businessman in the logistics field and a transportation expert, or so he said. His work meant he was constantly relocating throughout the region. A hundred years earlier, Ballard would have been part of the tribe of "lost" people always on the move, stripped of nationality, birthright or allegiance. In the modern world he'd been refitted with worldly tastes for fashion and international jazz festivals and expensive hobbies like polo. Men like Ballard were no longer thought of as lost but envied for their positions inside the small community of global money men.

Standing beside his guest at the balcony window, Calvino listened as Ballard staggered through the war cemetery of his buried loves, blurry-eyed, shell-shocked, and no longer able to tell a windmill from an enemy combatant disguised in a bikini. By the time Ballard stopped to catch his breath, Calvino had him figured as one of those cavalry officers whose horse had been shot out from under him. He didn't have to limp for Calvino to know he'd taken a hard spill.

In Calvino's experience, when a man kicked down the door to his past, vermin tended to crawl out, but in Bangkok a visitor could always find someone to welcome the creatures home. For the moment Calvino was happy to be that someone. That night, as they shared the view of the city lights reflecting off the lake below, alarm bells were as far from his thoughts as Brooklyn was from Kansas.

Calvino had met Ballard a couple of years earlier at a jazz festival in Bali. Calvino's friend Colonel Pratt, a Thai policeman turned saxophone player, was on the bill as a novelty. Calvino had gone to Bali like any other tourist, believing that the sun, beach and local women, along with the music, would recharge his batteries, run dry from following the protests and demonstrations in Bangkok. Pratt hadn't had to twist his arm.

On the first day at the festival, Ballard had sat down at the hotel pool bar, ordered a rum and coke and watched a couple of young women take turns diving off the board and into the pool. Calvino, outfitted in sunglasses, swimming trunks and a Hawaiian shirt, had hardly noticed as the foreigner had taken the stool next to his. Then he wondered why the guy was staring at him.

"You're Eric Marienthal," Ballard said.

Calvino knew of the tenor sax player by that name.

With a smile he lowered his sunglasses, so Ballard could see his mistake, and responded,

"A sax player in New York once told me he learned all there was to know about the sax from Albert Einstein, who said, 'You have to learn the rules of the game. And then you have to play better than anyone else.'"

"Einstein, that famous Jewish relativity player," said Ballard.

"He mapped out the rules for universal improv," said Calvino, watching one of the women climb out of the pool, water dripping from her body as she padded back to the diving board.

It was Ballard's turn to smile.

"Nice eye candy," he said, as he waved at the young woman on the diving board.

She looked Ballard's way but pretended not to notice him.

"She didn't see you," said Calvino.

Ballard shrugged and looked out at the sea.

"That's the story of my life. Women either ignore me or they obsess over my minor flaws. Not that I don't have a few. It doesn't matter if they're young, old, big or small, too poor or too crazy. I've got a Walmart warehouse filled with rejected merchandise."

Ballard and Pratt, when they met soon after that, had gotten along well immediately as Ballard had a Google-like command of modern jazz trivia and a couple of unusual theories about modern women. The three had struck up a friendship over the course of the three-day festival. At the end of the festival Calvino told Ballard that if he ever passed through Bangkok, he should look him up. It had been a casual invitation, the kind no one expects someone known for just three days to redeem.

Calvino had been wrong about Ballard from the start. As they traded war stories that first night in Bangkok, Calvino wondered if the Bali sun and beach had dulled his judgment when he'd befriended the man. He reminded himself that he had been wrong about many things in the past and buckled down to the fact that he now had an unexpected houseguest he hardly knew.

Ballard planned to stay on for four more nights before moving on to London. The following morning, Calvino could just arm Ballard with a key and plastic access card to get him into the building, and then continue his usual routines as if Ballard weren't in residence. It seemed that Ballard had a schedule of business appointments and wouldn't need babysitting, which was a relief.

But on Ballard's first night Calvino would play the good host. They went out early for dinner. After Calvino paid the bill, he could think of no good excuse to leave Ballard to explore the streets and the bars alone. They would soon be forced to switch off their neon and interior lights in any case. Maybe Ballard was right; in a few days the curfew would end, the military would recede to the shadows, and the girls and the bars would welcome the tourists with open arms, as if it had all been a collective nightmare they'd woken up from.

They left the restaurant and walked up and down Soi Cowboy. By then it was half an hour before curfew and they found few punters on the Soi. The bargirls, discouraged, talked among themselves in front of the bars, avoiding eye contact, as if a shame greater than commercial sex had fallen upon them and made off without paying.

"It's as if we're invisible," said Ballard. "Remember the hotel swimming pool in Bali? How the girl on the diving board looked through me like I wasn't there?"

"How could I forget her? But this isn't Bali. The mood on the Soi has changed since the coup," said Calvino. "The police will be around soon to enforce the curfew."

"That one looks defeated, but it'll pass," Ballard said as they faced a girl in an orange bikini who stared off into space.

"People adjust to their new reality quickly," said Calvino as they walked on. "They accept that they have to read from a different script, especially when those running the show give them no choice."

"You take me, okay?" said another bargirl, her large black eyes wild with urgency as she grabbed Ballard. "Na, na, na..." she added, the way a child softly pleads with a parent who has absolute power over her life.

"Desperation is not the way to close a deal," Ballard said, untangling himself from her grasp. "Either they ignore you," he said to Calvino, "or they try to inject themselves into your bloodstream. I can't figure out which of the two possibilities is the least worse."

He sounded frustrated, like a man whose humor tank was running on empty. There was something a little sad and defeated about the Ballard who had shown up in Bangkok.

They walked to the Asoke end of Soi Cowboy. Traffic was light on Asoke. They passed the worried, self-absorbed faces of more bargirls clad either in bikinis or in erotic showgirl outfits. The young women looked at their watches and played with their cell phones, killing time. Unless a customer offered an all-night buyout soon, they'd have no choice but to change back into street clothes and hurry back to their rooms. No after-hours second chance at a nightclub like the Thermae or one of the hundreds of small boltholes where customers had once drunk deep into the night and waited for the right woman to walk in.

The Soi Cowboy bargirls recognized the kind of man who came to the Soi weighed down with baggage. Who could have guessed that a man's history could be that heavy? Such men left the Soi alone because they hadn't drunk enough to find the courage to add more to their load. Ballard was such a man.

On both sides of Cowboy, rows of bargirls sized up each other and all passersby. In Ballard and Calvino they saw two middle-aged men who'd lost their appetite for a pre-curfew snack. The girls relied on hungry men, unburdened by their past, whose voracious appetites made them gorge and pay the cost. Ballard and Calvino stepped away from the Soi like light eaters, feeling the wrong kind of heat.

On the taxi ride back to the condo, Calvino listened as Ballard told him about a strange business in London, some time after Bali. He'd had an affair with a woman named Christina Tangier, an art school dropout from Essex who'd become an escort service girl. She'd told him a good story, all about how she had a plan to become a world-famous conceptual artist. Chelsea Monroe—her real name—had studied photography and multimedia at Wimbledon College of Arts in London, but she'd left that behind to sit in an Occupy London tent. Of course, she soon ran out of money. She decided to fund her lifestyle in a new way so she could carry on with her class project, even though she was no longer a student. Over time she had become "Christina Tangier," earning three thousand pounds a shot as an escort.

"That's a lot of money," said Calvino.

"She wasn't like other high-end escorts."

"What made her special?" asked Calvino.

"It wasn't just me. She eventually claimed to have slept with 284 paying clients over two years. I don't know which number I was in the overall total, but I know the number she gave me."

"What number was that?"

"That's getting ahead of the story," said Ballard. "From the start I knew she was gathering material for an exhibition. I took her for one of those arty-farty conceptual artists who live in a dream world. With a body like hers, I didn't ask her for details, which of course was stupid and reckless. We spent four crazy days in bed. One morning I woke up and found out what she meant by conceptual art, and I booted her out. Christina looked at me and smiled. There was none of that desperation we saw on Soi Cowboy tonight. I was cutting her loose and she didn't scream, threaten or struggle. She just got dressed and walked out the door carrying a teddy bear."

"What was she doing with a teddy bear?"

"Again, that's getting ahead of the story," said Ballard. "Anyway, she'd taken me completely by surprise."

"She pulled a gun?" asked Calvino.

Ballard shook his head.

"I could have dealt with that, but she told me she'd secretly snapped a series of pictures of me, sleeping. Nude. With a teddy bear."

Calvino shook his head, laughing.

"You're joking."

"She'd photographed dozens of sleeping men with the same fucking teddy bear. Out of the 284 clients, she photographed seventy-eight of us with the bear. From those photographs she selected twenty-nine for her exhibition. She colorized them."

"Paint by numbers," said Calvino.

Ballard shook his head. "No. She used Lucian Freud as her teacher. You know, the English artist. She blew them into one-meter-high portraits and painted them."

"With a teddy bear?" Calvno slowly shook his head. "Even by Bangkok standards, that's weird."

"Tell me. I watched her put an old teddy bear next to my head, next to my stomach, my legs and next to my dick. She said the teddy bear was more than seventy years old and had a history. It was slightly creepy. And it had this smell. Like something stored in an attic. She said Lucian Freud had painted a nude male with a rat on his thigh. Before each session he and the model got the rat drunk and it passed out, so Freud could position its tail near the model's penis."

"I thought I'd heard every story about sexual kinks," said Calvino. "You're making this up, right?"

"I swear it's all true. There's more. She called the exhibition *Crackdown: Teddy Occupies the 1%*. Catchy title. Good timing. I forgot to mention that she dressed the teddy bear in a tailored dinner jacket with a red bow tie and cummerbund. Remember she painted the photos. The red is really red. She put a black top hat on its head. Some of the 'Elite Johns' had the teddy with the top hat ramrod straight, with some the bear had a raffish look, with the top hat cocked to one side, and in one case the hat was pushed forward, covering the eyebrows—if a teddy bear had eyebrows, that is.

"The exhibition opened in London. You'd think, so what? Who cares? There are thousands of openings and galleries there, and ninety-nine percent of the work and artists disappear like rocks thrown in the sea. Who knows why Christina Tangier's exhibition didn't disappear without a trace? Fate? Who knows why the art critics were bowled over by it? One wrote that she'd made an artistic contribution equivalent to the impact of Thomas Piketty, that French guy. That was just the start. She was compared to Lucian Freud, of course, but also Madame Bovary, Amy Winehouse, Russell Brand and Camille Paglia.

"Stories about *Crackdown: Teddy Occupies the 1%* were suddenly everywhere. The social media went nuts over it. You must have heard about it." He waited for Calvino to say something.

"I might've heard something," Calvino said, trying to recall some fragment of memory. "We have enough weird here it squeezes out the foreign weird."

"Believe me," said Ballard. "It was big. One critic called it Paddington Bear porno for the digital age. A series of painted photos of fat and seedy billionaire Christopher Robins. She became an instant celebrity, an underground hero, queen of the Occupy movement. I can't believe you didn't hear about it."

Calvino shrugged. "I don't follow the art scene."

"It's more than art. She dropped economic, political and social bombs. She was everywhere on social media—Elite John Number 1 through Elite John Number 29. "

"Why did she choose the number 29?" asked Calvino.

"She keeps changing her story. She said it was a number some fortuneteller gave her. She told another interviewer it was in memory of 1929 and the start of the Great Depression. By then she had a professional publicist who coached her on what to say.

"Then there was a *New Yorker* piece about how Christina, I remember the quote: 'Christina had curated a village of the damned, a slaughterhouse of the super-elites, exposing their fleshy, ugly bodies as if inviting people into the abattoir that capitalism had created.' He went on to write there was nothing pornographic about any of the men. I'll quote again, 'These high rollers had been stripped to display their slack, flappy bodies, immobile and soft, with the teddy bear's paw reaching toward their penises.' "

"Very Freudian," said Calvino.

"Very Lucian Freudian, with a teddy bear's paw instead of a live rat's tail."

"I mean Freudian that you memorized those quotes."

"I'm part of it."

"Which number were you?" asked Calvino.

"Elite John Number 22. She had seven more Elite Johns after me before she launched her exhibition. Six months later it opened at a gallery in New York. More rave reviews. The photos sold out. By now Christina was a mega-celebrity. She was getting rich bashing the rich. Ironic, right? And me? My photo currently hangs on the wall of a Soho loft owned by an investment banker who must have lit a candle to thank whatever god he believed in that it wasn't him with a teddy leaning near his pecker.

"Once the New York exhibition took off, I was ruined. The whole thing went even more viral online. You might have missed but believe me most people didn't. Copycat exhibitions sprung up all over the world. But Christina's was the first. She was a legend. Her painted Elite John photographs were reproduced on shopping bags, T-shirts and bikini bottoms. Every hooker in New York and London wore them. I officially became Sleazeball Number 22.

"It was only a matter of time before my associates found out. Basically she fucked up my life. At that point I happened to be flying to Cambodia on business. Now I'm in Bangkok, like a million other fuckups trying to figure out what to do next."

"Sorry I missed it," Calvino said, not certain what to say next. "So tell me who else showed up in her exhibit? Bill Gates? Warren Buffet?"

"No. I was her token American. London is a playground. She had Russian oligarchs, Chinese billionaires, Arab sheikhs, a couple of South American drug cartel bosses... It didn't take long for each of them to be outed. Their shills showed up at the London exhibition and would have bought every original photo. Christina told them to fuck off and took the exhibition to New York. By then the prices had tripled and she was selling them to collectors. She knew the shills would destroy her work. One of the English papers called it one of the most brilliant blackmail scams in history, but that was wrong. She only used their bids to raise the prices in New York. Being an elite hooker, she must have picked up some financial skills from her investment banker clients."

"How does she manage to stay alive after that double-cross?" asked Calvino.

"She has three ex-special forces guys as bodyguards, and she never stays in one place long. Someone in a federal witness protection program has more freedom. She's famous, and she has a book and a film deal too, but she can never walk down a street like a normal person again. That's a high price, but not as high as the price I'm paying. You have no idea what it's like to be romantically linked to a famous woman."

"Her name doesn't ring a bell," said Calvino.

Ballard sighed and slumped back in his seat.

"I was involved with a famous woman," said Calvino. He'd kept a ring of secrecy around his relationship with Marley. Ballard who'd spilled his guts out about his relationship with a woman who became famous. It was like the false intimacy of a stranger next to you on a long-haul flight. You can tell them everything because you'll likely never see them again.

Ballard came back to life.

"Seriously?"

"Not a celebrity like Christina Tangier but someone internationally well-known."

"Not a hooker?"

"No, she's a mathematician named Dr. Marley Solberg."

"She sounds seriously smart," Ballard said with a nod, conveying the impression of making a mental note to Google the name later.

"She's a genius."

Ballard pursed his lips, pausing for a moment.

"I can see the problem—'Boy from Brooklyn turned Bangkok PI romantically involved with famed math genius' didn't compute."

"It was a little more complicated than that, but as a quick and dirty summary, that isn't wrong."

"Calvino, she taught you a lesson, the same lesson Christina taught me. A famous woman doesn't need a man. She doesn't even want a man," said Ballard. "Except, in Christina's case, as a bodyguard."

Ballard's bitterness was apparent in his voice. Whenever Calvino thought of Marley, it wasn't with bitterness but longing and regret. During their taxi ride together the two men had discovered an unexpected bond. Both of them had fallen for a woman who had turned out to be famous. Though their individual routes to fame couldn't have been more different, the outcomes had been comparable. For the first time Calvino thought that Ballard had showed up in Bangkok at an opportune time. If there was someone to distract him from the coup, it might be Elite John Number 22. Calvino worked over in his mind what Ballard had said about a famous woman not needing or wanting a man and wondered if it described Marley Solberg.

Back in the condo, Calvino pulled out *On a Mission* by the American saxophonist Eric Darius and put it on continuous play.

"I'm going for a swim," he announced.

He needed to wash away the Soi Cowboy gloom and the bargirls' fear before heading to bed, and more than that, to reflect on Ballard's story about Christina, her camera, the teddy bear in London and the exhibitions in London and New York City.

"You know where to find the single-malt."

He then carted his laptop computer to the seventh-floor pool area, where after a quick dip he Googled "Christina, New York, conceptual artist, Number 22." He clicked on images and scrolled through a dozen photographs of sleeping nude men with a teddy bear. It was plain to see that in a state of sleep men's faces become more vulnerable, innocent and childlike, and Ballard's was no exception.

The presence of the fluffy bear, with the red bow tie around its neck, cummerbund around its pear-shaped waist, large black-glass eyes and furry snout, added a dreamlike quality to the portraits. At first none of the articles, essays or blogs mentioned Ballard or the other "models" by name. That dam had broken when a Russian oligarch's ex-wife exposed him—for a second time. Within two weeks all of the men had been identified. The commentators concluded that they were, despite their wealth, ordinary men when stripped naked and representative of all men in the state of unconsciousness. Their heads resting on a pillow, hair messy, lips slack, eyelids pulled down like Chinese shophouse shutters, they lay on one side facing the camera, feet caught in a tangle of sheets like a Roman emperor's vestment hastily discarded, with a teddy bear as their companion on their dreamland journey.

Fifty minutes later Calvino closed his laptop and headed back. He walked into the sitting room, his hair damp from the shower, and poured himself a drink.

"I've been trying to figure out if this fits the definition of conceptual art," Ballard said, staring at a framed picture on the wall.

Calvino wasn't sure if Ballard was joking.

"It's an old map," he said, moving alongside Ballard.

Ballard touched his glass to Calvino's, registering the high-pitched crystal ping.

"A client gave it to me."

That statement was true as far as it went, and he hoped the explanation would suffice. Ballard nodded.

"From the look of it, I'd say your client wasn't Michelin."

He flashed his deal-closing smile, the kind Christina's photos never captured.

"The client was also a good friend," said Calvino.

"That's the best kind. Like my good friends in Cambodia."

"Doing business in Phnom Penh means good connections," said Calvino. "Good friends almost never have the right ones."

" 'Almost' is the key word. What you really want is my Cambodia story, right?"

"Only if it tops the story about Christina."

Ballard explained that in Phnom Penh he had brokered the sale of an oil tanker for $9.3 million and walked away with a nice commission. He'd had some last-minute luck with a Chinese buyer who had been blissfully unaware of Ballard's sudden fame in art circles, or the deal might have gone bad, and his good fortune had held. Now he was riding high in the saddle again.

"I have my fresh-start money. I've got a few matters to finish, and then I'm a free man."

"How are you going to enjoy that freedom?" asked Calvino.

"I'm working on that," he said. "This map... Was the artist on drugs, insane or just trying to fuck with you?"

Calvino rarely had houseguests, and when he did, none showed much interest in the artwork on the walls. He'd kept to himself the story of how Dr. Marley Solberg had given him a rare handmade map of the ancient world, along with the logistics of how a Japanese-Canadian mathematician who lived in Bangkok had acted as a map messenger. Marley Solberg had bought it at an auction in London. She had made the arrangements with Yoshi Nagata without involving Calvino.

"It's a fifteenth-century Italian reproduction of Al-Idrisi's *Tabula Rogeriana, 1154*," said Calvino.

"I missed that. Can you explain it to me in English?"

"Some say the original hand-drawn map is the first real map of the world. Ancient maps recorded Bible stories, myths and legends. The Greeks introduced geometry and mathematics, but Al-Idrisi drafted the first modern map."

"Al... what?"

Ballard looked at the bottom of his empty glass and glanced up at the map again.

"Al-Idrisi."

"An Arab made this?"

"A tailor on the Lower East Side of Manhattan. The kind of place an Upper East Side man wouldn't know," said Calvino.

"I get it."

"Get what?"

"How early terrorists didn't know much about the world back then."

Ballard scratched his chin and leaned closer to the framed map.

"Is it an original?"

"An original fifteenth-century reproduction, yes."

"When was the original 'original' made?"

"That was 1154, around the time of the Crusades. From the Arab point of view, our ancestors were the terrorists. You are looking at the first map showing Africa, East Asia and the Indian Ocean. At the time it was state of the art. Ships sailed and trade caravans traveled overland using Al-Idrisi's map.

"This Michelin-type reality lasted for about three hundred years. Then in 1492 everything changed. He'd left out what no one had known about until then: North and South America. Not that Columbus knew either. He thought he'd discovered another route to Asia. Al-Idrisi's map is a reminder that our reality lasts only until a new reality reveals the old one to have been an illusion."

"My sister's kid has autism. He draws maps that look like this. He gave me one once for Christmas. Maybe I should frame it and stick it on the wall. It'd be a conversation piece. That much I'll grant you."

He leaned over, picked up the whiskey bottle and refilled his glass.

"Though it might drive a man to drink too much," Ballard added. "So, when you look at this, what do you think?"

"Boundaries," said Calvino. "The ones that stop us cold, and the ones we breach to see what's on the other side."

Christina, the high-society hooker-cum-conceptual artist, had crossed some personal boundaries, taking an artistic crowd to the private place where the one percent lay exposed, cuddling a stuffed toy.

"Can't disagree," said Ballard. "Every map has a different set of boundaries. No-go zones. I once saw a map state by state of the highest-paid public officials in the States. They were all football or basketball coaches. Millions of public officials, and it's the coaches who are on the money map. When I saw that map, something snapped inside me. Broke. I saw that cash is just another boundary, and you could see who was rewarded and who was left on the bench. When a man sees that on a map, it does something to him."

"A good map always gets you thinking," said Calvino.

"And why not?" Ballard said. "One age looks back at an earlier time and tells itself that what people used to believe was stupid. And they think they've got it all figured out. After them, no one will ever have a better map of boundaries."

"That's why Marley wanted me to have this map."

"Marley? Isn't that the name of the famous mathematician you mentioned in the taxi?"

"The same woman."

"She gave you a valuable ancient map? All I got out of my brush with fame was a public exhibition of my dick next to a teddy bear."

"Life's not fair," said Calvino.

"You Italians have got flair. I didn't even get a T-shirt."

Calvino liked Ballard's mental agility, his ability to reflect on what had happened to him. It was as if he had no ego or opinions he cared enough about to fight for. Likely it served him well in selling old oil tankers to Chinese traders. He seemed to be working through a crisis and coming out the other end a better man for it.

"What kind of case did you handle for Marley? If you don't mind my asking."

"A missing person case."

"She must have been happy when you found who she was looking for."

"Not really."

"What happened?" Ballard said, looking over his glass at Calvino.

"A murder, another murder, a cover-up. Bangkok has its murderous dark side, but what place doesn't?" asked Calvino. "It's the art of the cover-up that makes Bangkok unique."

That made Ballard smile, and he pivoted to the sofa, lay down and with arms outstretched eyed the map on the wall again. He retracted his right arm to return the glass to his lips.

"Do you keep in touch, Marley and you?"

"I hear from her sometimes. What do you hear from Christina?"

Ballard tilted his head to the side.

"The bitch. I hope one of those Russians or Colombians finds her unguarded for a minute and half. Bam."

"Of course you're not bitter," said Calvino.

"Why would I be bitter? She only ruined my life."

Ballard flicked his hand in a gesture of dismissal. That she was worth no further discussion had been transmitted with precision.

Turning his attention back to the map, Ballard searched his memory for associations. What had first appeared like a child's misconception of things, mistakes in spatial arrangements, was now evoking something more down to earth.

"If you squint like this... Look at me, Vinny. Yeah, like that. Now look at the map."

"It's blurry."

"No, it looks like a butcher's block that's taken a burst of .20-cal rounds. And a couple of lucky .50-cal shots."

Calvino considered it through Ballard's eyes and thought he had a point. For centuries people had stared at a lie that looked like a shooter's target and believed it to be true. The consensus of truth had masked an illusion.

"People can't get enough of mapping the world," said Calvino.

He thought of Marley's words about how imagined places are an approximation, an average of reality, with most of the details stripped away. The history of maps was the history of the stripping process—what to take away, what to emphasize, what to underplay. Maps archived the human imagination's take on the reality of space and the boundaries between spaces. The reality show needed a stage on which to mount its performance. But fake maps, like fake performances, left an audience stranded in a fantasy land of make believe.

"Yeah, Google Cars, GPS, satellite photographs. We won't be making this Arab's mistakes again."

"The funny thing is Al-Idrisi in 1154 thought the same thing. He thought that he'd discovered every detail of the world, and that his *Tabula Rogeriana* would last forever."

"Nothing lasts forever," said Ballard.

"Including painted photos of nude men next to a teddy bear."

"I don't know about you, but I'm okay with what I know. About relationships, governments, money. And people. I hear what you're saying. I get it. Be on the lookout for a Christopher Columbus wild card. When the wild card's played, you see where you went wrong. Now," Ballard said, shifting his gaze back to the wall, "how much is that map worth?"

"In terms of describing the reality of our world, it's worthless. As an ancient testament to three hundred years of ignorance, it's invaluable."

"Give me a number, Vincent. I'm a businessman. I can't think without a number in my head."

"Try a mid-six figure amount."

"What currency?"

"Pounds sterling," Calvino said with a smile.

Marley had bought it at Sotheby's in London. Calvino had found a record of the sale online. The fact that the information was still there to be found meant that Marley hadn't stopped him from discovering the price.

"A gay New York investment banker paid Christina's gallery in Soho about the same amount for the original signed, a painted photo of me in the style of Lucien Freud hugging a fucking Mr. Teddy Bear. Who knows what it'll be worth in the future? But I got nothing out of it. After a losing deal like that, a businessman needs upbeat, positive people around him, who believe the future will be better than the past."

"How's that going, finding that kind of person?"

"Even after a coup people like that keep believing in the future. Someone who's powerful will play a future wild card," said Ballard. He shrugged. "A coup can be a good thing for someone like me. Chances are good that someone on the losing side with plenty of assets wants to liquidate and get out while he can. That's where I come in. And that's what I want to talk to you about."

"What's this?"

"People who might want to lighten up on their assets. After all, you got dumped. I got dumped. At least you have something to show for it. Sell the map. Forget her. Like you said in the taxi, famous women don't need us. What I need from you is some help. Maybe an introduction or two."

He fished in his pants pocket and handed Calvino a list. Calvino glanced at the familiar family names of well-known businessmen, politicians, senior government officials and their wives and children. He folded up the list and handed it back to Ballard.

"What do you think?"

Calvino returned his gaze to the map.

"I didn't take you for a vulture."

"If it's not me, it'll be someone else. And I won't cheat them."

"I can't help," said Calvino.

Ballard saw a man he couldn't buy.

"No hard feelings," he said. "Why don't I take you to dinner while I'm here at a restaurant I like near the Oriental Hotel? And you can tell me the story of how a private eye in Bangkok helped a famous woman like Marley Solberg enough for her to give him a priceless map.

"Often the backstory of a work of art is as important as the object itself, wouldn't you agree? Works of art come from inspiration. It's said that Edvard Munch was inspired to paint *The Scream* after witnessing blood-red clouds at sunset. And Grant Wood used his sister and his dentist in *American Gothic* to paint the farmer and his daughter. With your map, the story of the mapmaker may be lost in time, but the story of the famous mathematician buying it for a private investigator in Bangkok excites my curiosity."

That's how the conversation ended, abruptly and without any clear demarcation of the boundary between Ballard's business and personal life. As with most strangers, the parts of the story Calvino knew only made the unknown parts more intriguing. But life was too short to set off and cross every boundary line, and Calvino had a feeling that once Ballard left, he wouldn't hear from him again. Ballard had wanted something and needed Calvino's help to get it. Having failed, he would cut his losses and move on.

Calvino lay back in his bed, gazing through the window at the curfew-darkened skyline of Bangkok. He hadn't thought of Ballard as a man driven by obsessions. The way Ballard had focused on the framed map caused Calvino to wonder if his houseguest had an art connoisseur's eye. A lover of jazz who brokered ship deals: such a man might have an eclectic range of interests. But Ballard's interest in the map extended beyond the artifact to the person who had given it to Calvino. What story could Calvino possibility tell to someone like Ballard about Marley Solberg? They'd been mismatched. She was young, wealthy, a genius, and he was a middle-aged ex-lawyer, a private investigator who handled small-time expat cases that made him neither rich nor famous. He was another face in the Bangkok crowd; she was a mathematical superstar. Her photograph had appeared in the *Wall Street Journal, Wired* and *Forbes,* and her papers were published in the top journals. Ballard was right. He'd been out of his league with her.

She'd come into his life as a client. But no one, especially Ballard, would buy a story that a mere client would give him a thank-you worth a small fortune. Ballard must have seen there had to be something else to it, and there was. As with all good stories, understanding the power and force of the tale wasn't possible without knowing the pain behind it. The forced mass exodus of the Rohingya people from Burma had deeply affected Marley—the wanton cruelty and brutality at every step of their exodus, from their burnt-out villages to overcrowded boats and jungle detention camps, and the sale of many of them into slavery along the way. She'd created an underground network to smuggle some Rohingya out of Thailand. By the time she'd hired Calvino, Marley had experienced her own personal nightmare, one that lay beyond her control. Calvino knew that there is no grief to compare with that of a mother who loses her child. He had been beside her as she held on through that period of darkness. When a man and a woman share such a journey, they are fused together, bonded in the fire of human suffering.

As Calvino had stood before the map with Ballard, his mind had been pulled back to his last night with Marley, on her yacht, how he'd felt her breath on his neck in the dark stateroom as she'd arched her spine, moaned, her nails in his back, then let her hands go limp and slide down his sides. Afterwards, they had lain curled together on the sofa. In those minutes Calvino had felt closer to her than he'd ever felt with another human being. They hadn't spoken, nor could he have produced any words for the feelings that flooded through him.

The memory of that night had much to do with its location, sobriety, mood, perfume and music, but above all the newness of a beautiful body that remained a largely unexplored terrain. In the stateroom of Marley's yacht, all of those elements had lined up. The two had torn each other's clothes off and soon extinguished the world outside, clinging to each other as if to brace for a headlong fall into the void. The world had vanished, as if magically forgotten, shed like a skin, and two warm-blooded animals had sealed themselves together inside a new skin. The sadness of knowing that the transition was only momentary had made them all the more desperate. Afterward, she had put a finger to his lips, knowing he wanted to protest the loss.

"There's so much you want to say, and so much more than you ever could say," she had said. "More to say than would be possible in a hundred lifetimes."

She had paused a few seconds, letting the motion of the yacht fill the silence. When that moment had passed, she had re-emerged as her usual self, saying, "That was like discovering an unexpected, perfect and beautiful proof of $P=NP$. Thank you." Marley had begun her descent back to the world of algorithms and mathematical proofs, her home base. Her touch was once again like a pen stroke on a whiteboard. They no longer shared a common skin, and the separation came as a shock to him.

"What's this beautiful proof you worked out?" he'd asked.

"An entanglement between opposites."

"You mean the two of us?"

He'd felt her kiss on his neck.

"No, not about you and me. We aren't opposites."

"And we're still entangled," Calvino had said, tightening his leg around her thigh.

But the mood for playfulness had already passed. Marley had raised herself, leaned over and picked up her glass of wine.

"Anger and violence occupy the same orbit as desire and pleasure. There's an immense gravity that attracts them. Their orbits aren't stable. It's only a matter of time before they collide. And when they do, they annihilate each other."

"After they're destroyed, then what?"

"Peace. Silence. Like the moment we just had."

"But you're not in that space now. You're upset."

She had shaken her head.

"I've never been more calm. Thank you for that."

"You're still grieving the loss of your child. I can help you, but you have to want me to."

"A man gave an order to firebomb the refugee camp. I want him to experience my feeling of loss, not just for my child but for those who died in the camp. I know who it was. It would be so easy to have him killed. But that would be stupid. He'd be given a hero's funeral. He'd be remembered with honor, and not as the man who wiped out a refugee village in the North and trafficked Rohingya in the South. I want to take away what he treasures most—his reputation, his status, his identity. I want to strip him of his general's uniform, his rank and medals, and his friends. Do you still want to help me?"

True to her word, Marley had shared the General's Twitter messages with his minor wife, his two *giks* and his wife. What had surprised Marley was that the exposure, while causing the wife a public humiliation, hadn't ruined her life. She had been married not to the man but to his position and status, and that hadn't changed. It had been a valuable lesson for Marley.

A couple of months after that last night on the yacht, it was clear that Marley wasn't coming back. Calvino stopped waiting to hear from her. She'd really gone and he started to come to terms with that fact. He'd returned to those neon lit casinos where love was for sale and pulled the lever but never hit a jackpot.

This wasn't a story to share with Ballard over dinner. Their love had become a story of loss, and neither Ballard nor anyone else wanted to hear such a tale. What Ballard wanted to hear was how Marley was another famous woman like Christina who had done him wrong. The map she'd given to Calvino had simply raised a question mark about the nature of the wrong.

Ballard's last words that night had challenged Calvino to explain what extraordinary help he'd extended to Marley. Ballard had started with the wrong assumption. It wasn't about his private investigator services. The ancient map had another meaning for Marley. And if he studied the map long and hard enough, he might find a hidden passage that would take him back to their time together in the dark stateroom of her yacht.

TWO

"As we grow older, we no longer know whom to awaken, the living or the dead."—Louis-Ferdinand Céline, *Journey to the End of the Night*

AUBURN-BROWN HAIR dye bubbled along the coils of Alan Osborne's thinning white locks. In the dim light the effect was not unlike a healthy smear of African lion dung applied as a young man's rite of passage, the final purification ceremony. Osborne wore thin plastic gloves, and the blue veins running along his wrists looked like the excited jellyfish innards on a screensaver. As he passed from the bathroom into the bedroom, his eye caught movement on the computer screen, which showed live shots from a number of CCTV cameras positioned outside his house.

Osborne stopped, leaned forward and watched the image of a man outlined in the center of his computer screen. In his right hand was a gun. The gunman, dressed in black, pulled a balaclava over his face.

It was two in the morning when the gunman slipped inside the house. He must have had a map of the interior because he made his way directly and silently to the second-floor sitting room off the master bedroom. Osborne, according to the script, would be asleep. The intruder would creep into the bedroom, finish his job and return the way he'd entered.

Instead he saw Osborne dive to the floor from his desk chair at the end of the sitting room. The gunman fired a double shot from the 9mm that punched holes in the wall six inches above Osborne's head, dusting his wet, matted hair with powdery plaster. The chemist who had invented the hair dye hadn't considered that possibility when writing the warnings on the box.

The gunman crouched inside the doorway, aiming the gun for a third shot. Osborne had crawled behind the couch on all fours. He reached up to open a hidden panel and removed an M16 rifle with a full clip and a round in the chamber. He returned a burst in a nice cluster over the left side of the gunman's chest. Whatever heart had beaten inside suddenly had a series of new chambers leaking blood.

Alan Osborne raised his head above the couch and stared, blinking at the crumpled body, motionless on the parquet floor. Still holding the M16, he moved away from the couch toward the doorway. He knelt beside the body and then sat, legs crossed, while he pulled out his cell phone and auto-dialed a number. The M16 now rested against the dead man's shoulder.

Osborne saw a flicker of gold. He reached down and found the source around the gunman's neck. He held in his palm an amulet still warm from the dead man's body heat. Thai gunmen for hire believed amulets protected them from bullets.

"I trust this is still under warranty," Osborne muttered, letting the amulet flop back against the body.

He rose to his feet, picked up the M16 and walked back to his computer. Protection from death derived from mystical powers in Thailand, but when an amulet failed to protect the wearer, the true believers could always blame the dead man for failing to perform the empowerment rituals.

Osborne wasn't interested in amulets or blame. His concern was the body in the doorway. The only professional he wished to indulge in was not an astrologer but someone to help him clean up the mess. Osborne was a practical man.

As Osborne waited for Calvino to pick up the phone, he caught a glimpse of himself in the hallway mirror. A thin coat of plaster had stuck to the dye in his hair. It made him look like a nineteenth-century English barrister on his way to the Old Bailey criminal court in London to argue why his client shouldn't be hanged.

Calvino reached for the phone. It was two a.m. He saw that it was Alan Osborne's number. The thought crossed his mind to roll over and go back to sleep. He let the phone ring out.

A moment later Calvino's phone rang again. Osborne wasn't giving up.

"Are you okay?" asked Osborne.

"You're phoning at two in the morning to ask if I'm okay?"

"I need you to come around. It's a matter of some urgency."

"Can't it wait until tomorrow?"

"That's a bargirl's excuse. I thought better of you, Calvino."

Calvino sat up in bed, switched on a table light and checked his watch.

"I have a houseguest."

"Give her some money and throw her out."

"There's a curfew, Alan. Don't you read the papers?"

"I see. You're afraid. I rather overestimated you."

When Calvino arrived at Osborne's private compound, Alan was watching from his computer screen and opened the automatic front gate. He went downstairs and waited at the door as Calvino parked his car. He stood in the open door as Calvino got out and walked up the stone path.

"Calvino, I have a problem," Alan said.

"What's the problem?"

"My ex-partner is trying to kill me."

"Why would he want to do that?"

"Because he thinks I'm trying to kill him."

"Are you?"

"He deserves to die."

"You're sure it's your ex-partner?"

"No. It could be the crook I sold my nightclub to. He's out of cash and he's in arrears for the last two installments. Or it could be one of several ex-wives, or an employee or a customer with a grudge. The man I killed tonight was hired by somebody."

Calvino followed Osborne up the staircase.

"Was he a professional?"

"A semi-professional. If he'd been a professional, I'd be dead."

He led Calvino to the sitting room. Osborne stepped over the body that lay in the doorway. Calvino stopped, rested on his haunches and felt for a pulse on the neck. There was none.

"I don't handle dead body removals," said Calvino, looking up.

"I'm aware of the limits of your expertise. Removals require specialists," said Osborne. "They've been called."

Osborne poured Calvino a glass of whiskey and handed it to him.

"I'm afraid I don't have ice."

"You shot him?" Calvino said, nodding at the M16 on the sofa.

"He didn't shoot himself. I doubt he was competent enough."

"Why do you believe it was your ex-partner who sent him?"

"He hates me. But they all do."

"Where's Fah?"

"Sky is spending the night at a friend's. She couldn't get back before curfew."

Osborne could never get the tone right for his wife's Thai nickname and stubbornly insisted on calling her by its English translation: Sky.

"It just so happens that Fah didn't make it back on the very night a gunman slips into your compound?"

"I know what you're thinking, but no, Sky doesn't hate me. She loves me, and I make certain she knows I'm worth far more alive to her than dead. With women that's an essential precaution."

"Right," said Calvino.

"Don't be cynical. It warps your judgment."

Calvino downed the whiskey, wondering if Osborne was being ironic. He looked over at the body and the gun lying beside it. Osborne picked up the whiskey bottle and refilled Calvino's glass.

"Is that why you got me out of bed to see a body, so you could impart some of your homespun wisdom about women? Or was there something else you wanted?"

Osborne sighed.

"Frankly, I'm worried about Sky. Not that she wants to kill me. That I could understand. There's always someone who wants to kill you for your money. You can't get too bothered about it. If you do, give away your money and no one will care whether you live or die, let alone try to kill you. No, Calvino, I'm worried about Sky's state of mind since the coup."

"Any reason to worry?"

"She's been disappearing around two in the morning. Slips out of bed, thinks I'm asleep. I want to know if she's having an affair."

Calvino sat on a sofa ten feet away from the body that blocked the entrance to Osborne's sitting room. He wondered if Osborne knew the Thai saying that it was "Better to be a lover of an old man, than the slave of a youth." Fah would have known it. She was living proof of it or so Osborne had assumed until a doubt entered his head. Calvino gestured at the corpse.

"There's a dead body in your doorway, and your concern is that your girlfriend has a boyfriend?"

Osborne grinned and let out a long sigh.

"Yes. You can be quite perceptive when you want to be. That's exactly what I want you to find out. Let me know one way or another. In those first months after I became her sponsor, she was so grateful. She had good reason to be. Her father dead, her mother destitute—the usual family horror story—and there I was riding in on a white horse to save the day. The thing is, Sky was always polite, in that coy Thai way. Of course it's an act, but it never lasts, does it? I'm not that big a fool. Did I tell you before that her maternal grandfather is younger than me?"

He had told Calvino that. Up to now the age difference had been a source of pride for Osborne. The more years between him and his latest girlfriend, the happier it had made him.

Calvino had met Fah once. She was a university student in Bangkok. A week into her new job at an upscale restaurant, Alan Osborne had dined there. Fah seated customers, checking off their names on the reservation list. With all the demonstrations and protests, business was bad. The owner told her that he might not be able to keep her for more than a month. Then Osborne drove up in his Rolls Royce with his usual entourage of two dogs: a Jack Russell and a Golden Lab. The restaurant owner, being French, allowed customers to bring their dogs in and thought nothing of Osborne feeding them buns from the breadbasket. By the time the second course arrived, Fah was sitting at Osborne's corner table, petting the Jack Russell. When it jumped in her lap, she smiled and stroked its neck with her long, red fingernails. Osborne said that at that precise moment he fell in love with Fah.

On the third date Osborne offered to build a three-bedroom house for her family, give her mother an allowance, buy her a BMW and deposit more money in her bank account than she could earn in a lifetime as a university graduate. On the fourth date she moved into his house. That had been six months earlier. Alan had found her price. He'd used the word "grateful" to describe her acceptance. He'd spoken about his "Sky" like a man obsessed with a woman he hoped might change her mind about him. Given the age gap, his anxiety on that score wasn't entirely irrational.

"Why is it that women are filled with gratitude when you choose them, and after a year or so they have a secret life and late-night meetings? Gratitude never lasts. It inevitably collapses into entitlement. What have you done for me today? The only solution is to make them pregnant. Did I tell you that Sky has agreed to be the mother of my child? In those circumstances, you can understand why I can't have her out fucking around."

Before Calvino could reply, Osborne's phone rang. He spoke in English. A moment later there was a knock on the door.

"Could you get the door?" he asked Calvino.

Osborne had mastered the art of turning everyone around him into service staff of one sort or another. There was no guile or meanness in his request, just a deeply embedded sense of noblesse. Calvino walked down the stairs and opened the door.

Three men passed Calvino in the entranceway without so much as a hello and walked in as if they lived in the house. They gathered next to the stairs.

"Where's the body?"

Calvino pointed up. The men climbed the staircase to

the second floor and Calvino followed behind them. The crew had come prepared. One carried a quantity of large plastic garbage bags while dragging on rollers an oversized black piece of cargo luggage of the kind used by commercial enterprises to transport large items. One of the other men positioned himself behind the luggage to help steer it up the stairs. The third man carried duct tape, rope, box cutters and two handguns in holsters on his hips. He looked like the boss.

Osborne remained seated on the sofa, sipping his whiskey, as the three men approached the body lying at the door to the room.

"This doesn't look like a FedEx," Calvino announced from behind, "but these three men in dark glasses are here to pick up your shipment."

"He's dead," Osborne said to the men. "Step over him and get on with it."

Two of the men lifted the body out of the doorway and into the sitting room. Calvino followed them inside. In a moment Osborne was on his feet, gesturing to Calvino.

"While they clean up, let me show you something."

THREE

"Reality is not always probable, or likely."
—Jorge Luis Borges

OSBORNE'S SHOULDERS HUNCHED like an old man as he leaned over an electron microscope in a room he had converted into a makeshift lab.

"I want to show you my sperm," he said, with a mischievous smile.

It was the first time anyone had ever made Calvino such an offer. He looked up from a printout Osborne had insisted that he read. Other printouts lay scattered across a table. They were all copies of scientific reports. The one Calvino held had the catchy title "Motile sperm organelle morphology examination (MSOME) and sperm head vacuoles: state of the art."

"Some of them are beautiful. I'm collecting the perfect ones to make them into babies. If only I could have chosen who would have become Rob. What a difference that would have made!"

Rob, his son, had been killed in a Rangoon flophouse where Calvino had hidden him. Things had gone wrong, and the young man that Calvino had gone to Burma to find had been lost forever. Calvino was sure that if it hadn't been for that history, he would have been somewhere other than Osborne's lab just then, about to examine Osborne's swimmers.

Alan sat back from the microscope, rubbed his eyes and pointed at a chair a few feet away.

"Pull that chair over here and have a look."

Calvino took a deep breath and fit his right eye snugly into the hard rubber eyepiece, still warm from Osborne's body heat. Breathing slowly, he fixed his gaze on a mass of long-tailed sperm with massive heads, dancing in knots with no apparent purpose. The damaged spermatozoa, erratic freaks, had a fragile elegance as they struggled against the tide. The report he'd glanced at said the female genitalia were a hostile environment; sperm were likely to be picked off by scavengers or beheaded. The microscopic view revealed a battlefield where most of the wiggly combatants had suffered grave wounds and dismemberments. It looked like a defeated army with only a few healthy survivors swimming among the dead and dying.

"What do you see?" said Osborne.

"The way I see it, if you'd been the first alpha male, our species would have plateaued at around five thousand people," said Calvino, without looking up.

"Don't be negative, Calvino. You only need one strong one to make a baby. The rest are cannon fodder. You must understand I love children. It's when they grow up that everything can turn out wrong."

Calvino rose from the chair and ran his fingers through his hair, which had started to show grey. He worried if he'd end up like Osborne hunched over a microscope looking for one or two swimmers that could finish the course.

"Alan, look, I don't want to hurt your feelings, but you should consider getting yourself a hobby. Maybe travel."

"I already travel."

"Then chess. Or learn to read Thai."

Calvino sat back in the chair, arms folded, thinking of Osborne's son's body, slumped in a chair in the shabby room. When a bullet had entered his head, Calvino, his protector, had been across town sleeping with a woman in a bookshop once frequented by Orwell.

Osborne pulled an old man's startled face, like he'd been stabbed.

"I don't need to read their lies. It's enough to hear them."

"Collect art or coins or stamps."

"And wait to die?"

Osborne moved his chair forward and pushed his eye back into the eye socket of the microscope.

"You think I'm crazy. But I don't care what you think or what anyone else thinks."

Calvino believed him. He had never known a man who stood apart from society as much as Alan Osborne. Calvino watched as Osborne lost himself in the microscopic plane, casually shutting out Calvino and the rest of the world. He was travelling, following a flotilla of spermatozoa, deformed and directionless, as they coiled together in oblivion.

Perhaps on another occasion a survivor could be found, isolated and sent on a journey of Osborne's choosing, one where it would face the hostility within Fah's uterus. Reproduction was still possible for an old man like Osborne, but it was an expensive science project that required outside reading and plenty of homework. He pressed on, determined to take charge. Reproduction was far too serious a task to leave to the whims of biological fate.

"This time I will choose. I will decide who wins—"

Osborne stopped mid-sentence as Calvino's smile widened. Osborne hadn't said anything amusing. On the contrary, he had been quite serious.

"Vincent, what are you gawking at?"

"Your hair. Shouldn't you wash that shit out?"

Osborne touched his head and his finger recoiled like a Springfield rifle.

"I forgot about it in all of the excitement."

Osborne looked terrified, his eyes shifting wildly as if he were under attack by a swarm of hornets. He turned and quickly disappeared into the bathroom. Soon Calvino could hear the sound of a shower. A couple of minutes later, cursing and shouting erupted. Osborne emerged from the bathroom, toweling his hair with one hand and carrying the hair dye box in the other.

"It says leave the dye in for up to thirty minutes. I put the dye on almost three hours ago. Tell me, what has it done to my hair?"

Osborne drew air in until his cheeks puffed out, all the while slowly rotating his head side to side.

"I wonder if it's carcinogenic," Osborne said.

"I don't have a clue," said Calvino, "but 'life-enhancing' doesn't come to mind."

"I almost got shot. That thug made me forget."

"He's paid for it."

"If he hadn't, I'd shoot him again."

A noise came from the three men working in the next room. Osborne saw Calvino glance at the door.

"Don't worry about them. They're professionals," said Osborne.

Calvino turned back and found that he couldn't stop staring at Osborne's hair, which, like his sperm, seemed to have come from another dimension of reality. It had turned a cotton candy orange, a surreal color that would have been difficult to find on a color chart, no matter how extensive.

Calvino blinked and sat on a chair. This whole night had been like a bad dream. Osborne had roused him out of a deep sleep. He'd stepped over a dead body in a doorway, and now the killer had dyed his hair a brilliant orange. He'd been a private eye for many years in Bangkok, but this was something of a first. "The Orange Haired Killer" had a certain ring to it and might have sold millions of copies of the *Daily Mail* in Osborne's native England: "Ex-teenage bullfighter in flaming orange hair turns killer in Bangkok."

"Have you looked in the mirror?" asked Calvino.

"When you're my age, you avoid mirrors."

"I'd keep to that vow if I were you, Alan."

"Are you trying to be funny?"

"No need."

Calvino wondered why the worst damage a man endured in life was usually self-inflicted through momentary inattention. Given what Osborne had survived that night, though, he might be forgiven.

"You're smirking. That makes me curious."

Osborne disappeared into the bedroom.

"Follow me," he said.

He walked to the right side of the bed, opened a nightstand drawer and pulled out a mirror. To judge from the perfume bottles, cosmetics and tiny heart-shaped pillows braided with white ribbons, this was clearly Fah's side of the bed. Osborne sat on the edge of the bed and stared at his reflection.

"My hair's orange."

"It's called a bright punk orange. Fashionable. I think it suits you, Alan."

"Fah may leave me if she sees this."

"Increase her salary."

"That's a thought."

Distraught, he lay back on the bed and stared at the ceiling. Calvino turned as if to leave the room and the house.

"Wait," Osborne said.

He climbed from the bed, towel still wrapped around his waist like a Roman senator at the baths, and walked to the closet.

"There's something else I want to show you," he said.

He pulled a small suitcase from the top shelf. It was old, leather, worn, the kind of case that travelers had used a half-century before on long ship voyages. Calvino helped him carry it to the bed. Osborne worked the old release hinges with his fingers and dug through the contents.

"Would you believe this is me?"

He handed Calvino a small stack of photographs. He'd seen them before, but each time Osborne showed him the photos, he had to ask the same question.

"That's you?"

"That's what Fah said. She couldn't believe it. Look at my hair. Wasn't it a lovely color then? I was only fifteen."

Alan Osborne the teenager stood in a tight-fitting matador's outfit, holding a cape and gazing into the lens as if the bull were snapping the picture. Calvino looked up. Almost sixty years had taken a man and fashioned him into someone wholly different from the boy in the picture.

"I ran away to Spain to fight the bulls. I had twenty-three fights in sixteen months. My picture appeared in the English newspapers. It wasn't every day an English public schoolboy ran off to Spain to become a bullfighter."

He pulled out a matador's outfit and spread the faded pants, sequined vest and black matador's hat across the bed.

"I used to fit in that."

"It must seem like yesterday," said Calvino.

"Yes, it was just yesterday," he said, finishing his whiskey. "And I remember you before you went crazy."

Calvino smiled.

"I remember that me, too."

"You're up to the job of finding out about Sky?"

"If you have doubts, you can hire someone else."

"They might be crazier than you."

"That's always a risk."

"I'm a risk taker, just like you. We feed on fear. It's like this: if you haven't mastered your fears by twenty, you'll always be afraid and will die fearful, just like all the others paralyzed by the prospect of death, pretending they're still alive."

Calvino tried to take in Osborne's grand words about death and fear, but the sight of the speaker's orange hair was a circus act rarely seen. Calvino thought Osborne should find another private investigator to handle the case. Then he remembered the answer to that suggestion: what would another investigator make of Osborne? Fire-bright orange hair, an old suitcase full of photographs of him as a boy matador and a microscope charting ships to be sent on a mission inside Fah.

Osborne picked up the matador outfit and held it at arm's length.

"This is how I learnt about controlling fear."

FOUR

"The enemy is anybody who's going to get you killed, no matter which side he is on."—Joseph Heller, *Catch-22*

CALVINO HAD HEARD it before: Alan Osborne's sixteen months as a bullfighter in Spain had shaped him for the rest of his life. As a novillero, he had faced death in the ring. He had found courage to stand his ground. When he was a young boy, his father had told him many stories of his safari adventures and how they had made him a man. They'd taught him valuable life lessons, ones that had allowed him to understand the world and other people.

"My father said that in Africa, as he watched large herds of zebras, he wondered why no one had domesticated zebras, milked them, slaughtered them for meat or put harnesses on them and used them as beasts of burden. The Africans smiled and shook their heads at the white man's desire to tame the zebra. They knew zebras were nasty creatures. No one had ever tamed one. Later he found that the same held true of the panda in China. They were unpredictable, vicious and wild. Walt Disney, who'd never been on safari, made pandas and zebras look cuddly. He denied them their wildness.

"My father said most people were more like cows, easily herded, corralled and fed, but that made them profitable to own, rent, use or sell. They would stand for hours chewing their cud and never challenge a barbed wire fence. Cows submitted. Wildness had been knocked out of them. And I said to my father, 'What about bulls?' "

Osborne could see his father smiling as he thought about a huge black bull kicking up dust with its hind legs, nostrils flaring, eyes wild.

"The Spanish put the bull in a ring with forty thousand people in the stands, on their feet, cheering as the matador tests his courage against a beast that wishes to destroy him. The bulls test the resolve of a man who faces that which can't be tamed. The bull will not submit. He challenges, and men learn from that confrontation. The wildness of the bull will not save him in the ring. His nature is the instrument of his destruction.

"Every matador is a teacher for others who lack this courage. It is a rare man who can enter the ring knowing not only that his sword must be steady and true, but that the bull must be respected for his strength, brute force and determination to survive. Yet he must kill what we admire most in other creatures: the refusal to surrender.

"But bullfighters grow old," Osborne concluded.

What he didn't say, thought Calvino, was that you'll find no old bullfighters active in the ring. Instead they color their hair orange.

Calvino listened patiently to Osborne's story of youth and bullfighting, though he'd heard it many times before. How the new generation of bulls had lost nothing of their speed, reflexes, anger and strength. How courage was for the young. It flowed best when the mind was still forming and believed in its indestructibility. Old men, Osborne said, were the clowns that distract the bull when the matador stumbled and fell. The matador has helpers. Only the bull is alone in the ring. No clowns, no friends, not an ally to rush to his defense. When he dies, it is with honor and dignity, and in freedom. The audience rise to their feet, shouting encouragement, the ring of applause echoing in the stadium, a standing ovation to courage and death. The matador has redeemed them. Audiences live through their proxies, funneling their collective courage into the tiny figure in the ring holding a red cape, ice running through his veins as the bull charges.

"It's because of the bull that we appreciate the docility of the cow. The cow is the gold standard. I've tried to explain this to Fah. But even though she's in university, she knows almost nothing. Forget bullfighting, I said to her. Look at the stars. What do you know about the stars? She says Taurus is her favorite constellation. I defied her to find it in the sky. I offered her ten thousand baht if she could find it. She just smiled, took my hand and stroked it. Of course, I gave her the money even before we went out to look at the night sky. And what can you see in Bangkok anyway? You can hardly see the moon."

He seemed to be merely distracting himself by talking about the stars. He grinned then as if some random thought had returned him to his original complaint about Fah.

"The stupid girl studies political science at university. How she ever thought science could be found in politics remains a mystery. She should know better. Her father was murdered. He was one of those stupid political activists leading a demonstration against a mining company. Of course, a local mafia boss hired a gunman. No one was ever arrested, and his murder is an unsolved crime. What did he expect? Where did he think he lived? Of course they were going to kill him. I could have told him that. There's no science in the fact you don't go around challenging the military or big corporations.

"Afterwards, her mother fled with a boiler-room player to live in Stockholm. He threw her out after nine months, and she came back to Thailand broke. Now Fah supports her. I support Fah. You can see the chain reaction. Fah was stranded, working on a fucking worthless degree and no real job. Showing rich people to tables in a French restaurant was all she used to have to look forward to."

"That's where you came in," said Calvino.

"I offered to rescue her. And to support her mother. I admit it. Six months ago she appreciated what I'd done for her. Not now. She doesn't listen to me when I talk. She says things like, 'When the army overthrows a government, they know the water buffalo will chew and stare, and wait.'

"And I said, 'A water buffalo doesn't care who's in charge so long as it's fed. Its owners come and go. It's the big bulls that the owners fear. The possibility of an alpha bull charging, now that's serious business. That idea fuels the generals' sleepless nights. In their dreams they're in a ring with a dozen bulls charging, goring them with their horns. And as they lie there dying, not a single clown comes to their defense. She asked me, 'Where is the honor in the generals' martial law, curfew and guns?' And I said, 'You sound like what I imagine your father sounded like, and what happened to him?' She suddenly got very quiet. I think it hit her. She's her father's daughter."

"You've figured her out. What do you need from me?" asked Calvino.

"I can't believe for a minute that these thoughts are hers. She must be seeing someone, a radical who may be a lover. Some young buck as suicidal as her father. But I need evidence. I want proof. I want you to find out who it is. I want you to follow her."

"Like in the movies?" asked Calvino.

"Find out the truth."

Most of Calvino's cases were about someone lying, and the client hired him to find the truth. Only he knew that truth is like light; the purity of the white light we see is just an illusion, an impure mixture of colors. Osborne had dragged him out of bed and over a body to instruct him to follow Fah and to report where Fah went, what she said and who she slept with. But modern technology had disrupted the old romantic methodology used since the PI heyday of the 1940s.

"I'll give you an iPhone," said Calvino. "It'll be in the box. And you can give it to her as a present."

Osborne stared at him, his brow furrowed.

"How romantic."

"The phone will be loaded with software so I can see her, hear her and know where she is twenty-four hours a day."

"Trust and verify is the heart of romance."

Osborne lifted his weight to one side and removed a wad of cash from his pocket. It was hard to judge the thickness, but it looked like a couple hundred grand in thousand baht notes. He peeled off about a hundred notes and handed them to Calvino.

"Go on, take it. Get me the phone, and keep the rest for bus fare just in case the software doesn't work and you need to follow her in person."

He flexed his jaws and his eyes popped out as he stared straight into the distance, as if a bull had challenged him and was about to charge. Alan Osborne was a fifteen-year-old in an old man's body. He didn't care about anything other than putting a sword into the bull's neck and watching it die.

FIVE

"There was no telling what people might find out once they felt free to ask whatever questions they wanted to."—Joseph Heller, *Catch-22*

"THIS SUNDAY MORNING in Bangkok, the sun has risen, but its light does not clear the shadows falling on the path ahead of us." Fah's latest tweet reverberated in Calvino's mind as he headed to Osborne's house for the second time in forty-eight hours. This time the plan was to meet with the student who had agreed to enter the breeding program of a seventy-four-year-old, and to hand off to her husband the cell phone that would track her every movement and thought.

Fingering her long hair, barefoot legs pulled up under her, Fah sat on the leather sofa in the same sitting room where a murder had taken place the night before, her iPad open on her lap. She wore her university student uniform— tight-fitting white blouse with buttons down the front, and a tight black skirt hiked to her thighs. Fah elegantly extended her forefinger to flick back and forth between her Twitter and Facebook feeds. How her brain processed the two data streams simultaneously was a question Osborne had once asked her. "It's how we grew up," she'd told him. "Not all of us ran off to fight bulls in Spain."

Fah showed no evidence of noticing Calvino as he walked in and sat on an overstuffed chair a few feet away.

"Darling, remember Mr. Calvino?"

Slowly she lifted her head and nodded at Calvino. He knew that the attention a woman pays to a strange man who suddenly appears in her life can reveal a library of information about her. Fah's gaze reminded him of something his father had taught him: pay attention to crows, what they're looking at, where they're perched, how they move and how many of them have gathered in one place. Crows are incredibly smart, he had said. Watch them and they'll teach you a lesson on how to balance suspicion with survival. Fah watched him with a crow's leeriness, never letting him drift from her awareness even when she wasn't looking at him directly.

"Say 'Hello, Mr. Calvino.'"

"Hello, Mr. Calvino," she said, parroting Osborne's English accent.

"I guess you don't get a lot of visitors," said Calvino.

"You're the first one," he said, grinning.

Except the assassin who tried to kill him two nights ago, thought Calvino.

"Sky has her friends over, though, don't you, darling? She calls them her study group. Did you have study groups when you went to university, Calvino?"

"I don't remember. If they existed, I wasn't invited to join," he said. "But they're common in Thailand."

Fah glanced up, perhaps not expecting moral support from one of Osborne's friends.

"Didn't I tell you?" she said to Osborne.

"It's rubbish. Groups aren't good for studying any more than they are for sex. Too many distractions from people doing too many things to each other."

"Who do you speak for? Me or you?" asked Fah. "Tell me."

"Me, of course. Whom else would I be speaking for?"

After a couple of moments, Calvino noticed that the screensaver had popped up on Fah's iPad. An image appeared of the fifteen-year-old Alan Osborne in a matador outfit, holding a red cape, eyes fixed on a large black bull with its head lowered and frozen in the bottom right part of the frame. He stared at the youthful photo of Osborne on her screen and tried to imagine that the man next to her on the sofa was the same person. Age evidently had a terrifying ability to demolish a body and reconstruct it in grotesque ways that were only vaguely reminiscent of the earlier structure. It didn't help matters that Osborne's hair was now a deep orange. The boy in the long-ago photo, the teenaged Osborne wearing a matador hat, clearly once had naturally sandy hair.

What was it with the photos women selected of the men in their lives? Calvino had noticed that when a woman used an image of her man as a screensaver, that spoke volumes about the nature of her affection. Gazing at Fah and Osborne on the sofa, Calvino wondered how deep her affection ran. Other women had other ideas about photographs of their men. Christina Tangier's painted photo of Ballard had captured a private moment with the intention of displaying it to the world. That hadn't been an act of affection. It had been a kind of theft that had left Ballard feeling a victim. She'd found a way of gaining ownership of a man: steal and publicly display his most private face, the one only he possessed, the one that only a handful of people, including his mother, had ever witnessed, and sell his nakedness as conceptual art.

"Did Alan show you his lab?"

Calvino liked her already.

"I had the tour."

"Weird, right?"

"As a clinical education?" asked Calvino. "It was eye opening."

She shifted her legs around.

" 'Clinical.' I know that word. What's it mean?"

"If you know the word, then you know what it means," said Osborne.

"Give me a hint."

"As in 'clinic,' where you get tested for STD."

She nodded.

"Okay," she said, turning back to the iPad.

The matador screensaver vanished as she began flicking through her contacts online.

Not long ago there had been a dead man in the doorway. The killer had leaned over a microscope looking at his mostly dead sperm. Calvino tried to fit the pieces together and found that some puzzles resist solution. Calvino glanced toward the door. There was no evidence of what had happened there. Osborne's team of cleaners had done a thoroughly professional job.

"I told you Sky had spunk," said Osborne.

"You can call me Fah, Mr. Calvino."

So formal, yet she managed a smile.

"It means Sky, but a hippie name never seems quite suitable for a Thai," said Osborne. "She's been naughty. Haven't you, darling?"

"I am always good, my husband."

She pursed her lips and blew him a kiss.

"There, you see how polite she is? That's why I want her to have my baby. And I've come to accept that she has a hippie name."

It seemed to be Calvino's destiny, each time Fah came into the picture, to witness a tug of war over whether to use the Thai "Fah" or the English "Sky."

Fah's phone rang with the chimes of Big Ben. She answered it. For a couple of minutes she spoke in Thai.

"What's she saying?" Osborne whispered to Calvino.

"Making arrangements with her study group," he said.

"I want you to find out about this group. Who are they?"

"I thought they came to study here."

"Once or twice. Two skinny Thai boys who looked no more than fourteen years old. I asked them if they were really old enough for university. One of them looked quite pissed off. He thought I'd insulted them, but it was a compliment. Doesn't everyone want to look younger?"

"Not when they *are* young," said Calvino.

Fah ended her call and rose from the sofa.

"I have to go now, Mr. Calvino."

"There's a curfew," said Osborne.

"Not at eleven in the morning, darling," she answered.

"What are the names of the boys in this study group?"

"I told you a thousand times. Oak and Palm."

"Those aren't actual names of people. They're the names of trees."

She rolled her eyes, leaned over and kissed him on the forehead.

"Nice hair."

She stood up and smoothed out her black skirt. Calvino could see how her narrow waist, long legs and long, black hair would attract the attention of men and cause anxiety in Osborne each time she walked out the door.

"Is this really necessary?"

"We're working on a group term paper, and yes, it is necessary if I'm going to graduate."

Fah's electric smile dulled a little as if she'd rotated an internal dimmer switch. She appeared less sure of herself the more she tried to explain herself to Osborne. She packed up her iPad, tucked her phone into a Gucci bag and started to walk out. Her confidence gained altitude as she neared the door.

"I won't be late."

"Say hello to the Tree Brothers for me," said Osborne.

"They aren't brothers and they aren't trees," she stopped to say, "but I will tell them hello."

"Liar."

Then she was gone, and Osborne let his head collapse against the back of the sofa.

"Political science. There's no science in it, only guns, tanks and soldiers. She's young; she'll learn. Meanwhile, at my age I'm finding that Sky can be a handful. One day you too will be old, Calvino."

Calvino didn't need any reminders as he slipped a hand into his bag and retrieved Fah's new iPhone 6.

Seeing the sleek prize, Osborne nodded with approval, leaned to his side, stuck his hand into his side pocket, removing out the thick wedge of thousand baht notes once more. He licked his fingers, counted out several dozen notes and offered them to Calvino.

"At least take some money for the phone."

Calvino made no move, leaving Osborne's hand hanging midair.

"Don't pretend you don't want money, Calvino."

Calvino was still working off the karmic debt left by Rob's murder. Osborne was no fool; he was perfectly aware that guilt was a far more powerful currency than money. He folded the notes back into his wad and stuck it in his pocket again.

"You think I'm too hard on her, right? And you think I was too hard on Rob, and if I'd been easier on him, he wouldn't have run off to Rangoon to get murdered. You think I'm a bastard."

"It's time I headed back to the office."

"I can see in your eyes you think I'm a bastard. At least you don't lie, or your eyes don't. And I am a bastard. So what?"

He left Osborne seated on the sofa, his pants pocket stuffed with cash. The word "bastard" free-floated between them, seeking a response that wouldn't come from Calvino.

On the way back to Sukhumvit Road, Calvino thought of Osborne alone inside his mansion compound, not a stain of blood in the doorway or hint of violence anywhere on the premises. Osborne's great skill was knowing how to clean up a mess, make it invisible, but he never thought to ask himself if treating his wives and children like employees made him just another boss who would accept nothing short of servitude. Like political science, Calvino thought, Osborne's approach to personal relationships was less a science than an art. It required making a map of those close and those far as a guide for allocating the suffering, favoring those closest to him.

On the way out, Calvino passed the pale yellow, freshly washed and polished vintage Rolls Royce, the sun reflecting off the windscreen.

SIX

"The most effective way to destroy people is to deny and obliterate their own understanding of their history."—George Orwell

AT CALVINO'S CONDO that morning, Ballard had had a proposition. Calvino was only half-listening, his mind distracted by the image of *Elite John Number 22* asleep beside a teddy bear, its top hat cocked to the right. Ballard repeated the offer—he'd found a buyer from the Middle East who would pay double the previous auction price for the 1154 map. Was Calvino interested?

Ballard seemed to assume that finding a buyer in a cash deal was doing Calvino a favor, but he had only part of the map's story. If he'd had the full background, he wouldn't have bothered.

"It has sentimental value," said Calvino.

"She dumped you. How could it have sentimental value?"

"I thought you tried to buy the original *Elite John Number 22*," said Calvino.

"That was different. Self-preservation isn't sentimentality."

"I'd miss it," said Calvino.

"The money would help you forget."

"Thanks, but no thanks. If I change my mind, you'll be the first to know."

Calvino noted Ballard's frustration in failing to sell him on the deal. Why did Ballard care? The promise of a fat commission would be one good reason. Ballard was scrambling for money amid the wreckage left by Christina's exhibition. He would have to find his financial salvation somewhere else. Ever since the day Yoshi gave Calvino the map, he knew that, whatever the resale value, this was one asset he would never sell.

With most clients, after the case was finished, Calvino found there was little reason to maintain contact. The PI life was like life on a film set, where crew and cast bond during an intense six or eight-week period. They might vow to be best friends forever, but life usually intervenes, and a new set of best friends soon fills the space. Calvino knew that ad hoc clans focused on a common goal usually fall apart as soon as the goal is achieved. In the role of private investigator he was a bit actor in a client's drama. The client may cast him as a kind of hero when the case was solved, then the drama ended. The cast always disbanded and moved on to other sets, new dramas and a new set of best friends.

However, every ten years or so an exception to the rule came along. In the case of Dr. Yoshi Nagata—Japanese-Canadian mystic, mathematician, guru and yoga master—client and PI had by the end experienced what passed for real friendship. Still, in the days leading up to the coup, a year and a half had passed with no contact. He'd heard nothing from Dr. Marley Solberg either. He suspected that it wouldn't be a permanent silence, though, and that once it was broken, there'd be a blinding light like a supernova.

Then Calvino had received an email from Yoshi, inviting him to his condo for a drink. Yoshi had a gift he wanted to give him. The gift was from Marley, the brilliant mathematician who for a moment had remapped his life. Marley had left Thailand eighteen months earlier. Her departure had been abrupt, a surprise. She'd vanished, leaving behind only her mathematical version of a Dear John letter. As a formula for a breakup, she had reduced their relationship to a simple equation based on the indeterminacy principle—certain lives, once entangled, would always be connected no matter their distance apart in the universe. He drafted a response saying that, while her physics worked well on the cosmic level, it was a poor guide to maintaining a sexual relationship in Bangkok.

Although Calvino specialized in finding missing persons, he couldn't locate her. He assumed he could find her if he really tried. She had a public profile. But he never sent his letter. When she'd pulled up the ladder behind her, she'd made it nearly impossible to find which rabbit hole she'd disappeared down. Calvino accepted her choice.

The elderly yogi, in his white teaching outfit, stood framed in the door, a serene smile on his face.

"Vincent, I am pleased to see you," he said simply, as if the previous eighteen months had been a couple of days.

Calvino followed him into the sparsely decorated main room. Yoga mats, a series of ceremonial tables with small statuettes of Indian and Chinese deities, incense sticks, fresh orchids. A wrapped present lay on one of the ceremonial tables. Nearby was a low wooden teak table with a tea service set up. Yoshi nodded at the gift. The wrapping paper was a map of the five boroughs of New York City.

"Marley wanted you to have this."

He lifted the large rectangular gift and handed it to Calvino. Calvino scrutinized the wrapping until he found what he was looking for.

"I lived there in my last life," he said, pointing to a street in Queens.

"Open it."

"Do you know what it is?"

"See for yourself."

Calvino tore away the wrapping paper, the tear line cutting through the East Village. Inside was a framed map. It appeared to represent the world, but it was unlike any ordinary map. It looked like something from a children's book of fables. The map of New York City on the wrapping paper was realistic and to scale, but inside was a totally different kind of map, one that might have emerged under the influence of drugs or a crazy flight of imagination.

Marley's note inside read:

"There are people for whom the world is too big, and for others the world is far too small. For both, the map is not the territory. You will have found your past self on the gift wrapping, but can you find your present territory?

"This map is a prophecy written in longitude and latitude for navigation, and mostly that works. But we can never be certain which part of a map is true and which part is imagination. Only at the end of the journey can you know whether the prophecy is true."

Calvino looked up from the note. He handed it to Yoshi to read.

"She's right. You found yourself on the wrapping," said Yoshi.

"But on this strange-looking map? There's no New York. There's no America."

Yoshi read the note and nodded.

" *'Ceci n'est pas une pipe.'* And this map is not a map. That makes finding oneself all the more interesting a challenge."

Marley loved puzzles—making them, solving them, sending them into the world. She'd sent Calvino a challenge that was both a love letter and a riddle. Yoshi saw that Calvino was struggling to express a reaction that wouldn't make him appear as foolish as he felt.

"The map is strange only because we no longer see its world as ours. For a long stretch of time this map guided thousands of journeys. For hundreds of years it summarized our knowledge of the larger world."

As Yoshi watched, Calvino glanced between the framed map and the map made of wrapping paper, now torn. One printed on disposable paper while the other framed for the ages. He understood it took a wise man to digest the fundamental differences and the more he thought about the less wise he felt.

"Old maps are from an alien world," said Yoshi. "The past doesn't travel well when it comes to maps. When you study the features of a distant place and time, you discover how they are disconnected from our current knowledge. We smirk. We ask, why should I look at this cartoon? We look down on those who came before us as ignorant. But in the future, new generations will look down on us in the same way. Maps change. Human nature remains constant."

He traced a finger across the ragged blue mouth of a thousand-year-old Mediterranean Sea.

"Our modern maps chart genealogy, consciousness in the brain, politics, religions, ethnic groups, wars, coups, information and the cosmos. We are a mapmaking species, using them to find our way, even wrapping our gifts with them. From satellites to Google cars, we trace one boundary after another. But there is always a new, unmapped frontier. We long to explore the territory beyond any map. Again, this is human nature."

"Is that where Marley has gone?" asked Calvino. "Somewhere off the map?"

"Marley's quite good at doing that."

Yoshi's eyes slowly closed, and Calvino watched as the elderly man descended to a place deep inside himself. When his eyes opened, he gestured for Calvino to sit on the mat.

"Maps are a kind of intelligence report, one that is edited and updated. What if you could update your own intelligence? We have about ten thousand variants in our genes that correlate to intelligence. With the tiny disconnects, errors and flaws, a genius has an IQ of 150. Push those genes to their limit, and you might find a rare person with an IQ approaching 200. If you could edit the gene variants, and you had the possibility of arranging the nucleotide polymorphisms into a perfect grammar, then human IQ, in theory, might ramp up to 1,000. But what does that mean? We can't assume to know what it means to scale intelligence to that level. There is no precedent. We can't know whether our values, ethics, norms or ideologies scale to that level of intelligence."

"It's off the map," said Calvino. "By the way, are we talking theoretically or are we talking about Marley?"

"Both," said Yoshi. "If someone is ten times smarter than you, can you comprehend that level of intelligence? I have my doubts. Just as if I based my idea of the world on this map, and you told me there were other lands I hadn't seen."

"But Marley's told you that she's working on intelligence?" said Calvino.

"She's funded a private artificial intelligence project, and she's had some success. Major breakthroughs are years away. She's pushing at the outer edges of knowledge. But she feels no need to commercialize her findings."

A twinkle in Yoshi's eye signaled his agreement with Marley for her to keep the research results off the market.

"I assume Marley's found something," Calvino said, "and she's asked you for advice."

It would have been a natural thing for her to do. Yoshi had once been her professor and mentor. She would go to him.

"She knows human intelligence is only a temporary scaffolding to reach a much larger, complex structure. Perhaps we can enhance our intelligence tenfold. Impressive. But AI has even greater potential. There's no limit except the laws of physics. An intelligence that's a thousand or a million-fold beyond ours? It's possible. She's always been exceptionally intelligent. She knows, no matter how good the map, that we will always be one step short of our destination. We are one upload short of artificial intelligence. One funeral short to the end of history. I will confide in you Marley's conceit. She believes we can complete that last step, upload, or formula. So far Marley has found, what all before her have discovered—there is always one more step."

"Is there any way I can talk to her, Yoshi?"

"Not yet. The time isn't right."

"Meanwhile, her way to communicate is through maps?"

"Accept the gift, Vincent. Try to understand she truly cares about you. She has her own ways of communicating, and once you come to appreciate them, you'll find them richer and deeper than anything you have ever imagined."

When their visit had ended, Yoshi lifted the framed map and carried it as he escorted Calvino to the door. Inside the lift to the lobby, a young Thai couple stared at it, giggling at the map's absurdities. Another *farang* caught carrying an out of date, wrong-headed map of Thailand. Calvino returned their smiles but said nothing. He wondered how many ships had been lost taking this particular map as a reliable guide.

Maybe getting lost had a different meaning in the past. Had there been a greater sense of wonder and mystery, and an expectation that nothing was quite as it appeared? What he held was like a hobbit map. Marley had, for her own reasons, wished him to project himself into this hobbit-like world.

As he walked to the street, he ran Yoshi's parting words through his mind: "We can map most things, including violence, crimes, wars and hijackings. Now we can even assign probabilities that are updated each minute, as new acts emerge from a particular space. An interactive map of violence, one that is dynamic, allows the police to predict muggings.

"This map was a watershed. The world it depicts, which now looks like a wild leap of the imagination, was in fact a documentary representation of the world that people then believed to be true. See where the landscape pools, overflows and cascades down the side of mountains? That wasn't an idea from a dream state. That was once how the nature of the world was communicated between people. Marley wants you to travel with her, and this is her way of bringing you along."

SEVEN

"In a time of deceit telling the truth is a revolutionary act."—George Orwell

CALVINO ARRIVED IN his office on Sukhumvit Road early the next morning, nodding to Ratana, his secretary, as he walked past her desk. She looked dressed to kill in a gray vest worn over a sleek black dress and high heels.

"Nice dress," he said, as he turned to do a double take.

He was already eating a sandwich that he'd bought at the Villa Market around the corner: ham, cheese, lettuce and mayo.

"I bought you one," he said, laying a plastic bag on her desk.

She looked up and acknowledged him before turning back to her posting on Twitter. He'd bounded out of bed that morning with a mission, a new case, and he wanted to start working on the Osborne-Sky case map. Matrimonial cases were like trying to map a bowl of spaghetti. But then he was Italian, he told himself.

"I'm working on a new map."

She pulled a serious face. She didn't approve.

"I'm not certain if the time is right for you to accept a new client," she said.

"It's for an old client: Osborne. He thinks his girlfriend is cheating on him."

Any time she heard Osborne's name, Ratana sighed while maintaining her smile, one of those contradictions that Thais are masters at.

"He exploits what happened to Rob. That's why I don't like him."

"This case will square accounts. It'll close the books."

Calvino was thinking that Ratana was looking very good indeed.

"You've said that before."

"I'm certain this time."

He winked and disappeared into his office.

Taking a seat behind his desk, Calvino turned on his computer. He opened a modified software program that combined the traveling-salesman mathematical problem with a program designed for psychologists to map the relationships of couples seeking marital counseling. A blank template appeared on his screen.

Finding the shortest path between points wouldn't necessarily establish a connection between Fah and a male lover, if she had one. The blank map on the screen needed information of multiple contact points to assess the strength of any one point over another, and an algorithm to figure out the shortest path between Fah and the males mostly likely to be lovers.

He removed Marley's note from his jacket, smoothed it out on his desk and read it again. What was Fah's interior territory? He read another of her tweets for a clue: "Junta spokesman to foreign journalists: 'Thai people have different way of thinking to you. I have a different upbringing to you.'" When he'd seen Fah with Osborne, it seemed to him that was an opinion she might have shared with the junta spokesman. Calvino wasn't certain whether her tweets were intended to be subversive or sympathetic.

There was only one way to find out—leather on the pavement, covering the turf one step at a time. Such cases had taught him that lovers had a ninety percent probability of living within eight kilometers of each other. There was an irony in that while it was easy to maintain an overseas relationship, road traffic in Bangkok was bad enough to kill relationships separated by just ten kilometers. He keyed in Osborne's address and the addresses of Fah's university, her favorite restaurants, nightclubs and Starbucks.

Calvino sat back in his chair, hands behind his head, looking at the screen. It wasn't much of a matrimonial case map. There was too much missing information about the men in Fah's life to know where they met. He needed time to build a case map, starting with a representation of Fah's personal network—Oak and Palm, her fellow students. He would add her history with Osborne and her connections to others in his life. Then he would move on to the "hot spots," the overlapping communication tunnels that connected them. And when he had finished such a map, what would it tell Alan Osborne? That he had a picture of about the same level of accuracy as the *Tabula Rogeriana, 1154*, or something more like a detailed street map of the five boroughs of New York? If Marley had been trying to tell him anything, it was to follow how information was exchanged, saved, routed and used among a group of people. Sex was another form of social co-operation, but getting to that level of detail required a lot of work and a piece of good luck.

Fah was a beautiful woman. The old saying, "The menu isn't the meal," applied to beautiful women as much as to food. His first task was to understand Fah's territory, and that meant defining its boundaries. To figure out her intentions, he needed to understand how a young Thai university student kept by an older *farang* navigated through her Thai network, the cultural barriers and her political connections, and familiarize himself with the society she kept and the kind of people she communicated with.

If she was cheating on Alan Osborne, it would show up somewhere inside that complex social network. If she wasn't cheating but was up to something else, there would be signals showing a set of patterns suggesting the true nature of her relationship to other men. It was one of Calvino's Laws never to presume infidelity, because it causes an investigator to ignore or discount connections that don't support this theory. Osborne speculated that she was being unfaithful, but he had no solid evidence. It would be a mistake to accept Osborne's speculation as the investigation's fated destination.

When Calvino looked up from his computer screen, Ratana stood in front of his desk, holding out a cup of coffee.

"You may need this," she said.

"You forgot the IV needle."

He took the coffee mug and pressed it to his lips, keeping his eyes on his secretary, who sat in the chair normally reserved for clients. She had that concerned look of a mother, a wife or a close friend who carries a sadness or disappointment. An unofficial moratorium on new cases had been breached.

"Is that a new dress?"

"You notice the dress. But you don't notice how Osborne is using you."

"It's a minor investigation. Maybe a couple of days. It's not like I'm overloaded with work."

Calvino's maps had stirred up a set of bad memories Ratana had sought to forget. The thing with bad memories is they come with periodic reminders. His latest contact with Osborne reminded her of Calvino's creation of a montage of the Bangkok car bombing. Ratana associated that work of art with Calvino's mental breakdown and wondered if his thoughts were returning to the murder scene without his realizing it. If that was the case, was he on his way to a second breakdown? She worried about him but kept the depth of her concern to herself.

"Are you okay?" she asked, acting a little distracted, as if her mind was somewhere else.

"Don't I look okay?"

"I can't read what's in your head."

"Welcome to the club. Neither can I."

Calvino couldn't blame her. Many people he knew had fallen into silence and self-absorption after the coup, as they tried to wrap their minds around a life under martial law and a junta.

"Never ask a man about to pick a lock if he's worried what's on the other side of the door," he said.

He wanted to ask her if she was okay, but the time wasn't right.

"Osborne asked me to find evidence of his girlfriend's infidelity. I'm working on the lock."

"Khun Alan should be the last person to demand faithfulness."

"His girlfriend's been disappearing at night for hours. She's been using the curfew as an excuse not to come home. She doesn't tell him where she goes, who she's seeing or what she's doing, other than she's working on a paper in a study group. She's young."

"How young?"

"She's made about twenty-three orbits around the sun."

"Half a century younger than Khun Alan."

He hadn't thought of it that way. A century was a large number, more than a lifetime except for a tiny number of people who refused to die. Half a century remained a substantial historical marker. And maybe that was the way Fah thought of Alan Osborne, as an object of history.

"Alan's plan is to get her pregnant. He wants a baby. A replacement for Rob."

Calvino watched her smirk, something she rarely did to show her disdain.

"Crazy, right?"

"He's far too old for that," she said.

"He's dyed his hair orange."

Ratana laughed, unsure if Calvino was joking.

"Why would he do that?"

The hit man he'd killed inside his doorway was the answer. Calvino chose not to share that detail with Ratana.

"I don't think he intended it to be orange. Accidents happen."

Calvino sat in his chair, nodded and picked up a happy Buddha paperweight from Burma.

"You're right about the fertility issue," he continued, "but he's thought of that. He's bought the latest high-tech instruments."

For a moment he considered describing the electron microscope hooked up to a computer, and how he'd studied the technique of separating bad and good sperm. Too much information.

"It's all about Rob. I call it Vinny's guilt," she said.

"Guilt is a currency you should blow to the last baht before you die."

"When you are a guilty billionaire, that's not so easy," she said.

She had worked with Calvino long enough to know that it was foolish to lie when she delivered an unvarnished truth.

"Guilt comes with the Jewish DNA," he said, as memories of his mother's family flashed through his thoughts.

He also knew that guilt was like debt bondage. No matter how hard and long you worked, you never got close to reducing the principal.

"He's using it against you."

"I am using it against myself," said Calvino, raising his hands in a mock gesture of surrender. "I need to call McPhail."

"Which means you need a drink."

"Yes, I need a drink, too."

"My classmate's grandmother was detained yesterday," she said. "She was reading a copy of Orwell's *1984* and eating a sandwich."

"Why did they arrest her?"

"They said she had an intention."

"An intention to do what?"

"They didn't say. It was enough that she had an intention. She also wore a T-shirt with the words 'Respect My Vote.'"

"I'll phone Pratt. He's still got friends in the department who can get her out."

"You can tell himself yourself tonight. We have dinner with him and Manee, remember?"

His face showed that he had forgotten.

"That's why you have the new dress. Sure, I'll ask him at dinner."

Her face flushed red.

"It's okay. The police kept her five hours and let her go. They told her not to get in trouble again."

"It got sorted out is what you're saying."

"In the Thai way. Both sides saved face, knowing underneath that no one had won," she said.

Ratana returned to her side of the partitioned office. Calvino heard her settle into her chair and the soft tap resuming from her computer keyboard. There was a pause, then more tapping, and soon Ratana had gone down the rabbit hole of her own world, where hundreds of friends conversed over Facebook and Twitter timelines.

"Could you check if Fah is using the new iPhone?" Calvino said through the partition.

Replacing her old phone with a new iPhone 6 should be easy for Osborne to accomplish, Calvino figured, a task that even Osborne on a bad day couldn't screw up. Fah's face would expand to cover the campus in a dark shadow.

The previous morning Calvino had loaded up the new smart phone with the latest spyware apps. By the time he'd finished, the iPhone was enabled to take remote photos and videos, send copies of her Gmail, Twitter and Facebook accounts, and activate a voice recording of her phone calls. A GPS tracker would follow her movements between locations. Shoe leather manufacturers, like most industries, had taken a high-tech knock. Private investigators rarely had to leave the office anymore.

Ratana checked Fah's Facebook page. She had already scrolled through her two thousand "friends" and through an extensive photo album of selfies at university, Lumpini Park, nightclubs, restaurants and shopping malls.

"She turned on her new iPhone 6 an hour ago."

"It's not just an iPhone," said Calvino, who'd paid a small fortune to have the phone shipped from Singapore by one of the MBK gray market runners.

Ratana looked away from the screen.

"Then what is it?"

"A portable keyhole."

Ratana took a moment to reply.

"What if I said I was on her side?" she finally replied.

"Privacy is dead. Her generation never had a chance to know what it meant."

Like a clandestine radio station, Ratana went off air, turned silent, and that lasted for a couple of minutes. The silence was broken by a question that she'd been thinking about for some time and had only now mustered the courage to ask.

"Do you think Fah is beautiful?"

Calvino walked around the corner to her desk and looked over her shoulder. She felt his presence.

"Well, do you?"

That kind of question asked by one woman about another was always a baited trap, and he was in no mood to potentially chew off his own leg.

"She's a looker. But is she a cheater?"

As intended, Ratana had to puzzle over whether that was the equivalent of beautiful or some lesser state.

"By Thai standards, she has an ordinary face," she said.

"Trust me, there's nothing ordinary about her."

He noticed that Ratana was studying Fah's dress in a photograph, and that Fah wore a fashionable vest in the same style as Ratana's.

EIGHT

"If liberty means anything at all, it means the right to tell people what they do not want to hear."
—George Orwell

FOLLOWING DINNER CALVINO Calvino and Pratt walked down toward a sandy beach fifty meters east of his country house. When Calvino looked back, he saw Manee and Ratana framed in the window overlooking the sea, the light behind them as they sat on the sofa watching the two men slowly move out of sight.

At the edge of the sand, Calvino removed his shoes and socks. Pratt had already slipped off his sandals and strolled to the loam bubbling on the sand as the surf washed over his feet. He had retired to a beach house in Chon Buri province, about 140 kilometers from Bangkok. His new life with his wife might as well be a thousand light years away from Bangkok by the measures of power, wealth and influence. As Calvino pulled up beside him, Pratt looked at the sea, breathed in the fresh sea air and held it in for a moment before slowly exhaling.

"Do you remember this line from *Hamlet*: 'We know what we are, but not what we may be'?"

"I'm more interested in why on the beach tonight, with the moon and stars in place and a full belly, *Hamlet* popped into your mind."

"I've been thinking of that line for a week."

Calvino did a rough backward count.

"That must date from the time you would have heard the news about the coup."

This was their first meeting in person since the government had been overthrown. They had talked on the phone, but the conversations had contained too many silences and pauses, and what had been said had been thin, vague and tentative. Pratt hadn't come out and condemned the overthrow, but he hadn't celebrated it either.

Nodding, Pratt squatted down, facing the sea, and Calvino did the same. Pratt liked the quick connections that Calvino made from bits of information. *Hamlet*'s characters had been saying lines inside Pratt's head since the coup had been announced. He'd had a premonition the army would intervene, and ever since he had found himself changing his habits, choosing his words with care, leaving a trail of silence. He was watchful, scanning those who crossed his path for any small signal to indicate their feelings about the coup—a small gesture or a word, anything that revealed their true opinion.

He knew that coups give birth to new power holders, and that in such circumstances people will naturally be fearful and anxious about how the new bosses will shake up the political world of civilians. The military generals and their supporters had started to explain their plans, hopes, intentions and fears in coded language. Like an evolution, the new order had spawned an entirely new structure, an organism that had consumed its predecessor. But as with a revolution, the change had been immediate.

"I've been asked to return to the department," said Pratt.

Calvino sighed and stared ahead.

"You and the department are like a pair of mismatched socks. One's black and the other's white. Even if you're color blind, you can see they don't match."

Water lapped over their feet.

"I told them that I like my life by the sea."

Something in Pratt's manner suggested there was more.

"But they phoned again," said Calvino, figuring such issues are never resolved by one phone call.

"A senior person phoned and said my dismissal was something others had talked about. They held it up as an example of how corrupt the old government was, and it showed how unfairly the police department had operated under the former political regime. The politicians had forced out the good police officers, and that had caused damage. He said the only way to repair that damage was to bring back the good officers. In my case, they want to make me a department head. My job would be to sideline the bad guys in the department and help recruit back to the department the officers that the politicians had unfairly dismissed."

"Yeah? Here's the thing," said Calvino. "With a coup, the head guy gets to play god and appoint lesser gods. The department is a big place to patrol. They need help."

" 'Hell is empty and all the devils are here'—meaning, there is good and evil in the world. They're both all around us. We are living *The Tempest*. And people are taking sides whether they want to or not."

"The only Shakespeare quote I can remember is, 'Now I will believe that there are unicorns…' I forget the rest."

"That's from *The Tempest* as well."

"So… You're going back to the department."

Pratt nodded.

"Next Monday. It's probably not a big enough deal to be in the press, but there is that possibility. I didn't want you reading about it before you heard it from me. I wanted you to understand why I made the decision to accept their offer."

Calvino rose to his feet, arms folded over his chest. A necklace of lights from a dozen shrimp boats wrapped around the throat of the dark horizon.

"Now I *will* believe there are unicorns."

"I've been called back, Vincent. We need to give them the benefit of the doubt, to withhold judgment for now. We can't reverse what's been done, and we might have a chance to influence what happens next."

"Next thing you'll tell me is you've been promoted to general."

Pratt stared at the sea.

"The paperwork's been processed. Yes, they've promoted me."

He wasn't seeking a second opinion. Calvino had been invited for a friendly stroll along the beach to hear his decision. Calvino noted that the pauses on the phone during their earlier conversations were starting to make sense. Pratt was being called back to duty by those who had defeated his enemies. In a way that made them his friends. Among the coup makers no one felt weighed down with guilt that force had been necessary to overthrow the government. Why would they? Force, or the threat of it, had always been the essential requirement for every coup.

"Manee is looking for a condo in Bangkok."

"What about your new life here at the seaside?"

He figured that's what Manee had been talking about to Ratana when he'd seen them through the window.

"Growing orchids, playing the sax," Calvino continued. "The good life. What happened to those plans?"

"We'll be back for weekends."

"Charging at windmills during the week, and relaxing on weekends by walking on the beach. Ideal—if you're Don Quixote, that is."

"And Sancho Panza is my friend."

In such a time as they were in, Calvino figured it was enough that a man continued to value friendship. He knew that maintaining that value when friendships all around them were being devalued demanded persistence and patience. More than that, such friendship required the conviction that it mattered.

Theirs was a time when the generals ruled throughout the land. Who wouldn't want to join them in the creation of the new order, a new brotherhood? To salute the beginning of a time when strife and scandal and conflict ended? To usher in a time when the gentle breeze of happiness blew through the schools, villages, towns and factory floors, cleansing and purifying the squalid, corruption-infested politicians?

Calvino kept his misgivings to himself, but doing so disturbed him. He was already finding himself censoring what he said to close friends. It seemed to him that that might be the definition of submitting to power. He'd learnt that submission to power was toxic to truth and friendship. Those who value power over everything else have no true friends, only allies. He found himself studying Pratt as if seeing him for the first time, and wondering what he'd missed before.

"Manee will be worried," said Pratt. "We should go back."

He brushed the sand from his feet as they reached a fringe of wild grass. The shrimp boat lamps cast small pools of light swallowed by the vastness of the sea. Calvino stood watching the surface shimmer like a black mirror.

"Are you coming back, Vincent?"

He slipped on his sandals.

"I never left, General," he said, feigning reverence.

"Let's get a drink," Pratt said.

"No, let's get drunk."

" 'I have drunk and seen the spider.' "

Calvino sat on the grass and put on his socks and shoes.

"One eye on the spider and the other on his web," said Calvino.

"Ratana tells me Ballard has been your houseguest. I remember him from Bali. What's he up to in Bangkok?"

"It's a long story, involving a teddy bear, a camera and a conceptual artist who free-lanced as a hooker in London."

Pratt shook his head, laughing as he walked.

"I've lived a sheltered life by comparison."

"Compared to Ballard, we've all been living in small spaces."

NINE

"Let us cultivate our garden."—Voltaire, *Candide*

MUNNY LEANED OVER a small generator, using a damp rag to wipe the oil off his hands. He examined his fingers, dabbing a black speck of oil from the tip of his thumb. He stared at the machine as if trying to hypnotize it to his will, drawing in a deep breath as he pulled the cord on the side. A small plume of blue smoke rose, and he smiled as the generator sputtered and started to purr—a heavenly sound as the machine came to life.

Munny grinned, squatting on his haunches. He looked over at Chamey, his wife, and she nodded. She didn't have to say anything. Her husband had performed his magic and got the machine to work. Now she could cook a catfish on the hot plate for their dinner.

They'd saved for over a year to buy the small second-hand generator, and last month she had scavenged an old fridge, which Munny had got running again. But despite their efforts to get ahead, someone always got ill or some relative had a problem, and there was never enough money to pay for their needs. Life in the Aquarium was never easy. It was a place where dreams evaporated. At least Munny had found work, until that too had ended badly.

The past week had started well. A wealthy Chinese customer from Hong Kong had come into the Khao San

Road parlor and asked for a special Khmer-style tattoo, the Sanskrit lettering neat and in nine rows on the left shoulder. He had asked for Munny by name. Munny had been gathering a reputation as the magic amulet tattoo man to see among a small group of Khmer tattoo art aficionados. He worked for a Thai-Chinese man in a hole-in-the-wall shop off the main drag that had no neon sign or décor to speak of. The shop owner paid Munny 250 baht a day provided he did a minimum of three tattoos; otherwise a 150 baht sum was deducted from the payment, leaving him enough for bus fare and a bowl of noodles. The Hong Kong customer had known the score and slipped Munny a hundred dollar bill.

Munny had given tattoos to people of all different nationalities, but no customer up to then had ever been so generous—that is, until a few days after the Hong Kong windfall, when a young Thai woman named Fah had walked into the shop and sat in his chair. She sat flipping through a book of colored photographs of tattoos. From the way she turned the plastic pages of the binder with color photos inside, he could see she wasn't studying the details. She was biding her time, wanting something, but it wasn't clear that it was a tattoo. Munny thought that maybe she was nervous because it was her first time to get a tattoo. He'd seen the reaction before in young, conflicted kids. Wanting one, not wanting one. Tossing a coin in their mind, over and over, still unsure. Smiling, he took the book from her hands and put it back on a shelf.

"It's a big decision. You think it over. No need to rush into things if you've not made up your mind. Come back when you've decided."

"Isn't it your job to sell me a tattoo?"

He smiled again.

"I never was much good at selling."

She liked him and his smiling face. Her hands relaxed in her lap as she looked around the shop.

"You're Khmer, right?" she asked.

He nodded and whispered, "Yes."

She concentrated her focus on him like she was looking for something, and that made Munny nervous. She'd started her conversation neither with an expression of confidence nor with the usual questions about the inks, dyes or pain thresholds—and whether each person had a different one. From her chair, she'd managed to corner Munny with a stare. He had an uncle who could do that with dogs: make them stop in their tracks, tail between their legs, head lowered. He could see that she was working up to something, looking for the words. He couldn't decide if she was one of those who worried about suffering under the needle piercing their skin. Those people didn't have much pain tolerance. With their sheltered city lives, protected by money and family and friends, they didn't have much experience with pain. It was something Munny knew a thing or two about.

Fah pulled her new iPhone 6 from her backpack. She clicked open a photo app and scrolled through an album.

"Is this your work?"

Munny looked at the photograph of one of his tattoos on the right shoulder of an Englishman. He remembered his name: Colin—Colin from London, who had reddish uncombed hair and freckles over his nose and his shoulders, too. He was twenty or twenty-one years old and had been traveling for six months. Smelling of beer and pad Thai, he had stumbled into the shop a few months earlier holding a magazine. Alcohol-fueled courage commonly propelled a customer into a tattoo parlor for the first time. He'd plopped into the old dentist chair, crossed his legs, belched and opened a book at a dog-eared page.

"Can you do me this?"

His finger had pointed at the page showing a girl of four or five, in a dress, hair wind-blown, releasing a heart-shaped balloon.

"You know Colin?" Munny asked.

"He's a Facebook friend. He posted this really cool tattoo."

Munny nodded and looked up from the photo. He waited. There had to be more to the story.

"You want this tattoo?" he finally asked her.

"I like this one," she said, scrolling to another tattoo.

Colin had returned two days later for a second tattoo, one of Banksy's rat holding a sign that said "You lie."

Munny pursed his lips and nodded.

"So you want the girl and balloons or the rat and the sign?"

Before Fah answered, the shop owner, a Thai-Chinese man about fifty years old, stormed through the door. Taut anger pulled the man's face into a sneer of contempt. He grabbed Munny by the arm.

"I told you yesterday. Get out. Don't come back."

His gold incisor teeth showed as he began to shout.

"You are illegal Cambodian. The army doesn't like illegals in our country. The military warn us big problem if they catch us with illegals in our shop. I tell you. Why you come back? You want cause me a problem? I told you, go back to your home. No one want you in Thailand."

He spit on the floor just as he noticed Fah looking at him. He had ignored her up to then as some inconsequential girl. Now he flashed a fake smile.

"You want a tattoo? I can do. This man's not Thai. He's no good. No one like."

Munny edged toward the door, opening it.

"I'll come back for my pay," he said.

"I owe you nothing."

"You owe me two thousand baht."

"Get out!"

The Thais had a smile that vanished in the moment when all control over emotions shut down and pure anger and aggression was released. The Chinese owner was a ticking time bomb, hands made into fists, edging toward the door. "No impulse control" should have been tattooed on his forehead.

If that was the way the boss wanted to play it, what could Munny do?

"Okay, okay," said Munny, holding up both hands, palms out.

Thailand wasn't his country, and the boss could do whatever he wanted, and no one would say a word. He walked out of the shop and turned right down the street. He had money for a bus, but a bus wouldn't get him back in time to avoid violating curfew. Munny felt his world dissolving around him. He was screwed. There simply wasn't enough time to return to the Aquarium by ten p.m., and if he was arrested anything might happen to him. Rumors of beatings, detentions, disappearances as the army cracked down on illegals had spread like fire through each floor of his building. He shuffled along the sub-*soi* like a straggler from a retreating army, hands in his empty pockets except for a few coins for his bus fare. He pulled them out, counted them under a streetlight and stuffed them back in his pocket. Munny leaned against the wall of a building, his weight on his right foot, hands in his pockets, wondering what he should do next. Fah, who had followed him out of the shop, stopped beside him, startling him.

"You got fired," she said.

"That was yesterday."

"I have a job for you. If you need one."

"Doing what?"

"Graphic art. You can do graphic art?"

"Yeah, I can do," he said.

It was Munny's nature to always leave the door ajar, especially when he wasn't sure exactly what someone was offering in terms of a job. In his twenty-eight years he had acquired a lot of experience as a tattoo artist because he'd never turned down a challenge.

"You don't understand. I don't want a tattoo. I want an artist who can design graphic art stencil designs. Like the ones Banksy makes. If you can tattoo Banksy on skin, I am thinking you can make a stencil to use on a concrete wall. Like this one."

She touched the wall where he stood.

"Can you do that?"

"I'll need materials."

How hard could it be? Writing on skin prepared an artist for any medium.

She fished her wallet out of her bag.

"Take this," she said, as she pulled five one-thousand baht notes from the wallet and held them out. "You can start work tomorrow."

"Where do I work?"

She handed him a business card. He squinted at it. A barber's pole with red and white stripes was embossed on the front.

"A barbershop?"

"We have a room on the second floor. It's above the barbershop. Go through the shop and up the stairs. Tomorrow. One in the afternoon."

"You didn't say how much you'd pay me. This is enough for material."

He stared at the notes. That money would feed his family for a month and a half. But some instinct stopped him from immediately taking it. She saw how much control Munny exercised in not grabbing the notes. Osborne had taught her the control that comes from flashing money at someone who has none. The face of such a person would twist like that of a drug addict in withdrawal.

She counted out another five thousand baht.

"It's a down payment. Take the money," she said.

These were words she had heard Osborne use. They made him appear generous. She stuffed the ten thousand baht into his shirt pocket. He made no effort to hand the money back. That was the moment of truth—the moment when one person controlled another. She had witnessed that moment every day since she had been with Osborne. He demanded to be in control. Looking at Munny, she understood what that moment meant for him.

"You'll have a place to work, and I'll bring all the materials you'll need. The ten thousand is for you. You okay with that? Tomorrow we'll give you our ideas about design."

As she walked away, he was shaking. He didn't know exactly why. Maybe it was the shock of getting so much money from a stranger. He thought to call after her and ask who "we" was, but in truth he didn't care that much. She trusted him. He liked her for that. He looked at the name card before slipping it in his pocket. Then, stepping into the road, he flagged a taxi with the red vacancy light on. He was going home in time and in style. Munny felt his luck had taken a sharp turn for the better.

For the last two years the Aquarium had been Munny's family homestead. They lived on the third floor of an eleven-story building site, an abandoned, unfinished skeletal structure of gray concrete and rusting steel girders. Tucked away in back *sois*, the building had been largely forgotten by its rich owners. The Décor Hi-So, as it was officially known, had become an expensive folly, an orphan. For anyone in the family to admit they played a role in the catastrophic failure of its planning and design, including the lack of necessary approvals and the many license violations, would have resulted in a massive loss of face. For the guilty parties, to accept responsibility was clearly out of the question, given how toxic to their reputation and standing that would be. Munny had not been the first to spot the building's indeterminate status. Other Cambodians were already squatting there when Munny joined the community with his family.

Seven additional floors had been constructed beyond the four that had been allowed in the permit. This lapse wasn't the result of a little bit of cheating; it was hog-wild cheating at the buffet, the kind that could get the owner in trouble with the law. One or two floors over the quota, secured with a stuffed envelope, might have worked. All those extra floors triggered the predictable lengthy court battles and demolition orders, but in the end nothing much beyond administrative paperwork ever belched out of the great bureaucratic machine, and the uncompleted building remained standing. The authorities were perfectly content to process the necessary orders while taking their rewards for inaction, and the owners were perfectly happy to take delivery of the latest order or appeal and simply pay more money. Like a bad marriage that inched forward in ongoing instability, this uneasy state of affairs had lasted for fifteen years. Meanwhile the seven illegal joined the four legal stories of concrete and steel, nestled deep in a sub-*soi* off Phra Kanong—some floors with brickwork, others open on all sides—filled up with illegal immigrant squatters.

Seven years before the coup, the basement had flooded. Some said it was a sign of what was to come. A monsoon left behind ten meters of water covering a vast interior area. The unfinished structure lacked doors, windows, walls, electricity, water, toilets or lifts. The floors that were completely open to the elements gradually grew makeshift walls of brick, plywood or fiberboard, materials nicked from nearby construction sites. The basement remained underwater. No one had any reason to drain it. Besides, there was nowhere for the water to go. Mosquitos became a problem, and a few people came down with dengue fever.

The neighbors found a solution—stock the water with fish, which ate the mosquito eggs. Word got out, and other squatters arrived and released fish to make merit. Soon there were thousands of fish. By then, weeds and trees had grown around the building, cutting it off from street-level view.

Five years on, the first illegals from Cambodia had joined the squatters in the building. Their illegal community of nearly a hundred people was difficult to keep a secret. Because of this new influx, the early settlers in the more finished floors worried about the owner, neighbors or the authorities throwing them all out. A meeting by eighth and ninth floor members resulted in a decision to close off the top two floors from occupation. The six men at the meeting also voted to install themselves as lookouts and enforcers, the ones who dealt with the owner and the police. Politics had arrived at the community, and no one thought much about it at the time.

Munny hadn't gone to the meetings. But that was understandable, as he hadn't been invited. The meeting-calling men referred to themselves as the Eight-Nine Safety Council and made it clear to everyone squatting in the building that from now on they were the ones who ran things, and no matter what floor someone lived on, they had to obey their orders. A couple of men from other floors who challenged them were beaten up. After that no one, including Munny, risked offending the council. One day, out of the blue, the council decided the building needed a name. They decided after a long drinking session to call it the Aquarium. Most of the squatters welcomed the sense of stability that came with firm authority and rules. The squatters, before the Eight-Nine Safety Council appointed themselves, had been worn out by the temporary factions and unstable alliances and quarreling. As the time before the council ran things faded from memory, so did the beatings.

Munny dreamed of moving his family out of the Aquarium, away from the men the squatters had begun to call the Eight-Niners and into an apartment. He lived, alongside his wife Chamey and their son, Sovann, in a corner of the third floor. Their son's name translated, like most Thai and Khmer names, into a thing—in this case "like gold." Chamey told Munny he lived in a fantasy world with his tattoos. They had no chance of leaving the Aquarium, not now. Not since the coup. No one felt safe, and the Eight-Niners gave new orders about using fire and light at night so as not to draw attention. They also set a quota on the number of fish each family could take from the basement pool for personal use. Beyond the quota, residents now had to pay for the fish. Munny found out that the leader of the Eight-Niners supplied the fish market from the pool. They also collected a "tax" to pay off the police and the owner. But as the new rules and demands increased, Munny said nothing.

Chamey wasn't quiet. No one owned the fish in the basement. Anyone could see the massive numbers were sufficient for all to take as many as they wished. She complained, and her discontent reached the eighth and ninth floors. The Eight-Niners didn't frighten her. They watched her taking fish from the basement, and when they told her to stop, she flashed a knife. She threw her last hundred-baht note at one of them.

"Here's your tax," she said. "Now leave me to feed my family." She earned money frying and selling fish harvested from the basement.

"You owe us one thousand more. We want our money."

She glared at the two men, her jaw tight, moving up and down, as she thought of what she could do or what she should say. The last thing she wanted was to back down or even worse, cry. "Tomorrow," slipped out, and she immediately hated herself for giving in to their threats.

Chamey had memorized the details of the structure room by room—hiding places, empty and occupied places—memorized as if the Aquarium were a universe with eleven discrete but interconnected worlds. They lived on the south side of the third floor, overlooking the back of a row of shophouses with lights in the barred and curtained windows, trash barrels leaning against the common walls and motorbikes parked in the alley. Chamey's family laid claim to an area of about thirty square meters. One day Munny brought home a piece of chalk from Khao San Road and used it to draw the boundary in straight lines along the unfinished concrete floor. He mapped their territory, and soon others did the same. Then some of the chalk marks were replaced with concrete blocks.

Early the next morning, before setting off for his new job above the barbershop, Munny sat along the edge, taking a moment to admire his handiwork. The old chalk lines had become smudged, and he'd recently redrawn them. He thought about how working in ink on a person's skin had given him purpose and power. Chalk had a different texture and feel, but the purpose was similar. He looked at the outline of *their* space and felt the power it conferred on them. The chalk, like ink, had transformed a surface into a new creation. As the light streaked across the chalk lines, he also felt a bitter taste. Inside their marked-off space, they lived deep inside enemy territory. No amount of chalk would change that fact.

Munny walked over to the electric generator and squatted down beside it. It had conked out again at about three in the morning. The fan had stopped and the sweating had started, along with the buzz of mosquitoes in their ears.

"Can you fix it?" his wife had whispered to him as she turned on the bamboo mat in the dark.

Though he'd tried through the rest of the night, Munny had failed to repair the generator without some new parts. By morning his wife found him curled up next to it, clutching a wrench. She woke him up.

"You did all you could do," she said.

It hadn't been enough. Once the curfew time had ended, he'd dressed and gone out to buy parts at a junk shop. Then he'd had to return there again to buy a gasket. The generator, like his wife, kept up a steady stream of demands. Without the fan to move the dead air, they were both languid and irritable as they swatted at the bloated mosquitoes.

"Half an hour," he said, showing her the gasket. "Unless something else is broken."

Chamey's long night of frustration, discontent and anger had turned into a collective experience for the members of her work group, now assembled around her. Ten meters from Munny, Chamey stood at the table with a long knife, glancing back at him as she gutted a large red snapper. Her hands glistened with silvery fish scales. Some stuck to her skin and her black hair, and when the morning sun caught the scales, they sparkled like rotating lamps from a thousand tiny lighthouses. Her medium wasn't ink or chalk; it was blood. The smell of blood and piles of guts hung thick in the air. Two plastic buckets on the floor beside the table vibrated with flopping fish. Three other women and a man, in sandals and jeans, sweat rolling down their cheeks and necks, helped her fillet the fish, wrapped the strips of meat and stacked the packages in neat rows inside small wooden crates.

A silver streak of blood ran across the cheek of a boy no more than ten or eleven. Munny watched his son, sweat rolling down his face and neck, as he lifted a crate with gutted fish onto a trolley. He should have been in school. It wasn't possible. Like other families who lived at the Aquarium, the illegals had trouble getting their children into Thai schools.

They had to live like criminals. Munny thought how the Thai woman who'd come to the tattoo parlor and given him ten thousand baht had looked so young. She was only a couple of years younger than his wife, but they didn't look like they belonged to the same generation. That made Munny sad.

Though she was only twenty-five years old, Chamey showed no signs of youth. It had been dragged out of her by a hard life in the open, on the run, without money. The Aquarium had provided some degree of shelter, food and community but hadn't restored her youth.

She called out to the boy: "Wait until the crate is full before you move it! You are just like your father, impatient."

A trickle of fish blood ran down the side of his cheek like a red tear. The boy nodded, his head dropping in a sulk as he lifted the crate back to the table to wait for more fish.

Was it true that Sovann was impatient, Munny wondered. He hadn't told Chamey about the money the young Thai woman had given him the night before. He hadn't figured out how to explain that such a person had given him so much money. When she'd asked him if his boss had paid him, he told her that the boss had been angry, threatened to call the police and ordered him out of the shop. Any other woman would have cried. Not Chamey. She lay next to him quietly, eyes open, unblinking like one of the dead fish, her mind drifting off to some other place where the chalk lines of their world didn't smear and run in the rainwater. Munny had also reasoned that if news of the ten thousand baht leaked out, he would face a rush of people wanting loans. The Eight-Niners would sniff out the money then too and demand a new tax. There was no way Chamey could keep the money a secret. She was too open and honest for secrets.

At last he got the generator started again, and the plastic blades on the fan rotated once more. Chamey rewarded him with a genuine smile but said nothing. There was no need. His boy smiled at him too and raised his fist in the air. The others at the gutting and packing table looked like they'd won the lotto. "Thanks, Munny," fell from their lips.

He'd always been a solitary type, even as a child, and had grown into a man who didn't like trouble. He was also his wife's cousin. They shared the same grandparents on their mothers' side. Chamey's mother, Munny's aunt, was still in Cambodia. Munny had married Chamey when she was fifteen and five months pregnant. The other two women on their part of the third floor were his other aunties. After gutting and packing the fish, five members of the family went to set up a stall to cook and sell them. The family had come from Battambang, an old Khmer Rouge stronghold, leaving behind them a place of landmines, ghosts and hunger.

The family had outfitted their corner of the third floor with bamboo poles and canvas stretched between them for sleeping quarters; it was a family lair. Other floors had more families from villages along the border. They all sent money back home each month. No one living in the Aquarium ever used a bank. Cash was hand-carried to its recipients, and sometimes men in uniform would stop the courier, take the money and push him back across the border—if he was lucky. It didn't much matter whether what uniform the official wore. The result was the same. Pay. Munny's best friend, on the fifth floor, had lost his cousin on a cash run to Kampot. No one ever heard from him again or found his body. He vanished, and there was no one to go searching for him. He could have run away. He could have been killed. There were so many ways for someone to go missing. And there were many rumors of Thai authorities roughing up illegals, putting them in jails or selling them to fishing boat owners as crew. The stories were enough to feed their fears that life outside the Aquarium had as many dangers as a Battambang minefield.

The Aquarium was no holiday resort. Its lack of architectural finishes made it an elevated outdoor experience. They did have a roof and a floor, and that was something. But a coffin had those things too, and also sides. There was no satin lining in the Aquarium. Prisons at least had painted walls. Raw and rough interior concrete walls and floors gave it the appearance of an ancient cave. At night, shadows from lanterns and candles danced over the cave walls, and the sound of someone playing a flute—or vomiting or shouting—echoed as if demons had ambushed a victim, and the rattle of his last breath whipped through the structure.

The mothers of the Aquarium sometimes threatened their children with banishment to the watery basement if they misbehaved, and Chamey was no different. Some of the younger children were terrified of going down there. The guards even told them stories about how alligators had eaten two or three children. Because of the depth of the water, it seemed possible. Pillars shot up from the watery depths, and the dank vapors made the children's eyes water. Fish up to three feet long broke the surface, spraying everything around them.

Like fishermen back home in Cambodia, the building's residents lived close to their food supply, mended their nets and hung them out to dry. The community had been organized around farming the fish. Some of the men had escaped from Thai fishing boats, where they'd worked for months at a time but had never been able to repay their "loans." They knew about fish. They knew about the kind of men who owned boats to catch fish. And their history had taught them that the owners were as dangerous as the old Khmer Rouge. The squatters argued at night whether to put out Claymore mines like the ones around their village. They only knew one or two people who had died of old age. For their community death came calling long before the body was ready to go. Living like hermits, they played hide and seek with their fate.

At night they lay on their backs, as in their village, but could see no stars. Sovann asked his father to paint stars on the third floor ceiling over the chalk lines. Munny painted the Orion constellation, mixing fish scales into the paint. Each painted, cut-metal star in the constellation was the size of a soccer ball, beautifully designed, with sharp edges that caught the light. The stars sparkled when Munny pointed a flashlight at the ceiling. Sovann smiled at the heaven his father had made. Not everyone had such a high opinion of Munny's artwork. The aunties who'd watched him moving a bamboo ladder to climb up and reach the ceiling thought he wasn't right in the head. There was no money in it. Since he was a child, Munny had had the same reaction to his art from others in the family and village. Better to fish than to paint a sky that wasn't real.

After the first constellation, Munny had started on a second one, choosing Taurus the bull. No one but his son praised his work, but that was enough. Munny found that an artist needed only one admirer to sustain his faith. Within a few months he had added Taurus, Sagittarius and Pegasus, drawing on his memory of the night sky in all its detail. As if he were lying in the fields once again, his mind's eye moved across the curtain of darkness that stretched from one horizon to the other, remembering.

Having fixed the generator, Munny headed for the stairs.

"Where are you going?" asked Chamey.

"I have a new job."

Everyone who'd been talking stopped.

"What kind of work?"

"Art work."

"Tattoos?"

He shook his head.

"A Thai hired me."

Chamey looked doubtful.

"It might be a trick," she said.

"Maybe, but I don't think so."

"What kind of art? Stars?"

"I don't know. But I'll find out."

"How much is he paying you?"

Munny looked at all the faces studying him for the answer to the one question on all their minds.

"She'll tell me today."

Chamey and the others reacted with disappointment.

"Why didn't you ask her?"

Munny shrugged, wondering why he hadn't thought to ask the night before. But the shock of having ten thousand baht stuffed in his shirt pocket was a good enough reason. No need to ask too much with someone stuffing cash into your clothing.

"I think she'll be fair."

"When has any Thai treated us fairly?"

"Are you going to paint her stars?" asked one of the aunties.

The others laughed. Their laughter burnt a big hole through his pride. He thought that after a lifetime of taunts and rejection of his drawings, perhaps he should have developed a rhino hide, but his skin remained as thin as when he was a boy.

"Don't you have fish to sell?" Munny reminded them.

He didn't wait for an answer. He ran down the open concrete staircase to the landing on the second floor and nearly ran into an Eight-Niner guard climbing up the stairs from the basement.

"Where are you going, star man?"

"To look for work."

"Good. You come back and pay what your wife owes, okay?"

TEN

"Prostitution gives her an opportunity to meet people. It provides fresh air and wholesome exercise, and it keeps her out of trouble."—Joseph Heller, *Catch-22*

EVER SINCE THE wrecking ball had demolished Washington Square, McPhail had been on a personal mission to discover a new lunchtime hangout, one that would draw what was left of the old gang of regulars from the Lonesome Hawk. All kinds of new bars, cafés and restaurants had opened along Sukhumvit Road since the Lonesome Hawk had been reduced to matchsticks, loaded into dumpsters and hauled away. The problem was the new places were either too far away or too upscale, or they had rules against smoking and getting drunk, or waitresses who cadged drinks and checked off for a short time, dragging the customer up a flight of rickety stairs.

The fact was, most of the Sukhumvit crowd had forgotten Washington Square as quickly as a young woman who trades in a poor husband for a rich one. The expat culture had changed from the old days. It had been a long-running party without many rules or the need for much money. By the time the wrecking ball arrived, the bars in the Square were on life support anyway, fed by a group of regulars who had informally decided they would not go to a lot of trouble to live a long time. They'd all been around long enough, and waiting for the inevitable only pushed their drinking from evening into afternoon, and by the end of the Square's life, into late morning.

They'd made things up as they drifted through the long, hot days. It was a time when a man got lost for a long afternoon with a bottle and a woman, and no one could reach him. A time before iPhones and iPads, Facebook, Twitter and Line messaging. The Lonesome Hawk was one of those bars where stupid things got said and argued about. No evidence of those old conversations survived, only the failing memories of old-timers who'd lost the plot. Most of the time they shouted about the unfairness of not having enough money or women who wanted too much money. Maybe lifting a shirt to show off a war wound, they would bitch about meager social security benefits and advise listeners how to stay out of serious trouble. They had trouble adjusting to the modern world, where young foreigners compared their own scars not from violence but from bicycle accidents in the Bangkok traffic. They complained that finding a reliable friend among the new generation was as likely as stumbling over a Gothic pipe organ in an Isan brothel.

McPhail, though, never gave up hope of discovering a new drinking place.

"I found it," he said to Calvino as they took a taxi into Soi 49. "The perfect bar."

Calvino nodded. He'd heard McPhail say it before and with the same conviction. He had that Bill Clinton, I-did-not-have-sexual-relations-with-that-woman kind of sincerity. Even though you knew he was lying, you couldn't stop yourself from wanting to believe him.

"Time to bring along the 'Mission Accomplished' sign?"

"Fuck you."

McPhail saw that he had lost Calvino's full attention as his iPhone was distracting him.

"In the age of signs, everyone gets two words for their T-shirt. What do you choose, McPhail, other than of course 'Fuck you'?"

"I'm keeping an open mind," he murmured.

McPhail let Calvino's skepticism slide pass. There was no point arguing until Calvino saw the place—and either he could see the potential, or fuck him, he was a fuckwit.

"Did I tell you it's called the Happy Bar?"

"You did mention it. 'Happy' is the magic word of the moment. Have you heard about the detentions?"

McPhail nodded.

"It's just the locals screwing around with each other. I don't see any foreigners being taken in. Besides, the army says they're treating everyone well."

"Cookies and milk. What do you expect them to say? We tortured two academics today? They promised to change their footnotes, so we let them go?"

"Calvino, look. If you go around bad-mouthing the coup, they won't make it easy on you. They'll make it tough. Why do you care? The traffic's moving, people are going to work, eating lunch, drinking and screwing."

McPhail leaned forward and instructed the taxi driver to turn into a small sub-*soi* in a residential area.

"Almost there."

"The new bosses want everyone to be happy," said Calvino, reading from his iPhone screen.

Scrolling through Fah's Twitter timeline, he read one of her Tweets aloud: "Junta adjusts the attitudes of scholars who are unhappy with them."

McPhail's head had begun to resemble an ancient sandstone lion's head eroded by sun, wind and rain. He tilted his head to the side.

"What are you reading?"

"Tweets."

"I didn't think you did that shit."

"I don't."

"Right. ... I thought it was you talking."

"It was me talking, Ed."

"You know what I mean. You were reading someone else's words?"

"Alan Osborne's girlfriend."

"Stop," McPhail told the driver. "Go back. It's back there."

McPhail rolled his eyes because the driver had overshot the bar by twenty meters. They got out of the taxi and walked to the front of the Happy Bar, where half a dozen *katoeys* lounged in high heels, fishnet stockings and the larger-sized exotic sleepwear sold by street hawkers. He looked again. One or two might have been actual women who blended in with the *katoeys*. The right makeup, surgery and outfits camouflaged the original gender much as green-brown netting covered a tank in the desert. The staff lolled about in chairs out front, smoking and jabbing their fingers on their cell phones. Looking up to see real, live customers, they waved and smiled. Two of them made straight for McPhail, throwing their arms around him. One of them took a cigarette from her lips and stuck it between his, and then kissed him on the face.

"You've been here before, Ed."

"Man, I told you that. They know me. Don't you baby?"

"It's probably better that Old George isn't around anymore."

They walked into the bar. Calvino followed behind as McPhail strutted like a fighting cock, with a *katoey* on each arm, smiling as smoke spiraled out of his nose. The *katoeys* marched McPhail to a booth in the back near the kitchen. McPhail, distracted, didn't notice at first a man at the adjacent booth, seated with his back to them, curled up with a newspaper. The man turned around.

"Vincent. You're right on time."

Ballard held up his wine glass and toasted McPhail and his two escorts.

"Ed, this is Ballard."

"Your houseguest. I've heard about you."

"All good things," said Ballard.

"Why don't you join us?" said Calvino.

What was Ballard doing at the Happy Bar? Dressed in an expensive white shirt open at the collar and tan trousers with a perfect crease, he also wore a cologne scent that had one of the *katoeys* sniffing and sighing.

Changing seats, Ballard turned to Calvino and said, "I hope you don't mind if I join you for lunch. Your secretary said I could find you at the Happy Bar."

"You know how many Happy Bars there are in Bangkok?"

"I got lucky," said Ballard. "Only one deep into Soi 49. I took a chance and here you are."

He looked around the room.

"What do you think?" asked McPhail.

"An inspired find," said Ballard. "A place I'd never have found by myself."

"It's not in the guidebooks," said Calvino.

"Don't listen to Calvino."

The *katoeys* drifted over to the TV, connected to a DVD player, sitting like an artifact wired from another time. Covered under a film of dust, it still functioned like a museum display on a metal shelf bolted to the cheap wall paneling. One of them cranked up the volume of Beyoncé's "Dangerously in Love" video, and the *katoeys* started to dance and sing along. The walls were plastered with posters of Jimi Hendrix, John Wayne and Michael Jackson, some of them framed, others taped to the wall, their edges frayed and curling up like a sneering Elvis lip.

"Everyone needs a theme song," said Calvino.

"Mixing danger and love is risky business," said Ballard.

"I'm gonna like you, bud," said McPhail, "because that's exactly what I've been doing my whole life."

He turned to the waitress.

"Bring me a double vodka and soda, sweetheart."

"If I'm interrupting something, let me know," said Ballard.

"What do we look like? A couple of spooks?" said McPhail.

Calvino sat back in the booth, wondering exactly what Ballard wanted from him.

"Ed's been scouting for a new lunchtime hangout."

"A place with character," said McPhail.

"Some people confuse a place with character with one filled with characters," said Ballard. "Still, I believe you've found both."

"See, Calvino, what did I tell you?"

"I can't stay long," Ballard continued. "I have an appointment on Sathorn Road with an Englishman named Alan Osborne. He said that he'd known you for years."

"Yeah, I know him."

Calvino wondered how the two of them had connected, and the possibilities formed a succession of dodgy deals in his mind. Calvino had known Osborne for more than twenty years, but he kept that detail to himself.

"How do you know Osborne?"

"It's not all that different from how I came to know you. Pure accident. We both love flying, and it turned out we owned the same kind of plane. Piper Seneca V. Same year, 2001. Our planes were parked side by side in Phnom Penh a couple of years ago. We stayed in touch."

"You're meeting up with Osborne?" asked Calvino.

"Not Alan but someone he knows who wants to buy a yacht. Alan thought I might know a seller and could help broker the deal."

"Osborne knows a lot of rich people," said Calvino. "He would have loved Christina Tangier. Though he would have likely stolen the teddy bear."

"That was my impression, too. Seems that markets are much smarter than people who deal in them. Some people buy a ship like a racehorse because it will enhance their status in a certain crowd. While other men buy a ship like a draft horse, to build an empire. I know both kinds."

Ballard pushed back his chair and stood beside the table. Raising his half-filled glass of the Happy Bar's cheap red and looking at it, he then set it on the table without drinking from it.

"I should have ordered the beer," he said. "That's what I want on my tombstone, by the way."

He placed a five hundred baht note under the glass.

"We just arrived," said McPhail.

"I like your friend," Ballard said to Calvino. "I like all your friends."

"Let me order you that beer," said Calvino.

He shook his head.

"I'd like to, but I've got to go. I'll be in town longer than I expected. I've checked into the Oriental. Here's your key and keycard. Thanks for the hospitality. Let me know if you change your mind about the map."

Calvino felt ashamed. He'd been out most of the time since Ballard had arrived.

"Let's talk over dinner."

Ballard watched a *katoey* dancing to Beyoncé's video in front of the cash register. Her hips and arms moved with the precision of the captain of the North Korean synchronized swimming team.

"I've got that covered," said Ballard. "On Wednesday night I'm taking you to dinner on the river. I left the details in a note back at your condo. The restaurant might not have the atmosphere of the Happy Bar, but it is highly recommended."

They watched Ballard walk out the door.

"Buying and selling yachts," said McPhail. "That's something I should try. I know people. It sounds like an easy way to make money. Enough to buy a twin engine plane."

McPhail had Googled the model of Ballard's airplane on Calvino's phone. He whistled through his teeth as he showed Calvino the price tag.

"Ed, haven't you learned? There is no easy way to make a lot of money, and once you work to make some, it's even harder to hold on to it."

"That guy was smooth. Dressed like a movie star," said McPhail. "Come to think of it, he was a little too smooth, if you ask me."

"He's carrying around a heavy bag of troubles," said Calvino.

"Who isn't?"

"Exactly."

McPhail shifted his attention to his vodka and rattled the ice cubes. He didn't like to be reminded of Calvino's financial wisdom. He eased back in his chair, remembering how happy he'd been listening to Old George and Gator and the other guys, drunkenly telling stories at two in the afternoon.

Calvino twisted around and watched three more *katoeys* join in dancing to the Beyoncé song. We all need a hero, he thought, someone to inspire us to sing and dance. This crowd found its fix in songs about a world of suffering and hurt. Beyoncé delivered them to a better place.

"They're happy," said McPhail.

"It is the Happy Bar."

What it was, was a shabby, run-down hole where, for the length of a song, the *katoeys* could connect with happiness, and that was good enough.

"These girls don't care about politics. Those problems are a million miles away for them," said McPhail. "Their heads are filled with other worries."

Calvino shook his head.

"You're wrong, McPhail. Politics tracks them down like everyone else. It's a shadow over their lives. They know the man can walk in any time, turn off the music and push them around. And what can they do?"

" 'The man'? You mean someone like your friend, Ballard?"

"That's not his style."

But Calvino thought maybe he had been thinking of Ballard unconsciously. There are a hundred ways to push someone around, he knew, and some ways had more style than others. Still, for all Ballard's style, it had been unsettling to find him waiting at the bar, and disturbing to find out that Ballard and Osborne shared a history. Next to sharing spit, it was apparently hard to beat the bonding that came from finding out someone owned the same plane. Calvino doubted that it was a coincidence Ballard had decided to move out of his guestroom and into the Oriental Hotel once he'd discovered the Calvino and Osborne connection. Had Osborne told Ballard about the problem with Fah, or the story of how his son, Rob, had been killed while under Calvino's watch in Rangoon?

In Calvino's experience there were no secrets anymore except in a person's imaginary world. The grids in the network constantly evolved new nodes. And yet each time a new one arose, Calvino never failed to be surprised. Why was that? He wondered if that was a question anyone could ever answer, in a land where surprise coups were a regular feature of the landscape.

The Beyoncé video finally ended, and a reedy Thai voice came from the far corner. The boss barked at the *katoeys* to get back to work. In the man's attitude Calvino heard an echo of Old George shouting at the staff of the Lonesome Hawk: "Turn down that fucking music!" Calvino turned around in his chair.

Along with McPhail, Calvino watched the *katoeys* flip the man the bird as they filed out the door like a chorus line fired from a show. They gathered in front of the bar, sharing a cigarette and nursing their loss of face as they watched the street. Theirs was a life of watching and waiting, noting who came and went, and calculating what got left behind and what got taken away. They knew that although they had each other, they had lives that didn't add up to much, and it left them somewhere between anger and despair. All they knew for sure was the size of their cage, a home a bit larger than the communal prison cells some of them knew from firsthand experience. They counted off their steps inside and outside the Happy Bar with the same dull awareness of movement on a treadmill. What did they have to look forward to other than an occasional Beyoncé fix to keep them from going insane and doing damage?

After the *katoeys* left, a waitress came to the table. Calvino ordered the taco special.

"Tacos..." said McPhail. "Yeah, I'll have the same."

The waitress scribbled the orders down on a notepad and disappeared.

"You know some interesting people," said McPhail, "but have you ever noticed that most of them are criminals? Except for Pratt, of course."

"The department has hired him back. They've made him a general."

McPhail's jaw dropped.

"One honest man makes for a small fig leaf."

Every so often, *idiot savant*-like, McPhail broke to the surface like a blue whale, tail slapping the water hard. Calvino cherished those moments. McPhail saw straight through the bullshit with perfect clarity, and what he saw was the truth. He wasn't afraid to speak it.

The waitress shoved two plates of tacos across the table. Each taco shell was partly crushed, bearing thumbprint-sized holes, either from carelessness or vandalism. McPhail picked one up but it fell apart in his hand, expelling ground meat, cheese and tomato like shrapnel over the plate and table. Calvino watched his friend take a bite and chew.

"It's like this, McPhail. If you have too much crime, there's something wrong. The laws are outdated and unfair, or maybe the government is in the business of running illegal sidelines for their own benefit. When that happens, people have freedom but no safe space to be free. Everyone runs scared. They shoot and knife each other to take what they can get, or maybe for no other reason than they're fearful. If you have zero crime, it means the government is controlling everything using curfews and martial law. That keeps people off the streets. They are free but imprisoned. So... what's your poison?"

"You're saying, people are a lot happier when crooks other than the ones in government are raking in the benefits of stealing and shooting," said McPhail.

"Sometimes you're brilliant, Ed."

"Then why don't you trust me on a new restaurant?"

"There are limits to your brilliance."

McPhail started on his second taco.

"They don't look great, but they're good. Aren't you going to eat yours?"

Calvino slid his plate across to McPhail.

"You look hungry."

"What's with you? I never see you eat."

"I'm saving up for my post-taco life."

"Okay, you don't like Tex-Mex. So what's this about taking on a new case? When you told me and everybody else..."

McPhail finished by taking half a taco from Calvino's plate into his mouth.

"I've been hired to get the skinny on whether Osborne's girlfriend is cheating on him. I was about to tell you the story in the taxi when a *katoey* dragged you out of the back."

Calvino glanced at his phone, reading half a dozen text messages from Fah's phone.

"Get the bill. We need to go."

"What's the hurry?"

"Osborne's girlfriend is making a move."

"I've got to get one of those phones. Will it tell me when to make a move?"

"Get the bill, McPhail."

"Okay, I take your point. As long as I hang around you, I don't need a smart phone."

He'd lost Calvino, who was focused on the iPhone screen.

McPhail looked around for the waitress. She'd vanished. The *katoeys* were outside and there were no other customers. McPhail stood up and walked toward the counter and the cash register. There, lying on a cot, he saw a bony-chested, shirtless man, whose rolled-up jeans exposed a pair of spider-thin legs and shoeless feet sticking over the edge. A copy of Orwell's *1984* rested on his sweaty ribcage, which heaved with his groaning and moaning.

"Noi, what are you doing over there?" said McPhail. "Are you okay? We walked right past you."

Calvino left the table with cash in hand and laid a five hundred baht note beside the cash register. He stopped next to McPhail.

"This is Vincent Calvino, a good friend of mine. Noi's the owner of the Happy Bar."

Mr. Happy himself looked like a hunger striker stretched out in his final lap around the wasting-away track. Under a backwards Red Sox cap, a pair of aviator sunglasses dwarfed his thin face, making it bug-like. Dark bags spilled down from his eyes toward oversized lips that vibrated around the butt of a cigarette like strings on a harp.

"What's wrong with you?" asked McPhail. "Tell me it wasn't the tacos."

That broke Calvino's attention from his cell phone and he looked up. Noi seemed to be seriously ill.

"Half right. It's food poisoning from last night. There were some bad crabs in the *som tum*. Been puking all morning."

Another victim of the irresistible raw crabs, thought Calvino. He had seen it before.

"Man, you shouldn't eat that shit."

"But I love it."

"Have you seen a doctor?"

Noi held up a bag of medicine and lowered his sunglasses.

"I went to the clinic. See that plate behind you?"

Calvino turned to where Noi pointed and picked up a plate with a few tiny pellets of dry food.

"Right, that's it. Let me see it."

"Someone's taken half the food," said Calvino.

"It doesn't look like food," said McPhail.

"Can you feed what's left to my fish? He should have been fed an hour ago. The *katoeys* are on strike. They're trying to starve Dylan."

"Dylan?" asked McPhail.

"After Bob Dylan. The *katoeys* hate Dylan. Don't ask me why. They're pissed off with me. And the curfew, no customers and no tips don't help the situation. They've been out front most of this morning plotting against me. They sabotaged the tacos. Refused to feed my fish."

A huge silver-bellied fish hovered in an aquarium two sizes too small for its body. Dylan turned like a supertanker in a pond, tail brushing one end and the lips the other.

"I'll feed him, Noi," said McPhail.

He sprinkled taco shell crumbs into the top of the aquarium.

"Thanks, Khun Ed," Noi said.

"I've put the money we owe on the counter," said Calvino. "We've got to go."

"You'd better give it to me. They'll steal it if you leave it out in the open," said Noi, motioning with one hand. "Not one of them is honest."

Calvino retrieved the note and handed it to McPhail, who slipped it into Noi's English-language copy of *1984*.

"Big Brother says keeps the change," said McPhail.

Calvino led the way out of the bar. The first thing he noticed was that all the *katoeys* had disappeared. McPhail joined him on the street.

"Where did they run off to?"

"McPhail, the old Lonesome Hawk Bar crew isn't gonna flock to the Happy Bar. Best to keep looking."

Twenty meters away from the bar, McPhail stopped in his tracks and turned around.

"Looks like the cavalry has arrived."

Calvino followed McPhail's gaze and spotted a black police van and military vehicle screeching to a halt in front of the bar. Doors opened and shut as two-way radios squawked with static. Half a dozen soldiers in green combat gear, bearing M16s, clambered out. Four uniformed police, two of them senior officers, emerged from the van. Calvino and McPhail watched the group march into the Happy Bar.

Ten minutes later they came out again. In the procession two soldiers, weapons slung over their backs, carried Noi on his cot. One of the military officers walked behind, carrying the copy of *1984* and showing one of the cops the five hundred baht note McPhail had left inside. Another soldier held up Noi's Red Sox cap like a prize catch.

"Man, that cap's got the word 'Red' on it," said McPhail.

Anything red or with the word "red" attached was unlawful.

Calvino walked a few steps toward the armed personnel carrier, and one of the soldiers rushed up to block his path.

"What you want, *farang*?"

A soldier behind him displayed a Che Guevara poster ripped from the wall—along with the book and the cap, damning evidence of Noi's crimes. The soldiers looked proud that they'd apprehended an enemy of the nation. Calvino was certain that if he'd not been prostrate with illness, Noi would have been handcuffed and frog-marched out of the Happy Bar.

Noi smirked as they loaded him into the police van. At the vehicle's rear doors one of the cops and a soldier stood guard. Nothing Calvino could say or do was going to change Noi's fate. He'd just been inducted into a seven-day attitude adjustment program. But that didn't stop Noi from raising himself up and catching Calvino's eye.

"My own staff did this for revenge," said Noi, nodding toward a couple of the *katoeys* who had drifted back and were giving statements to the police. "Can you believe it? I should have seen it coming. Stealing Dylan's food was a sign. It's not right. It's not fair. I ain't done nothing but read a book."

"You should've stuck with the New York Yankees," said McPhail. "Wearing a Boston Red Sox cap was dumb, Noi."

Raising his head again, Noi lowered his sunglasses and flashed a victory sign.

"At least I'll get to see a real doctor," he said.

Noi's head rolled to the side and he vomited. The sound of his dry heaves rose above the burst of static from the two-way radios. The van door slammed closed. The other police climbed in front, and the driver followed the armored personnel carrier as it made a sloppy U-turn, the wheels climbing the opposite curb. As quickly as they'd arrived, they were gone.

"You think Noi is a Red Sox fan?" asked McPhail.

"My guess is he couldn't find Boston on a map."

"Or explain what 'S-O-X' means," said McPhail. "But he bought it for the word 'Red,' so the soldiers probably are right."

Like the poster, the cap was a kind of signature of support for the losing side. At least in terms of baseball, he'd picked the right team.

Calvino and McPhail exchanged a look and slowly walked away. Despite scenes like the one they'd just witnessed, life in Bangkok wasn't anything like a movie. That was the weird thing, Calvino thought. None of it felt abnormal, when deep inside he knew that it was. What happened in the Happy Bar and in the street should have pulled alarm bells in a normal person. He looked closely at his friend.

"Did that seem strange?" he asked McPhail.

"Don't start on about the tacos."

Calvino was reassured.

"You're right. Not another word about the tacos."

A man living in Bangkok soon discovered that he needed to understand entries and exits, knowing the right lines to say at the right time. Even with those skills, things could sour quickly, attitudes darkening. From out of nowhere an unlucky card could get played, and that normal, abnormal thing fell on a man like green snakes from the trees. Calvino quickened his pace. He had work to do, and a solid lead had dropped on him in the Happy Bar. All he could think of was rushing to the main *soi* and finding a taxi.

ELEVEN

"Political language is designed to make lies sound truthful and murder respectable, and to give an appearance of solidity to pure wind. "
—George Orwell

FROM THE MOMENT Munny headed upstairs from the barbershop, he had the feeling that whatever awaited him there wasn't going to be easy or friendly. As he stood framed by the doorway, Fah called to him.

"It's okay. These are my friends, Oak and Palm."

"I'm Khmer," Munny said, when Oak asked him about his heavy accent.

There was no hiding he was a foreigner. He let that word, Khmer, sink in as the room went silent. Oak pulled Palm, the third member of their cell, to the side.

"Is she crazy?" Oak asked him.

"Let me show you something," Fah said to her friends.

She opened a new window on her laptop, and photos of Munny's tattoos filled the screen. She scrolled down to Munny's Banksy-inspired tattoo of the schoolgirl pulled airborne by balloons.

"Tattooing isn't the same as graphic design. Can he do graphics?" asked Oak.

She looked at Munny.

"We'll soon find out."

Fah opened a second window and scrolled through a slide show of Banksy's street art: a homeless man holding a sign that said, "Keep your coins, I want change"; a man with his face covered, right arm cocked like a bomb throw ready to unload, only the bomb was a bunch of flowers; and a succession of rats and Mona Lisa-inspired designs. The last work in the slide show had been stenciled on a wall: an English policeman holding a flashlight and a leash attached to a poodle, under a sign—"This wall is a designated graffiti area."

"Can you do this sort of thing?" she asked. "What I mean is use the idea. Don't just copy it."

Munny studied the policeman and the poodle.

"Yeah, I can do that."

She handed him paper and pen, and Munny drew. He stopped, wadded up the paper and started again and again until he had his own version of the policeman and then the dog. Palm and Fah came up with new words for the image. Oak had the idea of a fake phone number that accessed a junta hotline. He also criticized the policeman's cap. Munny did another version.

Oak shrugged his shoulders, shaking his head like a man unconvinced. What had started as their personal study group was now expanding. The addition of one person might not seem like much, but that was paying too much attention to the single-digit number and not the role of the new person. Oak fancied himself—and he'd sold himself to Fah and Palm—as Bangkok's Banksy. When they had hatched the idea of a guerilla street art group, he'd told Fah and Palm that he was the man to make them all proud. He'd gone on about how his private art tutors had always complimented his talent and imagination.

Oak's face grew and grew with the talk, all before he'd showed them any of his artwork. He had promised to show Fah his portfolio of his award-winning graphic designs, including the hard-hitting stuff he'd bragged about. When the time had come, she'd just flipped through it, thinking the next one had to be better. One after another, the pages were filled with crude cartoons of vampires, dragons and giants showing lots of fangs and long nails, and exploding coffins. She looked for elements of protest. What she found was blood and gore.

"Where's the Banksy stuff?"

His jaw had tightened, softly grinding his teeth.

"You're looking at it."

She had been afraid that would be his answer. As their study group had broken up that day, Fah had remembered seeing a guy with a Banksy tattoo. She'd made it her mission to find this artist who'd used a tattoo needle to channel into human flesh the Banksy urban vision of the powerless caught in a vice of repression. She'd hunted down the *farang* on Khao San Road who had the Banksy tattoo, and he'd given her Munny's name and shop address. She'd handed Munny the ten thousand baht and the barbershop card. Then she'd worried he would skip back to Cambodia with the money and kicked herself for giving him so much. Osborne had taught her never to give an employee enough money to do a runner, but what was done was done. To cover the possibility she'd misjudged Munny's character, she'd said nothing about him to either Oak or Palm.

The soldier and dog had proved Munny could channel Banksy. Fah now grabbed his elbow and guided him to the long table, instructing him to take it to the next step. After that, Munny had no question in his mind about who was calling the shots inside the room. Banksy was the superstar and Fah the coach who believed that a rookie like Munny could play at Banksy's level. He let himself be led. He wanted to believe her because he wanted to believe in himself.

"Now I want you to draw a Thai soldier, instead of a British policeman, and have him holding a Thai dog on a leash. We need big images, so people will notice them on a wall."

"What kind of dog?" asked Oak.

Fah thought for a moment.

"A *soi* dog." Turning to Munny, she asked, "Can you draw a sad-looking street dog?"

"Come on. He's probably eaten a dozen *soi* dogs," said Oak.

"The Vietnamese eat dogs," said Munny. "Cambodians don't eat dog."

Fah shook her head.

"A *soi* dog and a Thai soldier. Could you just let him draw?"

Munny used the better part of two hours to sketch out a one-meter tall soldier and life-sized *soi* dog, right down to a pair of floppy ears. Fah and Palm taped it to the wall and they all stood back, imagining the effect when applied in spray paint on the side of a building. Palm stuck up two fingers in a victory sign.

"Looks good," he said.

"Thanks," Munny replied.

"I want the words to go with it," said Fah. "Have a look at this for the style."

She handed Munny the Banksy book with the designated text graphic he was to emulate. When he had drawn the text and cut the stencils, Palm's easy, relaxed smile registered his approval. Munny had won him over. Palm's thick, black-rimmed glasses magnified his eyes, giving him an owlish look. His neatly trimmed rat's-tail beard framed each side of his face, dead-ending just short of his jaw. The finely maintained facial hair carried the hint of a medieval duelist, sword in hand, committed to slaying infidels. Palm's square-shaped head, set off by a curtain of black bangs, added a touch of the mad scientist.

Fah, hands pressing each of the stencils against the wall, taped and secured them. When she was finished, the combined stencils read, **THIS WALL IS A DESIGNATED.**

"What do you think, Oak?"

"Okay," he said.

That was the closest to a compliment Oak was willing to give.

"Position it at eye level," he added.

Appointing himself as spatial consultant was better than being left out in the cold.

Munny, hearing no further objections, leaned over the table and, working freehand, began to cut the next stencil word: **HAPPINESS**. With the font this size, it took a good eye to navigate the sharp curves of the S's. Any slippage and it would send the whole eighteen-wheeler tumbling over the side of the mountain, requiring a fresh start.

Luck seemed to be on his side. Fah's studio was on the third floor over a barbershop. Munny lived on the third floor of the Aquarium. Another three-floor walkup was to become the story of his life. In Bangkok there were hundreds, maybe thousands of buildings with hundreds of stories. Fate was sending him a message: Munny, your place in life is on the third floor. Deal with it. The Eight-Niners are always going to be coming down your staircase asking where there money is.

The floor area beneath the table was littered with wadded paper, throwaways of earlier drafts and discarded acetate stencils. Oak, his hair tied in a ponytail, circled the table in his black T-shirt with the Batman signal against the night sky of Gotham, while his jeans and his white cloth bag on the floor gave away his university student identity. He sported a tiny trail of a moustache above his upper lip.

Rather than regret his inflated view of his own graphic art skills, Oak just wouldn't give up. As they stopped for a coffee break, he talked up his résumé and how he had just about landed a graphic designer's job with an international company.

"I've followed Banksy for years," he said.

Fah drank her coffee and stared at the stencils on the wall.

"Can I see your work sometime?" asked Munny, in a polite, genuine voice.

"So you can copy it?"

"Only if Fah wants me to."

"Time to get back to work," she said.

Beyond a stencil that said, "2 + 2 = 5," Oak would never master Banksy's world. Fah knew that and also understood that when discussing Banksy with him, there were limits to what she could say. How could she tell Oak that his images were stillborn, tainted with dull echoes from established brands? She couldn't. Any more than she could tell Oak that he lacked the talent to stretch his mind into another realm. He also lacked the flare to realize the artistic potential within the existing political state of play, unable to see the paradox. Banksy effortlessly visualized a larger truth. He knew exactly where to position cops and soldiers against the world of innocent children and animals for maximum impact. Like her hero, Christina Tangier, Fah saw that Banksy used art to tell the truth.

Oak still resisted bringing in an outsider, and that meant anyone who wasn't a classmate. He knew that what they planned to do might get them into serious trouble. Only those very close could be trusted. Had Fah considered the risk of being thrown into a military prison? Sensing his disapproval, she touched his arm, with a look in her eye that said he should trust her judgment. Oak sat looking at her, saying nothing, lost inside his world. Since the coup, he'd changed in subtle ways.

"What are you going to do with this?" asked Munny, gesturing toward the stencils on the wall.

"It's for our term project paper," said Palm.

"That's how we started," said Fah, "but it's time that we've moved on."

She glanced at Oak, who remained in a suspended state of half-acceptance, half-denial.

"You're studying art?" asked Munny.

"Political science," said Fah. "The art of governing."

Munny scratched his chin, wondering what kind of art Fah meant.

Fah then watched as Munny used a knife to cut the image of the soldier and the dog into the surface of a clear sheet of acetate. Earlier, he'd experimented with cutting the image into thick paper and then cardboard. Acetate made the best stencil material, as it could be reused, but it required a sure hand when the image was taped over the surface. The real skill, though, was drawing a design that, when quickly spray-painted on a wall, a bridge or a building , would be immediately recognizable from a distance. The trickiest parts were getting the edges clear and precise, and the contrast and brightness right.

The group then worked together to assemble the stencils on a whitewashed wall. Munny shook a can of black paint spray. He felt their eyes on him as he sprayed over the words cut into the stencils. He stopped to check his work, moving in close, eyeing the density of the paint. Only then did Munny resume the spraying, taking special care with the cutouts of the soldier and the dog.

They let the paint set for a few minutes before Oak and Palm moved in to take down the stencils. The four of them stared at the wall for a minute. No one wanted to be the first to say anything. Finally it was Fah who broke the silence.

"It's beautiful." She turned to Munny as if examining him for the first time. "We have a saying in Thai that 'A bad situation makes a hero out of an ordinary person.' But I'm getting the feeling you're no ordinary person, Munny."

She held out her iPhone and snapped a series of photos. She took a selfie with the wall behind, her head between the soldier and the *soi* dog on a leash.

THIS WALL IS A DESIGNATED HAPPINESS AREA

**REFORM UNHAPPY PEOPLE
Help Line: 911189**

TWELVE

"We know that no one ever seizes power with the intention of relinquishing it."—George Orwell, *1984*

CALVINO SCROLLED THROUGH Fah's tweet timeline from the previous night and found, "Curfew locks my door for the night, no kiss goodnight, my thoughts like a stranger in silence." Wasn't she supposed to be a political science major? Apparently she shared her inner thoughts with a couple of thousand people, but Osborne wasn't one of them. He clicked onto Fah's Facebook private messages and read the last half dozen, which had been left while he'd been in the Happy Bar.

For the modern private eye, there was no assistant to track the thoughts, movements, plans, desires and craziness of people who could match the data streams of Twitter and Facebook. Fah continually self-reported her location, how long she'd be at that place and her future meeting places and times. It was now hard to believe how difficult it had once been to follow a person in Bangkok in a time before smart phones and social media. The new generation demanded to be followed online. It was in their digital blood. A small investment in a few specialized apps, and not even Sherlock Holmes in his most inspired opium dreams could have imagined the possibilities—such as remotely switching on Fah's iPhone mic. He listened to voices speaking Thai, young male voices. When Fah spoke, he recognized her voice.

Calvino clicked on another app to turn on her iPhone camera. This one required some analog good luck. The phone had to be at the right angle. If the camera was inside a handbag or next to something blocking the lens, nothing but a black void would come through, as if Alice had fallen down the rabbit hole. A video image of the people behind the voices moved across Calvino's cell phone screen.

The upper floor of the Chinese-style shophouse was open, loft style. Fah sat cross-legged on the edge of a double bed, using her thumbs to type on her screen keypad. She looked up from the phone and said something inaudible to one of the men. On the chairs near the bed, two Thai university-age men watched as a third man, a bit old for university, studied a large stencil spread flat on the surface of the long table. He held a box cutter in his right hand, and Calvino then saw the three of them, backs to the camera, looking at the wall where the words **THIS WALL IS A DESIGNATED HAPPINESS AREA** appeared alongside a soldier and a dog.

Palm leaned in closer to examine the word **DESIGNATED**.

"The word is 'designated'?" asked Oak, waiting for a translation into Thai.

"It's perfect," said Fah, looking at Oak. "It means the official place."

McPhail lit a cigarette in the back of the taxi as it made a left turn onto one of the many forgettable higher-numbered *sois* where Sukhumvit Road snaked toward Chon Buri Province. They drove under a flyover bridge for one hundred meters and passed shophouses until the road took a sharp U-turn. As the taxi headed back to the main road, Calvino leaned forward and told the driver to stop. The barbershop was about twenty meters away on the left-hand side. McPhail, cigarette between his lips, climbed out first and stretched as Calvino paid the driver.

"Man, I'm hungry," McPhail said.

"Let's see if they have tacos."

At a roadside noodle vendor's table, the two occupied small plastic stools with a clear view of the barbershop. The noodle vendor stared at them, smiling broadly. Not many foreigners had ever stopped to order a bowl of noodles from his stand. In fact, they were his first *farang* customers. But his smile collapsed a little when they ordered in Thai, as this immediately limited the price inflation he had in mind. The *farangs* he'd seen before had all been in the back of taxis that stopped and asked for directions. The tourists were clueless that their driver was giving them the famous roundabout tour of Bangkok to increase his fare.

"Man, this is a rat hole paradise," said McPhail, looking at the building behind the noodle stand. "An infinite number of drainpipes to run up."

Just then the head of a large rat emerged from one of the drainpipes. It surveyed the landscape before dropping out and scurrying along the side of the building to another drainpipe.

"Did you see the size of that fucking rat? The size of a cat."

Calvino looked up from his bowl of noodles.

"Cats never get that big."

"You gonna eat those noodles?"

"As I missed lunch, yes, I am eating the noodles."

His attention was on the surveillance app on his cell phone.

"You talking to me or your phone?"

"They're about to leave. I want some photos of them in the street."

McPhail pushed his bowl of noodles to the side and lit another cigarette.

"What do you think they're doing to Noi? The poor bastard."

"In his condition, there isn't much more they could do," said Calvino.

"They'll let him go, right?" said McPhail, looking for some assurance.

"After they beat his taco recipe out of him."

"That's why you brought me here. To punish me for the Happy Bar tacos."

"Let's agree this hasn't been a good food day."

He listened to Fah's voice and the voices of her friends coming through his cell phone. They were about to leave but then changed their minds and started to cut another stencil.

"I thought we were leaving the *wai kru* until tomorrow," Calvino heard Palm say.

Munny looked up, holding the box cutter.

"I need to go home, too."

"Soon," said Fah.

That's what she'd said an hour earlier. Oak saw an opening.

"Go, Munny. I can finish up."

Munny looked over at Fah, who was lost inside a social media world where she starred under the handle of ZenMeBot.

"Okay, let's pack up," she said, opening her bag.

Fah walked over to Munny and stuffed three thousand baht in his shirt pocket.

"Tomorrow, same time."

That left Oak holding the box cutter as the curtain came down.

Calvino looked up from his cell phone.

"McPhail, they're coming out."

"Nice neighborhood," said McPhail, blowing smoke out of his nose.

The local community of lower-income Thais lived and worked in shophouses. The neighborhood was lost, out of time, waiting to be discovered by developers. The unbroken line of shabby tenements, a prison complex of cramped, airless rooms cooled by electric fans, wrapped around the U-turn. No one got into or out of the *soi* without a hundred eyes watching.

The residents peered out from their pre-Internet world of small shops as the two *farangs* sat eating bowls of noodles on the pavement. Their version of the social media was the analog world of windows, sidewalks, taxis, cars, motorcycles and people on the street. Through the large glass window of the barbershop, Calvino watched a man getting a haircut. The barber, even at that distance, had a distinctive, round Chinese face. He wore a plastic Panama hat. His stomach, swollen by too many late-night snacks, gave him a sumo wrestler appearance but with a happy Buddha smile. Fah and her friends had a floor in his building.

Calvino had tracked Fah easily. She hadn't bothered to change her phone setting from the default—Show location. Whatever she was up to, she was carrying on without any awareness that her movements were being tracked. Was it the innocence of digital youth, or was it the new normal for young people not to care? Calvino caught the vendor's eye and gestured with his hand for the bill.

"Big spender," said McPhail.

The two bowls of noodles came to sixty baht. The vendor wiped his hands on an oily rag and held out the change from one hundred baht. Calvino waved it off.

"You come back tomorrow?" asked the vendor, smiling at the tip.

"Hey, with your homemade noodles from a packet, how could we resist?" teased McPhail.

The irony was lost on the noodle vendor and his pregnant wife, who dipped the *farangs'* bowls in a plastic tub of soapy water. The couple were an important set of eyes and ears in the neighborhood, well positioned to give the first warning alarm in the event of trouble. They'd be gossiping about the two *farangs* for days.

First Munny strolled out of the barbershop. He looked like a day laborer—long legs, lanky arms that swung as he walked. Calvino snapped several photos. Nothing in the photos captured the real Munny, the artist, the Khmer tattoo genius who lived in an abandoned building, where his wife and family, along with others, farmed fish in the basement. Or Munny's son, Sovann, waiting for his father to return home to help him with his homework. Nor could Calvino read Munny's thoughts as he passed by their table without giving the two *farangs* a second glance.

Munny in his mind was already home. Sovann helping his mother like a good, respectful boy, doing his studies under a fluorescent light connected to the generator. The picture clouded as he thought of the Eight-Niners. There was no future for him and his family in the squatter's building. Now that he had some money, things would be different. After the hate campaign against the Khmers, Chamey had packed up their stuff, three old roller-wheel cases that remained beside the bamboo mat where they slept. They could move out on short notice. They had a few things—clothes, some old family photos, Sovann's schoolbooks, identity papers, good luck charms and eight boxes of cheap noodles. When the time arrived to run away, their belongings wouldn't slow them down.

He regretted having to leave behind the electric generator, but he thought that before they got to that point, he'd try to sell it. News of the generator being for sale would alert the Eight-Niners that Munny was up to something, though, and that was sure to cause trouble. Munny went back and forth in his mind about how best to get his money out of the generator. Chamey, always the practical one, had said they'd better leave it behind. They'd had a fight about it, another regret he felt as he walked along the street. He looked around. He was in a foreign land. He laughed, he had money in his pocket and, inside his head, that thing pigeons had, a built-in navigation system to guide him home to his roost. Instinct was the original mapmaker. Munny's father once told him that people, like birds, lions and zebras, had a map imprinted in their minds. Soon it would be time to go home.

Oak emerged next from the barbershop. The barber in the Panama hat nodded and said something as he passed. Oak pointed behind. Palm and Fah walked into view. The large plate-glass window turned the barbershop into live street theatre. Calvino saw Fah dip a hand into her bag and hand over money to the barber. He counted it as a customer sat in the chair, watching Fah and the barber in the mirror.

As Fah and Palm appeared in the street, Calvino snapped a series of photographs of them talking in front of the barbershop as they waited for a taxi. After a few minutes a taxi pulled up and they piled into the back.

"Another bowl of noodles before we go?" asked Calvino.

"I thought we were friends."

THIRTEEN

"Don't you know, if you don't step outside yourself, you'll never discover who you are."—José Saramago, *The Tale of the Unknown Island*

"I HAVE GOOD news and bad news," said Calvino. "What do you want to hear first?"

Osborne pursed his lips, trying to decide. He examined Calvino's face for some clue. There was none to read.

"Let me have the good news."

"When Fah disappears, she's not hiding away with another man to cheat on you."

Osborne looked physically relieved.

"Okay, now give me the bad news."

"Let me show you. You can see for yourself."

"Show me what? Why do you have to be so mysterious? If she's not cheating on me, how bad can the bad news be? She's not seeing another woman!"

Calvino shook his head as he opened an app on his phone.

"Not another woman."

He opened a photo folder with Fah's name on it. Osborne watched the screen. Calvino scrolled through dozens of photographs of Fah, Oak, Palm and Munny as they walked out of the barbershop, waited for a taxi and climbed into it, as well as a close-up of Munny, who had left first and walked right past Calvino's table on the street.

"What were they doing in a barbershop?" asked Osborne, mystified.

"Nothing. They use a room upstairs."

"A gambling den."

Calvino thought how a twisted mind might draw that conclusion.

"No gambling."

"It's looks like a slum. What would Sky be doing in such a place?"

"They're producing political art to protest the coup."

"You're telling me this is all political and not sexual?"

Calvino nodded.

"That's some relief. They are silly students."

"Alan, there's been a coup. The army could detain her if they found out about her activities. They're not messing around. Dissent and you get an attitude adjustment. That's how it works."

"Do you have pictures of this illegal artwork?"

Calvino showed him half a dozen shots of the soldier, the dog and the lettering: "By Junta Order, THIS WALL IS A DESIGNATED HAPPINESS AREA. REFORM UNHAPPY PEOPLE. Help Line: 911189."

Osborne studied the images and text that had been spray-painted on the wall.

"Sky's always been a rebel. And who are those young men she's with?"

He took Calvino's phone and held it in both hands, his eyes darting between Oak's face and Palm's.

"That's Oak. And this is Palm. They're her university classmates."

"I recognize them, the Tree Brothers from her study group. They've been in my house."

Calvino had run the photos through a facial recognition program that linked to Fah's university database. There's no place left to hide once someone has your picture, thought Calvino.

Osborne stared at the screen on Calvino's phone, shaking his head and sighing.

"And that third, sinister-looking man? I've never seen him before."

Nothing in the university database had turned up for Munny. Calvino had relied on the data dump he'd downloaded from Fah's phone, including the voice recordings of their conversations. She'd called Munny by his name as he worked in their room above the barbershop.

"His name is Munny. He's not a student. Munny's a Cambodian tattoo artist."

"An illegal migrant. That could be trouble. And what's this nonsense about him being an artist? He looks like a laborer. She told me this was a group project for her class. Why would they have an illegal tagging along?"

"They give him directions and he draws the artwork they describe."

"Of course, Fah and her Tree Brothers are exploiting him to get a good mark. Is he also writing their paper? Disgraceful little weasels, don't you think?"

"Have a close look at his artwork, Alan. What do you see?"

"He's cheating them. He's ripped off Banksy. You do know Banksy? He's a famous English street artist."

"Fah hired him precisely because he's mastered Banksy's style," said Calvino.

Osborne rubbed the bald spot on top of his head as if he expected to find hair there.

"I once lent Banksy's dad money. I remember even then his son was spraying graffiti on walls in Bristol, and I was thinking what a waste of a young man's talent. He should get a job. But he was right and I was wrong. Once the right people discovered Banksy, his art sold for a bundle at auction. Sotheby's got him millions of pounds for graffiti images of rats. He became rich defacing other people's property. A criminal, an outlaw, and now you're telling me that my sweetheart is pirating his graffiti in Thailand? Now my beloved is stealing with Banksy? Why does this always happen to me?"

"Did he ever repay the loan?"

"Who?"

"Banksy's father."

"He gave me one of his son's paintings. It was a picture of a rat in a matador's outfit, fighting a bull. I kept it and forgave his old man's debt."

"I listened to their conversation as they worked on the art. As I told you, the ideas came from Fah, not from this guy," Calvino said, pointing at Munny.

Calvino sat back in Osborne's large sitting room, thinking that Fah hadn't stumbled onto Banksy through some random Google search. Her interest must have come after a bottle of wine, with Osborne all relaxed and bragging about how he'd pulled off a once-in-a-lifetime deal.

"Do you still have the Banksy painting?"

"I just told you that I kept it."

"I'd like to see it."

Osborne rolled his eyes.

"Follow me. It's in the guest bedroom."

He led Calvino into one of the other bedrooms, and on the wall over the king-sized bed was a large framed drawing of a rat in a matador's outfit, waving a red cape at a charging bull. Calvino stood at the foot of the bed, staring at the drawing. The bull's flared nostrils emitted a blue smoke that stopped just short of the cape.

"I've been offered ten million baht for it. I told the Chinaman to piss off."

"Does Fah know the background to this painting?"

"Sky. Please call her Sky. Of course, she's seen it. She lives here. How could she not see it?"

"You told her the story about the loan to Banksy's father?"

"I told her that one of Banksy's artworks, far inferior to this one, sold for four million baht. Her eyes lit up. What is it about the Thais that a discussion of big money makes their eyes go all shiny and electric? And she said to me, 'Darling, you are giving me five million baht to have your baby.' She must have thought that I was cheating her. A street artist of rats was getting almost as much for a painting that took him a couple of hours as she was getting for nine months of hard labor. Thank God I didn't tell her I'd turned down ten million baht for this one. If she thought a Banksy picture of a rat and bull was worth double what I was paying her to produce a baby, there would have been a scene. I hate having a scene with a woman I am trying to artificially impregnate. Their emotions can pollute the environment where egg meets sperm.

"And you know what she asked me? 'Darling, how many drawings can Banksy make in one day?' And I said, 'I don't know. He might be able to do two. He has a big studio and all kinds of people working with him. It's big money.' And then she says, 'Christina Tangier is even more famous as an artist. I like her. She would like Banksy's rat. Elite Johns were all photographed with a teddy bear, not a rat, but same, same.' I asked her to stop talking in fucking code. And I said, 'Just explain, who is this Christina Tangier?' And she looks at me like I'm from the Stone Age, and she says, 'She's super-famous, a woman artist. And I love what she's done.' She told me the story about the teddy bear. Have you ever heard of this artist or about the teddy bear?"

"All I know is Tangier photographed some very rich men sleeping nude with a teddy bear," said Calvino.

"Did she tell you the teddy bear used in the photos was an exact replica of Alan Turing's teddy bear, the one they have in a museum at Bletchley Park? Turing was a brilliant mathematician. He broke the Nazis' secret code in World War II, and in his spare time he practiced delivering lectures to his teddy bear. Apparently he was a shy man. After saving us from the Nazis, as his reward we castrated him because he was gay. We can be quite nasty about sexual enigmas. Apparently Christina Tangier destroyed the lives of twenty-nine men because they were rich. I've met one of them: Oliver Ballard. Do you think this Christina Tangier might be saying he's gay?"

"He's no Alan Turing," said Calvino.

"No, he isn't."

Calvino smiled, thinking of Ballard and the idea that no one is more than six degrees of separation from anyone. Sky wouldn't have been the first woman inspired by Christina Tangier's rags to riches story.

"None of this seems to come as a surprise to you," said Calvino. "I thought you'd be shocked when I told you that Sky was making political art," said Calvino.

"The day you shock me, Calvino, is the day they push my coffin into a crematorium and you light the fire with the wrong end of a Roman candle."

"I'll be sure to wear gloves."

Osborne cracked a smile.

"Don't get ahead of yourself, Calvino. Of course it's not political. She's Thai. They don't understand their own politics. It's all guns and uniforms and medals. They love saluting and *waiing* each other. Why would anyone protest?

What's the point? There's nothing to say. It's stupid, all of this protesting. Just salute and move along. That's what I've told her. She listens to me, Calvino.

"As far as I know, Sky loves guns, uniforms and medals. And an English artist named Christina Tangier. So I'm sure she's in it for the money. Like all the Thais I know, she wants to break into the financial big league, and she's using these three amateurs to do her heavy lifting.

"In a way I'm quite proud of her, but in another way I want her stopped. She can't become pregnant and stand near all of that paint and paint cleaner. All this trouble I've gone through to select the perfect sperm, and then they get polluted with chemicals? Sky's engaging in criminal conduct isn't the point. But her exposure to these dangerous fumes is a problem. My child might be born retarded. Or deformed. Or turn out to be another Bristol City thug, one who can't paint or draw anything beyond rats."

Only a blurry line separated Osborne's world of horror and tragedy from humor. That was not unexpected. After all, he was English. Calvino made for the front door.

"Where are you going?"

"We've finished our business."

"I haven't paid you."

Calvino's eyes narrowed.

"We're square. The books are closed."

"Come, Vincent. If you don't want money, what do you want?"

Calvino tipped him a hint of a smile. There was something he wanted from Osborne.

"How do you know Ballard, and what are you doing arranging a yacht deal for him?"

"You know Ballard?" said Osborne. "Why didn't you say so before?"

"His name never came up until today."

Osborne's wily smile flashed.

"Don't be secretive. It's one of your highly unattractive traits—except I suppose that in a private investigator it's an asset. But we aren't finished. I need more information about Sky. To tell you the truth, I'd rather that she was seeing another man than going political, if that's what's happening. I can handle another man fucking her. That's nothing. She's already pregnant, so what can it matter? But politics—that's inside her head, it's likely genetic, something she'll pass along to our baby. That would only mess him up, like Rob, and he'd end up before some firing squad before he's turned nineteen or found dead in some squalid guesthouse in Rangoon. Follow her for a few more days. That's all I ask. After that, I'll answer any question you have about Ballard and my little ship deal in Phuket."

Calvino figured that was as much as he would be getting out of Osborne for now.

"That's blackmail," said Calvino.

"In the time of email, do people still go around using old terms like 'blackmail'? I am surprised. But you're not that young, so that means you're the wrong person to ask. I'll ask Sky. I sense she may be something of an expert on blackmail, judging from what you've found out so far. The Thais are a sinister lot. But your colonel friend must have taught you as much."

"He's a general now."

"There you go. He's made 'sinister' a career path."

On the way out of Osborne's compound, Calvino thought about whether to forget about Osborne and his young wife. There were clients who screamed "mission creep" from the moment they walked into the room and opened their mouths. No matter what information you brought them, the lies and dead ends never stopped with people like them. There was always a new angle, some other problem that came up, sometimes related, sometimes not, until they started to hand over every loose end in their life. It was like finding a tailor and giving him a wardrobe of suits to alter and then asking if he would paint the house and fix the air conditioner while he's at it.

The reality was Calvino wanted something. He wanted an answer to his question about Osborne and Ballard. Their personal connection gave him a feeling he was being played.

FOURTEEN

"All men who repeat a line from Shakespeare are William Shakespeare."—Jorge Luis Borges, *Labyrinths: Selected Stories and Other Writings*

CALVINO HANDED A wrapped gift to the steely-eyed security detail, who viewed him with a combination of disdain and suspicion. A *farang* bearing a gift at police HQ was unusual. The officer stared at the wrapping paper. Calvino had special-ordered paper with hundreds of rows of identical images of Shakespeare in his finest Elizabethan splendor. Just the right touch for Pratt, he thought.

"A gift for the General," he said to the police officer.

"What kind of gift?"

The officer held the package, looking at thousands of cloned Shakespeare images.

"Something for the General's office."

The officer frowned, wondering what this *farang* could possibly bring for a police general's office. The security guard pointed a finger at Shakespeare.

"This looks like Osama Bin Laden."

"William Shakespeare."

The officer examined the beard.

"Terrorists have beards."

"So do bards. Shakespeare was an English *farang*."

The name rang no temple bell inside the security guard's head, but the idea of an English *farang* seemed to register. He looked Calvino up and down, squeezed the package, turned it over and squeezed it again with both thumbs pressed against Shakespeare heads. He lightly tapped the gift against the side of a metal desk. It was as solid as a brick. The image of the Happy Bar tacos flashed across Calvino's mind, and he smiled as the cop turned the package over, trying to look professional but losing the battle. The scanner behind the cop wasn't working. That meant he had to make a decision. Should he make this *farang* unwrap his gift for the General?

The gift, which Ratana had wrapped, was a long, flat, solid object.

"You can open it," said Calvino. "I'll let the General know you thought that it was necessary to spoil the wrapping."

The cop stared at Calvino for a long moment. Then he pushed the gift back into Calvino's hands.

"Go!" he said, waving him through with a look as if he'd just scraped dog shit off his shoe.

On the other side of the checkpoint, a young female officer waited for Calvino.

"You're Khun Vincent Calvino?" she asked.

He could see that she had a printout of an old photo and was trying to match the image to him. He nodded. She requested that Calvino follow her.

"Expecting someone younger?" he asked.

He saw the lieutenant insignia on her uniform.

"Follow me, sir."

She was all business.

"Lieutenant, do you have a name?"

"Pim."

She was the quiet type, the kind who might answer with a single noun when a verb or a few more words might have disclosed a hint of personality hiding inside the uniform.

He followed Pim up a flight of stairs and down a long corridor with rows of office desks on both sides. Behind most of the desks were women officers looking at computer screens. Halfway along the corridor Calvino blinked twice as he saw a folded bedroll under one of the unoccupied desks. He looked closely and saw more bedding rolled up and stuffed underneath other desks. Bedding looked strangely out of place in the police department. Most of the bedrolls were positioned in such a way that they would normally go unnoticed, but once Calvino had spotted one, he couldn't help notice they were as common as computer screens.

One of the bedrolls had unfolded, and the edge of the blue and gray fabric had caught on the wheel of an office chair. He stopped, leaned down and untangled it. The young, attractive woman cop in the chair blushed and flashed an electric smile. Pim looked slightly embarrassed as she watched him stand back up with an amused expression.

"When's nap time?" he asked Lieutenant Pim.

She ignored his question.

"The General is waiting," she said.

The corridor was chilly from overactive air-conditioning.

"I'm going to ask Pratt to show me his bedroll," Calvino said. "Does a general get to choose firm or soft? Or are they standard issue?"

"Feel free to ask General Prachai any questions," Pim said.

"I'll do that," he said.

Pim seemed ready to jump out of her own skin. She gave the impression that depositing him at Pratt's office couldn't happen soon enough. She would certainly avoid being dragged into a discussion of sleeping gear. As they continued, Calvino counted several more bedrolls.

"That makes eight," he said. "It's like fleas. You find one, and you know they come in colonies."

She pretended not to understand him. For some reason, there wasn't just one cold cop with a comforter but a whole dormitory of mainly young female cops who kept camping gear under their desks.

He tried a different tack.

"How long have you been a cop, Lieutenant Pim?"

"Eight years."

He looked at her. The number eight had appeared twice in a row. It was time to buy a lottery ticket, he thought.

"How old are you?"

"Twenty-seven in two months and three days."

"I'll remember to send you a birthday present. Maybe some fresh sheets."

Finally she delivered Calvino to Pratt's door, where she lightly knocked. General Pratt had a private, enclosed office. Like a big shot, he sat behind a door that closed off the rest of the world. And he had a young, attractive woman cop to screen his guests and escort them to his door. What more could he want? Again, the Lieutenant softly tapped her knuckles on the door. Calvino heard Pratt's command voice, muffled by the door, granting permission to enter. She opened the door and gestured for Calvino to walk inside. She remained outside and quietly closed the door behind him, slipping away before Calvino could thank her.

"As McPhail might say, eye candy wrapped in a tight-fitting uniform plucks the rebellion out of a man."

"She's single and looking for a husband."

"I'm single and looking to stay that way, so that leaves me off Lieutenant Pim's short list."

"You got her name."

"She's not much of a talker, your Pim."

"She's not used to a *farang* coming to my office."

He gestured for Calvino to sit in the chair in front of his desk. Pratt's eyes danced over the Shakespearean wrapping paper.

"You shouldn't judge a gift by its wrapping," said Calvino. "But in this case, make an exception."

The banter finished, Calvino placed the present on Pratt's desk. The General leaned back in his executive chair, his fingers touching in a bridge, admiring the paper.

"Ratana wrapped it," said Calvino.

"Of course."

Pratt wore the brown uniform: the star on the left epaulet and colored bars across the pocket on the left side. A black nametag with his name in white Thai lettering rested above his right pocket. The official Pratt was packaged for his new position as a police general and smiling for a photo op.

"We had pictures taken this morning," said Pratt.

"No Shakespeare quote?"

Calvino handed the gift to Pratt.

"What is it?"

"Open it."

General Pratt used a letter opener to slice through the tape and dozens of images of Shakespeare. He peeled back the wrapping paper and read the words on a plaque:

The robbed that smiles steals something from the thief;
He robs himself that spends a bootless grief.
— William Shakespeare, Othello.

"Shakespeare on your desk," said Calvino, watching Pratt's reaction. "He's always been your partner."

"Indeed he has."

The General studied the fine black lettering in New Times Roman font and, turning the plaque around, set it on the desk facing Calvino. Pratt folded his two hands in a *wai*. A smile emerged on his lips, and he leaned back in his chair.

"There's been a problem with your friend Ballard," said Pratt.

"Is he in trouble?"

Pratt drummed his fingers on the Shakespeare wrapping paper.

"He's dead."

Calvino realized his summoning to Pratt's office hadn't been a social invitation after all. Bringing a gift was now making them both feel awkward.

"That's terrible."

He'd been blindsided. Ballard found dead? A numb feeling began to set in. Pratt had had time to adjust to the idea.

"For him, yes. But for you, the trouble fuse has been lit, and it's burning."

"What's that supposed to mean?"

"Ballard worked undercover for the DEA."

"Selling and buying ships?"

"That was his cover. In the drug business you want to get in close to the logistical side of the operation."

"When did this happen?"

"Two nights ago."

"I was supposed to have dinner with Ballard two nights ago. He didn't show up. I've been asking myself why he didn't bother to take time to email or phone me. I was pissed off, to tell you the truth."

"Now you know why he stood you up."

"You remember Ballard from the jazz festival in Bali, right?"

Pratt nodded.

"I remember him. It occurred to me then that he might have had an agenda other than music. You can profile people who love jazz. He didn't fit the profile."

"What happened to him?"

Calvino started to sweat. He loosened his shirt collar and necktie. His heart raced as he waited for Pratt to answer.

"His body was found in the Chao Phraya River, a hundred meters downriver from a French restaurant called Ruea Farang-set. He'd booked a table overlooking the river for two people. A police boat fished his body out from five meters of water, his head bashed in, throat cut. He was badly mutilated. You said something about meeting Ballard for dinner?"

Calvino brushed a line of sweat from his brow. The location of the restaurant was not far from the Klong Toey ferry pier.

" 'Meet me at Ruea Farang-set,' he said. I walked around for half an hour waiting for him. When he didn't show, I left."

Pratt picked up the plaque that Calvino had brought and studied it for a moment.

"The American embassy has already gone through his personal effects. They found your name in his diary, and your dinner appointment. They also read a note in the diary about his stay at your condo."

"They think I killed Ballard?"

"They are diplomats. At least some of them are. No, they say you are a person of interest. The embassy has followed up with the department, with the usual request to keep them informed of our murder investigation. They have offered the services of the FBI, the DEA, the CIA and the rest of their alphabet. Of course, we declined. It's a sensitive time. The Americans don't approve of the coup. They weren't expecting we'd be jumping at their offer."

He went quiet for a moment and put down the plaque on his desk.

"Vincent, I have to ask you…"

"I didn't kill Ballard. Why would I?"

"Someone from the embassy is likely to contact you. You should be prepared for that. If that does happen, let me know. They shouldn't be meddling, but they have a right to talk to their own nationals. We can't stop them."

"Their intelligence officers stationed at the embassy read Ballard's diary and decided I had something to do with his murder? That's crazy."

"If you were in their shoes, what would you think?"

"You're right. I'd want a conversation with me."

Pratt leaned back in his chair, studying Calvino. He pulled a wad of tissue from his box and stretched his arm out.

"You don't want to walk out of my office with sweat rolling down your face."

"You're sure Ballard was murdered?"

"It doesn't look like suicide. Think, Vincent, did Ballard say anything before he left about having a problem with someone?"

Calvino ran the tissue over his face, wadded it into a ball and put it on Pratt's desk. He stood up from the chair and paced, running his hand through his hair.

"Nothing like that. Well, there was this escort, Christina Tangier, that he met in London, who took some pictures of him sleeping nude with a teddy bear. She got famous by destroying his career and that of twenty-eight other johns."

"He was involved with a prostitute?"

"He told me that he was working on a case, and that she was connected to a big-time operator in Colombia. Maybe that guy killed him. Or maybe the investment banker in New York killed him, the one that bought Tangier's portrait of him."

"Why would he do that?"

"To increase the value of the painting of *Elite John Number 22*."

"Was that Ballard's code name?" asked Pratt.

"This Christina gave all of the johns she photographed a number. It so happened that Ballard was number twenty-two. Her painted photo of Ballard helped establish her reputation as a conceptual artist."

"Slow down, Vincent. Teddy bear. Conceptual artist. Escort. London. New York investment banker. A woman named Tangier."

He looked up from his notepad and put down his pen to hold his fingers together in a bridge. He studied Calvino.

"She photographed him sleeping in the nude with a teddy bear in a top hat cocked to the right side. Google the name Christina Tangier and *Elite John Number 22*. See for yourself. It's Ballard. Or kind of looks like him. After she painted him in the style of Lucian Freud, the face looked like a lot of people. But you study it long enough and you know it's him."

"Some Cupid kills with arrows, some with traps."

General Pratt quoted *Much Ado About Nothing* as he scribbled on a notepad.

"There was no Cupid. This English art student used him. If anything, he was the one with a grudge. He said this hooker artist had ruined his life."

"How do you spell her name?"

Calvino obliged.

"It's not her real name. But it doesn't matter. She's famous. She's been on TV and in the newspapers."

"Never heard of her."

Pratt looked at the name and seemed a little disappointed. A celebrity in London didn't sound like much of a lead in a Bangkok murder case. But an effort still had to be made to verify her connection with Ballard.

"Anything else that Ballard said that seemed strange or unusual during the time he stayed at your condo?"

"You hung out with him in Bali. Everything about Ballard stood out as strange and unusual. I thought those covert guys worked in the shadows. Ballard appeared to live under a spotlight."

"Sometimes the best place to hide something is in plain sight."

Pratt shook his head in frustration. Calvino was right; Ballard had more stories than an Irish alcoholic trying to settle his bar bill on charm and flights of imagination.

"There is one thing, Pratt. I had lunch with McPhail. We walked into a dive called the Happy Bar. And who's waiting for me? Ballard. Ratana had told him I'd be there, and he got there before me. That got me thinking. He had some special training. He told me he'd moved to a suite at the Oriental Hotel and invited me to dinner. Later that evening, after returning to the condo, I checked the guestroom. Ballard had left a copy of *The Quiet American*, the Graham Greene novel, on the bed. It had a note inside."

"What did the note say?"

"The name of the restaurant and a line about the novel. I can't remember it for sure, but it was something like, 'It's not the quiet American you have to watch out for, it's the Fowlers who get the woman at the end.'"

"What does that mean?" asked Pratt.

"I never got a chance to ask him. Does that mean I'm in trouble, and I need a patron to vouch for me?"

"I'm not your patron, Vincent. But I am your friend."

"Same, same," said Calvino.

Pratt watched Calvino sit back down in the chair. Pratt's expression showed he disagreed.

"A patron protects you from your mistakes, while a friend helps you face up to them."

"What's my mistake, Pratt? Having a houseguest who left a cryptic note in an old novel?"

His response came across more heated than he'd wanted.

"In Thai culture we share a hatred of criticism. A patron doesn't care about his *luk nong*'s run-in with the police. The nature of a *luk nong*'s transgression is irrelevant. If someone makes a big deal out of it, you know what we think?"

"Someone powerful has a grudge."

"Right. It exposes an enemy. Only an enemy would use the mistake of a *luk nong* to strike at the patron."

"Maybe someone wants to embarrass you or test where you stand? You're a newly minted general who may have jumped over some other candidates. Someone might be jealous. Or maybe it's revenge. Think how it looks from their point of view. What will Calvino's patron do? Cut him lose or protect him? Either way you lose."

Pratt had taken the American embassy's inquiry personally.

"I'm not worried," Pratt said. "I can handle it."

"And you have. But things are different now."

"It's always different. But one thing stays the same. A patron is the one with the most to lose. That's why there's always so much at stake in Thailand."

"Ballard's murder is giving someone an opportunity," said Calvino. "They'll have dug a bit and found you knew him too. So you can't be impartial. You've got colleagues and maybe people working out of the embassy looking at how you handle yourself. What are you going to put in the report you kick back to them? I'd report what I told you. They aren't looking for the truth. It will only confuse them."

"I have the full support of the department."

"You don't believe that. No one in your department has full support. Everyone's watching their back. There's nothing else I can give you to pass along, Pratt. Ballard mentioned someone in Phuket wanting to buy a luxury yacht, and he was looking for a commission on the sale. Who knows if that was bullshit? He didn't show me his agency ID. Maybe he was unlucky and caused a hoodlum to lose face, and a few of the hoodlum's friends jumped him. Which agency do you think was on his badge?"

The tone of Pratt's voice bore a hint of weariness.

"DEA, but I saw an intelligence report that indicated his real boss was DARPA. Let's say his true affiliation is a bit of a mystery."

The Defense Advanced Research Projects Agency funded all kinds of technologies that had possible military use. It reported on scientific and technological developments directly to the senior officials in the Department of Defense.

"Given what happened in London, his own agency had a reason to get rid of him," said Calvino.

"The thought crossed my mind. Are you certain he said nothing about seeing someone? Maybe the buyer of the boat or another American?"

Calvino shook his head.

"If I'm in his diary, wouldn't he write the buyer's name in the diary? He didn't tell me and I didn't ask. He'd banked a big commission on a Cambodian ship deal. You'd think he'd be on top of the world. But the photo exhibition in London and later in New York followed him. He couldn't shake it. It was plastered all over the Internet. Send the embassy links to the photos. Of course, they already know about that. It should tell you something that they didn't share it with you."

"He didn't happen to ask you about Dr. Marley Solberg?"

"Why do you ask that?"

"I had a call from the embassy. Their liaison officer asked me if I had any information about Ballard finding information on the whereabouts of Dr. Marley Solberg," said Pratt with a hint of a smile.

"They're fishing."

"They're fishing in your pond, Vincent."

"Does it matter who Ballard worked for or what his mission was?" asked Calvino. "His life was in shreds. He'd been caught sleeping naked with a stuffed toy, and the photo went viral. That photo finished him. Whatever he was doing in Bangkok, he was a man in a hurry to grab some money and disappear."

"The embassy's story suggests something else was going on."

"And that Ballard had done some fancy footwork, and I fell for his hard luck story?"

"They might have played you, Vincent. That photo exhibition could have been a setup. Would Ballard be that stupid? He comes to Bangkok with the story and it takes you right in. He was taken in by a successful woman. Just like you. The two of you could get together, share stories and plot your payback."

"You think I've lost my edge?" Calvino said, leaning forward. "Okay, if it was planned and executed as a setup, why is Ballard dead? Why go to all that trouble only to have their man killed before the mission was finished?"

The fact had caused General Pratt the same doubts. He'd tried to explain the unusual facts of the Ballard case to his own bosses. They'd written Ballard down as a crazy *farang* who might be a cause of public embarrassment for them. While the government had been changed by the gun, the fundamental fear of his bosses remained unchanged—a public sex scandal linked to the murder of an American agent working undercover as a businessman. Had the London affair toppled over Ballard's life, left him disoriented and dazed, stumbling through the twisted wreckage, or had it been staged to give that appearance? Ballard had walked into Calvino's life, admired his art, left behind a book and then ended up dead in the river. Calvino reminded himself not to invite any more strangers to stay at his condo.

Picking up the plaque that Calvino had given him, Pratt looked at the inscription.

"For future reference, if you ever buy another present with a Shakespeare quote, you should consider, 'That's a valiant flea that dare eat his breakfast on the lip of a lion.' From *Henry V*, Act 3."

"Who's the flea in this story, Pratt, and who's the lion?"

The General had always worked inside the Thai system of periodic coups, which like California earthquakes were not precisely predictable but over time become inevitable. It was only a question of time before the tectonic plates shifted and the ground started shaking again. Since the coup Pratt had witnessed close up how those inside the department had adjusted to the new power grid. After searching how the newly constituted department functioned as it fired up for business with anxiety high as those who'd been excluded waited for the axe to fall. Not everyone emerged safely inside the circle of winners. *Luk nong* continued to be the cannon fodder in the aftermath.

He handed Calvino a handful of fresh tissue.

"I heard you're helping Osborne in a personal matter," said Pratt.

Ratana had been talking to Pratt's wife again.

"He's a character, one who's never short of problems. You know the type."

Pratt waited for a further explanation. None was forthcoming.

"Please give my greetings to Ratana," Pratt said, signaling that the meeting was over.

"I think she's going through a mid-life crisis," said Calvino.

"Why?"

"Short skirt. Wearing one of those fashionable vests sold to young women. New high heels. A new shade of lipstick. The stuff that women do to shed years."

"It's a phase."

"She'll work through it."

General Pratt nodded.

"I have no doubt."

Calvino stuffed the tissue into his pocket and stood up to leave. His conscience had been bothering him. Alan Osborne. He asked himself, looking at Pratt, if he should tell him that Ballard knew Osborne. Their connection didn't appear to have gone into Ballard's diary. Forget the diary. Ballard's job required him to file all contacts to his bosses. If he hadn't done this, then Ballard was going rogue. It was also possible that the DEA or DARPA had that information and were testing to see if the Thai police could provide them with independent confirmation.

Ballard had been at his condo the night Calvino had been called to Osborne's compound. He'd found Osborne, hair matted with dye, standing over an armed dead man crumpled up in the doorway to his sitting room. Had the same person who had sought a hit man to kill Osborne taken care of Ballard?

As Calvino reached the door, he thought of something else and turned to face Pratt again.

"Back in uniform," said Calvino, thinking his friend had made his choice. "I didn't think I'd see this day, General Pratt."

"If you think of anything else Ballard said about his friends, colleagues or enemies, phone me."

"Sure thing, Pratt."

They locked eyes for a moment. Ballard had asked him, "How's your friend, the sax-playing colonel?" He'd been irritated that Ballard hadn't remembered Pratt's name, and said, "His name is Pratt." Ballard had said, "Now I remember." Calvino had said, "He's been promoted to general." And finally Ballard, with a smile, had said, "If he plays the sax as well as he plays the system, he'll end up in the Jazz Hall of Fame."

Calvino waited for the usual invitation to dinner, but Pratt remained silent.

"I'll give your regards to Ratana."

Pratt smiled with a slight nod of his head.

Calvino had withheld information about the Osborne and Ballard connection, telling himself that the information would lead to Fah and the Tree Brothers appearing on the police radar screen. Before the coup he wouldn't have hesitated to share that information with Pratt. But things had changed since the 22nd of May. Calvino looked at the man behind the desk. Why had they called him back? It was no secret. Who better to put in charge of a witch hunt than someone who'd been witch-hunted himself? Part of the coup cycle was to recruit men abused by the previous regime and watch them beat the bushes, exposing more members of the witches' coven.

As Calvino opened the door, he almost bumped into Lieutenant Pim, who waited on the other side. She stood straight as a rail, ready to escort him out of the building.

"See you later, General."

Nothing like giving Pratt face in the presence of his *luk nong*. It was the system. Calvino glanced at the Lieutenant, who looked straight ahead. She was all business as they walked away from Pratt's office. Where did she fall in the life cycles of a flea and a lion? She gave no indication.

Pratt could rely on the history of how he was forced out of the department. He wore it as a badge of honor. That was necessary but not sufficient for the junta. The military would be watching him for any sign that he couldn't be trusted to be a true team player. They seemed to assume that Pratt's suffering at the hands of the previous overthrown government made him one of them, but things were a lot more complicated than that.

Alone in his office, General Pratt picked up the gift from Calvino, opened his desk drawer and slipped it inside, closing the drawer. Western authors had become suspect. Thais who quoted them earned a place on a watch list, or a black list, or a social invitation list—there were many lists to take the names of Thais marching to the tune of Orwell, Huxley or Shakespeare. Pratt made a mental note to add Graham Greene to the list.

Calvino hadn't fully appreciated this basic, fundamental shift in ground rules about permissible attitudes, opinions and beliefs. The alternative was that Calvino knew full well the situation and had brought the gift as a reminder of how Pratt often quoted Shakespeare. Clearly it also had another message: the censorship of Pratt's spiritual mentor came at a high cost, and he ought to bear that rising debt in mind as he helped the junta right the wrongs of the old regime. Pratt knew well that Shakespeare had lived during a time of plots and conspiracies. He felt that the Bard's legacy was to question whether modern society had emerged with its lessons learned from the Elizabethan Age—or had there been a regression into a prior age that was much darker?

FIFTEEN

"Everything that belongs to the past seems to have fallen into the sea; I have memories, but the images have lost their vividness, they seem dead and desultory, like time-bitten mummies stuck in a quagmire."
—Henry Miller, *Tropic of Cancer*

THE MAIN ENTRANCE to the police HQ in Bangkok was a colonial-style adaptation. Isolated amid a grove of the languid tropical trees and bushes that lined parallel roads in and out of the spacious compound, the administrative offices enjoyed a peaceful setting far from the commerce and shopping malls of the big city. A large water fountain added a touch of Versailles.

Before the coup, protesters had swarmed through the compound, trampling the grass and flowerbeds, tossing rubbish in the fountain, removing the letters on the HQ nameplate and spray-painting slogans on walls. Only small traces of the earlier vandalism now remained. A committee of generals' wives had self-assembled after the coup with the mission of overseeing the renovation and redecoration.

The committee had started before the coup. After the coup it had grown from three to fifteen members, all drawn from the ranks of the official wives of high-ranking generals. They decided a post-coup blessing of the fountain was in order. Manee, Pratt's wife, had been invited to join even though her husband was not a senior general. His sterling political pedigree apparently compensated for her *mia noi*-like collection of jewelry and a five-year-old car. As with most decisions in Thailand, the official reason for establishing the committee was designed for public consumption. The real reasons lay elsewhere.

Throughout each day, by phone and via Facebook and Twitter accounts, the generals' wives exchanged private messages about people inside their husbands' offices—who worked around their husbands, their gender, rank, family background, education and affairs. They'd established a credible intelligence network, cross-checking their husbands' stories about official life with what other wives were learning about their husbands' associates, meetings and activities and who was on their way up or on their way out. Memories of the *annus horribilis* of the previous year remained fresh. An anonymous tipster had used social media to expose hidden relationships with senior police officers, and a covey of minor wives and *giks* had been flushed out like quail from the undergrowth. The generals' wives vowed that this year would be an *annus mirabilis*—a wonderful year, restoring the balance between yin and the yang.

The wives had other reasons to monitor their husbands. At night, after working hours, the office lights burnt late into the night along with the flicker of TV screens. The lights dancing against the windowpanes could be seen through the trees from the road. Tongues wagged. Who stayed behind? What were they doing inside the offices late at night? It had been no secret to the wives that the department had recruited many young, attractive and educated women into the police force. Politics had its own set of serious risks and threats, but no general's wife would have ranked the political risk faced by her husband higher than the threat of a younger woman who worked inside his office.

The committee traded gossip about what went on at HQ at night. The female office cops who couldn't afford to rent a room unfolded their sleeping mats from behind their office desks and slept coiled up with their desks as their roof and walls. The committee members worried about the temptation this presented. Lingering suspicions from the previous year ensured that the wives had not forgotten what social media had revealed about their husbands.

As Calvino came out of the main building, he passed a group of middle-aged women dressed to impress—the thick black helmet of hair, the diamond rings sparkling, necklaces of diamonds, emeralds and rubies, and designer handbags, shoes, dresses and sunglasses. From inside the group one of the women waved at him. At first he didn't recognize Manee. Near the water fountain, the women had broken into several discussion groups of two or three. It was hot, and none of them looked happy standing in the sun. Manee broke away from the others and walked up to him.

"I just saw your husband. He didn't mention you were here."

"He doesn't know," she said mischievously. "It's a secret."

"Looks like you've made new friends," said Calvino, glancing at the other wives standing and talking nearby.

"I'm on the blessing subcommittee."

"The one that gets to decide which big fish to bless?" asked Calvino.

"Sort of. It's true. We've expanded our mission. We will recommend what to do with the fish in the fountain. How did you know about that?"

He hadn't until then.

"Lucky guess."

"Vincent, someone told you."

"Aren't you hot?"

She pulled an umbrella out of her handbag and opened it.

"I'll walk with you a bit," she said.

Calvino looked over at the other women, who watched Manee.

"You should get back to your friends. This is no time to be seen walking with a *farang*."

"Pratt told you about the fish, didn't he? We were just talking about the fountain last night. It must have been on his mind."

"That must be where I picked it up."

It was common knowledge that the fountain was filled with exotic fish. Each time the Japanese or Chinese generals arrived, they brought expensive tropical fish as gifts, and a brief ceremony to release them was held at the fountain. It was a way of making merit. The fish multiplied, and the fountain became a frothy fish pond. The protesters had taken fish, but they had only made a small dent in the teeming population.

"I heard the Chinese carp eat the smaller Thai fish," said Calvino.

Manee looked back at the fountain and her new friends, who were now pointing at the water.

"That's funny, Vincent."

She explained how both Thais and foreigners had released different species of fish into the fountain over many years. The fish had prospered until the fountain boiled with exotic breeds, sucking the oxygen out of the water. The committee of generals' wives then took it on themselves, in the spirit of the new order, to undertake a total cleansing of the fountain. What could be more noble and worthy than the restoration of purity, order and tranquility to this living symbol, this jewel in front of the police HQ? The chair of the committee urged the wives to press forward, applying the full force of their will and determination to the task.

Manee stopped talking. She was distracted as two non-commissioned officers walked past, both attractive females. Calvino could see that the middle-aged women at the fountain were no longer interested in the fish as, whispering among themselves, they watched the two officers disappear into the administration building.

"Looks like the committee has some other fish to fry."

"You must have met Lieutenant Pim," said Manee. "Do you find her attractive?"

"I hardly noticed."

"You are a terrible liar, Vincent. I say that as a compliment."

"I wouldn't worry about Pratt."

Calvino wanted to say that Pratt had learnt his lesson in Rangoon, but he couldn't bring himself to mention the infidelity that had happened there a couple of years earlier. Besides, he'd already been labeled a poor liar, and digging up a graveyard of lies would serve no purpose.

She squeezed out a smile. The reassurance of a friend had been what she'd come searching for, and she had found it. He watched Manee rejoin her group, which had retreated from the sun and the fountain to the shade of a tree. She held the green umbrella over her head as she walked. Pratt was a lucky man, he thought, as he turned and walked toward the main gate.

Manee's fears reminded him of Cambodia years before. A missing person case had taken him inside the old Khmer Rouge stronghold. He'd joined a group of landmine-clearing soldiers on a UN payroll. Their wives had set up camp on the opposite side of the road. They'd realized that all that UN pay in a place with too many poor women was giving the landmine clearers funds to set up homes for minor wives in villages near the minefields. All it took was a lousy $168 a month salary. And what a cover: a humanitarian reason to disappear into the countryside for weeks at a time to kick back with the minor wife. The Phnom Penh wives had caught on and walked through minefields to follow their men like shadows. Everyone watched everyone, as hidden landmines waited a misstep away. Memories of atrocities were buried deeper still.

By the time he reached the street, Calvino had thought through the possibilities surrounding Ballard's death. The last time he had seen Ballard had been in a sleazy bar. It had never occurred to him that it would be the last time, but then it never did. In Calvino's experience life never issued a red alert—this will be the last time you see me before I'm dead. Only afterwards would he feel a regret that he hadn't paid more attention or given the person a hug.

He remembered Ballard leaving the Happy Bar after paying his bill, walking past a *katoey*. That was Calvino's final memory of him, an unguarded, private moment, when the man's mask had slipped off. It wasn't the Ballard in the heavily painted Lucian Freud-like face, the one that hung on the wall of an investment banker's brownstone in New York to generate pre-dinner conversation. As with Calvino's own 1154 map, the story in the portrait was incomplete. The image of Ballard's journey into sleep included an innocent child's cuddly teddy bear, a spirit guide with unknowable boundaries.

Ballard, an enigma in life and death, had left an image for others to puzzle over. The deeper one probed into the mystery, the more unreliable and uncertain the information, and each new layer of information came with more questions. Calvino no longer felt certain what had actually happened in London or in Bangkok, what were the causes, who were the principals, who were the agents and who was responsible for the outcomes. All of it was coming apart in his hands. What he was left with, as he walked out of police HQ, was an enigma, a kind of information loop, traveling fast but never going anywhere it hadn't already been before.

SIXTEEN

"I shut my eyes and she was again the same as she used to be: she was the hiss of steam, the clink of a cup, she was a certain hour of the night and the promise of rest."—Graham Greene, *The Quiet American*

CALVINO CAME BACK from the ferry terminal at Port Klong Toey and uploaded his photos. Leaning with his elbows on the desk, he shifted his weight toward the computer screen. He compared his photos with the Street View images in Google Maps, zooming in on the buildings near the ferry terminal. Google Maps couldn't pick up the spot inside the terminal where he'd waited for Ballard that day he'd been killed. He'd stood at the end of the pier looking up the river for Ballard's private launch. Ballard had said in the note he'd left at the condo that he'd be arriving at the terminal by boat, and then they would set off together for the restaurant, where they could dock. No Ballard, no boat, no French meal. Calvino had paced up and down the pier until it was clear Ballard had stood him up.

He concentrated on the Street View photos. Each time he saw the same row of flat-roofed two-story concrete buildings, a 7-Eleven sign stretched across one, a dozen motorcycles parked in front, the green and white striped awnings, a red pillar postbox and a woman vendor behind her stainless steel cart selling sausages. Time stood still. The traffic and people were motionless. The street-level picture looked much as it had on the day he'd gone to the ferry terminal, only at the time of the failed rendezvous it had been after dark. Streets and lights from the buildings left large shadows. Google Maps only showed the daytime scene. What the photos couldn't tell him was whether Ballard had reached the pier before him. Maybe one of the motorcycles on the Google Maps images belonged to Ballard's killer. Calvino studied the photo, thinking the embassy's intel staff would have examined the same images, looking for a valuable detail in the snapshot of the past, wondering if Ballard had been part of that past and left some trace of a connection.

What Calvino needed was a Google Map of the river. There were only Google cars; as far as he knew, there were no Google boats. He clicked through Street View to the ferry dock entrance. The images stopped there. Maps had their limits, and computers had theirs. In Calvino's mind Ballard's story started to fall apart. Something about his inquiry felt counterintuitive—the more information he had about the man, the less he knew and the more questions remained. Calvino was realizing that he hadn't fully absorbed that Ballard—which probably wasn't his real name—had worked undercover running covert ops for the DEA. He must have been working some angle at the jazz festival too. Or had he just been a jazz lover? Calvino looked at Christina Tangier's famous photo of him, *Elite John Number 22*. Like Ballard himself, the title of his photo had a certain anonymous feel of the gulag about it, an impression that fitted the image of the man sleeping on the bed. "What in the fuck were you doing at the jazz festival?" Calvino asked out loud, as if the man in the photo would wake up and give him an answer.

Nothing about Ballard's behavior at the Bali Jazz Festival had been exceptional. Dead end, thought Calvino. What about Alan Osborne? He had a reputation of hating drug addicts and had forced Rob, his son, into rehab twice before he ran off to Rangoon. Did Osborne think that his friend was DEA? Why would Osborne be involved in a yacht deal out of Phuket, connecting the potential buyer with Ballard? Had the deal turned sour? Why had a hit man been sent to kill Osborne just when Ballard was staying at his condo? Which side was the hit man working for? Calvino leaned back from his computer screen and looked out the window at Sukhumvit Road in the distance, lighting the night sky. With so many unanswered questions, Calvino told himself he needed some advice. One person came to mind.

He auto-dialed Yoshi Nagata's number and listened to it ring. On the computer screen he stared again at the Google Street View photo of the terminal—the Thais captured there, a taxi, its registration plates easy enough to read, and vans, trucks and buses all frozen in the amber of Google time. He glanced at Al-Idrisi's *Tabula Rogeriana* hanging on the wall as he waited for Yoshi to pick up the call. Calvino lost track of how long his phone had been ringing before Yoshi answered.

When he did, Yoshi said that he had nearly finished meditating as the ringing started.

"Vincent, I was waiting for you to call," Yoshi said calmly, "and I knew it was you before I answered."

How many times had someone said that to him, Calvino thought. Except this time seemed different.

"You saw my name on your phone. That's how you knew."

"If you wish," said Yoshi.

"Why were you waiting for me to phone?"

Yoshi laughed.

"Marley has arranged a surprise for you. Of course, she hasn't told me precisely what she has in mind. As you are aware, there is no point in pressing her."

"Why doesn't Marley phone me directly?"

"If I could look inside her mind, I might be able to provide an answer. But I can't."

"She once told me that you were a good influence and I should keep in touch," said Calvino.

"That's not unusual. She once said the same thing to me about you."

"So you have no idea what kind of surprise?"

Yoshi read her invitation: "Please ask Vincent to come to your condominium on Thursday at 8:30 p.m. I have something for him."

"Her message came in only a few minutes ago. She insisted on that time."

It was an odd hour. And it was also the anniversary of the last day and time they'd been together in Banglamung. Her clothes had lain scattered on the floor of the stateroom of her yacht, her breasts pressed against his chest. He'd stroked her hair. Shifting her weight, she'd looked up in the dim light, the sound of the sea breaking against the hull, a gentle rocking motion, comforting, promising a secure passage. One of her legs had been wrapped around one of his. She'd pulled him in tightly.

Afterwards, she'd judged Calvino not to be sentimental. Sex and the lapping of the sea had synchronized like a perfectly constructed block of code inside an algorithm that allowed her to read his thoughts. He'd felt her inside his head that night, opening doors and windows, climbing into memories of places he'd forgotten. One thing he was sure about: she was aware of things inside his mind no one else had seen. No one ever forgot the significance of that kind of experience of body and mind. She had never really left that space. He felt her presence even now and couldn't explain how or why she was never far away. So much time had passed since she'd vanished from Calvino's life. Like a magician, Marley had made herself disappear. No place on the map had enough gravity to hold her for long. It was the way of Marley's world—paths converging, diverging and running in parallel.

"I'll be there," he'd said. "This is Thursday, and 8:30 is an hour from now."

"Yes. I only received the message just before I started my meditation."

"Marley doesn't give people a lot of lead time."

"She exists inside Marley time. That's true. Can you make it?"

"Yeah, I'll be there."

They didn't exchange another word. The retired professor ended the call first. Calvino wondered if Yoshi smiled as he looked at his shrine of deities. They had power, much as Marley had power over Calvino. He had received his invitation to Yoshi's condo and that had been the purpose of the call. It didn't matter that Marley had made it easy; there had been no need for him to invite himself. Deep down, he thanked Marley for her remarkable timing. Marley time—he liked Yoshi's phrase.

Calvino checked his cell phone apps for an update on Fah's movements. He located her inside Osborne's compound. He put away his phone and thought about how to play along with whatever Marley had waiting, and with that business out of the way, how he'd ask Yoshi to guide him through the maze of questions that Ballard had left behind.

Calvino's taxi pulled up to Yoshi's condo. The front-desk security buzzed him in as he reached the door. He was expected. As his name was checked off the guest list and he was escorted to the lift, he thought about Marley, who was living proof that a super-intelligent, beautiful woman with a fortune at her disposal was indistinguishable from a god. Most children figured out by the time they reached eight years old that it was pointless as well as exhausting and fruitless to waste time bonding with a personal god. Gods didn't do well in relationships. Marley was no exception. When she'd left Thailand, Calvino had happily rejoined the world of women who were ordinary mortals. He liked that world, belonged to it. But nonetheless, when an old god summoned, he was quick to become a relapsed worshipper for his private audience.

The lift doors opened on Yoshi Nagata's floor. Calvino wondered whether others in the building knew that a famous retired mathematician lived there. He walked the few steps to a large wooden double door. As he reached for the recessed brass doorbell, the door opened and Yoshi greeted him.

"Vincent, hello. We can talk later. Marley's little show is about to start."

Calvino took off his shoes and followed Yoshi into the condo. In the large main living space, the yoga mats were rolled up neatly and stored near the ceremonial table and shelves of statuettes of deities. Yoshi sat down on the floor cross-legged in front of a massive TV screen hanging from a wall. Calvino squatted on a mat beside him. On his left a Mac computer screen had gone to a screensaver photograph of Hong Kong Harbor. Yoshi positioned the mouse as his left hand tapped on the keyboard. A live cam shot of Hong Kong Harbor filled the TV screen. A stream of boats and ships crossed the water, along with several tugboats and an old-fashioned junk, its distinctive red sails visible. Beyond the waterline, on the Hong Kong side, stood a forest of high-rise structures adorned with large letters and logos fashioned from neon. It was like a Street View map of the seats of the city's economic, social and political power—the signs reading HSBC, Jardine House, Bank of China and Hong Kong Convention and Exhibition Centre—with the ridges of the low hills rising behind.

"You're about to see the nightly performance of the Hong Kong Symphony of Lights," said Yoshi.

"Why don't I hear any music?" asked Calvino.

Yoshi touched Calvino's arm.

"The lasers and LEDs are the notes in this symphony."

"If it's nightly, what's so special about tonight?"

"Patience is rewarded. Trust her a little, Vincent."

Calvino sat on the floor beside Yoshi, trying to think of the last time patience had sent him a reward. As the third scene in the show started, it became apparent that there were three cameras on different boats in the harbor, each focusing on one of the luminous high-rise structures.

"This part is called 'Heritage,'" said Yoshi.

The laser lights created on the front of one of the high-rise buildings projected an image from Calvino's own life. The lights had been programmed to reproduce Galileo Chini's 1913 painting *The Last Day of the Chinese Year in Bangkok*, the best-known artwork of Calvino's great-grandfather. The painting in light hung, so to speak, over the Hong Kong cityscape—a blaze of glowing lanterns against the sky, a man running through a stationary crowd of lithe, pigtailed figures in black pajamas, one of them in a conical bamboo hat. The digital image erupted in a fire show that captured the painting's fine detail, spilling its reflected light across the harbor as it filled the TV screen. Then the painting's title appeared.

The image dissolved a couple of minutes later, replaced by a rainbow of lights, dragons and lions. Once, in a long conversation about his family, Calvino had told Marley the story about how during the day of the 2006 coup, he had come into his great-grandfather's inheritance, including the man's paintings. Pratt, a colonel at the time, had ensured their safe passage. Calvino had no means of updating her on the differences between the 2006 and 2014 coups. He'd become suddenly wealthy in one, and a person of interest in a murder investigation in the other.

"Someone once said the medium is the message," said Calvino.

"Marshall McLuhan," said Yoshi.

"My great grandfather's painting splashed across Hong Kong Harbor. I am impressed. But she could have sent a postcard and saved a lot of money. So many people are competing for my attention—Pratt, Osborne, Ballard, each one inside my head, knocking me around. Now Marley comes into the ring to finish the head job?

"Help me understand, Yoshi. I am trying. First she spends a fortune on an old map and has you deliver it. Now she's produced a huge light show in Hong Kong, reproducing my great-grandfather's most famous painting. And again, you're the middleman. What are you two planning next?"

Calvino waited for an answer as Yoshi switched off the TV. When he decided Calvino had calmed down enough, he spoke.

"She expected you'd have questions. Let's start with the 1154 map. A map doesn't have any intrinsic meaning. What matters is its use. What you want to use it for gives it a function. Where you want to start, and where you want to finish—those decisions are up to you. The business of a mapmaker and a painter are the same. They create the space you wish to play in, spend time inside, eat, sleep, make love and die in; it's a representation of a location in space and time. Where is time on a map or in your great-grandfather's painting, *The Last Day of the Chinese Year in Bangkok*? It's there. Infused in every aspect of the space, pigment, design, lines and details. It invites you to enter."

Calvino looked at Yoshi's collection of deities.

"Like your bronze and gold gods?"

Yoshi smiled.

"They are other portals into the realm of imagination, companions with which to explore the regions and borders. Maps, paintings, idols remain caught in particular times and spaces, but you possess the power of movement inside time and space. An ancient map, like an old painting, is a fossil of a unicorn, presenting us with a contradiction: we never have found a fossil of a unicorn, and yet people—many people—believe they exist. They can point to drawings and paintings and stories of unicorns and argue that the images prove the correctness of their belief. The time and space of Bangkok in your great-grandfather's day is no longer accessible except through art. His painting transports you back to 1913."

"In 2006 the great hope of the coup makers was to find passage to the mystical world of my great-grandfather's art. They failed," said Calvino.

"This is their second chance. There won't be a third one," said Yoshi. "Their belief in unicorns is difficult to extinguish. They keep searching for a way back to that past Chinese New Year. That's a challenge. Like finding MH370, the Malaysian plane that vanished over the south Indian Ocean. We forget that large uncharted parts of our planet remain as inaccessible as in the past. We have no map to guide us. Such searches are hit and miss. Each time it appears that success is around the corner, and then..."

"They start over again, covering the same territory with the same result," said Calvino.

"Like the man running against the Chinese New Year's sky lit with fireworks. Dramatic, colorful—and he will never be a step closer to his goal no matter how long we look at the painting."

"I have a similar problem, Yoshi."

Calvino explained how he'd found Osborne with a gun and a dead body in the doorway, and how Ballard had been found dead on the night they had agreed to have dinner. He also told him how Pratt had been promoted to the rank of general, and now his superiors, along with the American embassy, the DEA, DARPA and no doubt others, had taken a sudden interest in Calvino, his movements, activities and associations. There had been a lunch at the Happy Bar, and McPhail and he had arrived to find Ballard inside, and after lunch the military and police had arrested the owner, carted him out on a cot and loaded him into the back of a police van. Finally Calvino showed Yoshi the graffiti art in the style of Banksy that Osborne's girlfriend had engineered with her friends.

"It seems that you are caught in the same cycle of karma as your great-grandfather. He tried to paint his way out. When I see his great painting, I see him making a run for it. The Thai generals live inside their world and try to reconcile it with the larger one outside, but the two don't match. They don't accept the contradictions between Galileo Chini's painting and the modern world. They believe they can bring the society in that painting back to life. But they can't quite manage it. And you, Vincent, are in the middle of the scene, the man running as the others wait."

"Where exactly am I running?"

Yoshi Nagata smiled and bowed his head slightly.

"Where is the man running to in your great-grandfather's painting?"

"I don't know."

"We have no reason to believe that your great-grandfather had the answer either. There is no hint of a destination. To our eye he's running blind. Or you can infer whatever you want. The Thais love to say, 'Up to you,' though they don't really mean it literally. It makes them uncomfortable if someone is running off the grid. It means he's lost or without purpose, but when you closely examine his stride you feel a rising panic is moving him forward.

"Don't get lost, Vincent. Don't panic. Keep your wits. Isn't that Marley's message? You aren't alone. She's there beside you. She has faith you will find the way and discover the place the runner is sprinting toward. It's off the border of the canvas. The runner's forward motion is forever captured in the painting. What if his painting isn't a finished thing but a dynamic work that comes to life inside your own heart? It's your turn to take the baton through a Bangkok skyline aglow with fireworks."

"You're saying my legacy is to finish his race?"

A sparkle shone in Yoshi's eyes as he sat in silence for almost a minute, a time that seemed like forever to Calvino.

"A race to find yourself. Just like your great-grandfather before you in 1913, and long before him there was Al-Idrisi in 1154. It's your turn, Vincent. It's your time to run through the fireworks and darkness and be free. I am the Buddha, Mohammed, Jesus, a Sufi mystic, a Hindu sadhu, and so are you. So is everyone. We come into the world with enlightenment already inside each of us. In every life the journey is nothing more than finding your way to switching on the light. The ego isn't a flashlight to guide you through the void. Our ego is by its nature a product of the darkness. Let it go, Vincent. Time only appears to slip away. In reality it is always now. The runner? Where is he? How fast is he traveling? Movement at the speed of light appears to us no different from frozen motion. Your great-grandfather passed you this message."

Calvino saw a light in this small, fragile man's eyes. Marley and Yoshi had gone to a great amount of trouble and expense for him. He thought of himself as an ordinary man, as someone no different from the next guy on a barstool. Why would they waste their time on him? He had killed men and done other deeds that no Buddha would have done.

"Why tell me this, Yoshi? I think you've mistaken me for somebody else."

Yoshi acknowledged the question with a smile.

"I've been waiting for you to ask that question. If Vincent Calvino can break the cycle of hate, anger and fear, that will change something important. Hate shackles the hater. He will never wish to leave his chains because he doesn't see them. His lack of freedom defines who he is, and all of his friends hate as much as he does. To hate less draws suspicion. Failing to hate makes you an enemy. That world is passing into history. It will soon be gone.

"You are a chosen one. If Vincent Calvino can pass beyond the horizon of hate and fear, everyone has that possibility, too. A coastline can't be truly mapped to the reality. The fjords of Norway are an example. The smaller and deeper you go, at each stage, you find a fractal that contains the whole coastline. Our whole being and nature is expressed in each fractal representation. Do you know how ancient mapmakers expressed their fears?"

Calvino shook his head.

"They drew fire-breathing dragons at the edge of the known world. Their flights of imagination and the world of the supernatural was their default."

"How would you draw your fear," asked Calvino, "if you were a mapmaker?"

A wisp of a smile passed Yoshi's lips.

"My fear is about a different kind of dragon at the edge of a new kind of map. A dragon that the members of our species, and in the billions, are daily drawing with every keystroke, search, comment, like and photograph. With these things we construct a map of our reality.

"Like the slaves who built Angkor Wat, we are the legions hauling the stones from the quarry with no idea of what the final structure will look like. Unlike the slaves at Angkor Wat, we believe we are educating ourselves, communicating our thoughts to friends and others, growing in knowledge. This is our grand illusion. What is the purpose of this artifact we are creating for the future? Our time will be over soon enough. Our historical place will be alongside the slaves of Angkor Wat, whose stones we admire and whose names no longer matter. It will be a map. A temple. A Stonehenge. An Easter Island. A painting."

A painting of Elite John 22, thought Calvino, hanging on an investment banker's wall in New York City.

SEVENTEEN

"2 + 2 = 5"—George Orwell, *1984*

"NOoooooooooo. NO!" SHOUTED Fah.

The barber touched the brim of his Panama hat, his head tilted as he glanced at the ceiling, listening to the plaintive female voice crying out beyond it, half in anger, half in frustration. The customer in the barber's chair stared at the barber in the mirror.

Fah's lament split through the walls and floors of the shophouse. The structure amplified voices, in this case the voice of a woman, mingled in a chorus of male voices. A silenced followed.

"Someone must have lost a hand at cards," said the barber, as his scissors resumed the cutting of hair.

The silence wasn't to last. The loud thumping of feet moved overhead above the barber's chair. A door slammed and raised voices, muffled by the building, were impossible to decode.

"Sounds like a bad loser," said the customer.

Oak had ripped up one of Munny's sketches, and the shredded paper lay scattered across the floor. He stuck his face close to Munny, glaring at him. Fah moved between the two of them.

"We make joint decisions," she said. "No one has the right to tear up anyone else's work."

His act of vandalism had erupted out of a cauldron of frustration with a large pinch of envy stirred in. Oak had demanded that his vision should be used as the symbol of their protest, and it was driving him mad that Fah failed to appreciate the brilliance of his work. How could a Cambodian design an image that sprung from the heart of an oppressed Thai? In Oak's world true Thai art could find expression only through a Thai bloodline.

"Only a Thai can express this moment," he had said.

"Bullshit!" Fah had answered. "And you know it."

Oak had lost control at that moment. Having run out of vocabulary and argument, he had grabbed Munny's drawing and destroyed it, ripping it into smaller and smaller pieces, as if at the end nothing but paper dust would remain.

Each day, after their classes, the members of the study group made their way separately to the bridge community. They had to be extra careful. Palm's idea was to give the appearance that their study group had disbanded for the day.

They had worked in their hideaway for many days, locking the door behind them. It was their world. The walls soon filled with graphic protest images. As the number of images proliferated, so did the competition for approval. The matter of money complicated things and created tension. Oak and Palm couldn't help but notice Fah slipping cash to Munny at the end of each night of work. Did she think they were stupid and couldn't see what she was doing?

The cascade of Munny's talent and the money stuffed into his pocket, along with the maddening absence of ego on Munny's part, acted as an incitement for Oak. But no amount of baiting worked on Munny. Oak's best verbal punches landed on Munny as on a soft pillow. He felt no sting, no pain. He didn't even feel anything when Oak tore up the drawing. It made no difference to him whether they used it or not. Show the tattoo or don't show it: it had always been the same for Munny.

After an hour Oak had finished a stencil of a laughing water buffalo, with a speech balloon above its head that said "Joke."

"Joke?" asked Fah. "This isn't a joke. It's not funny."

"You don't get it," said Oak. "The joke is on them."

"Who?"

"The army."

Fah rolled her eyes.

"Okay, the coup is ... is what? Something that makes us laugh?"

Palm and Munny stared at them like a tennis match audience, their heads following the action from one side to the other, waiting for one of them to put the ball into the net. They fought over what worked in "making" protest art. Oak argued that graphics inside a small room couldn't be relied on. The graphics had to be field-tested. Fah argued it was too soon to start spray-painting them on walls and buildings. They first needed an arsenal of high-grade graphics, and then they would hit all at once. They'd only get one or maybe two chances once they went into the street. She shouted at Oak that he was being reckless. Didn't he know the military had eyes and ears watching everywhere?

Palm found a compromise.

"Let's wait until curfew is lifted. Less hassle."

Fah went silent. Oak blinked. It made obvious sense.

"What do you think?" Fah asked Munny.

"Who cares what the fuck he thinks?"

"I care," she said.

"Whatever you decide," Munny said.

No one Munny had tattooed had ever asked him what he thought about showing the tat to a mother, a wife, a friend, a boss or anyone else. The subject never came up.

Palm's compromise was a godsend, a face-saving formula, and the three of them agreed to wait until the curfew was called off before hitting the street with the stencils and spray paint. Rumors were circulating that the curfew would end soon. Fah checked online for the latest rumors about it.

"In two days, if there is no conflict," she said, reading from her iPhone screen. Looking up, she added, "If we started before then, they'd never end the curfew. And we'd be in some military camp."

Oak glared at her, thinking she was blaming him.

"But we won't fall into the trap," she said.

"It's our chance," said Palm.

A sense of excitement pulsed through the room. Even Munny allowed himself to show what might have passed as happiness, thinking about how his artwork would look on the walls of the city. After they went back to work, Oak eased off Munny and, in return, Munny credited Oak with a stroke of genius—the group's trademark graphic would be a water buffalo with a Guy Fawkes mask strapped on its ass. It hadn't really been Oak's idea, but that didn't stop him from accepting the credit. Munny wasn't such a bad guy after all, Oak thought.

"How are we going to choose?" asked Fah, her laptop screen displaying a half dozen of the best of Munny's graphic illustrations.

The others looked over her shoulder. Each of them had a favorite except for Munny, who remained neutral. He allowed their group to trade and bargain amongst themselves. They looked up from the screen at the walls where each of the short-listed graphics dried. Each day after Munny finished cutting the stencil, the others taped it to a vacant space on one of the walls, shook the spray paint, the castanet-like sound from the can echoing around the room, and stood back to let the paint dry. They'd painted white over a couple of graphics that they'd rejected so they could start over with a fresh graphic on a clean surface. Munny's skill was making it difficult to choose. Precisely because of that difficulty, the problem facing them came down to who should choose in the absence of a unanimous vote, and how many would be chosen. None of the questions could be ignored. Oak picked out five of his own graphics from a neat pile of photos stacked on his side of the table.

"We can go out on the first night with these," he said.

He flipped through the images as Fah, Palm and Munny looked on.

"We've scouted three locations," said Fah. "They're on a *soi* off Thonglor, an abandoned building on Soi 101 and a wall near Sathorn Bridge. You can see it from the river."

"That means three graphics. Shit, that's nothing. All this work for three?" asked Oak. "And putting them up in places where no one will see them? Fucking waste of time."

"It's too dangerous to spray-paint outside. We'll have a crowd around us in minutes," said Fah. "Police and military checkpoints are up everywhere."

Palm cleared his throat and looked at Fah and then at Oak, as if he'd been holding something back.

"We go outside. But we won't spray-paint the artwork."

Fah stared at Palm, jaw dropping as if he were crazy.

"What did you say?"

"Spraying-painting is so analog. It's the old generation. Banksy risked getting caught on the street with stencils and spray paint. He's done. Guilty."

They looked at him.

"Okay, genius," said Oak, "if we don't paint them, then what? Put them on T-shirts?"

"I mean we don't use stencils or spray paint."

"You're not making sense," said Oak, shooting a knowing glance at Fah.

"You haven't let me explain. This is something new. No one else has it. But we have it. It projects images, and others can project them too, wherever and whenever we want. All we need is this."

He held up his cell phone.

"Here's how it works."

He pointed his phone at the wall. Munny's water buffalo with a Guy Fawkes mask on its ass appeared on the wall.

Palm watched them stare at the image on the wall. He was enjoying the moment of glory. It would have been hard to wipe the thin smile from his face.

"Palm, you are a fucking genius," said Oak.

Palm smiled and continued: "We decide where we want to project the image. We go to Google Maps and search for a location. Say, we decide to show it at six p.m. at the Asoke BTS station. We do it as a flash show. Hit and run. The graphics are mobile. We move, the image moves too. The cops come, we stick the phone back in our pocket and walk away."

"This is so cool, Palm," said Oak shaking his head.

"Let me finish."

Fah reached out and touched Palm's arm.

"Where did you get this app?"

"Does it matter?"

"No one else has it. Why do you have it?"

"Someone wants to help us."

"Who?"

"I don't know."

Oak sighed.

"It doesn't matter, Fah. Palm's right. No one is asking for money or credit. It's ours to use. Why wouldn't we use it?"

Fah, seeing she was outvoted, shifted her approach.

"Why use it at Asoke BTS station?"

"It doesn't have to be there. We can project the image anywhere we choose. And you know the best part?"

"Tell us," said Fah.

"We won't be alone. Others will help us. We'll send a message to our Line contact list. We'll tell them to go to such and such a place at a certain time. We choose the time and place. All they have to do is use an app we give them to 'open' our message. They point their phones at a wall and a drop of water appears, they click on the drop and boom, what do you know? There's the water buffalo and cop on the side of a building."

"Palm, Oak's right, you're a genius," said Fah.

"Thanks, but I didn't invent it. Someone loaded the app in my cloud and texted me to check it out."

"So who sent it?" asked Fah.

Palm shrugged.

"Anonymous. Don't know, don't care. It's ours to do with as we wish. Listen, I've figured out how to crowdsource the image in a group message. That way we can send it to hundreds, thousands of people who go to a hundred locations and project it. Or they simultaneously open their phones and, without projecting it, just show the image to those passing. Either way, bam, we have our message out. There are too many people, too many locations for the police or military to round up everyone. Think of hundreds of commuters at a BTS station showing the image, projecting it against a wall, shining it on ceilings, floors or the sky.

"Amazing," said Fah.

"People will notice."

"I don't know," said Oak, having second thoughts. "Maybe we'd better stick with spray-painting walls, Palm. It's what Banksy does. He's the man to follow."

"Sorry, but Banksy's no different from the average cave painter in one way. He paints a single wall at a time. We need to get these images on a thousand walls. And we don't want to get caught," said Palm. "With this app we'll leave no trace. They can't catch us."

Both of the men looked at Fah, waiting for her to say something.

"What do you think, Munny? Real wall? Digital wall?"

Munny had been doodling on a piece of paper and not paying much attention as they debated. Pushing aside his sketch, he scratched his cheek with the end of the pencil and looked at his fingernails.

"You can be a street artist or you can be in the movies," said Palm. "You tell me who reaches more people."

"Oak, this is a miracle," Fah said. "This is our generation's way to get the message out. Palm's right. We break with the past because we want freedom. I like the plan."

She turned to Palm.

"Are you sure no else has used this app to protest against the Juunta?"

Palm smiled.

"We'll be the first. We can add a voice or music, too. Try that with spray paint and a stencil."

"Music, yes!" said Fah, clapping her hands and dancing like a schoolgirl.

"Why would someone hack your cloud account and leave the app?" said Oak.

Palm blushed but loved the attention.

"I've thought about that too," said Palm. "I don't know. At first it troubled me."

"And now?" asked Oak.

"I say we use it. What do we have to lose?"

"What if it's a setup?" said Oak. "We could go to prison. If someone wanted to trap us, this would be a good way."

"You're wrong," said Palm. "There are a hundred better ways. No, this doesn't feel like a trap. It's a gift."

"Dropped in our laps from the sky," said Fah.

Fah reached forward to connect a knuckle bump with Oak.

"You have some music to go with your graphics?" she asked.

"I might have a couple of tunes, yeah."

Oak paused, turned to his left, reached over and slapped Palm on the back.

"And you, why didn't you tell us sooner?"

"I only just found it."

"When?"

"When you two were fighting, I was surfing. I downloaded it from my cloud. I got a text message, read it, opened the app. Thank you, whoever you are, guardian angel."

Fah checked her Dropbox and found the same app.

"I've got it too."

Oak opened his cloud account.

"Same here."

They shared their cell phone screens.

"I've searched for information about the app online," said Palm. "I figured someone must be making a fortune selling it."

"What did you find?" asked Fah.

"Nothing," said Palm.

He shrugged, pursed his lips.

"Impossible," said Oak.

"Google it. ProTemp_Beta_2112."

Not a trace of ProTemp_Beta_2112 showed up in their online search.

"Spooky," said Palm.

"Someone's gone to a lot of trouble to help us, but who, and why?" asked Oak.

The questions made Fah's head hurt.

"It's an omen. Like finding Munny. All the pieces of our karma are a perfect fit."

The three of them turned and looked at Munny. No way it could be him. But if it hadn't been one of them, who else knew about their plans except the Cambodian? Could the tattoo artist have written the code for ProTemp_Beta_2112 and sent it to them? What did they really know about Munny?

"Have you ever designed software?" asked Palm.

Munny blinked, picked up a pen.

"Describe it and I'll draw it."

Fah laughed.

"Munny, you are special."

"Does that mean I can go home?" asked Munny.

"Munny, come here," said Fah.

He crossed over to the table, hands pressed against the edge like a man on a boat steadying himself against a breaker wave.

"Oak, *wai* Munny," she said. "And you too, Palm. We've done this together. Munny deserves some respect. He's not a piece of equipment. He's a human being."

She *waied* the Cambodian, Palm followed, and that left Oak. Chuckling to himself, he bridged his hands together into a traditional Thai *wai* and nodded his head slightly.

"We couldn't have done this without you, Munny," said Palm.

For the first time in Thailand, Munny felt hope.

EIGHTTEEN

"When you write, you should put your skin on the table."—Louis-Ferdinand Céline, *Journey to the End of the Night*

SKY HAD GIVEN a draft of their group paper to her professor. A day later she was called, alone, into his office. He sat behind his desk, the paper in front of him filled with red marks. She saw how he broke out in a cold sweat as he began going through the contents with her.

"Did you write this?"

She nodded. The English wasn't Fah's, and the professor questioned whether Fah had paid someone to write it. It was a valid question as Fah had a history of outsourcing her work. Hiring Munny was typical of her readiness to get things done by bringing in the right person for the job. The academic papers in her university had a history of being outsourced. In this case her professor wanted to hear that someone not connected with the university had written it. It opened the argument that his students had no idea what had been written and had turned in a paper written by a professional, one they couldn't fully understand.

"Is this your work?"

"Along with Oak and Palm. Is there a problem?"

She smiled innocently.

"You always tell us to use critical thinking. So we did."

"In theory, yes. Critical thinking is good."

"But?" she asked after a long pause.

"It can make some people unhappy."

"Have we made you unhappy, *ajarn*?"

He looked miserable, his head slowly moving from side to side, as he stared vacantly into space like a man facing a firing squad.

"Have you shown it to anyone else?"

"Should we?"

"No, please don't."

"Okay. Was there something else?"

Such innocence, beauty and potential, he thought. Her question echoed through his mind.

Yes, he thought, there's a lot of something else. The authorities had been watching him. Waiting for a misstep, seeing if he'd show his true colors as a critic of the coup. As an outspoken professor of political science, he had every reason to be anxious. He had a history of publishing articles on freedom, democracy, human rights and elections—all subjects considered sympathetic to and in support of policies of the overthrown regime and hostile to the junta. Fah and her classmates had unwittingly given him a chance to redeem himself.

When he'd contacted a military officer about their paper, he'd expected they would embrace him as, not a hero perhaps, but as someone who understood what was required in these times. The officer said that his action would be noted, but he should be aware that turning in his students wasn't a decisive factor one way or the other. It was one piece of the puzzle in a cloudy picture. One strike against him was his less-than-candid answers to a particular line of questioning. Had his lectures encouraged her and her conspirators? Hadn't he urged his class to use critical thinking? He had to admit he had. The second strike against him was his timing in disclosing this rogue cell of rebels.

Why had he waited? Why hadn't he acted immediately? Why had they already received information about their term paper from an independent source? Was it possible he had learned that the military already knew of the paper and he was belatedly contacting the authorities to save himself? Was his appearance before them merely a front, a pathetic effort to appear that he was engaged in rooting out the old corrupt regime? His academic history showed his leanings. Had he had a change of heart?

During the interrogation, inside a military camp, several soldiers circled him in the small room, asking questions about events, timing, personalities, motives and beliefs. His answers from the day before, and an hour before, had been written down, and any variation of the story was noted. A story of what his interrogators called his "involvement" had been twisted, pulled apart and reassembled in a strange and alien narrative. Even the professor agreed that what they'd determined had happened seemed wholly plausible. That was the problem. It didn't matter that it was nothing but lies. It didn't have to be true; it had only not to appear absurd.

At three in the morning, they woke the professor up and asked him again about the substance of his students' term paper. Had other students written and submitted similar papers? If so, why hadn't he reported them? Or was he going to lie to them and say this was an isolated incident?

The professor repeated what he had told them from the beginning. He freely admitted that Fah had written the paper for his class. Once his suspicions had been aroused, he'd made inquiries, gathering information about her daily activities and friends, and he'd placed Fah, Oak and Palm on his personal watch list. The intention of reporting her anti-coup activities had never left his mind. What more could he tell them?

His interrogators had something more to tell the professor. Their intelligence unit had discovered a working copy of the term paper almost a week before the professor had contacted them. Fah had gone online and hired an Australian expat ghostwriter to write it for the group. She had instructed the scribe, giving him an outline of points drawn from the professor's own writings. Her hired hand had worked out the details using those core ideas.

The young woman, in the view of the military interrogators, was more of a dangerous ideas person. They hated her ideas, the professor's ideas, and they despised the practice of delegating the execution of work to foreigners. Wasn't it the responsibility of university professors to impart the right knowledge, the right ideas and the values of the good people?

The professor was told he must share responsibility for what happened. The sooner he confessed, the faster his request to be released would be processed. Of course, it was entirely up to him. His detainment was voluntary. But he understood that leaving detainment required him to agree to their definition of "voluntary."

Meanwhile, he had homework to do—to mark the term paper with special attention to the errors and falsehoods of his students. Several officers then read the professor's critique of the paper. After signing a document that he had voluntarily agreed to meet them and would desist from any further political activity, he was released.

USER PRIORITY LEVELS
Political Science 201
Term Paper

> All over the planet, throughout history, the real power over life and death has resided in the hands of the Users. They had the weapons. They commanded the armies, navies and air forces. Their power hovered drone-like above the life of

the Used, whom they controlled.

[False premise. True premise: Unity came from the people; the guardians of the people protected them against their common enemies.]

In the analog world the Users held all the agricultural land, and the Used tilled the land, planting and harvesting the crops, building the temples, halls and cathedrals. Trade and commerce created a new class, as did the industrial revolution, and as the Users became more powerful, the Used sometimes revolted.

[All of our people benefited from the land and co-operated for mutual harmony. Rewrite accordingly.]

[Graphic illusions are NOT allowed in university term papers. Offensive graphics

such as this one are unacceptable in all cases. Please remove.]

Security, police, militia repressed the Used, intimidated them into submission. They imprisoned them behind a Great Wall, sheltering them against the contradictions of the outside world. The wall was breached. The evil of the outer world flooded in along with their stories that contradicted what the Users taught. People became agitated and confused and angry. All of their emotions bottled up until they took to the streets. This caused unrest and disturbance as the Used started to openly discuss how the official story had inconsistencies, lies, falsehoods and make-believe leaps. They were stories about ghosts, but the larger world said that ghosts, especially ones without a navel, only existed inside the imagination of people and were not real. Ghost stories infected school textbooks, teaching the students to believe in authority, magic and superstition.

[False premise. Those who don't understand our culture diminish our rituals, beliefs and values. To reject heritage is to lose identity. Rewrite accordingly.]

A grand circle was drawn with the Users at the epicenter and the Used moving out from the center as spokes, connecting the center with the rim; the circle rotated along a stable, slow-changing technology. Once the smart phone combined with Facebook, Twitter, Line and Skype, it was much easier to spot the ghost stories. The Users had invented this wheel. It had been built into every social, political and economic wagon.

Now the wheels are falling off. Wagons are breaking down. One at a time the roads are clogging with the wreckage. Eyes are being opened. People see clearly what is happening. You become an oracle or you remain blindfolded. You can choose. You stop, think and ask yourself, "Can I stop this from happening? Will everything roll out exactly according to the generals' orders? Let's run the movie back to the part we like."

[Geometry, technology and vision all mixed up! Nothing is falling except in your minds. They need adjustment for them to see the perfection of what we can build together in Happiness. Rewrite accordingly.]

Only by the time the Users figured out that they don't like the future and want to reshuffle the deck and play a new hand, it's too late. It's not like the old times, when divide and conquer was easy—the Users had all the schools, textbooks, radio, TV pumping them with their messages. That world is still there, but a new world has cast a very long shadow over it.

[See above. Rewrite accordingly.]

Think of sudden climate change, or that the Great Wall of China is now a dike, holding back a huge ocean of water, and on the other side is an alien technology, exploding in all kinds of new directions, algorithms opening thousands of precisely bored holes in the wall, and watch as the water splashes through. How do you shut down thousands and thousands of gaps that allows a tsunami of truth to wash away your statements, evidence or your forecast? How can you control that which is beyond your capacity to control? The uber-Users never had to answer that question before.

[Delete all text in this paragraph. See above. Rewrite accordingly.]

Our leaders face a full frontal attack from those outside our borders, who use the new technology to challenge their views and power. What is their response to the modern world? The evidence is clear—they lack understanding of our generation's age. They've seized power in the old way and believe that what worked in the age of the Cold War is the way forward.

[False, false, false! They assumed power on behalf of the people. Rewrite accordingly.]

The frog's life in a coconut shell is a traditional Thai parable. It is our story warning of living in an illusion of reality. We know this parable by heart. So how did our world become filled with frogs that refuse to stick their heads out of the coconut shell? What are they afraid to see in the world outside?

[Delete all text in this paragraph. This is political science, not biology or a course in fables and mythology.]

"You, the big world. I am running to embrace you. Wait for me."

You don't hear the junta using that slogan. It doesn't play to the audience of frogs living inside the coconut shell.

[False! They embrace all of the people. Rewrite accordingly.]

Their deepest fear is of being absorbed into the Used class. Technology has undercut the sources of their wealth, power and influence, transferring them to a new group of Users. No one voluntarily joins the Used class, and they will fight to stop it from happening. They will use all available means to stop it. Users understand better than most what it means to be relegated to a lower division of play—where they are just another Used person who struggles to determine levels of access.

[False premise. Do not use the word "fear" in this context. It is wrong. Our leaders are motivated by love and kindness. They wish nothing but happiness for all of the people. Rewrite accordingly.]

The model of the future is Wikipedia. The Administrators get all kinds of tools that empower them to delete pages, protect pages, block and unblock, modify pages, remove accounts, roll back, confirm users and limit manager rights to other Users. These sysops appear, in their world, more powerful than military generals in their world, but sysops fall under the authority of Bureaucrats, who can add and remove an Administrator. At the top of the digital power structure are the Stewards.

[Delete. Irrelevant.]

Don't you love that title? Stewards, whose name is an elegant term recalling both the Bible and *Star Trek*, are appointed from all around the world. Theirs is a truly world-governing body. And what is the power of those who occupy the top realm of Wikipedia? They have limited power over the lesser Users. Stewards grant and revoke permissions to or from any other User. They can shut them out, shut them down and grant access levels. They act as overseers, the final check in the system.

[Delete. Irrelevant.]

The Thai generals who acted as the Stewards under the old regime don't want to lose that job in the new system. They want control at the meta-level, granting and denying access, deciding who gets banned or their access denied. The power to delete is true power.

[Delete. Irrelevant.]

That's me above in the drawing. We are writing down good things I've done in my passport of good deeds. You see, we are Stewards, checking the system, and you can see how the doves I've released are checked. How can you make people happy if you come to power through force? Can anyone ever force someone else to feel happy? We don't believe it is possible. We are stuck in the mud of hate and suspicion on a bumpy road, jammed by tank traffic hogging all of the lanes. The signpost reads: OVERTAKE AT YOUR OWN RISK.

[Delete and rewrite with no less than twelve examples of how happiness has been returned to the people.]

[Final Mark: F. I don't believe you wrote these words. You hired some foreigner and paid him money to write this paper. No one can believe you wrote it. I give you a second chance to rewrite it in your own words as indicated in my notes above. Otherwise, you will not graduate. The paper as written is filled with wrong thinking, bad assumptions and dangerously provocative misunderstandings.]

NINETEEN

"Don't talk unless you can improve the silence."
—Jorge Luis Borges

PALM SYNCHRONIZED THEIR cell phone clocks and demonstrated how to use the mysterious graphic projection app. He handed back Oak's phone and then returned to Fah her new iPhone 6—a novelty that had burnished her reputation.

Fah checked her phone and pointed it at a wall. Munny's graphic of a schoolgirl with her Merit Passport Book appeared.

"Cool," she said. "Okay, here's what we do. Tomorrow at five p.m., meet at BTS Asoke station. I'll be there with my iPhone."

"Why isn't this a collective decision?" said Oak. "If one person decides, it should be me. I know Bangkok better than anyone here."

"Fuck off," said Palm. "There are only a dozen places in Bangkok on anyone's protest short list. These are the sensitive spots. These are the locations we need for maximum exposure. The journalists go to these sites and report what they see."

"How do you know that?" asked Oak.

"Because that's where the police and army have concentrated their forces. They aren't in the middle of nowhere, guarding abandoned buildings, are they? Otherwise we've wasted our time."

Having lost that argument, Oak lost no time before moving on to the next obstacle.

"Okay, what if Fah is detained?" asked Oak. "Then what?"

"If any of us is arrested, the system has a fail-safe installed," said Palm.

"Show me," said Fah.

She handed over her phone.

"I've saved your login and password."

She leaned forward, her long hair touching the table.

"Then what?"

"You see cops coming, press the star key, the dollar key and the question mark key, in that sequence."

"What happens then?" asked Oak, moving in closer for a look.

"It's programmed to automatically send an email to kwaibaby8@yahoo.com, and when Oak or me log in, we find your 'goodbye' message. Once you do that, all of your information and apps are erased. Gone. Can't be recovered. What the cops find is an empty phone with a high-level encryption. They'll think you're hiding stuff, but even if they could break the encryption, which they can't, they'll find nothing. Zero."

"Why do that?" said Oak.

"It buys time."

"Who made this?"

"I don't know," said Palm. "And I don't fucking care."

"How did a nice guy like you become so sinister?" asked Oak.

"Practice."

"All of Munny's artwork is stored in my Dropbox, and yours too, Oak," Palm continued. "And you have it, Fah. We're backed up."

"There's a big hole in this," said Fah, folding her arms, looking between Oak and Palm.

"Which is?" asked Palm.

"What happens if all three of us are arrested?"

She glanced over at Munny, who stood with arms at his side, expressionless, as if waiting for the three of them to finish their arguments and get on with the business at hand. The other two turned and stared at him. Munny shifted uncomfortably under their stare and their judgment. Was he really part of this group?

"No way," said Oak.

"Why no way?" asked Palm.

"Munny, are you following this?" asked Fah.

"You trust him?" asked Oak.

Fah rolled her eyes.

"Munny's one of us. He's part of our group. Who do you think made these graphics? Of course I trust him."

"The high-tech stuff isn't like drawing water buffalo or cutting stencils," said Oak.

"Can you work a cell phone, Munny?" Fah asked as she opened her handbag and fished around, waiting for him to reply.

She removed her old iPhone 5 and handed it to Palm.

"Load it with the app and show Munny how to use it."

Palm took the phone and moved beside Munny.

"If I go too fast, tell me and I'll slow down. We'll go over it until you can do it in your sleep. You do sleep, don't you?"

Munny smiled.

"When I can."

With these new friends Munny was having some new experiences. He listened with great intensity, taking in all they said. Something important was about to happen. And they'd decided to not spray the stencils on walls after all. The plans had changed. All of their talk about the apps, Dropbox and logins wasn't that different from the world of diagrams and instruction manuals he studied to repair generators or tattoo parlor equipment. Palm taught him how to use the iPhone and how to log in to the email account, and Munny only had to ask Palm once to repeat how the failsafe worked. Palm then slowly drilled him again on how to use the projection software.

"And if Munny forgets what to do?" asked Oak.

"What if you forget?" asked Palm.

"I'll remember," said Munny as both of them turned and looked at him.

"Do you have a better plan?" asked Fah.

That shut up Oak, who had nurtured the ability to blow up other people's bridges but failed as a rule to take the time to build any himself.

"Then we're agreed," she said, holding out her clenched fist.

Palm gave her a fist bump and exchanged a second one with Oak. Then all eyes were on Munny as he joined their little ritual as a full-fledged member for the first time.

"Keep your phone safe, Munny," Fah said.

Fah had found Munny at the tattoo parlor in Khao San Road, trying to collect his back pay. He'd signed on to their venture not for political reasons—he'd drawn what he'd been asked to do for the money. It had been no different from designing a tattoo; the mission was to please the customer. Underneath, all Munny really wished for was enough money from his work to feed his family. Fah had made sure he'd be able to do that. All of the group's preparation, which had caused him to run hours late, was about to yield dividends.

TWENTY

"In circumstances of real tragedy you see things straight away... past, present, and future together."
—Louis-Ferdinand Céline

THE ROUGH, UNFINISHED concrete staircase was jammed with the sweaty bodies of several families and their belongings, each claiming the right of way. Munny pressed his back to the wall so that a fat woman from the fifth floor could squeeze past.

"Hey, Munny, you're going the wrong way!" said the woman.

Her eyes were open wide with anxiety, and her jaw trembled.

"What are you running from?" he asked.

"The soldiers are coming for us. Haven't you heard?"

She continued down the stairs before Munny could respond, moving fast for a big woman carrying two suitcases. He climbed several more steps to find a woman carrying a baby in her arms, and in front of her was a kid of about five or six cradling one of the doped-out puppies the beggar kids used as sympathy props in their daily street performance. Behind them the husband juggled a battered suitcase with a busted lock on the right side. Their terrified faces resembled those of their countrymen back home when the Khmer Rouge had emptied Phnom Penh. Sudden evacuations seemed to all play out according to the same script. Another man followed, weighed down with two large garbage bags of clothes and bedding.

As other fleeing residents shoved past Munny, all sharp elbows and bony arms, he recognized the man with the garbage bags.

"What happening? Why the rush?" he said, touching the man's chest with his hand. "What's wrong?"

The Khmer shook his head.

"We've been given forty-eight hours to leave the country or the army will come for us. No one knows what the soldiers would do with us. No one wants to find out."

Coming from a country with a history of an army "taking" people, which was code for killing them, the man was leaving no room to chance. He told Munny hundreds were already fleeing toward the border, carrying what they could and abandoning everything else. Rumors circulated about how the army had set up roadblocks and was arresting anyone who didn't have a Thai ID card, loading them into trucks and driving them away. One man, they said, had run had been shot.

"Are you sure?"

In recent times there had been many rumors, most of them false, of Khmers who had been detained, "disappeared," jailed or deported. Most of the time the person had turned up with a sheepish grin and no money in his pockets.

"This time is different," the man said. "The soldiers are tearing up documents and saying they are no good now. Go home, or you have a problem. Give me three hundred baht, they say."

Shakedowns were nothing new. Neither was a rogue cop or soldier tearing up valid documents for no reason other than he could. What was different this time no one could say. It was more a deep, instinctual feeling that the lion cage had opened and it was feeding time. The man scurried off carrying the plastic bags on his back.

On the way up to the third floor, Munny heard the sounds of children playing, a baby crying and pots and pans rattling, along with the chopping sound of fish heads severed against a hard wooden board. Sewage smells from beneath drifted lazily across Munny's dark path, making his eyes water. Now he could hear the sound of mahjong tiles slapping against a hard surface. On the third-floor landing the narrow beam of a flashlight panned across the wall and the walkway and stopped on Munny.

"Munny, is that you?" asked his wife.

"A lot of people are in a big hurry."

"We've been waiting for you. We gotta leave this place tonight."

He pulled her closer and, taking the flashlight, turned it toward her. Caked tears showed on her face. Her hair smelled from gutting fish, and her hands were raw. For the first time, he thought she looked old and defeated.

"We have some money. So don't worry."

"They'll just take whatever we have."

"I'll hide it."

"They'll find it."

"Who?"

"The army, the Eight-Niners. Two of them have taken off, but the others are still in the building with clubs and knives, and they're demanding an exit tax."

"I won't pay."

"They'll kill you."

"I don't think so."

"Munny, what can you do? You are one man. They are a gang. Pay what they want or they'll take away our son. They have children they've taken already. They told people they'll be selling the children to fishing boat captains in the South."

Her talk about children being taken as hostages made Munny feel numb as he leaned back against the wall, pointing the flashlight toward their space and calling out his son's name.

Sovann shouted back, "Father, I won a prize at school."

He could hear the pride in his son's voice as he walked over and hunched down next to him, arms hanging loosely at his side.

"What kind of prize?"

"For mathematicians."

Munny stroked his son's hair.

"That's good."

"Mother says we're going to Cambodia. I don't want to leave."

He saw that his wife had packed the clothing, bedding and kitchen stuff. The cases were stacked in the far corner of their space. He'd seen across the way where neighbors had already left. Looking around with the flashlight, his gaze stopped at the generator. It wasn't among the things they could take home.

Munny pointed the flashlight into the darkness ahead of him.

"Hello?" he called.

"They're gone, Munny," said his wife.

Only then did it sink in. They were the only family left on the third floor. Munny suddenly felt guilty for spending the whole day and most of the evening at the shophouse with the Thai university students. Fah had said it was probably the last time they'd meet. Their business was done. She'd mentioned a problem with their professor. None of those matters concerned him.

Just before he'd left the room for the last time, each of them had *waied* him. He couldn't believe his eyes; it was a moment Munny would never forget. He felt he'd won a prize. Indeed he had, and a rare one, too. His father had taught him that a genuine display of respect was the only gold medal worth getting in life. All the rest were silver medals. Second prize. Munny thought maybe that was why men fought so hard to win it.

Munny hugged his son, kissed his hair. His hand reached out to his wife. She grabbed it with both hands and put it against her lips.

"What are you gonna do, Munny?"

Three of the Eight-Niners arrived with flashlights running their beams over the walls, floor and ceiling. The three flashlight beams settled on Munny and his family.

"You working again today, Munny?"

The men held weapons—an ax, clubs and knives.

"Looking for work."

He stood up and walked toward the light.

"Nobody's hiring, just bosses firing people like us," Munny said.

He hadn't intended this as a play for pity but a statement of fact. The Eight-Niners had no time for excuses or sob stories. They held to a basic reality of illegals: no matter how down and out, people always held something back in case they had to make a run for it.

"What do you have for us?"

Munny glanced over at the generator. The machine was the envy of others in the building and the only power source for four floors.

"Take it," he said.

"Munny we don't need your permission to take what is ours. But you need our permission to leave. You understand us? We have to be fair. If we make an exception, what will the others say?"

"I can't give what I don't have."

The iPhone 5, Fah's old phone that she'd given him earlier that night, vibrated in his right sock where he'd hidden it. Munny had had a bad feeling as he'd headed home. He couldn't say why he had it, but there it was, to be acted upon or ignored. He'd hidden the phone while sitting in the back seat of the taxi. He'd come to the Aquarium prepared for bad news. Over the taxi radio he'd heard a report about the Khmer roundups. He couldn't understand it entirely, but he understood enough to know that trouble was brewing for people like him.

The eyes of the Eight-Niners were on him as he tried not to react to the vibration that was tickling his calf. He hoped the sound of the vibration would be masked by the background noise coming from the stairwells. The one with the ax waved it at Munny.

"Give me your wallet."

Munny pulled his wallet out of his pocket and made an underhand toss to the man with the ax, who put it down and shone the flashlight inside, finding two hundred baht notes, one fifty baht note and three twenties. Just enough money for a mugger, a thief or a man with an ax, Munny had calculated. The rest of the money was stashed inside his clothes. The Eight-Niner's head tilted into the beam of light and he sighed as he spread the wallet apart to find two thousand baht notes stuffed in a hidden compartment.

"Munny, you're a sneaky cocksucker."

One of the other gang members pushed the generator on its wobbly rubber wheels.

"And we'll be taking this as you already gave it to us."

His wife sobbed as the Eight-Niners laughed and made off with Munny's cash and generator.

"You are stupid, Munny. You didn't think we'd find the two thousand? Well, we did."

"Let's go," Munny said, picking up two cases. "Sovann, you carry that bag."

His wife had a shopping cart filed with mats, pots and pans, and clothes.

When they reached the ground floor, two large trucks stood before them with big funnels directed into the basement. The pumps groaned, and several men stood around smoking cigarettes. Munny looked over the side. Hundreds of fish flowed out of the funnels and into the basement aquarium. One of the men working a funnel said he had loaded the fish from a fountain at police headquarters. Someone else from the building whispered that was plain crazy talk. They'd tell us anything, he said, because they think we'd believe it. Why would the police have so many fish in the first place? Not to mention hiring a truck to suck them up, transport them across the city under martial law and flush the whole lot into an illegal basement pond in the bowels of an abandoned building.

Munny saw the building owner standing near the truck with his nephew and counting out money to the two drivers. The man might be losing his Khmer squatters, but he had some good news, too. He saw the potential of a thousand or more exotic fish attracting the tourist market. People loved looking at fish, especially in a half-natural, half-urban sinkhole. Rather than a break in continuity, the transfer from police fountain to slum skeleton basement seemed to be happening smoothly, with no apparent warps or wafts in the fabric of the world seen through the eyes of the fish.

What the observers didn't know was that the owner's nephew worked at police headquarters and had been tipped off that the fish in the fountain were looking for a new home. He'd offered a committee of generals' wives a solution to their problem; he would remove the fish for free, leaving behind a few rare species of Chinese carp. Hearing the news, his uncle had shaken his head and spit, complaining that he'd blown the chance to have the rich wives dip into a secret fund to pay for the cost of transportation, plus assorted overheads and a twenty-percent profit margin. His sister's boy might be a fine cop, but the sideline extortion rackets clearly hadn't prepared him for real business. But even with the cost of the truck, the owner had seen an opportunity to profit from his folly of a building. The second aspect of a great business mind, he believed, was to find the right formula to turn lemons into lemonade. The owner had a lifetime of experience in applying just the right pressure to squeeze the last juice from the lemon.

As they watched the fish pouring into the basement, a new idea flashed through the nephew's mind. Surely all the exotic fish from the police had released a lot of karma over the years. Should his uncle decide to sell the Aquarium, a buyer might be persuaded to pay a premium for all of that good karma. This was further proof that, as the nephew said, there really was no downside. Meanwhile, they were free to collect admission from the Chinese tourists who had already been posting Facebook pictures of the best aquarium in Southeast Asia.

TWENTY-ONE

"We are all alone here and we are dead."
—Henry Miller, *Tropic of Cancer*

AS MUNNY, HIS wife, son and relatives—two cousins, one aunt and his father's broker—filed into the street and turned the corner with the Aquarium behind them, he pulled the iPhone 5 from his sock. Logging in to the email account just as Palm had showed him, he found three messages:

"Goodbye: Palm 21.48.25."
"Goodbye: Fah 21.49.26."
"Goodbye: Oak 21.49.39."

All three of the Thais had been picked up, less than a minute apart. Something had gone very wrong, but Munny had no idea what it could be. What mattered was the fail-safe system had worked as Palm had said it would. He marveled at the three brief goodbyes stacked one above the other in his mailbox. Short death notices. Nothing long and drawn out. So direct and to the point that they could have been uploaded to Twitter.

The news of the group's arrest, or worse, left Munny feeling alone and scared, even though he had his family around him. He cursed himself for not thinking about them before taking the iPhone 5 and getting involved beyond drawing what they told him to draw. Standing in the street with his wife and son and everything they owned, Munny sighed.

"Let's go," he said, taking his son's hand.

As their group walked, Munny heard a small voice inside his mind. It was telling him to forget those Thai students. But another voice was broadcasting a contradictory message— "Munny, they are relying on you. You got paid for the artwork. Is that all you wanted? Was it just for the money? Doesn't it matter that other people might be inspired by your art?" The voice turned into Fah's voice inside his head, saying, "Munny's one of us."

Chamey could see that some demon other than fear was eating away at her husband.

"We'll be okay once we reach the border," she said. "Where'd you get the phone, Munny?"

At first he was going to say, "My employer," but that didn't sound right.

"From a friend," he said.

"That's an expensive gift. We can sell it."

"No, I can't do that, Chamey. It's got a use."

"Who you gonna call? Not that woman who was paying you?"

He heard the jealousy in his wife's voice.

"She's in jail."

The words spilled out of his mouth before he could consider what he was saying.

"If we don't get moving," she said, "that's where we're going to be, too."

They increased their pace down the street, but the suitcases slowed them down. Sovann complained about being tired and hungry. They all looked to Munny to set the pace and to tell them everything was under control.

"We've got money," he said. "We'll be all right. Up ahead we'll find a van."

After that, Chamey stayed quiet, leaving Munny to return to his thoughts. The others in their group were silent, too. They would have followed Munny anywhere. He had worked for days on the generator—painstaking work in bad light with basic tools and makeshift parts—and after failure upon failure, one night he'd plugged it in and the power had suddenly run lights, fans and TVs. Munny, for his part, admired Palm, who could do something like that with a phone—reach out over space and time, and no one could stop him.

It's up to me, Munny told himself. Fah had been right about that, and everything else. Damn her, he thought. If only she had cheated him or treated him like dirt, then it would have been an easy decision to make. But that hadn't happened. They'd *waied* him. Given him a gold medal. Munny couldn't get those three *wais* out of his mind. He could hear Fah's voice saying, "Munny, you're not a frog in a coconut shell. You're talented. You belong to the world. You're our Banksy. You're going places."

To a shallow unmarked grave, thought Munny. He looked at the driver seated in a van parked on the curb. The bearded man wore a Muslim skullcap.

"*As-salamu alaykum*," said Munny. "Peace be with you."

That was one of the few Muslim phrases Munny had learned from a Muslim prisoner when he'd been jailed along the Thai-Cambodian border for illegal entry.

"*Wa alaykum as-salam wa rahmatu Allah*," said the driver automatically. "May peace and mercy of Allah be upon you."

He looked Munny up and down. There was nothing to suggest that Munny or his family were Muslim. The driver was curious about this thin young man trailing a village of relatives behind him with their personal belongings.

"Where you go?" asked the driver, as Munny set down his cases on the pavement and leaned toward the window.

"How much to drive to Aranyaprathet?"

From there, the city of Poipet lay just across the border in Cambodia, and once they crossed the border, they'd be safe.

The driver's eyes widened as he stared at Munny. That was a long drive from Bangkok—six, seven hours, and there would be roadblocks and checkpoints. He sized up Munny and the people standing behind him, trying to calculate the entire cost, including fuel and the bribes if they were stopped by the police or army. He decided to start out with the nice round amount of ten thousand baht.

Munny stayed patient and calm, as he'd learnt to do when someone with half a tattoo started screaming that it hurt or it wasn't what they wanted. The main lesson was not to throw gasoline on an emotional fire. Munny slowly shook his head and smiled as he leaned in through the window.

"*Wa alaykumu as-salamu wa rahmatullahi wa barakatuh,*" said Munny, "May peace, mercy and blessings of Allah be upon you."

They settled on four thousand, two hundred baht. He returned to his wife and told her the amount the driver had agreed to accept.

She squeezed his arm, whispering, "Munny, we don't have that kind of money."

"We'll be okay. Besides, we don't have any choice," he said. "Look at all the people around, they all want to go home. If we don't pay, someone else will. And there are seven of us. It's not too much."

Chamey searched her husband's eyes. He was a man who had always told the truth. She wrapped an arm around her son.

"You hear your father, Sovann? It's going to be okay."

Munny was happy to sit back in a van with his wife and son on the long road home. Soldiers in full combat uniform stopped the van at a military checkpoint outside of Pattaya and shone a flashlight on Munny and his family. He handed over five hundred baht and the soldiers waved them on. Why are they making it difficult to leave Thailand, Munny asked himself. If they don't want us, why don't they let us go?

"It's all about money," said Chamey, as if she could read his mind.

They'd entered Thailand illegally. Paying some cash on the way out was a kind of exit tax, he decided. They could have come out a lot worse. Munny wasn't too upset. Half an hour later, when his wife had fallen asleep against the window, Munny slipped out Fah's smart phone. He put a finger to his lips as Sovann watched him operate it.

The screen light switched on. Munny covered it with his hand. He wondered what had happened to Fah and Oak and Palm. Where had the soldiers taken them? How long would they be detained? If it were only a few days, they could carry out their plans and they didn't need him. But he was fooling himself, he thought. Once someone got arrested under martial law, it was serious. That's why they'd made pledges to each other. It was up to Munny to follow through. But it wasn't that simple.

Munny considered the possibility that his friends might be tortured. As he was the last man standing, perhaps one of them would give him up to stop the pain. That was the purpose of torture. Pain was meant to retrieve information from someone who refused to give it freely. Pain, question, pain, question repeated in a loop, with interrogators replacing one another and no break in the process, until an answer other than "I don't know" stopped the cycle. Sooner or later the person broke. In the torture business, that was known as the bingo moment. The torturers had a winning number.

Munny thought about rolling down the window and throwing away the smart phone. His little interior voice told him to wash his hands of all that. It wasn't his country, his fight or his problem. He had his family to think of. But it seemed to have come down to Munny to be the one to send out the messages to others through Line. Five hundred numbers had been queued up by Palm on his phone. Those people would receive the invitation to participate in a collective exhibition of Munny's art. From his phone Munny would then push the graphics through five hundred phones, pointed at walls in a hundred locations.

"That's how to project people power," Fah had said.

He thought of Oak leaning over the table, looking at the walls covered with spray-painted images Munny had made. Oak had turned, looked him in the eye and performed a *wai*, bowing slightly. The image of Oak ran like a film clip inside Munny's head. He couldn't turn it off, and Palm *waiing* him, too. Both of them *waiing* him like he was a monk. Fah had started something unexpected. She'd broken a taboo, and it made him feel free in a way that he was still coming to terms with. What was Munny going to do with all that respect coming at him from all directions?

Munny pushed the sequence on the iPhone, waited a moment, and then put the phone back in his pocket.

"What are you doing, father?"

"Figuring out how it works."

His son lowered his head, looking at the screen.

"Does it have games?"

"Plenty. When we're back home, I'll teach you how to use it."

"You can teach me now."

"I have to keep the battery from running low," he said.

Besides, there wasn't a signal. They were either out of range or the system was down. It didn't much matter as the phone wasn't co-operating, so he slipped it into his pants pocket.

"Get some sleep. We have a long way before we reach home."

By the time they arrived in the border area, they found thousands of other Khmer already there. As far as the eye could see, people on foot, on motorcycles or in vans or buses or trucks edged along. Their van pulled over to the side of the road. It was hopeless to continue a meter or two every ten minutes. Munny and his family unloaded their possessions, and Munny went around and told the driver to wait a few minutes. The driver shrugged, looked at his watch.

"Fifteen minutes, I go."

It wasn't much time. Munny and his family joined the stream of Cambodians heading to the immigration booth at the border crossing. He squeezed a thousand dollars in Thai baht into his wife's hands.

"Hide this money somewhere."

"Munny, why you doing this now?"

His arm around Sovann's shoulder, he replied, "For our son. I've got to go back to Bangkok."

"You can't! They say the soldiers are killing Cambodians who stay. Don't talk crazy! You can't go back."

"I made a promise to Fah and the others."

She shook her head.

"That don't matter, Munny. What about us?"

"Don't you think I've been thinking about that? What I'm doing is for Sovann. What kind of man is his father, if he teaches him to break his promise to help someone? If a father has only one lesson to teach his son, it's don't make a promise unless you intend to keep it. Once you learn that lesson, the only thing of value in the world is being true to those who trust you."

He took a deep breath as his wife hugged him.

"It doesn't matter, Munny. We're going home."

"And you wait for me at the border. I promise I'll be back. And I just told you how important it is to keep your word."

When Munny reached the van, he looked back, but his wife, son and other members of his family had already been swallowed up in the blur of the crowd. All the people he saw looked as if their lives depended on getting over the border as soon as possible.

TWENTY-TWO

"The word in your mouth is anarchy."
—Henry Miller, *Tropic of Cancer*

IN THE DARKNESS she watched the blades of the ceiling fan rotating slowly. They made a soft whirling sound. No cool air blew from the air-conditioning unit on the opposite wall. No light, no sound came from the unit, and there was no remote control. Fah lay on her side, looking at the light slipping from under the door a few feet away. Sweat had run down her back and neck, soaking through the mattress of her narrow bed. The room, still and humid, was like a tropical hothouse at midday. She slapped at a mosquito and missed. She started to cry.

One of the women guards had taken away her clothing. She'd been given just a towel to cover her body. The room lights had been shut off an hour ago. The voices of men came from the corridor. Now they were talking outside her door. She rolled to one side on the bed, folding her arms over her stomach, Osborne's baby inside her. It was too soon to feel anything. An image of Christina Tangier's Elite John exhibition flashed through her mind. What would Christina, her role model, have done if the military had put her in detention? Christina had made achieving fame, wealth and recognition look easy. How many idealistic students wanted to be her? Thousands? Millions?

Fah had one "elite john" in her life, and her request to phone him had been rejected.

"No calls. It's the rule," she was told.

"It's cruel not to tell my husband that you've arrested me."

"We haven't arrested you. You've been invited to come here."

"I don't want your invitation."

Belligerence was easy at the beginning of detention, before the awareness sank in that nothing she said or did would allow her to hold on to any minimal amount of power over what happened to her. She had none. She remembered the reply she'd been given.

"You don't have a choice."

No truer words had ever been spoken. It took her a few hours to realize that there was no point in arguing. Osborne's temper would flare as he waited for her call. She'd promised to phone him if she was going to be late. She'd sworn an oath, but in the sin business, there were always extenuating circumstances, such as being arrested. She told herself it would work out. Her captors had nothing but suspicions. They'd have to let her and her friends go in the morning with a warning. And once Osborne found out the army had detained her, kept her overnight, sweating under a towel, he would turn his rage on them. It would be the same violent emotion but directed at a different target. Or would he? She wondered.

The soldiers inside the camp were young, tough and pumped up with a high-octane rage of their own. Osborne was an old man. He'd be no match for them. Yet she knew him well enough to know that he never showed fear. That's why people avoided getting into a fight with him. It would be a battle to the death, and nothing would stop him from charging ahead. She saw the young matador, buried in his old man's flesh, roaring to go back into the ring, shaking his orange hair. He was both matador and fighting bull, waging war against old age. Lying in the darkness, she found it comforting to think about his fierceness, not when it was used against her but when it became a sword and cape wielded to protect her honor. She missed him.

He'd taught her a great deal about life, but nothing had prepared her for the long, hot night locked in a room along a hallway patrolled by soldiers. She heard their heavy boots pacing outside her door. They preyed on her like wolves on a lamb, and she imagined that other, higher-ranking men preyed on them. She'd learnt how to read men from Osborne, who had the instincts of a predator, one who had survived countless battles. He knew better than most the masculine landscape of the Bangkok night filled with its bands of distracted men, made stupid with booze, drugs and lust, licking old, self-inflicted wounds, searching for a tunnel out of the command structure of their lives and seeking release in pleasure.

What had made the soldiers outside her door submit to the chain of command? It was the dirty little secret of life. Osborne whispered it to her one night when they were in bed together. It was their fear, their naked fear. There was a fortune to be made in making people fearful. Night after night, men returned to the bars not for the sex but to purge their fear and to find power over someone they paid money to fuck. The lure of a new excitement promised a moment when they wouldn't have to be afraid.

She rolled on her other side, facing away from the door. What had happened to Oak and Palm? Oak's face had flushed red when a soldier slapped him. He looked deeply wounded by the act of violence. Its quickness and power made further force unnecessary. He already looked fearful.

A military unit had set up an ambush point on the street that led out of the bridge community and back to Sukhumvit Road. The unit commander had planned it well. They had only moments after their taxi was stopped to activate the sequences that would wipe their iPhones. Ten soldiers blocked the street, and the driver of the taxi pulled over and rolled down his window. Oak looked over his shoulder as another army truck came from behind them.

"Some serious shit," said Palm. "It's time to say goodbye."

He pressed the sequence on his phone keyboard. Fah followed next, and Oak a few split seconds later as the soldiers ran toward the taxi, flung the doors open and pulled them out.

They were frog-marched back in the direction they'd come from. Two soldiers flanked them as they entered the barbershop and walked up the stairs, through the door and into the room where they'd worked.

They'd cleaned the room before leaving. When the door opened, the soldiers found a long table, chairs and a single bed with a thin sheet and two pillows. The white walls smelled of fresh paint. The officer in charge walked around, looking under the table and bed. Two of the soldiers took photographs of the room. It looked like a room some old *farang* might stumble into to sit at the table and slowly drink himself to death. It was the kind of room where, if someone died, no one would know until one of barber's customers complained about the bad smell. The kind of room a landlord might quickly repaint to make it a bit easier to find a new tenant. The soldiers walked around the empty space, looking for something. No incriminating evidence was visible.

"Who paid you?" asked the officer.

"No one paid me," said Fah.

It was inconceivable to the officer that anyone would voluntarily challenge authority without a financial payment from someone. Why would a student write a hateful paper unless someone had slipped her a fistful of cash? The presumption remained that she was under the protection of someone powerful. His mission was to get her to confess to the amount she'd received and finger the person who'd paid her. At the same time, he was hitting resistance, so his psych op training told him the best strategy was to change tack, hoping to catch her off guard.

"What were you doing here?"

"Studying for our lectures," said Fah.

"Why don't you study at university or at home? Why come here?"

"We were praying for the junta as instructed, sir," said Oak.

That earned him an open-hand slap across the face.

"Why does the barber say he smelled paint from this room?"

No one said anything.

"What were you painting in this room?"

"We wanted to return it to the landlord in perfect condition so we could get our deposit back," said Palm.

That made Fah smile.

"Why are you laughing? This is serious," said the officer.

Two other officers showed up, and one of them had their phones in clear plastic bags.

He asked, "What did you do to your cell phones? They work but there's no record of calls. No contact list, no apps. Nothing. Clean. What are you hiding?"

"Is that why you were laughing? You think you can make fools of us?" asked the original officer who'd taken them upstairs.

"Are we in trouble?" asked Fah.

"You are going to learn the meaning of that word before the night is over."

They were taken back to an army vehicle, pushed inside and blindfolded.

The officer leaned into the back and touched Fah's shoulder, saying, "If you can tell me the phone number of your two friends, I'll let you go."

She couldn't. The numbers had been on auto-dial.

"You can't remember," said the officer. "So how do you phone each other?"

"It's a scientific fact that when a person is terrified, they can't remember numbers," said Palm.

That earned him a slap across the face.

"Stop with the bullshit!"

Palm shook his head. He should have left a small backup phone directory. There were a lot of things they should have done. That was becoming the clear takeaway lesson about life in the back of a military vehicle on the way to a secret location.

TWENTY-THREE

"Through endless night the earth whirls toward a creation unknown..."—Henry Miller, *Tropic of Cancer*

OSBORNE LOVED DINING at any French restaurant where the owner permitted customers to bring their dogs. He had a regular table and two leather-cushioned chairs for his Jack Russell and Golden Lab. The dogs sat at eye level with the table and sniffed the air with the arrival of every new dish that came.

Calvino had phoned him to say he had news about Fah but wanted to talk in person. He'd told him he should bring along his friends Cesar and Charlie. Osborne admired the way Calvino used a code to suggest meeting at Osborne's favorite French restaurant. The private investigator must have assumed someone was likely listening to his conversation. Calvino could be theatrical at times, like most Americans, but he had good instincts for survival, important to making it in Bangkok in his line of work.

"Cesar and Charlie are with me and send their fond regards."

Osborne was an old pro in a city where pros and cons weren't different sides of an argument but descriptions of the people who ran things. He'd understood Calvino's message.

He'd told Calvino about the restaurant and the routine of the dogs dining with him once a week.

"You are more clever than you look, Mr. Calvino," he'd said on the phone.

"Thank you for your confidence, Mr. Osborne."

"I recommend the lamb," said Osborne, chipping in without missing a beat, a requirement to disguise the uselessness of the information. Disinformation had its own code of conduct, and Osborne had learnt the code by heart.

"Cesar and Charlie are quite fond of lamb, too."

"Let them know. I have a bone for them," said Calvino.

"That should motivate the two of them to sit up and take notice."

Calvino terminated the call and put his phone down beside his computer. Let them try and track him. He slipped out of his condo, putting on his helmet as he stepped out of the lift and onto the fourth floor. He rode his motorcycle down through the parking area and headed out through the back *sois* of the neighborhood. Calvino had memorized the shortcuts, the small, crowded *sois* where cars, vans, chairs, tables, potted plants and vendors expanded their territory, claiming part of the street as their own. In the best of the small *sois*, traffic was reduced to one lane, perfect for a motorcycle. Fast-track predators loved the cover of Bangkok's big darkness.

He looked into his rear-view mirror, checking for a tail. He saw none. Weaving in and out of traffic on dimly lit sub-*sois*, he passed streets lined with hotels, condos, shophouses, bars, restaurants and 7-Elevens. The topology of the city changed at nightfall. Darkness shrouded the landmarks, and the signs were difficult to read, the dim street lighting falling short. People suddenly appeared out of shadows, stepping out of their shophouse or car, not looking at the street, only to be swallowed up in darkness again.

Thirty minutes after leaving his condo, Calvino pulled into the French restaurant driveway, a narrow passage buried among dozens of other entrances along a sub-*soi* off Thonglor. He tossed his keys and then his helmet to an attendant, who caught them each with one hand.

"Khun Alan's Rolls Royce," said Calvino, drumming his fingers on the driver's side window.

He recognized Osborne's pale yellow 1970 Silver Shadow alone in a reserved parking area.

"Park my bike next to Alan's Rolls."

Calvino handed the attendant a hundred baht note. He then turned and walked toward where two more attendants held open a door. A wall of chilled air greeted him at the threshold.

Calvino stopped a few feet within the entrance and looked around for Osborne. He found him seated at a far table beside a large window overlooking an illuminated flower garden. Osborne sat between his dogs, smoking and glancing out the window at the garden. Beyond Osborne, with Charlie, the lab, perched on his right and Cesar, the lower-slung Jack Russell, nudging him to be scratched from his left side, the empty restaurant teemed with staff trying to make themselves useful.

"Looks like business can only improve," said Calvino, sitting down opposite Osborne.

"Just tell me where she is," said Osborne.

No preliminaries, no greeting or banter.

"She's in military custody."

Osborne rolled his eyes, his jaw slack like he'd been shot in the guts.

"No."

"Yes."

"Why? They've lifted the curfew."

"Martial law, Alan. That's how it works. They can do whatever they want to anyone, anywhere. Not knowing that is dangerous. Not knowing that means you haven't been paying attention."

"Don't lecture me, Calvino. Just tell me who I have to pay and how much they want. What's their price? Nothing else is relevant."

"You surprise me, Alan. Weren't you one of those who wanted a coup?" asked Calvino.

"This isn't helping me. Just tell me the amount I need to pay."

Calvino studied Osborne's expression. It was clear he really believed it was that simple; he wasn't putting on a front, joking or being ironic.

"Alan, this isn't business as usual. The military is running the show. Handing someone a bag of money isn't going to fix it."

Osborne butted out his cigarette, lifted his chin and blew out a column of smoke. The wheels in his mind were spinning. He lit another cigarette.

"Don't you have a friend who's a general?"

"He's police, not army."

"You told me they called him back from retirement. He must have powerful friends in the military or they wouldn't have bothered with him. You're right about the military. They aren't particularly sentimental. If your job is to shoot people, sentimentality isn't useful."

Osborne the angle-shooter had called his shot. He now waited to see if the ball he visualized rolling toward Calvino dropped in the side pocket or missed. He could see in Calvino's face that he'd sunk the ball. He'd been right. Unless someone high up in the army had supported Pratt's reinstatement and promotion, he would still have been stretched out on his beach chair looking at the tide coming in.

"He might be able to help, but you'll have to give something in return."

"Okay, now we're talking. How much does he want?"

"No money, Alan. Give him information about Ballard and what he was doing in Bangkok, something specific—places, names, meetings, deals. That's the kind of thing I'm talking about."

"He stayed with you. I suspect you know much more than I do, Calvino. Besides, I wasn't exactly his blood brother. Ballard was just someone I knew. It's like you—what do I really know about Vincent Calvino's connections, past or secrets? People are a mystery. And in this town their mystery only grows deeper."

Calvino watched as Cesar snatched a bun from Osborne's plate. A cute waitress dressed in a short black skirt flashed an inviting smile as she rushed to the table with a basket. She used a pair of silver tongs to lift another bun onto the plate. The Jack Russell gulped down the bun, and the thump of Charlie's tail against the window sounded like a sudden hailstorm had moved in from the garden. She moved around Osborne and placed a bun on Charlie's plate.

"There's not much he can do for you in that case," said Calvino.

He caught the eye of the waitress.

"Bring me a double Johnnie Walker Black on ice."

As the waitress turned to leave, Osborne said, "And tell the chef I want to buy a cigarette."

He tipped her with a hundred baht note. He lifted his right hip and slipped his thick wad of notes back into his pocket.

"You were saying your general wants information in exchange for the release of Sky? That's outrageous. What basis do they have for detaining her?"

"Wrong attitude, wrong intention or just the wrong information on her Facebook timeline," said Calvino.

"But she's only a student. She's pregnant with my baby, and I want her back. Tonight. After we finish with dinner."

Not even Osborne, in a rational moment, could believe that was remotely possible. But Osborne was like a dog paddling around a pond looking for a place to get out. He barely noticed as his pedigreed pets wolfed down another round of dinner rolls.

"Do you have any idea what she and her friends have been up to, Alan?"

"You've been tapping her phone, so you have that information. Tell me. Get it over with. I can take it."

"What has she told you?"

"She tells me everything. She goes to university. She studies. She fucks me. Three things."

"She's said more than that. You told me she did. What did she say?"

Two days before her detention, Osborne said he had confronted her when she had come home late, smelling of paint. He had sniffed her neck, arms, hands and blouse.

" 'Paint. Why do your reek of paint?' I asked her. She glared at me. I grabbed her wrists, forcing her down on the sofa. And she said, 'You're hurting me.' And I said, 'Why are you doing this? Surely you're not moonlighting as a house-painting contractor. Who are you taking money from? What's his name? Is it one of the Tree Brothers? Or is it that Cambodian tattoo guy? Tell me the truth.' "

Calvino waited as Osborne let the word truth hang in the hair.

"What did she say?" asked Calvino.

"She said, 'I'm not taking money from anyone. No one but you.' I said she'd been lying to me. 'I have proof. Who is this Munny, and what are you asking him to draw?' "

"She's going to wonder how you know his name," said Calvino.

"You only develop that level of paranoia when you grow older, Calvino."

Aside from the Tree Brothers, Calvino had supplied him with the name of this Cambodian. Osborne had been turning the three names over in his mind, imagining orgies, drugs and loud music thumping in the background.

"What did she say?" asked Calvino.

"The usual. 'And you only tell me the truth?' and 'All you care about is money.' She said I don't pretend to care about the truth. She's wrong there. I hate it when someone lies to me. If she wasn't in it for money what possible reason could she allow herself to have wild political ideas? Democracy is just a word. I told her that it had nothing to do with her. I said, 'Stick to your books and lectures. Look after my baby.' And you know what she said?"

Osborne padded Charlie on the head and sighed. He looked up at Calvino with sad eyes. "She said, 'To show the true reality of things takes courage.' How I'd told her what I'd learned that at age fifteen in a bullring in Spain. She believed me. She said, 'I admired you. You said that courage is hard and people will say you're a fool. But you don't care what they think. You know the truth, but don't expect anyone to thank you for pointing it out. It embarrasses them that you know they live a lie. To give in to their make-believe reality is the easy way out.' She told this Munny what I'd told her: 'If I'm going to be hated, let it be because I told the truth.' And then she said, 'Or were those just words told to a schoolgirl?'"

"She said that?" asked Calvino as Osborne finished.

"Word for word. See what I've created? What was I thinking? This is Thailand, and the bull wins. The matador dies. Why didn't I explain that to her?"

True to character, Osborne's attention shifted as he smoked the cigarette sent out from the kitchen. He called over the waitress and ordered a rack of lamb with seasoned vegetables. He looked up from the wine menu and gestured to the sommelier, who looked as forlorn as a standup comic playing to an empty house. When Osborne ordered a bottle of 1986 Lafite, the sommelier almost kissed him.

"Tell the chef I need another cigarette."

Talking about bullfighting, Spain, coups, paint and detentions had put him in the mood to order a thousand-dollar bottle of Bordeaux. Calvino wondered whether, if Osborne ever tried to stop drinking, as he was trying to give up smoking, he'd be sending requests to the kitchen for single glasses of wine.

"Sky showed me that Khmer tattoo artist's work. I didn't tell her you'd already showed me."

He stopped as the sommelier handed him a cigarette, holding the wine bottle in this right hand.

"Give it to me," Osborne said, sticking the cigarette between his lips and chomping down as he snatched the bottle and examined the neck. "You see that, Calvino?"

Calvino looked at the label on the bottle.

"It's wine. Lafite Rothschild, '86."

"Is there any other Lafite?"

Osborne dismissed Calvino's ignorance as a failure of the American education system.

"I meant the wine in the neck. When it's low, that means it hasn't been properly stored."

He looked up at the sommelier.

"Bring another bottle. A bottle with the wine at this level."

Osborne pressed his thumb at a high level on the neck of the bottle.

"Leakage, Calvino. That is the bane of our existence. What isn't properly stored leaks over time, it spoils. And not just wine—women, family, politics... Deals, too."

The sommelier returned with a bottle of Lafite '73.

"An inferior year for Lafite," sighed Osborne.

Calvino watched the poor man in the starched shirt and necktie endlessly shuttling from the wine cooler to the table with bottle after bottle, trying to please. Cutting things short, Osborne gestured his surrender. The sommelier smiled at his victory and uncorked the chosen bottle. Osborne smelled the cork and nodded. The sommelier poured a finger of wine in the glass. Cesar grabbed the cork from Osborne and ducked under the table.

"Powerful but not brash, a gentle nose," he said. "Long and intense. Pure and well-defined. An elegant, sensual body. I could be describing Sky. Indeed, I am."

The sommelier filled Osborne's glass before attending to Calvino and then departing swiftly.

"You can see why they do no business. The sommelier doesn't know enough to decant a Lafite. Even an inferior year deserves time to breathe before being drunk. It's the same with women. They too need space to breathe before you drink them. I sat Sky on the sofa and told her that I'd given her a great deal of breathing space. And that seemed to make her happy. As I talked to her, I realized it was like seeing someone for the first time. This stranger was carrying my baby. How did that happen? Was I dreaming? Have you ever experienced that feeling of strangeness in the presence of someone you thought you knew?"

Osborne had managed to also describe Calvino's feelings about Marley. But sharing those feelings with Osborne would have given him the distraction he needed next after already stalling with the Lafite saga.

"Let's move on to Ballard," said Calvino.

"We'll come to him in a moment. Let me finish. I don't mean 'strange' in a bad way. It's just that there was a whole part of Sky that I knew nothing about. I had thought she was a rather silly girl, someone who was after my money. But I was wrong. She has substance. Why hadn't I seen that before? Later that night, she showed me a term paper that she'd handed in to her professor. He'd written a load of nonsense in the margins. His favorite word was 'false.' From the pen of an academic, that's enough to make you want to vomit.

"It wasn't even her idea. Palm ripped off the idea about the Users and the Used from the Internet. Instead of writing the paper, she hired a grifter named Lee Welford, who is from Perth in Australia and lives in some squalid room off Petchaburi Road. Mr. Welford, an Open University dropout, ghost-wrote it for them. Where did she get the money to pay him?"

Osborne used his finger to stab himself in the chest.

"I paid the fee. She told me no one has time to write term papers. Not to mention the lack of the English skills to write one. Their final mark would rest not on the caliber of their argument, she said, but on a forger's perfect grammar. It's all appearances with these people. I thought about it and concluded that I should be proud of her. Sky was showing a deep insight—the importance of carefully selecting competent partners in a criminal enterprise. Most people don't learn that lesson soon enough, and they go to prison.

"But now it turns out she didn't learn it well enough, that bitter lesson about the importance of making quality judgments about strangers. That doesn't mean she should be thrown in some dungeon to be tortured by troglodytes. It's unbearable, Vincent."

He grabbed the bottle of wine by the neck and refilled his glass. He looked dejected as his rack of lamb arrived.

"How is your lamb?" he asked after while.

Calvino hadn't touched his plate.

"Others have been detained with her," said Calvino.

"I don't fucking care about the others."

"Frankly, the people holding her don't fucking care about you."

"It's a standoff. I am not the one who will give way."

"Rolls Royce against a tank. Who wins that standoff, Alan?"

Osborne sipped his wine and paid attention to the Jack Russell.

"I will win."

"Give me something about Ballard, Alan. Anything."

"Aren't you eating?"

"What do you know about him?"

Calvino shook his head in frustration.

Osborne leaned over the table, stuck a fork into the lamb rack on Calvino's plate. He picked up a knife and cut meat off the bone, picking up the cooked flesh with his fingers and feeding it to Cesar and Charlie.

"I love the honesty of dogs. They never have any moral problem eating what is offered. Ballard was not that different from Cesar and Charlie in that regard."

TWENTY-FOUR

"Any man who knocks on the door of a brothel is looking for God."—Graham Greene

OSBORNE RECOUNTED HOW he'd spent time, capital and old IOUs to bring rough justice to the mastermind who'd ordered the murder of his son, Rob. In planning for the revenge killing, he'd discovered a mutuality of interest with Ballard. He decided they were two of a kind. Osborne needed to square accounts over his son's murder in Rangoon. Ballard seemed to have no problem working with a man like Osborne if it meant eliminating a common enemy, and he'd seen an opportunity. An influential person with a good personal reason to bring down a big-time illegal drug smuggler had appeared out of nowhere. A black bag operation was set in motion to get the dealer. It had been a work in progress when Ballard had suddenly been pulled off the case and reassigned to gather intelligence on Dr. Marley Solberg. Only Ballard hadn't told Osborne of the sudden change of his assignment. He'd only told him he had to sort out a couple of problems first.

"I didn't even know he'd come to Bangkok," Osborne told Calvino.

Calvino let that information sink in as a waitress arrived with another basket of bread. Osborne's two dogs took no notice.

There had been a number of things that Osborne hadn't known about Ballard, but that hadn't seemed to matter at the time.

"I sized up Ballard the first time we met as one of those men who worked for himself. It didn't matter what it said on his name card. Ballard was self-employed."

Osborne had passed information on to Ballard about how Calvino had had his own teddy bear moment with Marley. Calvino had also been in Rangoon when Rob Osborne had been killed. From Ballard's point of view, it must have seemed as though Calvino's name just kept cropping up in unexpected ways. Osborne, who couldn't let go of his son's murder, played along. Osborne had seen too late that, for Ballard, the chance to bag a big player in a major drug smuggling operation could wait. The pressure had shifted to finding Dr. Marley Solberg. He had come to Bangkok not to arrange a deal with a smuggler but to find the rogue software programmer that DARPA had at the top of their "persons of interest" list.

Osborne had first laid eyes on Ballard at an airport in Madagascar. It was sheer chance. If the timing of their flights had been off by a few minutes, they would never have crossed paths. But Osborne's flight was running late, and Ballard's arrived early, giving fate a chance to set the clock so that Ballard arrived in a private plane a few minutes before Osborne landed his private jet. Osborne had heard traffic control give the go-ahead to Ballard, so he had circled the airfield, waiting for Ballard's plane to land. He wondered who this person was to merit priority landing.

"I'm in the shipping business," Ballard had told him as they walked through immigration and customs. "And your line of business is...?"

"Night entertainment."

"Brothels?"

"I also sell alcohol. I find most men need alcohol before sleeping with a whore. I'm a middle man," said Osborne, "the one who introduces the buyer and seller."

Ballard smiled and nodded.

"You tie both ends of the rope."

"I take it you don't build ships," said Osborne. "You procure ships."

"Procuring is a term more appropriate to your line of business."

"All business is the same. Give a man enough rope and his competitors will drive him to hang himself."

They exchanged enough information to size each other up. Giving away just enough but not so much as to destroy the mystery. What sealed the friendship was Ballard asking if he could bum a cigarette. Osborne tapped a cigarette from his pack, handed it to Ballard and lit one for himself, passing the lighter's flame in front of Ballard, who leaned into it.

"Almost everyone I know who smokes has quit or is dead," said Osborne.

Only later did Osborne discover the reason Ballard had flown into Madagascar. He was on the trail of a drug smuggler who controlled a supply network operating between Bangkok and Los Angeles. Intelligence reports showed that the market was expanding. Osborne explained that he was in Madagascar to spend time with a local French-speaking woman named Sylvia whom he'd recruited into his personal breeding program on a previous trip. Sylvia was nineteen years old, green eyes, dark skin—a mulatto, with a black mother and a French father. Sylvia spoke no English, and Osborne had planned his trip to coincide with her ovulation cycle. He was determined to get Sylvia pregnant.

The trifecta—plane arrival, smoking and hotel—was enough to bind them. Osborne was booked at the same hotel as Ballard. The first morning in the hotel dining room, there was Ballard again. Osborne caught Ballard's eye, which was difficult as his eyes were trained on Sylvia. Osborne invited him to join their table.

"Do you speak French?" he asked Ballard.

"No," he said.

"Good, join us. Sylvia speaks no English. Communication with women should be limited to meaningful glances."

Osborne's Madagascar wife sat mute at the table, occasionally asking Osborne something in French. She lasted ten minutes before drifting back to their room to change into her bikini for a swim.

Once she'd gone that first morning, Ballard had opened up. He didn't need much persuasion and even came across as someone who didn't have many friends he could confide in. Every man comes to a point in his life when he can't keep it all inside and the first person who is prepared to listen is going to hear something normally heard only by a priest at confession. That first morning he got to know Ballard over fresh-baked croissants and double espresso at the hotel café. They swapped stories about music, women and wine in Bangkok, London and Rangoon, and they smoked cigarettes and talked about private airplanes in foreign airports and, finally, cargo ships.

Over the course of five days, like a cat with a ball of yarn, Osborne had unspooled Ballard's personal story. Each day Ballard waited until Sylvia kissed Osborne on the cheek and left the two men alone at the table. He'd pick up his story where he'd left it the morning before. In high school Ballard had played tenor sax in a jazz band in Spring Lake, New Jersey. The band, called the Lemurs, had five members. Ryan, the lead singer, disappeared one day into a daytime TV show and didn't return their calls. Ryan's sudden departure left a gaping hole in the band and a lot of hard feelings. Ballard and the others were still basically kids with big dreams, and it looked like the dream had ended.

Abandonment has never been a medicine anyone can swallow without tasting the bitterness rising up in the back of their throat—something you can spit out but can't stop from poisoning your opinion of life. The band unraveled like a cheap suit. Gradually the band members lost contact with one another. Ballard graduated from Yale with a Bachelor of Arts degree, majoring in Southeast Asian politics. The DEA recruited him, saying he had a bright future in making the world a better place. For a year or so he actually believed that was possible.

In his first year with the DEA, he set up a sting operation. The targets included two members of his old band—Willy Joe, a black guitar player, and Arnold, a keyboard player who'd moved to San Diego. The two of them walked into a trap. They had half a kilo of cocaine and at the point of sale were arrested with half a dozen agents pointing guns at them. Ballard had stayed undercover and wasn't present when his ex-band members were arrested, but when their trial came up, he testified against them. Of course, it came out in cross-examination that they knew each other from high school and had played in a band together. Ballard received a commendation for putting his friends in prison. That was the day he figured out there was no such thing as a bright future in friendship.

His testimony had locked up two old his friends in a federal prison. Both of them were released a few years later and disappeared from the grid. It worried Ballard some; he found himself looking over his shoulder. Their prison time had hardened them, he heard on the grapevine, setting them up with the right contacts in the drug business. During their nine years in prison, the drug world had changed in a dozen ways. There was a lot of money to be made online.

"Are they in Madagascar?" asked Osborne.

Ballard shrugged.

"Don't know. Don't really care."

The last DEA intelligence report on them, slipped to Ballard by a friend, indicated that Willy Joe and Arnold had been active in Macau, Phnom Penh and Bangkok.

"I saw Willy Joe at the Bali jazz festival a few months ago," Ballard told Osborne. "He threatened to kill me."

Osborne's eyes brightened.

"But he said it wasn't necessary, that I'd get what was coming to me."

"Meaning?"

"Meaning a hooker name Christina."

"I thought drug pushers were stupid," said Osborne. "This one seems quite brilliant. Finishing off someone with a hooker. Not original but still brilliant. I often wondered who fell for that scam."

"I suspect your business worked on a similar model."

Ballard had been planning his resignation from undercover work for more than a year. He'd saved money from selling cargo ships. He worked in the same part of Asia as the friends he'd betrayed and had figured it was just a matter of time before they ran into each other again. In Southeast Asia, settling a score cost less than a bottle of 1986 Lafite.

"Just quit," said Osborne. "You have enough fuck-you money. Walk away."

"I can't."

"Why not?"

"I've been fired."

He told Osborne the story about Christina Tangier, the hotel room in London, the teddy bear, the photographs, the conceptual art exhibitions and the hedge fund manager. Christina had bought Ballard's act that he was one of the super-rich. His mission was to get information about a Colombian cartel boss she'd slept with. And he'd bought her story that she was just another high-class hooker. Two liars were fucking each other for their own reasons that had nothing to do with sex. Ballard played the big shot;

he bragged about his shipping interests. He didn't disabuse her of the fantasy she'd built around him in the first half hour of their exchange. He liked playing the international jet setter and had used the role as a cover. Impressing her was a collateral benefit. She'd sworn an omertà to him, an oath of silence, which turned out to be a lie. She didn't tell Ballard the oath only applied to Christina the hooker, and Christina the artist had no obligation to follow an oath that interfered with her art.

"Have a cigarette," said Osborne. "I certainly need a smoke."

On their last day together in Madagascar, Sylvia had lingered at the table. Ballard, though he had obviously been attracted by her beauty at first sight, seemed disappointed that she made no effort to leave.

"If you're ever in Bangkok, look me up," said Osborne.

"And if you ever come across anyone wanting to buy or sell a ship, here's my card," said Ballard.

Osborne studied the gold-embossed business card, which showed both New York and London addresses. He pocketed it.

"I don't carry a business card," said Osborne, "although that's bad manners in Asia, I know. Frankly I don't want people calling me about the next deal of a lifetime. As it happens, I do know rich people who might be in the market for a yacht, but since you're in the cargo ship business, that's not going to help you very much. Why don't we joint-venture a contract on the man who was responsible for the murder of my son? He's the major drug guy in Southeast Asia."

"I'll think about it," said Ballard.

Having finished the story, Osborne stroked Charlie's neck as he ate the last rib from Calvino's rack of lamb. Cesar had fallen asleep on his chair with a belly full of buns.

"But you didn't eat," said Osborne.

Calvino smiled, thinking McPhail had said the same thing. It hadn't been the tacos. He just lived in a time and place that robbed him of his appetite.

"When Ballard phoned," said Calvino, "he told me he'd come to Bangkok with a deal to sell a ship to someone in Phuket. Any idea whether he was telling the truth?"

"An American named Damon was introduced to me at a party. It turned out that he wanted to buy a yacht. He made his money in show business and had a luxury home in Phuket. I said I knew someone I'd met in Madagascar who might be able to help him get a good deal. I passed along Damon's information to Ballard."

Osborne poured the last of the wine into Calvino's glass.

"If I'd known Ballard was in town," said Osborne, "I'd have assumed he was here to kill the man who killed Rob. That would have been good news. But it wasn't to be. Is that enough for your friend, the general? Ask him to order the army to release Sky and send her home."

Cesar and Charlie slept off the buns and lamb on separate chairs. Osborne was a little drunk. Calvino didn't need to tell him that no one in the police or anywhere was ordering the army to do anything that the army didn't want to do.

There was an old saying about letting sleeping dogs lie, but Calvino knew it wasn't the kind of fable that Osborne wanted to hear.

TWENTY-FIVE

"Sooner or later... one has to take sides. If one is to remain human."—Graham Greene, *The Quiet American*

GENERAL PRATT'S WARNING that the US embassy was pushing the department to make an arrest of Ballard's killer haunted Calvino. He knew he was on their short list. It was just a matter of time before he received a visit. The best strategy was to convince your enemy to underestimate your available resources and capability. Calvino's law on ego swallowing—show less than you possess to stroke the ego of your enemy, feed his sense of superiority. Never starve it. In the digital age, the act of returning his office to its pre-digital splendor of twenty-five years earlier made him appear as a housefly caught in an amber tomb. Or as the Thai said, he looked like a frog trapped in a tropical coconut shell. The trick was not to overdo the show. For that reason, Calvino decided against the fedora and double-breasted suit.

Instead he dressed in a Hawaiian shirt, one with a pattern of dark blue leaves and vines among the large white Hibiscus blooms, the top two buttons undone, showing neck and the hint of chest. A five-baht gold chain, a Buddha amulet in a small case rested just below his throat. His beige slacks were freshly press and he wore a pair of new brown dockers without socks. The choice had been between the dockers and bedroom slippers given to him by an old Chinese client. He'd never worn the slippers. Inside his closet, pristine white slippers, tiny red dragons on the sides, were still in the box. He wanted the man-out-of-time look. The bedroom slippers would have pushed him over the edge into the crazy man category. That wouldn't work. When he had examined himself in the mirror, Calvino saw a man who could have passed for a late middle-aged captain washed ashore from the old analogue world.

Ratana assisted in the removal of his computer. In its place was an electric typewriter positioned on his desk. She was wearing a sleeveless, hip-hugging silk dress with a narrow red belt showing off her waist and red high-heel shoes. The hemline reached around a full hand above the knee. She looked far too plugged into the digital age to fit the image of an old-fashioned private eye's office.

John-John, her *luk krueng* son sat in a chair facing her desk. John-John was reading a book. Not just any book. But Ronald Dahl's *Charlie and the Chocolate Factory*. Calvino had given him the book for his seventh birthday. Ratana had helped him choose his clothes: a grey T-shirt with a silhouette of T-Rex on the front, green baggy shorts, and yellow racing shoes.

He *waied* Calvino as he came into the office, "Hi Uncle Vinny," he said.

"Found that golden ticket?" asked Calvino.

"Still looking," he said. "Aren't you supposed to be in school?"

Ratana said, "The school is closed for a teachers' outing."

He walked into his office. Having John-John in the office, Calvino decided, worked to his benefit. It would downgrade his operation in the estimation of the agents from the embassy. A seven-year-old was an analog bonus.

He sat at his desk. Ratana had plugged the typewriter into the wall socket and watched as he threaded in a piece of A4 paper and typed: "The only Lafite is a Rothschild. Good nose. Elegant and sensual body. The '86 is superior to the '73. Both bottles should be decanted for an hour so they can breathe." He stopped, satisfied with what he'd written, smiled and looked up at Ratana who had slipped inside.

"The touch of the keyboard comes back quickly," he said.

"You don't need to convince me. You'll need to convince..."

She broke off.

"Who is it you need to convince, Vinny?"

"Your dress."

She stood with her hands on her hips.

"What about my dress?"

"It looks like you belong behind a computer."

"That's because I work behind one."

"Not for the next few days."

"You want me to go home and change?"

He shook his head.

"It's okay. It's not important. I don't mean your dress isn't important. I mean... I don't know what I mean."

"I don't think I've seen a typewriter in years," she said.

Calvino nodded, looking at the machine.

"That's the point. We judge time by technology. We judge information by the date of the technology. Time is an exact messenger. I've decided to be a typewriter fundamentalist. I don't change with the times. You don't hear much about us, but of course you wouldn't. We're not online or in a chat room. But we know we're out there."

"You won't last. You'll be back on the computer before the day is over."

"That depends on the other people I'm expecting."

"Will they come today?"

"I don't know. People are unpredictable. Sometime between eleven seconds and twelve days from now, they'll come through the door. Give or take ten percent on either side."

"And meanwhile, you're planning to work on that... that typewriter?"

She stuttered, looking slightly amused and horrified at the same time.

Calvino ditched his smart phone in his office safe and removed from the second shelf of the same safe a vintage Nokia circa 1998. The black dumb phone fit like a glove with the electric typewriter. He'd gone back in technological time. His office had a Sam Spade, Philip Marlowe look, as if an ancient film set had materialized. The image of the Maltese Falcon passed through his mind. But his secretary looked like Taylor Swift.

"I want to give them the feel of time travel. Welcome to a Bangkok when the generals stayed in their barracks."

Ratana shook her head.

"When was that?"

"Figuratively speaking."

Shaking her head again, she said, "Let me know if you want to check your email on my computer."

"Don't blow my cover, Ratana. Could you do your hair up in a bun in the back? And remember, I don't use email."

"Right. You want me to lie for you and change my hair?"

He grinned.

"Of course. Both are part of your job description. I am glad you brought John-John to the office today."

"He asked to come."

Ratana waited for a knock on the door, but no one came around except for McPhail, who was looking for a top-up from the bottle in the bottom drawer of Calvino's desk. After McPhail had gone, leaving behind him a whiff of whiskey, Calvino assured her that a couple of strangers in suits would likely come around asking for him.

"Your appointment with General Pratt has been changed to 1:32 p.m."

"Is he using the department astrologer for lunch appointments?"

She didn't answer him. Nor did he expect her to.

"I told you he sent his regards, didn't I?" said Calvino.

"No, you forgot."

"He sent them. Messages in the old days took longer to be delivered."

Pratt had rescheduled the appointment for the second time. Calvino read the cancellation and rescheduling as evidence that his friend was under pressure, and getting away from his office wasn't as easy as in the old days. Generals had different clocks from colonels. He had told Pratt on the phone that he had something about Ballard for him. Pratt had insisted on meeting him outside his office.

Too many foreigners were against the coup. Allowing one to circulate in police headquarters had raised a couple of well-plucked eyebrows. After Calvino had left, another general had asked him about the foreigner. The messenger was more important than the message. The logbook showed Calvino had been to his office; having his name appear there twice in a week would bring more questions. Since Calvino was a person of interest in an open murder case, Pratt could report that Calvino had information for them. Even with that excuse, the suspicion would still have fogged their thinking. Pratt had a long history of association with this foreigner named Vincent Calvino.

Other senior officers regularly stepped out of the office for meetings with astrologers, monks or gurus who forecast their future. Fate readings, always popular, had taken on a sense of urgency in the department. It now took a week to book an appointment with a famous astrologer. Martial law was a time to monitor future threats so those in the prediction business had more business than usual. Such an orientation fit well with a belief in astrologers, who predicted disasters, misfortunes and the intentions of enemies. Pratt never dismissed the predictions of certain astrologers outright. He was, after all, Thai, and he said there were over a hundred references to astrology in Shakespeare. There were probably a thousand references to swords there as well, but that seemed beside the point. Something deep inside the new general told him that astrology, like swords, had limited use in the modern world. Yet astrology made for a great cover story. Checking the karmic weather report was a good reason to leave the office.

General Pratt told his orderly, Lieutenant Pim, "I haven't paid my respects to Brahma at San Phra Phrom Erawan. One thirty-two p.m. is an auspicious time. Please arrange for a car."

Her smile signaled her approval.

"Yes, sir."

He'd be left in peace to pay his respects. Calvino would be just another *farang* gawking at the devotees carrying out ceremonial offerings at the base of the four-headed Brahma statue. The shrine, it seemed to Pratt, was an inspired choice for a meeting venue. He wasn't above wishing to impress Calvino with his improvisational abilities, which weren't limited to the saxophone.

Before Calvino had a chance to leave the office and join Pratt at the auspicious time, two visitors inauspiciously arrived, flashing US embassy ID cards.

Ratana looked up from her computer.

"Do you have an appointment?"

"Tell your boss we're from the American embassy and we're here to discuss the death of Andrew David Ballard."

"Mr. Calvino only sees clients by appointment."

"We aren't clients, and we aren't asking for an appointment."

John-John looked up from his book, cocked his head to the side. The younger agent smiled at him. "No iPad?"

"My son likes books," said Ratana, a cold ripple coloring her tone of voice. "As I said, you need an appointment."

Calvino stood in the doorway.

"It's not a problem, Ratana. Why don't you come into my office?"

The two men in suits stared at him.

"Are you Vincent Calvino?"

"Ratana, these gentlemen want to know who I am."

"You're Vincent Calvino."

They looked disappointed.

"Does that answer your question?" said Calvino.

"You've got an attitude."

"Pre-adjusted attitudes are the latest problem in Thailand," said Calvino, gesturing toward his office. "Please come in."

The agent in charge looked forty years old, and his partner a decade younger. Clipped nails, short haircuts, wedding rings, and when they opened their mouths, American accents, flat and angry, carried an echo of menace. The senior agent filed in first, his junior a step behind. Calvino closed the door after them and sat down behind his desk.

"Give me a moment," said Calvino. "I was just finishing a letter."

On the other side, Ratana heard the sound of Calvino's electric typewriter. The two men, still standing, exchanged glances, the junior guy biting his lip as he tried not to laugh. The blond-haired agent, the senior suit, nodded at his brown-haired, blue-eyed partner, who whipped a line of sweat from his forehead. The typing stopped and Calvino read the line, pulled out the paper, crumpled it up and threaded in a fresh sheet.

"Made a mistake. It's hard to type when someone's watching. It's like taking a piss in a public restroom. It's one of my personal quirks. We all have them. Let me have one more try," he said.

Picking up the handset of a rotary phone, he dialed Ratana.

"Tell my guru I'm running a little late."

"Guru?" asked the senior agent.

"My astrologer. I've been in Thailand a long time," said Calvino.

"Sorry. Take a seat," Calvino said.

"We want to ask you a few questions about Andrew Ballard," said the senior agent, ignoring Calvino's request, "and we'd appreciate it if you'd give us your attention."

Calvino looked at his typewriter and sighed.

"Okay, I'll finish the letter to my mother later."

"Your mother? You expect us to believe you're writing a letter to your mother?" asked the junior agent.

Calvino nodded, looking at the younger man, who was close to drawing blood as he pinched his own arm, half a second away from losing it.

"What, you don't write your mother?"

The senior guy raised a hand.

"Stop. No more of your corny bullshit, Calvino. We have a thick file on you. Stop trying to fuck us around. It isn't funny. We aren't laughing."

"What do you want to know?"

"We already know that Ballard stayed as a houseguest at your condo. Two nights after he left your residence, he was dragged out of the Chao Phraya River. A couple of slum kids skinny-dipping not far from the ferry pier found his body. According to the autopsy, Ballard drowned, but his face was beat to a pulp. Whoever killed him was a professional. We take the loss of an agent personally. We won't let up until we find his killer. Am I making myself clear?"

The senior agent snapped his card on Calvino's desk like it was the ace of spades and he'd hit twenty-one. He slid it across the desk with two fingers as if he wished to avoid any direct contact with Calvino.

"I thought the DEA fired him. Or was it DARPA? You should retire the letter D in the agency racket. It's confusing."

"You still don't get it."

"I was sorry to hear what happened."

So much for the exchange of pleasantries. There would be none. That was how they'd decided to play it.

Howard, the blond with the kind of attitude that came with a diplomatic passport, a gun and a badge, displayed a look at contempt.

"Sorry? If that's the case, you won't mind helping us with our inquiry."

"Whatever I can do."

Calvino blinked as he looked at Howard.

The other agent, named Davenport, reached across the desk and handed Calvino his name card. Calvino stared at the two US embassy cards. He made a point of studying the cards, giving each of the men time to size up his office. From a puzzled expression on Davenport's face, Calvino guessed he'd never seen a typewriter up close.

"Feel free to take a picture, Agent Davenport."

"Are you really typing a letter to your mother on that?" asked Davenport.

"It was a graduation present from her," said Calvino.

Howard shook his head.

"We aren't here to discuss your mother or your typewriter."

Calvino's old-model mobile phone rang and he answered it, pressing it against his ear. Osborne was on the other end, wondering what General Pratt had told him about Fah.

"I haven't seen my guru. No, I don't have a lucky number to give you. And yes, I am in a meeting."

He cut the connection to Osborne, visualizing him at the other end shaking his phone and wondering if he'd experienced a weird connection to another universe.

Davenport snapped a photograph of the old phone.

"No Facebook, no website, no Twitter," he said. "Is that what you wish us to believe?"

"Distractions. Time wasters."

Calvino laid the old mobile phone on the desk. He carefully picked up each name card; each one showed an affiliation to the political section at the embassy. Americans from that section had been trained to make local house calls when necessary to find information beyond what technology could capture. Up to five years ago, men just like them had supervised enhanced interrogations at safe houses in Bangkok.

"The Internet killed the last Philip Marlowe in your line of business years ago. You should get out more, watch more TV," Davenport said, shaking his head.

"I don't have a TV, Mr. Davenport."

"You're one of those analog holdovers I read about on *Huffington Post*. What they call pre-Internet *farang*. Someone who got lost in the shuffle of time," said Davenport. "How do you receive the alerts the embassy sends US citizens by email?"

"I look out the window, and if I see riots in the street, I know it's time to be alert."

Davenport clenched his jaw like a Hollywood action hero.

"I'm probably wasting your valuable time," Calvino continued. "You could be writing alerts or checking your email or your Facebook timelines."

Davenport hadn't smiled once since coming into his office. Calvino made him for one of those hard young men who had no doubt about the nature his assignment. Only the technical, operations parts mattered—and of course, muscle. And Calvino, in Davenport's assessment, was no more or less than another name in a power point presentation with the heading "Ballard." What Calvino had missed was the self-inflicted pain that kept Davenport from dissolving into a puddle of hysterical laughter.

"I've known a fair number of Americans who've died here," said Calvino. "But this is the first time a delegation from the embassy comes to my office with a briefcase stuffed with questions. I met Ballard at a jazz festival in Bali a couple of years ago. When I was drunk, not an uncommon state, I invited him to stay with me should he ever come to Bangkok. He was drunk too, but not so drunk as to forget my offer. He showed up out of the blue. I could've told him to get lost. If I knew he was going to get himself killed, that's exactly what I would've done.

"The fact is, Ballard didn't stick around long, and I didn't spend much time with him for the few days he was there. I gave him a key and he came and went as he pleased. Then he moved to the Oriental Hotel. I guess my place wasn't good enough. Maybe he needed a bottle of '86 Lafite. It's a good year. Same number as the embassy car registration plates, and much better than the ordinary plonk I poured him. Who he saw or what he did or what he planned to do are questions I can't help you with. It's too bad he's dead. I liked him."

"How do you feel about the coup, Mr. Calvino?" Howard asked, retaking control of the questioning.

"I thought you were here to ask questions about Ballard," Calvino said.

The two agents were under the cover of the political section. Neither of them looked like political scientists.

"Unless you think Ballard had some connection with the coup," said Calvino. "Now that would be interesting news."

"Answer my question. How do you feel about it?"

"Feel? I don't feel much of anything. I've been through three coups. It's like getting a divorce. After the third one you're no longer shocked. You get the idea that it's hard to make a marriage or a coup work out the way you'd hoped. And the divorce is always messy."

"But you personally came out on the side of the winners. Isn't that right, Mr. Calvino?" said Howard. "You've got the power on your side."

"You're talking about my friendship with General Prachai, right?"

"General Prachai can do nothing for you. Dr. Marley Solberg is another matter," said Howard.

"She's the one who gave you the encryption no one can break," said Davenport.

"Dr. Solberg could have sold it for a fortune. Instead she chose a different way, one that isn't in anyone's interest but hers."

Finally they had produced the business end of the official sword.

"I've got no immunity, special or otherwise," said Calvino. "Does it look like I need encryption?"

He tapped his typewriter.

"Let me share what I've learned about Thai politics. Keep a distance from those doing a victory dance in the end zone unless you understand their game, how it's scored and how many players each side has. If you can't figure out the rules of game, you won't know when the game has started and when it's over. 'Don't put a bet on a game you don't understand'— I had a cousin in Queens who used to say that.

"My cousin, according to my mother, made his share of lousy bets. When he was killed in the Vietnam War, I thought about what he used to say. Don't you find that in your line of work? It's one of those things people used to say years ago, and seemed kind of stupid at the time, but later on you think there was wisdom in it. The past comes back to haunt us. You probably don't remember, but half a dozen years ago, maybe before either of you could find Thailand on a map, there were people in the embassy and JUSMAG honing their water-boarding skills at a black site here in Thailand. When I heard about it, you know what I did? I shook my head, and said, 'Can't be true.' "

Davenport leaned forward, but Howard stopped him from a knee-jerk reaction.

"You're playing to an audience that isn't in this room. We don't fucking care about your politics except if it links to Ballard and his investigation into Dr. Solberg."

"You asked about the coup."

"We are only interested in your relationship with Dr. Solberg and subsequently with Ballard."

"I didn't have a relationship with him. Nor do I know whether he was gay."

"Why do you say Ballard was gay?"

"It's like with Alan Turing. Things turn up unexpectedly, and suddenly the state decides on an official castration."

The two agents exchanged a glance.

"Who is Alan Turing?"

"Someone who delivered lectures on mathematics to a teddy bear."

"Mr. Calvino, are you trying to convince us that you're crazy?"

"My mental state, like my clients' business, is confidential."

"The facts indicate otherwise."

"Meaning?"

"We know you have a history of mental health problems. Dr. Apinya says you've improved, but improvement is a matter of degree," said Davenport.

"In other words, you can cut out the bullshit and answer our questions," said Howard.

Calvino sat back in his chair, hands on his desk. They'd visited his old psychiatrist, Dr. Apinya. He wondered what she'd told them, or had they found another way to access her psychiatric patient files?

"Go ahead. Ask your questions."

"What were Ballard and you planning to discuss over dinner? You were going to give him information about Marley Solberg, isn't that right?"

"I don't know what Ballard intended to talk about. I had an idea of what I wanted to ask him."

Howard leaned forward.

"And what was that?"

"In between keeping up with the latest advancement in waterboarding technology, do you and Agent Davenport find the time to read novels?"

"You're not answering the question. What were you going to discuss with Ballard?"

Calvino opened his desk draw, took out a copy of *The Quiet American* and slid it across the desk to Howard.

"This."

"I thought we agreed, no more bullshit."

Calvino pulled out the note Ballard had left with the book.

"Ballard left a note with this novel. When I got back to my condo, I found the book and the note in the guestroom, where he'd left them."

Howard read the note and handed it to Davenport, who read it.

"Ballard had time to read novels," said Calvino. "Could that be a reason why he didn't fit into your outfit?"

Calvino picked up the novel and turned to the opening passage.

"At the beginning of the book Fowler waits for an American agent named Pyle to show up."

"And what's that have to do with Ballard?"

"Fowler finds out later from the police that Pyle is dead. In the water near the restaurant where they planned to meet," said Calvino.

"You're saying he left you the novel as a suicide note?" asked Davenport.

"I'm saying he left the book and the note. Draw your own conclusions."

"You are way outside your league, Mr. Calvino. Whatever you know about Solberg, you'd be wise to disclose it to us," said Davenport.

"What he means is either you co-operate or you're in for a world of hurt," said Howard. "Have I made myself perfectly clear?"

He played with the wedding band on his left hand, pausing mid-spin.

"You might want to see your shrink again," said Davenport.

"Why would I want to do that?"

"Talk to her about your crazy ideas."

"One more thing, Mr. Calvino," said Howard. "Tell us about your meeting with Osborne, Cesar and Charlie last night."

"Cesar ate a basket and a half of buns. Charlie ate ribs from a rack of lamb like there was no tomorrow. And Alan Osborne drank a fifty thousand baht bottle of wine and talked about spotting lemurs in Madagascar. That's the place where you'll likely find Ballard. As for Marley Solberg, I have no idea where you'd find her, and I suspect you don't either or you'd not be wasting your time in my office."

"You're a smart guy. Maybe a little too smart," said Howard. "My partner's right, you should give Dr. Apinya a call."

As they left, Calvino sat back in his chair and looked out the window, watching Howard and Davenport climb into a chauffeured car. He thought about the man running in his great-grandfather's most famous painting. The fire in the sky, the balloons, the fireworks, the stationary figures waiting in the foreground.

Ratana walked into Calvino's office carrying his computer. She had combed the bun out of her hair, and it fell in waves to her shoulders. John-John followed behind his mother.

"I like your shirt," John-John said. "But I didn't like those men very much."

"Which shows you are wise beyond your years," said Calvino.

"I'll have you back online in five minutes," she said.

He came around from his desk and took the computer from her.

"Wait a day or two before you hook it up," Calvino said.

He carried the device back to her side of the office and put it on the side table. She followed behind.

"You're worried they'll come back?"

Calvino stared at the computer, the monitor and keyboard.

"I can't be sure. But that's not the point."

"What is the point, Khun Vinny?"

"While I was typing on the Selectric typewriter, I had a feeling of being liberated."

"Liberated from what?"

He didn't answer, and after an awkward moment Ratana returned to her desk. He heard her typing on her modern keyboard.

He stared at his Selectric typewriter. It had been a private place. No one could access, record or analyze his movements, his contacts, messages and search history. The typewriter caused him to remember being happy in another time and place. He'd typed his daily diary on that typewriter—his homework for when he was seeing Dr.

Apinya. He associated it with opening up to his inner self. He'd learned important things about himself, including what made him happy. Not the happiness the junta preached, but being centered, happy with who he was and what he was doing and what life meant. The computer reminded him of the person he'd become: distracted, focused on eight windows at a time, trying to make sense of twenty things at once and losing the thread.

There was another reason: Marley. It seemed she couldn't stop herself from leaving a sign she was near. The high-level app that Fah, Oak and Palm had downloaded from their clouds had Marley's fingerprints all over it. Was it her way of helping while staying in the background? If so, he was sure she wouldn't look at her involvement as interfering. Marley looked at things through the other end of the telescope. He felt her presence whenever he logged on. She was always there, somewhere, in the background.

Calvino walked out to Ratana's desk. John-John sat cross-legged on the floor, looking bored. "You want to go to the park after I meet Uncle Pratt?" Calvino asked him. A smile flashed across John-John's face.

"Yes," he said, rising to his feet, looking at his mother.

Ratana nodded.

"The typewriter is my way of taking a time-out, a rest from the game. Like sitting in the park and reading *Charlie and the Chocolate Factory*." He picked up the book from the desk and headed to the door.

She looked up from the screen.

"You won't last two days," she said.

"Thanks for the vote of confidence."

"You can't stop the game just because you don't want to play," she said.

"I am still in the game. I'm off now to meet Pratt."

"No matter how hard you try, Vinny. You can never go back."

TWENTY-SIX

"If this is the best of possible worlds, what then are the others?"—Voltaire, *Candide*

CALVINO WALKED TOWARD the main gate of the Erawan Shrine. A police BMW never looked out of place in that area, but something told him this wasn't just any police car. Was Pratt waiting inside the idling car, keeping cool in the air-conditioning? Calvino looked through a side window. Lieutenant Pim Suttirat worked her thumbs on an iPhone keypad. He lightly rapped his knuckles on the window. He didn't have to wait long. She immediately popped her head up and shot him an annoyed look, before she recognized him and let that annoyance deepen. She powered down the window.

"Sorry, miss, you're double parked. You'll have to move right along."

"The General is inside."

"Any particular dream you want to come true? Let me know, and I'll put a word in with Brahma."

Lieutenant Pim smiled coldly and powered the window up. A moment later, her head was bowed over her iPhone again.

Right, said Calvino to himself. She wasn't going to admit to being a dreamer, something that would have been drilled out of her as a precondition for her job as the general's assistant at the department.

She'd parked the BMW around the corner on Ratchdamri, with the left front tire turned and digging hard into the curb. The distance from the car to the shrine was only a few steps. Generals don't seem to walk that much, thought Calvino. Ordinarily, a long line of tourist buses would have been parked along the same curb, but he saw none. The coup had diminished their numbers. Calvino examined the faces of the devotees. Tourists from Hong Kong, China, Japan or Taiwan were absent. Ratana's Facebook friends speculated that the coup had rattled their confidence in the holy shrine.

As he entered the shrine, Calvino found the usually busy stall vendors looking bored and frustrated. He looked around for Pratt.

"How's business?" he asked a vendor as he bought a set of candles, incense sticks and flowers.

"No customers, no business, no money," the old woman said, as if she were reading a T-shirt mantra.

She saw no irony in complaining about business in the shadow of Brahma. Commerce and mysticism were joint venture partners in this large spirit house. Over the old woman's shoulder Calvino spotted Pratt.

Pratt knelt at the first of four positions at the base of the golden Brahma image. Calvino carried the sticks of incense, candles and flowers and knelt next to him, offering a *wai* to the god.

"It's always bothered me that the Thais have no trouble believing in Hindu gods, Buddhism and animism," said Calvino. "They see no contradiction, yet in politics they end up as doctrinal purists. Maybe that's inevitable."

"How you think about your next life is one compartment. What you think about politicians is another. People don't confuse them."

"Have you had lunch?" asked Calvino, positioning one stick of incense into the sand in front of the shrine.

It was the most acceptable opening gambit in a conversation with a Thai. Above their heads a train roared through the Chitlom BTS station.

"What did you say?" asked the Pratt.

"I haven't eaten. What about you?"

"Sometimes, Vincent, you are surprisingly Thai."

"That's what the two American embassy guys who showed up at my office thought. They'd talked to Dr. Apinya."

"No surprise. They're trained investigators, and following up on the mental health of a suspect is part of their job."

Ratana had already told Pratt what had happened.

"What did you tell them?"

"That I was writing a letter to my mother."

"Your mother?"

"I played to their Freudian side. And that was before I knew they'd leaned on my shrink."

"What did they say?"

"That I was a person of interest."

"And you've turned that into being an interesting person."

Calvino smiled, thinking Pratt hadn't lost his sense of humor as they walked clockwise to the second kneeling place, to face another Brahma head. He told Pratt about the conversation the evening before with Osborne and everything he'd learned about Ballard. He also told him how Osborne had ordered a bottle of wine that would have been a month's salary for someone in Pratt's position.

When they'd finished the fourth and final installment at the base of the shrine, Pratt asked, "This story Osborne told you, did you tell the embassy officers?"

"I thought I'd let you handle it. I had to give them something, though. So I showed them the Graham Greene novel Ballard had left and his handwritten note. Neither of the agents seemed like novel readers. Maybe a book with pictures, but a novel, no. But it was enough to get them out of my office. At least for now."

Pratt liked Calvino's ability to quarantine problems, shuffle them into the right container and pass them along to the senior person in charge as in Thai tradition, but he had upped the game by making sure his friend received full credit. In some ways it made Calvino invaluable. Either Calvino occupied the best of both worlds, or the worst, and Pratt had gone back and forth on the matter many times. He'd long since resigned himself to never eliminating that uncertainty.

Calvino walked with him to the BMW.

"If there's a way to fast-track the release of Osborne's girlfriend from military detention, I'd be grateful."

"She's being held at a camp in Chon Buri."

Events following the coup had moved fast, with a lot of people rounded up. No one was sure how many would be hauled in, who would be next or how long they'd be detained for. Information was sketchy, and no one was willing to stick their neck out to guess when the arrests and detentions would end. Pratt had inquired about Fah and been told that she was in a military camp. She and two classmates had been invited to the facility in Chon Buri. The word "invite" had acquired an Orwellian twist.

Pratt nodded.

"She was picked up with two university classmates. There was an issue with a term paper they'd written. The military wanted clarification of their intentions."

"Have they clarified things?"

"It's not that simple. It seems the paper was anti-coup. The group wrote it together. All three names were on it."

"How did the military get a university paper?"

Calvino saw Pratt look away.

"From their professor?"

"It's a difficult time," Pratt said. "Things will settle down soon. People need to be patient and trust that the right thing is being done."

"Davenport and Howard are right. I should make another appointment with Dr. Apinya."

Getting Fah out wasn't something Pratt had the power to arrange. The military were watching the police for any evidence of loyalty to the old regime or to certain groups. He had to be careful.

"Her release is up to her. All she has to do is sign a document promising not to engage in any political acts or write any criticism of the junta."

"That's it?"

"They've asked her to rewrite the paper, following the notes made by her professor. Once she's rewritten it and signed the release, she is free to go."

"What the hell did they write?"

"An essay that showed a bad attitude."

"And until she shows an attitude adjustment…"

"Her invitation is extended."

"That's fucked, Pratt."

But matters could have been far worse for Fah and the others. Had her professor done the bare minimum, ratting them out on the paper while withholding information about the street art? He might not have known about the graphics, but one of them was right in the paper itself. Pratt had mentioned nothing about the Banksy-inspired graffiti images Fah's group had produced to protest the coup. Calvino interpreted Pratt's silence as meaning that neither the military nor the police had any such information. None of the three had divulged their existence as a protest art committee that used a room above a barbershop to produce its graphics.

"What's the delay?" asked Calvino. "She won't rewrite the paper or sign off, is that it?"

"They haven't finished with the interrogations."

"Meaning, if someone has written a paper like this, she's shown her intention. They figure she'll continue doing other things, and knows other people who share her intention. Will they get together and cause trouble? And after she fills in those details, you think they'll release her?"

As Lieutenant Pim held the car door open, Calvino remembered there was another question he wanted to ask Pratt.

"By the way, what did Manee's committee do with all the fish in that fountain?"

"They found a new home for them. No killing. That was their main goal."

"I like a story with a happy ending," said Calvino, glancing over at Lieutenant Pim. "I hope Brahma grants your request," he said.

Pratt smiled.

"I hope so, too."

He watched as Pratt's BMW weaved into the traffic. He'd forgotten to ask Pratt what he'd asked Brahma for. That was the point of the ritual, making a deal with the god of creation to bring you a winning lottery number, a cure for some illness or a beautiful wife or rich husband. A long, happy life rounded out the usual dinner order. What had Pratt prayed for? Calvino suspected that, whatever it was, he'd ordered a wish that wasn't on the menu. Calvino had put in his own request on the god hotline—to double the size of his database on Ballard's killer.

Halfway along the pavement to the stairs leading to the Chitlom BTS station, Calvino saw a Thai in a university uniform standing near the gate to the shrine, holding an A4 sheet of paper with what looked like a large QR barcode on it. When he reached the top of the stairs to the station, he saw several other students near the railing overlooking the shrine. At 3:39 p.m. a dozen university students raised their smart phones and pointed them in the direction of the shrine. Calvino looked at the cell phone screen of one student and saw what looked like the QR code on the sheet of paper he'd seen the first student holding. When he looked again, the incomprehensible pattern had been transformed into a piece of art projected onto the station wall. He recognized it as one of the protest artworks from Fah's workshop. A young, slim Thai in a white shirt and black trousers, his back to Calvino, aimed his cell phone at the station wall with a calm, firm hand. A small crowd gathered around the image, holding hands, saying nothing, standing in silence. When the police and soldiers ran up the stairs, the image vanished.

What they had missed had gone back to being a QR code and dissolved into thin air. But for thirty seconds the group had shared the experience of the image. Marley had even discovered a technical solution that made the images stand out under a tropical sun.

In the image a girl lobbed an unhappy face emoticon into the back of a dumpster. Flashing in soft neon-green tones on the side of the truck were the words "Unhappiness Recycle Unit."

Calvino's path had crossed Munny's at the shrine, but Calvino had failed to recognize him. Munny was another face in the crowd. Munny watched the office commuters who'd gathered in front of the turnstiles, transfixed, admiring his art. And he saw a middle-aged *farang* man who might have been an old customer on Khao San Road. When Munny looked closer, he thought that Calvino clocked the platform like a cop; he didn't have the scared or perplexed look of the other *farangs*.

Once the police arrived, Munny slipped his token into the turnstile and moved to the train platform side. He rode the escalator up to the train. He was headed back to the outer edge of the city. He'd done his work—opened his one-man show, his first public art exhibition. There was more to come. He felt a mixture of pride and terror. Munny had no way of knowing where Fah and the others were. He wished they could have seen the crowd and the happiness and hope that the art had inspired. He'd sent out a coded map to a hundred people, and he knew that the same art must have appeared on walls in twenty separate locations across the city. More than that, he knew that by spreading the images through the social media, Fah, Oak and Palm had sown digital seeds that would be carried as through the wind to the screens of many thousands of people around the world, until the digital seeds had grown into a dense forest. That's what Palm had proudly announced—the images would be shared from London to Moscow.

Munny looked down from the platform as the train arrived and saw the flashing police lights below. Something had happened at the station to change things, and Munny had played a part in that process. He felt giddy, and he felt sad and guilty, too. In his school a French priest, who had been sent by his order as a form of punishment to teach in the countryside, had reminded his class on their first day that Cambodia had once been a French colony. The priest told them that meant the French had once owned their country. The priest had one book he rated one level below the Bible, and it was Voltaire's *Candide*. He told Munny's class that Voltaire was one of the great philosophers of all time, saying, "Forget about righting the wrongs and the sorrows and heartache of the world. Withdraw to your garden, tend it, and erect a wall between your tiny corner that shuts you away from the wars, disease, hates and tragedies on the other side of your wall."

At the border, when Chamey had wrapped her arms around Munny, she had reminded him of what the old priest had taught him. As the train doors closed, Munny stood looking out at the platform, thinking about the faces in the crowd, the image he'd drawn and the look on Chamey and Sovann's faces as he'd walked back to the van that would take him to Bangkok again. He was a long way from his garden gate.

TWENTY-SEVEN

"It's a beautiful thing, the destruction of words."
—George Orwell, *1984*

THERE WAS NO number on the door or the frame. Had Palm expected to find the number "101," that iconic number made infamous by a single book? George Winston had had his attitude readjusted in Room 101. "1984"—Palm knew that was more than a number, too. But real interrogation rooms were never like the ones in books, at least in the books Palm had read. He had no idea if Fah and Oak had been taken to the same room before him. He'd been here before. He assumed that the camp complex had other such rooms. He imagined that this one was just one among many other, similar rooms along a long corridor.

The walls in the room were bare, as was the room itself except for three wooden chairs. Two soldiers, whose uniforms bore no nametags or rank markings, had escorted Palm to the room and told him to sit in the middle chair. They said nothing, and having finished their job, left and closed the door behind them. He stared at the blank surroundings and at the other chairs. Perhaps it was a setting for musical chairs, where a guard would remove them one by one until the room was totally bare—except for the moment Palm seemed to be the sole player. The strange solitude didn't ruin the suspense of the game but only deepened Palm's sense of mystery.

His mind started to wander. His thoughts flew like moths to his parents, his sister and his two brothers, and then to Fah, Oak and Munny and the graphics they'd spray-painted on the walls of the room above the barbershop. He wondered now, more than ever, who had sent the photo projection app. What did he or she look like? Was the person Thai? Why had he and the others been chosen? None of the thought fragments stayed for long; they were more like disconnected images coming and going on their own timing. Was it the intention of the interrogators to get him to think too much? To get him to remember the first time he'd been in the room, when there had been a single chair? He saw in his mind Fah and Oak being led through the door to occupy the other two chairs. The image vanished.

He stood up from the chair and sat down again in the one on his left. A little act of protest, he thought. Sanity was finding meaning in such small gestures. It told him he had choices, even if it was just moving from one chair to another. Blinds covered a bank of windows against the east wall, but crack in them allowed some sunlight to spill onto the floor. He guessed it was mid-afternoon. A long fluorescent light on the ceiling made the room a sickly yellow like the body of a hepatitis patient. He turned his head to the other side and then shifted in his chair. A calendar hung on one wall. It was turned to the month May, the month of the coup, and no one had bothered to flip the pages over as time passed. Time had stopped in May. He thought of Somkit, an activist from Korat who was one of the people who shared his room at the camp. "Good luck is being run over on your way out of a brothel, and bad luck is being run over on your way to the brothel. I was on my way out when they invited me to the camp. How about you?" Having walked out of a barbershop, Palm decided his capture had bad luck written all over it.

Before Palm's interrogators appeared, another soldier entered to blindfold him and handcuff his arms behind the chair. He came and went without saying a word. A few moments later Palm heard voices and his interrogators entered the room. They didn't introduce themselves. One of officers spoke with a slight Isan accent.

"I haven't done anything, older brother," Palm said to him in Isan dialect.

The officer slapped him across the face with an open hand.

"Speak Thai," he said.

His tone had the high-pitched foghorn sound of bad luck moving at a hundred and fifty kilometers an hour.

Palm figured that the officer was under intense pressure to prove his loyalty, and speaking Isan in the interrogation room might be viewed as subversive. He'd had to slap Palm to prove himself.

"You will answer our questions, is that understood?"

Palm nodded. This was his sixth interrogation. The times varied from six in the morning to midnight. There was no pattern. He guessed the standard psych ops books must have taught interrogators ways to maintain the prisoner's insecurity, cause him psychological stress and make him vigilant for the physical punishment that was coming. The possibility of violence filled the empty room.

"Fah says you wrote the term paper. Is that true?"

"We all wrote it."

"Are you saying Fah's lying? Why would she lie?"

The interrogator removed Palm's blindfold.

"Look at me. Oak tells us the same thing. The paper was your idea. They went along with you. They say you were the ringleader. Why do you deny it? I thought you'd be proud."

Palm's eyes followed his interrogator's arms and hands, which moved like large cats covering the floor. The other officer leaned against a wall, opening a crack in the blinds and looking out. He seemed bored. Asking the same questions over and over was numbing for them, too, Palm thought. As before, neither of his interrogators wore nametags or bars or stars. Nameless and rankless, they worked in teams, never staying still. They walked around the room as if they owned it and he was an intruder who had better come up with the goods or something bad would happen.

They blindfolded him again and left. After a while a new shift came in and started from the beginning. An interrogator only had so much juice. Rotating them in and out of the room helped them keep up routine—blindfold, then no blindfold, questions, a slap, the smell of cigarette smoke and silence, followed by a new shift. It was a nightmare sequence that promised to destroy his will to resist.

The strangest part was that although the interrogators appeared to improvise their questions, nothing could be further from the truth. They were actors performing scripted roles. Interrogations balanced a number of elements with a fine precision—terror, fear, empathy, disbelief, support and threats. Always, at the end, came an interrogator's rapid volley of threats of violence. The words bubbled, heavy and bloated, floating like cartoon panels overhead, waiting to explode. It was like a tennis champion rushing the net to put the ball away. It was not safe to resist, they were saying. He should understand that there was no limit to what they could do to him. The violence escalated gradually, sending another message: co-operate and the pain will vanish. They warned him each time that they were nearing the end of their patience, that he was pushing them and they didn't like being pushed. If he refused to answer their questions, they would have no choice but to go to the next step.

Then the interrogators shifted their attention to the professor who had turned the students in. Or were they only pretending interest in the professor, to throw Palm off balance? They could have lied. In an interrogation room, the line between lies and truth dissolves. Palm had no evidence other than his interrogators' words that the professor had fingered them. In the first session he had asked one of the interrogators why one of his university professors would denounce him as a traitor. The interrogator had smiled, suggesting he'd been prepared for that question.

"You are from Isan," he said, launching into the standard humiliation. "You are a *kwai*, you are red, you love the corrupt people, and you do not love the land of our birth. Your professor is a good man. He did his duty as a citizen."

Being called *kwai*, a water buffalo, was standard-issue disdain, and it was why Palm had joined Fah and Oak in the first place. Water buffaloes don't fight back. They wander through the muddy field to graze. Palm sought the courage to fight back, to prove they were wrong to judge him. From the first session he promised himself to take a stand, to show them he was made of better stuff. By the third or fourth interrogation he was questioning himself. By the sixth session he understood how fragile his ideals were. The interrogation seemed to be designed to show him how futile, dangerous and silly abstractions about democracy and freedom were inside an interrogation room. How could abstractions or ideals protect a man when he is handcuffed and blindfolded? Such a man is less than a water buffalo, and this lesson was their objective. He looked at the eyes of the interrogator, who waited for his response. The man's pupils were dilated as if he took pleasure in his work. Palm looked straight ahead and said nothing.

"Fah and Oak have co-operated. They've taken their name off the paper. That leaves you, Palm. Alone. Your friends are going home. What about you? Don't you want to go home?"

On one level he refused to believe the interrogator, but on another level the words played to deep-seated doubts. He felt the unease of inner conflict as his mind raced from one end to the other like a child in a game of tag. "You're it," he thought as the interrogator circled his chair. None of the interrogators had mentioned Munny. If Oak and Fah had defected, they'd have given Munny up. The interrogators would be questioning him now about Munny's artwork. All the questions were about the paper and why their cell phones had been erased.

The drill, the treatment, varied little from one interrogator to another, as if they were all clones of the same person. At the end of time, they'd still be mouthing those same words, which floated over the room like bubbles, speech balloons, with one popping and another coming into existence.

One of the interrogators reapplied Palm's handcuffs and blindfold.

"You should prepare yourself," he said and left the room.

"Prepare for what?" Palm asked, as his imagination ran wild.

But the interrogators had gone. They had left him alone in the room to think.

The silence faded as Palm heard noises from beyond the walls of his room, murmurs and shouts coming from other rooms. Weeping. Banging. The unseen world of sound fed his imagination with a library of images from old TV shows and movies—horror stories, mysteries, thrillers. Interrogators knew how to start the reel inside a person's head and let the mind do its own takedown into imagination. Palm felt the sweat under the blindfold as his mind raced through the possibilities.

He had come to Bangkok for university. His Isan heritage was as visible as one of Munny's tattoos. He wasn't one of them, and he saw that message in their eyes. He had an unmistakable face from the Northeast, one he could never change, any more than he would ever be taken for a Thai-

Chinese. His look was as distinctive as a signature. He hated them, and he hated himself. They had filled him with hate.

Thirty minutes passed. Then Fah, blindfolded and handcuffed, was brought into the room by two female soldiers, who seated her next to Palm. Oak, also handcuffed, his blindfold pushing back his long, flowing hair, followed a few minutes later. He stumbled and cursed. The others recognized Oak's voice as he was pushed into the last empty chair.

"Are you okay?" Palm asked him.

"Fine," whispered Oak.

"Shut the fuck up! Silence!"

Palm recognized the interrogator's voice. He remembered it from a day earlier. His blindfold had been removed on that day, and he was allowed to see the officer who ordered the others around in a firm voice. One of the military officers from earlier was also back, the one who spoke with an Isan accent.

"You have one more chance to tell the truth before we take you away."

"Are you going to shoot us?" asked Oak.

"If you disappeared, who would ever know?" the officer said.

"I told you the truth," said Fah.

"If you don't believe us, then by all means shoot us for writing a term paper that even you said had one or two valid points," said Palm, speaking to the officer in the Isan dialect. "They'll always think you're a watermelon soldier, no matter how many Isan people you slap. Just like me, older brother, you are trapped and can only pretend to be free."

"You should go back home," said the officer.

"You're probably right," said Palm. "There's no place for me here."

The officer nodded for the interrogators to remove the blindfolds and handcuffs.

"Before we release you, all three of you will sign a document saying that you came here on your own, were treated well and will not engage in any social media until further notice from us. Do you understand?"

Three heads nodded. They just wanted out and had no choice about the conditions. The time for arguing had passed. They signed the documents, passing the pen down the row. An officer collected the documents and checked the signatures. He then left the room, and the other officers followed. The three were alone together for the first time since being arrested.

"Are they really going to let us go?" asked Oak.

"Shut up," said Fah.

She made a point of lifting her eyes to the top of the door. A small camera monitored the room.

"When was the last time you ate?" asked Palm.

"Can't remember," said Oak.

"Wait," said Fah.

Their confinement at the camp had become cramped. There weren't enough beds. New people arrived day and night. A steady stream of people, famous and anonymous, came through the door, and the sleeping spaces got smaller and smaller as students, activists, politicians, teachers and entertainers were shoved in.

At first Fah, Oak and Palm had thought they'd be interrogated together. But the interrogators had wanted to pick them off one by one, throw them head first into the Prisoner's Dilemma, find a winner and move on. From that first day the interrogators had pounced on inconsistencies in their stories and lied about the intentions and actions of the others. None of it had worked. Information the students had found on the Internet had prepared them for such strategies. They were each aware after the first interrogation that the military had nothing on them but the term paper, and that the interrogators' ignorance of the graphics would remain unless one of them caved in and told them about the art project and Munny.

All three of them had stuck to the cover story that their group had formed as a study group. The goal had been simply to work on a group assignment for a university class. They had researched, written and rewritten the paper together and handed in the finished assignment on time to their professor. What had they done wrong? What crime had they committed? "Why did you delete the apps and files from your cell phones," they had been asked, to which they'd responded, "How is that a crime?"

The soldiers said the students had had an "intention," and that was what mattered. Until they changed their intention, they wouldn't be let go. That standoff had lasted until the moment that the students at the Chitlom BTS station had magically held up their cell phones to project anti-coup art for all to see, creating quiet chaos near a sacred shrine. Similar reports had come in from more than a dozen sites around the city. Students, taxi drivers, vendors, office workers and farmers had been rounded up with their cell phones, but no trace of the software that had enabled the protest could be found on the devices.

In interrogation centers there was always a top boss with the highest level of authority on-site, who lorded it over his subordinate, who in turn ruled over his own fiefdom, all the way to the bottom of the ladder. Except for the top boss, everyone had a boss to worry about. Policy adjustments filtered through the system, orders were handed down, meetings and briefings were held to inform the ranks of their duties: what to look for and what lengths they could go to, to obtain information.

A day after the first of the cell phone flashers had arrived at the detention camp, a new order had pulsed through the chain of command, and that had changed things for Fah and her friends. A big boss had decided that in the greater scheme of things, writing a term paper with anti-coup sentiments wasn't so serious, given what had just happened. It was only a university paper. They'd used no social media in sharing their dissent. Papers and assignments written by students in universities, for the moment, would have a lower priority, he said. "The bad apples are online." He told his second in command: "If we decided to detain every student who wrote about politics, we'd be housing more students than the universities. It would demoralize the soldiers to have so many young people locked up for writing offenses." Also, the foreign press was hammering them for human rights violations. All that pain for so little gain, he concluded. Public displays of dissent, like that art splashed all over the Chitlom BTS Station, was hitting the country like an unstoppable freight train. Those protest messages of resistance had to be stopped. They could pull a switch and blame the subversive term paper on the *farang* ghostwriter. That would solve that problem.

Last but not least, a police general, with credentials approved by the Junta, had made inquiries about the girl. It all added up to the same thing—let the three of them go and keep an eye on them. If they were genuine troublemakers, they'd slip up again soon enough. Meanwhile, the big bosses had bigger fish to fry. "Send them home," was the order the military officer from Isan delivered in person. The three students had signed on the dotted line.

Palm thought about what his signature meant—submission without consent, form over substance, lies over truth.

Once they were outside the military camp, Fah broke the silence.

"We have three days to rewrite our paper and submit it."

"If we don't?" asked Oak.

"We'll be 'invited' back."

Palm shook his head.

"They've given us a standing invitation."

"Let's give them what they want," said Oak.

"On that day, we are no longer human beings," Fah said.

TWENTY-EIGHT

"If you live in a place for long you cease to read about it."—Graham Greene, *The Quiet American*

WHEN CALVINO ARRIVED on Soi Cowboy, the first *farang* he came across was Jerry, a regular from the Lonesome Hawk back in the day. Just emerged from the hospital after a hip replacement operation, he hobbled alongside Calvino for a while.

"The place always reminded me of a field hospital in Vietnam," he said. "I'm sending that one to Glover. It should win his weekly contest," he said, shaking his head.

Glover ran a popular website read around the world, and punters sent him hundreds of emails a week to win a five hundred baht monthly prize. The latest prize entries were for metaphors to describe the coup.

Jerry patted his hip.

"You don't waltz through airport security with all these metal screws holding you together, so I guess I'm stuck here for a while," he said. "I wish the Lonesome Hawk hadn't closed. I could sit there for hours and talk to people. Now I can't sit for long anywhere, and there's no one to talk to anyway."

In its own way, the old Lonesome Hawk in Washington Square had been the last Vietnam War field hospital. Calvino watched Jerry's face twist as he slipped into a seat at an outside bar, laid his cane on the table and started scanning the foot traffic for a familiar face.

An hour later McPhail sat on the stool next to Calvino's, nursing his third gin and tonic and smoking a cigarette. Another customer nearby sat entranced with peeling off the paper label from a bottle of Singha beer. The customer made no eye contact with the girls. He was a peeler, lost inside his own head. His thoughts were in some other place and time, where the beer flowed freely, the army stayed in the barracks, and the girls were scented, sweaty and sensual.

"You think that guy will order another beer?" said McPhail, blowing smoke. "A hundred baht says he's just spinning his wheels. He's not drinking any more, and he won't take a girl either."

Calvino slapped a hundred baht note on the table. McPhail looked at it.

"He'll buy one more beer," said Calvino.

McPhail put down his bet.

"I say he's a cheap Charlie and will eat that bottle after he peels it like an orange."

They watched the female performers go through the motions, pretending there was an audience.

"We've been here before—2006," said McPhail. "Coups are bad for the bar business. How can you seriously think about getting laid when there's a curfew? It destroys the mood. Everyone asks, where are the tourists? Well, I know where they are."

"Where are they, McPhail?"

McPhail raised his glass.

"In their rooms, wanking."

Patterson Roy, owner of Mama, Don't Call, came out with another bottle of Singha and a fresh gin and tonic.

"This round is on the house," he said. "And don't ask how business is."

A waitress in high heels and fishnet stockings, wearing enough lipstick to paint a half-kilometer of road divider, had spotted the money on the table and whispered to Patterson that their only two outside customers were about to pay up and bolt. Like most rumors, it wasn't true. And like most rumors, truth was never the point, and rarely mattered. Patterson was taking no chances. He needed a couple of loyal regulars like Calvino and McPhail as front men to draw in other long-time expats, who were drawn to their own kind.

"Patterson, Calvino would like to buy you a drink," said McPhail.

"Thanks, Ed. I should say, thanks, Vinny."

"We're waiting for Glover."

"I heard that after the coup he left the country," said Patterson.

"Rumors, Patterson. You live and die inside them."

"Tell me about it, Ed," said Patterson.

Calvino raised an eyebrow as Patterson ordered the waitress to bring him a Belgian beer in a frosty mug, the one he kept in the back of the fridge for special occasions. Friendship and business blurred on the Soi. Patterson had supplied Calvino with information in the past. He knew that an informant feels a bond to his handler not unlike what a bargirl feels toward a regular customer. They convinced themselves they shared more than just a business connection. Money flowed like electricity down the lines of that lie.

Patterson made a big show of pouring his Belgian beer slowly, tilting the frosted mug just right and letting the foam slowly rise on the inside.

"You're a little quiet tonight, Vinny," said Patterson. "You've got a lot on your mind. I can see that. It's the same for everyone. I was thinking the other day, whatever happened to that little Rohingya who sold nuts, watches and cigarettes on the Soi? Now's my chance to ask the man who'd know."

"You mean Akash," said Calvino.

He hadn't thought of him for months, and he remembered him as a bamboo-reed face blinking back tears in prison, asking only for the right to peddle his tray of nuts on Soi Cowboy.

With a film of Belgian beer on his upper lip, Patterson nodded.

"He's working the front desk of a hotel in Oslo," said Calvino.

"No shit?"

"He's been to England twice on his new Norwegian passport."

"Now you're fucking with me."

"Okay, maybe it's not a Norwegian passport. But he went to England. He's given testimony to the British parliament on human trafficking."

Calvino left out that this activity had been arranged and financed by Marley.

"I'm glad to hear he came out of it okay. Most don't," said Patterson. "You remember Nui. You know she married a guy in Berlin. Six months later she shows up here asking for her old job back. She lasted a week. The good life had made her lazy. She wouldn't dance. Came in late to work. Mouthed off to customers. Got into fights with the other girls."

"Is she working tonight?" asked Calvino.

Patterson shook his head.

"I had to fire her. She was doing drugs."

"Too bad," said McPhail. "I remember Calvino bought her out a couple of times."

"She claimed her wreck of a life was Vinny's fault."

"Yeah? How so?" said Calvino.

"She said you destroyed her confidence. Kept buying her out, taking her home, and instead of ripping off her clothes and charging out of the gate in the bedroom rodeo, you paid her without taking a bull ride and sent her home. So she married the German on the rebound, but her self-esteem never recovered."

"Nui's slippery slide into the gutter was my fault?" asked Calvino.

"You know how women are, Vinny. It's always your fault."

McPhail butted out his cigarette. "I remember her sister, Nok."

"What do you remember about Nok?"Patterson asked.

"I'd had a lot to drink. And the oral sex, if my memory serves me, was like one of those aborted mid-air refueling missions in high turbulence."

They drank is silence and watched as three girls grabbed a *farang* in his sixties. He was slow to break free and the girls wouldn't let go. He dragged them as he took short, wobbly steps on his sandaled feet, sweating in baggy shorts and a T-shirt with the slogan "Same Same But Different" printed in Times New Roman. The action on the Soi was like an alien version of the Discovery Channel where a pride of gazelles jumped on an old, weak lion.

"He's a goner," said McPhail.

"It's my kind of euthanasia," said Patterson.

"It's more like amnesia," said Calvino. "We've been here before. But we keep on thinking it's the first time."

"It's the coup—part euthanasia, part amnesia. Drink it down slow," said McPhail.

The Singha beer bottle peeler called over the waitress with the big lipstick. Calvino nudged McPhail as they waited for the moment of truth. She removed the chit out of the cup and waltzed into the bar with a smile on her face. A moment later she came out with another bottle of Singha and put it down in front of the customer, slipping the chit back into the cup. Calvino picked up the two hundred baht notes and called the waitress over.

"This is for you," he said.

After she left, Calvino said, "Patterson, the business is changing—for the bar owners, the girls and the customers. It's never going to be like the old days. That time has come and gone, like Washington Square."

"The Square was a slum filled with rats and drunks."

"Hey, Patterson, don't say that," said McPhail. "Vinny and me had lunch there for years."

"Not many guys from those days who are still alive," said Patterson.

"Did I tell you that I saw Jerry coming into the *soi*?" asked Calvino.

"He's still alive?" said Patterson.

"He had a hip replacement. Certain parts are alive, others replaced," said Calvino. "At some stage it's hard to tell if a person is alive."

"There's a limit to what can be replaced," said Patterson.

"That's the point," said Calvino.

McPhail wrapped an arm around Patterson's shoulder and quoted Ecclesiastes 3: "The Bible says, 'To every thing there is a season, and a time to every purpose under the heaven: a time to be born and a time to die, a time to plant and a time to pluck up that which is planted, a time to kill and a time to heal, a time to break down and a time to build up, a time to weep and a time to laugh, a time to mourn and a time to dance, a time to cast away stones and a time to gather stones together, a time to embrace and a time to refrain from embracing, a time to get and a time to lose, a time to keep and a time to cast away, a time to rend and a time to sew, a time to keep silence and a time to speak, a time to love and a time to hate, a time of war and a time of peace.' "

Calvino exchanged a glance with Patterson.

"You memorized the Bible?" said Calvino.

"Not the whole thing," said McPhail. "In ninth grade, we had an assignment to memorize a poem or a page from a book. My daddy said this was the only part of the Bible that ever made any sense to him, and I should memorize it. So I did. I've forgotten almost everything else I ever learned. But I remember Ecclesiastes 3, yes, sir. I'll remember it until I draw my last breath."

He drank the rest of his gin and tonic and held up the empty glass for another round.

" 'A time to get and a time to lose' pretty much describes Bangkok," said Patterson.

The quote had sobered them up. Calvino stared at his glass. The thought slipped back into his mind that he'd been mapping the distance between Bangkok in the old days when they were all young and Bangkok now.

"When I think of the old gang at Washington Square, I think of that passage," said McPhail.

"A time to check your timeline and a time to sleep," said Calvino.

"Have you been to our website?" asked Patterson. "I just paid a guy from Denmark for a makeover. Everyone says you need a platform."

In 2014 websites were like 1970s flared trousers. Yesterday's fashions and yesterday's technology were equivalent sources of embarrassment, pinning a man in time like a beetle on a display board.

"I've seen it," said Calvino, "but..."

"But what? Give me some feedback."

"No one is talking about the amount of traffic on websites, Patterson."

"What are they talking about?"

"Big changes."

"Like what?"

"Start with the slide in the quality of the girls coming through the bars. Ask yourself why that's happening. There are reasons."

"If you read Glover, he says they're working in factories now."

"Some," said Calvino. "But there's more available pay for play than ever. So how do you figure that's happening?"

Where was Glover? He was more than forty minutes late for their meeting.

Patterson sipped his Belgian beer, thinking for a moment, as bar owners prided themselves on having an answer ready for any question.

"More nightclubs, after-hour places, more money for the high end. More choice than the old days."

Patterson was in denial, thought Calvino. But who wasn't?

"The choice is much wider and deeper than new joints opening," said Calvino. "Commercial sex is online. You're running something like a bookstore, and readers want e-books, cheap instant experiences. Guys like Alan Osborne saw the hand-writing on the wall and sold out."

"What does Osborne know about social media?"

"Not much, but what he does know saved him," said Calvino. "He saw that big change coming and bailed."

"So where are they?"

McPhail wasn't talking about alien life forms.

"Online," said Calvino.

The owners and punters on Soi Cowboy had laughed at the news that Washington Square was to be bulldozed. They weren't laughing anymore. They blamed the coup and the curfew, and those hadn't helped anyone in their business, but they were just a distraction from a fundamental change in the nature of the game. They had once owned the night game, but that world had changed while they were waiting for the bar-fined girl to get out of the shower, towel off and return to the bar. The quick turnaround of girls had been the name of the profitable game. Now the girls were realizing that the bar wasn't their friend; it was a middleman that could be cut out. Online commercial sex teemed with angel investors. When the Soi Cowboy girls gossiped about their colleagues, their envy focused on the one who had punched her digital ticket to freedom and left behind dancing, boredom, cat fights with the other girls over a customer, *mamasans*, drunks and waiting for a bar fine. The change was all upside and just a Skype screen away.

"My girls can't figure out how to read a clock. Forget about a computer," said Patterson.

"It's the new generation that's making the move," said Calvino.

Fah's generation, he thought, Christina Tangier's inspired rebels.

"That's years away, Calvino."

"The future is already here, Patterson. Online you've got amateurs, semi-pros and professionals working out of their apartments. Mothers, aunties, grandmothers, students, office workers, civil servants—women in just about all lines of work have figured out that this money makes a good supplement. No need to ask you for a job."

"Vinny's right," said McPhail. "Going to the bars for women is like buying a copy of *Playboy* or *Penthouse*. When is the last time you bought a dirty magazine or a porno DVD?"

"Sex and politics have moved online. There's no going back."

Patterson yawned and sighed.

"You're saying I'm fucked?"

Calvino grinned.

"It looks like the old business model is busted. Think of the hot women. Where are they? I don't see them on Soi Cowboy. They aren't looking for jobs here or Patpong or

Nana. Not now. How long will the bars last, once their supply of women is cut off? Once they're online, you can't control them. That's what you and the coup makers have in common. People only submit when they have no choice."

"Gun to the head."

McPhail pressed two fingers to his own temple.

"This is why I support the coup," said Patterson. "We need to slow things down."

"Let's see if those brakes work," said Calvino.

No middleman ever thought his head was on the chopping block until the cold blade struck home.

Patterson rubbed his neck and moved his jaw. He didn't look well. Maybe he'd seen the ax for the first time. It wouldn't fall tonight or tomorrow night, but his fate was sealed.

TWENTY-NINE

"There is nothing as sad, nothing as unutterably sad, as an old man crying."—José Saramago, *The Cave*

IN LATE MAY, following the coup, Glover had voluntarily shut down his website. Farang_Lost_in_Thailand had become famous for featured letters from foreigners whose relationships with Thai bargirls had exploded like Chinese fireworks on New Year's Eve, or who had suffered a visa, financial or job loss. The list of problems was endless—police, immigration, cable connection, girlfriend, wife, job, money, children, friends or apartments. Mainly, though, the broken-hearted limped into the letter room, sharing stories of failure, despair and desperation. Glover posted their cries from the heart along with brief recommendations and advice. Some of the posters came back with updates, and these exchanges between the heartbroken and Glover were followed by hundreds of thousands of readers who emailed their comments from around the world. Glover created an interactive *Hunger Games* column for expat men, stragglers from the rebellion against a world of servitude.

Repeat letters came in from the yo-yo *farangs*, the men caught in the cycle of leaving and returning over and over again. Each change was different from the previous one. This time they'd adjust to reality. Only it rarely happened. Glover concluded that people were wired one way and that rewiring them was beyond the current knowledge of science.

After the coup Glover had received a call saying his website was drawing anti-coup letters and that violated martial law. The caller said he should think long and hard about continuing to run a forum for lawbreakers. The warning was Thai-style: not a warning per se. It was up to him. The junta wanted people to be happy, and Glover's crowd were spreading too many unhappiness stories. Did he understand? No more letters of hearts broken by lying, scheming, emotionally volatile girlfriends, hiding the existence of their boyfriends, husbands, addictions and the constant pump-handle action of relatives waiting for the cash flow. Letters from happy *farangs* were okay. Glover understood, only he rarely if ever received happy letters. It wasn't that kind of website. Glover pulled the digital plug and wrapped the message board with a black funeral wreath and a message—publishing under censorship suffers the same limitation as a blind eunuch reporting from an orgy.

Social media buzzed with rumors why he'd walked away from a row of slot machines that consistently produced a small weekly jackpot in advertising fees. But what good was the money if he was thrown in prison or booted out of the country? He tried to write some fake "happy" letters but ended up deleting each one. They didn't pass the projectile vomit test, and he knew that his readers didn't come to read testimonials from the so-called winners whose lives had been cleared of all obstacles. His readers demanded "agony" followed by mental collapse into a state of pure solipsism. With the coup, the agony business had been abolished, and solipsism nationalized.

"Here comes our man," said McPhail, spotting Glover strolling on the Soi, a string of bargirls tailing him like a superstar.

He shook hands with Calvino and McPhail.

"Sorry I'm late. Some men in green insisted on taking away my computer. If I objected, they said I could come along to keep my computer company. I declined."

"You had everything backed up?" asked Calvino.

"In the cloud," said Glover. "That means only people with top-secret clearance can read it."

Patterson blinked.

"It's a joke, Patterson. Surveillance, spying, NSA. Do any of those words ring a bell?"

"Right... What are you drinking?" asked Patterson, who had advertised on Glover's website.

Glover ordered a vodka soda and sat down with McPhail and Calvino.

"You brought it?" asked Calvino.

"You aren't big on foreplay, are you?" said Glover, pulling several A4 sheets out of his pocket and unfolding them on the counter. "Luckily for you, I printed these out before the army showed up and removed my hard drive."

Glover sipped his vodka soda as Calvino read through the emails.

It wasn't clear whether Howard and Davenport, the agents from the US embassy, had traced Ballard to Glover's website. They'd promised to leave no stone unturned in their quest to narrow down Ballard's death to one of two options—the murder would be unsolved, which would be a stain on their field operation capability, or they would catch or kill the killer, which would earn them a commendation, a promotion and a pay grade increase.

What was missing from their binary world of options was a third option—that Ballard hadn't been murdered, that he'd killed himself. Virginia Woolf might walk into a river with stones in her coat pockets, but Ballard, a seasoned field agent, even one who was fired, killing himself? That hadn't computed for Calvino until McPhail had run into Glover and asked him if he'd heard about the *farang* they'd pulled out of the river. And Glover had said, "Yeah, I saw something on ThaiVisa. I thought that guy was one of my readers. In the back of my mind, I remember some emails from him." "Can you check?" McPhail had asked.

It turned out that Ballard had been a regular contributor to Farang_Lost_in_Thailand using the handle ShipGuruAdrift. On the terrace of Mama, Don't Call, Calvino read through Ballard's emails. His last one had been written a couple of weeks before his death. He must have been using a proxy-serve in Cambodia at the time, thought Calvino. If Howard and Davenport had read through Ballard's emails to Glover, would they have showed up at Glover's office? Or could the intelligence people have dismissed ShipGuruAdrift as another piece of driftwood floating on an endless sea of mainly useless information?

Calvino reread one of Ballard's last emails several times. Each time the message was as unambiguous as balls on a dog.

"My ship deal collapsed."

That was the opening line. Ballard had lied about closing the ship deal with the Chinese billionaire.

Ballard's email continued: "I have no desire to stay in Phnom Penh. There's nothing to keep me. Returning soon to my girlfriend in Bangkok, and I'll have to tell her the bad news. The money is nearly gone. The deal didn't happen. I have to face that.

"I am sitting in my room reading *The Quiet American*, thinking I am too old to be Alden Pyle. Like him, I have a girlfriend who has her dreams. I'd be kidding myself to think she won't return to her old boyfriend, just like Phuong did after Pyle died. For Phuong it had been a tragedy. Pyle had been her ticket out of the war, a safe passage to America, the ship she'd board that would take her to another place. Can you call that love or calculated opportunity? Does it matter in the end? Does any of it matter when you've seen up close the greed, sorrow, pain and disappointment? What happens when everything you've believed to be true turns out to be a lie. All the talking points seem like bullshit. I have a theory that Alden Pyle felt the same thing. He committed what we'd call 'cop suicide,' and Fowler and the others never figured out that angle.

"If you've walked in Alden Pyle's shoes, you know how his mind worked, how he planned things in advance and how he knew what was waiting for him that night in Saigon. The world is happy to co-operate in your murder. It doesn't take much training to make the necessary arrangements. When you reach the end of the pier, you have a choice. Turn around and walk back, and join the parade of the lost, or go over the edge and end the search.

"Graham Greene got inside Pyle's head. He wandered among Pyle's thoughts, ideals and dreams. He saw how the gravity of life compressed these elements into the fundamental particle of sadness. Fowler accepted that condition. Pyle refused, until one day it hit him that Fowler was already dead to the world; his acceptance was his tombstone. Every Pyle needs a Fowler to hear his confession before he goes to the pier for the last time. Don't leave, don't leave is what Pyle had wanted to say to Phuong. It's what I want to say to Mai, my girlfriend, until I remember she, too, has her Fowler in a safe harbor. She'll be okay, filling his opium pipe and watching him stretch out on his bed, and it will be as if I never existed."

After he finished, Calvino folded the papers and put them in his pocket. When he looked up, he found McPhail, Glover and Patterson waiting for his verdict.

"Have you shown these emails to anyone else?" asked Calvino.

Glover shook his head.

"I have thousands of emails in the archives, though this guy stuck in my head. I thought at the time that he was thinking of killing himself. Over the last seven years, I'd guess that I've received about a dozen suicide notes emailed to my site. If my advertisers had found out, it's not something they would have appreciated. There was little that I or anyone else could do. If you run a website like mine, you're going to attract some unstable people. I'd like to think blowing off steam kept a fair number of them from killing themselves. Maybe I'm justifying myself for not talking about the suicide notes. In any event, you have these. I feel better someone else has them. Whether any of this helps, I don't know."

"It helps," said Calvino.

"Got to run," said Glover.

"Hey, buddy, good luck, and stay in touch," said McPhail.

They watched Glover walk into Soi Cowboy. The night swallowed him like an angry, raging river as he disappeared down the Soi 23 entrance.

"Thanks, McPhail," said Calvino.

McPhail touched the rim of his glass to Calvino's Jack Daniel's, which had gone watery with melted ice.

"What was in the letters?"

"A map of the long goodbye."

THIRTY

"When I look up, I see people cashing in. I don't see heaven or saints or angels. I see people cashing in on every decent impulse and every human tragedy."
—Joseph Heller, *Catch-22*

MUNNY HAD MEMORIZED two phone numbers. The first was Fah's, and the second belonged to Heng, a friend from his district who squatted in the southwest corner of the Aquarium's sixth floor. Fah's phone was dead and showed no sign of resurrection. As he listened to the recorded message, the female voice electronically modulated with dabs of honey and sugar on the vowels, telling him the phone wasn't switched on. That fact led him to one explanation. She and her phone were in different places. Once they were in the same place, he was sure Fah would phone him and tell him what to do.

He had promised to carry out the two assignments. He didn't read any newspapers or followed the news in any other way, and that meant Munny had no idea about the success of the first operation and how the authorities had thrown a lot of resources into finding the mastermind. All that Munny told himself was that he had one more job, and once it was done, he would be free to go home. In between, though, he needed a place to bunk for a couple of nights.

He phoned Heng at seven a.m. Munny had been wandering the streets near the Aquarium, trying to decide what to do. Heng was joyous to hear from him. He had been up since five, sitting in his corner, watching the sunrise. Heng had lost a leg to a landmine in Battambang. When the others in the Aquarium had left for the border, he had volunteered to stay behind, and no one had argued too much, knowing Heng's missing leg would slow down everyone. They remembered from the Khmer Rouge days that getting out fast meant staying alive. The slow ones, the cripples, the old, the infirm had been the first taken to the killing fields—there hadn't been just one; there were many—where they were slaughtered like livestock. Heng had smiled as his neighbors had left, telling them not to worry about him. He told them the Thais wouldn't shoot a one-legged man.

"You didn't make it home?" Heng asked.

"I had some business," said Munny.

"That means you're making some money."

"Not sure about that," said Munny. "My family's gone back."

"You got two legs, Munny. I thought you'd be running as fast as you could. It's dangerous for men like you. I'm a cripple. I got an excuse. Soldiers don't see a man with one leg as a man or anything other than a useless man."

"I am going back, as soon as I'm finished here. I need a place to stay until then. It's temporary."

Silence fell on the other end of the line as Heng was perplexed, wondering how someone like Munny hadn't returned to his village, and what kind of unfinished business would keep him in Bangkok when it didn't involve money. It was a mystery, like most things that had happened in Heng's life. He accepted it.

"The generator broke down again. I could hear them cursing from the eighth floor," said Heng.

"I'll have a look at it," said Munny.

"Can I tell them that, Munny? It will make their day."

"How many Eight-Niners are left?"

"Only two. Kiri and Nimol."

After Munny pocketed his cell phone, he couldn't help but worry about meeting Kiri and Nimol again. He had to decide whether going back was worth the risk. Kiri was barrel-chested, tall for a Khmer, with a muscular neck and shoulders that fit the profile of a man who liked to throw his weight around. And then there was Nimol, whose brain ran circles around the others in the gang. He was always plotting, planning, figuring out intentions and the best angle to exploit. He decided who deserved a beating and who needed a warning. Kiri was his enforcer. The Eight-Niners' little empire had greatly diminished over the last forty-eight hours. Munny wasn't surprised those two had stuck it out when the other members of their club had packed up and left. Kiri and Nimol didn't have anywhere to go; they had no family. The two of them had worked on construction sites, and Heng had explained that their troubles had got worse when they'd lost their jobs, followed by the disappearance of the other half-dozen members of their gang. Heng said they'd been living on a diet of fish and rice and had become even more mean-spirited and violent.

Munny, hands in his pockets, came to a bus stop and sat on a bench. He watched the traffic pass. Looking directly ahead, spotting one luxury car after another, he asked himself, "How much did that BMW cost?" A showroom of expensive cars sped by close enough for him to reach out and touch them. But of course, he knew the rules: look but do not touch; envy but don't covet. There was always the fear that such a god, talking into his phone behind tinted windows, could run a man like Munny down, and he'd dig into his pocket and pay what for him was small change to the victim's family. Munny sat back, waiting for the bus to the Aquarium, closing his eyes. In the darkness he saw his wife, his son and the Aquarium, with Heng sitting in his corner on the sixth floor, waiting for him.

Dread passed through his body like an electric current. He shivered as if a cold wind had caught him by surprise. He saw the bus coming that would take him to the Aquarium, and he got up, pulling a handful of change out of his pocket. As he climbed onto the bus, he squeezed into the crowded aisle, reaching for a strap from the ceiling. He could hardly breathe. He asked himself if he'd ever met anyone in his life who had made things easy for him? No name floated into his head. As the bus turned into the flow of traffic, Munny took his time thinking, telling himself he must have missed someone, starting back with his father and mother. The main lesson of his life so far had been a simple one—a man needed to surround himself with people who controlled their greed and violence. He looked around at the other people on the bus. He found dead, expressionless faces, lost in their cell phones. They were all searching for a connection to someone.

Munny talked aloud to himself, whispering as if he were talking to someone else: "Be careful. See what's happening around you. It's not on a screen. Life's an elbow about to break your ribs if you don't watch out. "

An old woman with heavy shopping bags stared at him as if he were crazy or dangerous or both. He'd been talking in Khmer. He smiled, but she turned away. Munny got off the bus at the next light and walked fifty meters down Sukhumvit Road.

He checked the time on his cell phone—it was almost nine-thirty a.m. when Munny turned into the sub-*soi* and saw a crowd of *farangs* lined up outside the Aquarium. He'd never seen such a large group of foreigners in the front entrance to the urban ruins. It spooked him, thinking something bad must have happened.

Munny moved closer, stopping a few meters from the Thai-Chinese owner and two of his employees. The *farangs* handed money to one of the employees. A young blonde woman with a tattoo of a Chinese dragon on her right arm, the tail winding down to her wrist, held out a one hundred baht note. One of the foreigners grabbed Munny's arm.

"Hey, buddy. There's a queue. Go to the back," said the man with a Lincolnshire accent.

"I live here," said Munny.

"Nice try, buddy. Go to the back of the queue."

Munny tried to catch the eye of the owner, but the old man with thinning hair and a turkey neck stared right through him as if he were a ghost. Munny went to the back of the line.

"What's going on?" Munny asked two strangers.

"There are thousands of tropical fish inside," said one of the teenaged girls. "It's amazing."

Her companion, a redhead, nodded.

"It's brilliant. They're in the basement of this derelict piece of shit. Can you believe it?"

Munny took a fresh look at the crowd. They'd come to look at the fish? By the time Munny reached the head of the queue, one of the employees recognized him.

"What are you doing here?"

He handed him a hundred baht.

"I've come to see the fish."

"That's another forty baht for the rice."

"I've already eaten," said Munny.

"It's for the fish, stupid water buffalo."

He held up a five baht bag of rice and thrust it into Munny's hands.

"Give me forty baht."

Munny handed him two rumpled twenty baht notes and entered through the front. Another employee in the newly formed enterprise led the tourists to the basement. From the look of the customers, they averaged around twenty-two years old. They were a group of backpackers who'd taken a bus from Khao San Road.

In twenty-four hours, the fish-in-the-basement story had taken off on the social media. The first photographs of huge, exotic tropical fish caught suspended midair as they jumped, breaking the surface of the brackish water, appeared on thousands of screens. Tourists dropped their bongs, plans and bottles and rushed to be among the first to locate and photograph the post-apocalyptic future. Selfies with exotic fish in the basement of an abandoned relic high-rise without walls—it was the must-have photo for the gap-year student of the day.

Munny shook his head as he walked up the stairs away from the basement. Halfway up the flight, a young backpacker in jeans and a faded "I Am Awesome" T-shirt blocked his path. Behind him was another backpacker with blue eyes and long, unwashed black hair tied into a ponytail.

"I know you," said the guy in the T-shirt.

Munny blinked, thinking that the man, who was a foot taller than him, had made a mistake.

"Munny, remember me? I can't believe you don't remember."

He sounded a little hurt by Munny's blank stare.

Munny had no recollection of the *farang* until he rolled up his right sleeve and displayed a tattoo—a map of Vietnam. The Mekong Delta started at his right elbow and Hanoi rested near his shoulder. For the words, written in Cambria font—the customer had insisted it had to be that font—Saigon, Hanoi and Da Lat, he'd used a special neon blue ink.

Munny's memory flooded back. It was the tattoo map guy from Melbourne. He had wanted a two-color tattoo. First blue, and a week after that healed up, he had come back for the red lines. The map with rivers and mountains as well as three cities had turned out well. The customer's uncle had been in the Vietnam War. After he finished the tattoo, the Melbourne guy had given Munny an extra two hundred baht tip. Backpackers rarely tipped. He'd even hugged Munny, saying, "My uncle will love this."

The Melbourne guy on the stairs grinned at him as if Munny were one of those MIAs who'd finally been found.

"Meet my friend, Roger. He wants a tat of England on his bum," he said, giggling. "Back home he plans to flash the Poms. I said you were the man. But where did you go? I went back to your place, and the owner said you'd left the country. Lying bastard."

Munny looked the friend over.

"How many colors?"

The friend hadn't given much thought to the colors. He palmed a joint, passing it back and forth with the Vietnam tattoo guy.

"Whatever," said Roger.

Munny noticed the nose ring that fit the ponytail image.

"More than one color—three thousand baht," said Munny.

Multiple colors were complicated. It couldn't be done in a single session. A separate session was needed for each color on a tattoo. First the black ink, after a week the red ink, and a week after that came the final color. Like a root canal, a multi-colored tattoo was built over time—one stage, one level intricately connected to the next. The friend looked like a single-color map customer, not a connoisseur of the art, a man who simply wanted a message on his body that made some personal statement burning through his head. Roger looked like a one-session customer on a mission.

The friend pulled a face like he'd taken a fist in the gut.

"Discount?"

The guidebooks advised a tourist to always bargain. Munny didn't see himself as a street vendor.

"Maps take time," said Munny. "Show me the map you want."

"The map of England," he said, giggling. "You know, that map."

He raised his hand and traced England with his finger in the air.

"Just like that."

Munny looked at the sky. He didn't see any map. His old customer intervened.

"Roger's stoned. Just give him the standard tat of England. Nothing fancy. Hey, Roger, don't fuck with him. He's the best. You want England on your ass, try and find someone else who'll do that for a hundred dollars."

In dollars it didn't seem so much.

"A hundred dollars? Shit, why didn't he say so? Okay, you got a deal."

There was a problem, Munny told them.

"I can't go back to my old shop. I had a fight with the owner. He owes me money."

"No worries, we go back to Khao San Road, and you can make a deal with another shop to use their stuff," said the Aussie with the Vietnam tattoo.

Not a bad idea, thought Munny, but it wasn't that simple. The shop would want a cut of the action: at least fifty percent, probably more. He had an idea of his own. He had a friend who worked out of a hole-in-the-wall tattoo storefront off Khao San Road. He'd let him use the inks and equipment for five hundred baht.

"Three thousand is for me," said Munny. "Five hundred for the shop. That covers the ink and needles."

He built some margin into the price.

"Man, there you go raising the price," said Roger.

"Up to you," said Munny.

After a few months in the business, he'd been able to tell when a customer had made the irrevocable decision. Deciding was the hard part. Once he'd decided, the chances were he didn't want to wait just in case he might start to have second thoughts.

"You cheap fuck," the Vietnam-tattooed *farang* from Melbourne said.

"How long will it take?" asked Roger.

Munny tilted his head, looking down at the fish.

"Three, four hours, maybe."

Looking at a customer, he could never figure what kind of tattoo they wanted. This guy didn't look like someone who'd drop his pants and flash a map on his ass. But Munny had lived long enough and tattooed enough people to know he could never judge what a man or woman wanted to display, or hide, and how much shock and awe they were willing to pay for.

"Four hours? Jesus, that's forever!"

"He could do just an outline of London," said Munny's old customer.

"That wouldn't mean shit," said Roger.

"Or how about the London underground map?"

Roger rolled his eyes.

"The point is to flash England."

"Got it."

They turned to Munny, who'd watched passively as the two *farangs* argued about the kind of tattoo that would cause the most outrage for a drunken Englishman in a Sydney pub and then over whether four hours was too long or not long enough.

"You've got a deal," Roger said, taking a long drag off the last tailing of the joint. "Three hours, okay?"

It would take as long as it would take. Why did foreigners want an exact time for something like finishing a tattoo? It wasn't a race. It was art, and art, like the fish in the basement, lived outside time, in a strange mental space that was hard to get to and hard to comprehend once you got that far. Roger leaned over the edge just as a large Banjar red Asian arowana broke the surface of the water.

"Hey, can you tattoo that fish on my chest? I want that fish on my flesh."

A young boy came up from behind Munny and tugged his hand.

"My father waits for you," he said.

Munny look down to find Heng's son looking up with large, brown searching eyes.

"Vichet, I thought you'd gone with your mother."

Vichet shook his head.

"Who would look after father?"

The boy was about the same age as his own son. The two had played together, and Sovann had helped Vichet with his homework. Complications of life kept adding up to large sums of misery, thought Munny, draping an arm around Vichet's shoulder.

"Hey, where are you going?" asked Roger.

"Got some business upstairs."

"We're going with you. No way we're going to lose you, man," said the Vietnam-tattooed *farang*.

They climbed the stairs to the sixth floor. Heng sat in the southwest corner, his crutches leaning against the wall, shirtless, sweating, holding a bottle of water. The boy ran to his father and toweled off his father's neck. Munny squatted down beside him.

"You don't look so good," he said to Heng.

"I want you to take my boy. I can't look after him."

Heng had made money begging on the streets, dragging his body along the pavement, one trouser leg empty, holding a cup. Foreigners dropped ten baht in the cup and hurried along. A final sideward glance was enough. Since the coup, though, it had become too dangerous to go out in the streets to beg, and he was nearly out of money for food.

"I was doing okay outside, but the owner didn't like me begging there," said Heng. "He called Kiri and Nimol to carry me upstairs."

From the look of him, they'd roughed him up a bit on the way up.

Once Munny had arrived with two foreigners, it didn't take long for word to spread, and Kiri and Nimol marched down the length of the sixth floor. The presence of the two large, young *farangs* standing on either side of Munny caused Nimol to reassess his approach.

"Munny, my younger brother, so good to see you."

Munny stared through him.

"Vichet's going with me," he said.

Nimol pursed his lips, looking at Kiri.

"Nothing's stopping you. But first, have a look at the generator. It's busted again."

"Got some business to do."

Munny saw from the way Kiri was clenching and unclenching his fists that he was waiting for the signal from Nimol to persuade Munny that the generator was a matter of great priority.

"People are living here? That's fucking insane," said Roger, looking around, holding his breath from the stench in the air. "Where do they shit?"

"You want us to look after Heng, you come on back after this business of yours is finished," said Nimol.

In Thailand most people experienced that feeling of the hair raised on the back of their neck as they saw how others were held hostage by circumstances—believing it could never happen to them, as they held their last patronage card to be played against such a misfortune. The Khmers had no such cards, and a hostage without a patron was a dead man walking. Vichet wanted to stay. His father fought back tears and told him that he had to go with Munny. They had no choice.

The second digital protest moment happened at Victory Monument. The local press only gave it a few lines. But on social media the coverage, with comments and photographs, circulated widely as it was shared and passed on. Five students, two housewives and a taxi driver had been arrested. They had been standing on the walkway with cell phones. Someone on the scene had captured Munny's image of four squatting peasants—he'd used his memory of Heng, Kiri and Nimol and himself for the models—who watched as two overbred toy dogs, one with a red ribbon, the other with a yellow one, each stained with blood, looking dazed from a street brawl. The commentators asked if the peasants had placed bets, wondered whether the dog owners also owned the peasants and speculated on what it was that one of the peasants was pointing at. Munny's art had started an endless conversation.

The image had been projected for a few minutes from the cell phones at Victory Monument and then vanished. An hour later it had reappeared for a performance at a dozen other venues scattered through the city, only to disappear again after a few minutes. Munny's art had the social media gurus scrambling to label and tag it—#HitNrun,

#BanskyBKK, #BKKWall, #NoCoup. The authorities found no solid evidence against the people whom they'd arrested. The image survived as a screen capture and had circulated on Twitter and Facebook. Munny's talent at last had been released into the world. Computer security personnel were ordered to deploy all necessary resources to track down and suppress the source of the art. A reward was offered for the first person to crack the code that led to the arrests of the persons responsible. In the bowels of the IT departments of a dozen agencies, a trace to the source code, only to find the GPS had been encrypted and all the back doors locked. It wasn't going to be easy to pinpoint Munny's location.

THIRTY-ONE

"We'd forgive most things if we knew the facts."
—Graham Greene, *The Heart of the Matter*

MCPHAIL, AFTER HALF a dozen attempts, had resigned himself to the fact that he might never find a replacement for the old Lonesome Hawk in Washington Square. He'd been in the middle of an afternoon massage, and it was just as the kneading by the twenty-three-year-old masseuse's thumbs slammed into a nerve in his left buttock that McPhail sat up with an epiphany and a throbbing woodie.

"Why didn't I think of that! It doesn't need to be a restaurant."

He arranged to meet Calvino the following day.

Calvino thought about McPhail's solution as he looked in at the former site of Washington Square. None of the buildings remained, most of the rubble had been carted off, and the ground had gone feral with tall trees, leafy bushes and wild grass. Nature had reclaimed the Square, turning it into a mini-jungle sheltering wild cats and dogs in the heart of the city. A hundred meters beyond, Calvino wandered down a narrow sub-*soi* that ran next to the Imperial Queen's Park Hotel. He glanced at the house numbers. McPhail's great hope was hidden down the sub-*soi*.

The sub-*soi*, no wider than a driveway, had been encroached until it became a narrow walkway between motorcycles parked against buildings. The access to Soi 22 Sukhumvit Road was a point in its favor. It was inside the old defunct Washington Square country. The old-timers would go to a new place in the same area. The Lonesome Hawk regulars were men who liked things they knew and hated anything new. The first indication that McPhail might have overlooked a detail materialized as Calvino passed a Muslim-Thai restaurant halfway inside the sub-*soi*. The Lonesome Hawk crowd had too many rednecks to pass a Muslim-Thai restaurant without pulling a face, spitting, waving a fist or cursing, wanting to punch a wall. Anything Muslim made them lose their appetite. Farther along, Calvino stopped in front of a shophouse and checked the number above a grand wooden door, the kind that might be seen in a brownstone in New York or a terraced house in Burlington Gardens, London. It matched the address McPhail had given him.

A small sign above the door read "Cinépolis." The second reason many of the old Lonesome Hawk regulars would shun the place was the foreign name over an imposing door that signaled a swank private members' club. Jerry, the Lonesome Hawk regular whom Calvino had recently seen on Soi Cowboy, would look at the sign in Arabic for Muslim food, a woman in the window wearing a hijab, and then a sign with the word "Cinépolis." The words "What the fuck?" would run through his mind. What's with the funny comma hovering like a drone over the E? His hip would ache and he'd turn around and limp home. But Calvino was prepared to keep an open mind as he stood tall in front of the three-story terraced house, ringing the brass bell. He waited a minute or so until someone inside peered at him through a peephole. A moment later the door opened a crack. He saw the face of a young Thai woman looking at him. She asked his name and business.

"Vincent Calvino. I'm meeting Ed McPhail."

"McPhail," she said.

She smiled as she opened the door.

"McPhail" is the password, Calvino thought. He'll be happy to know that.

As he stepped inside, he caught a whiff of leather and expensive single-malt whiskey.

"Khun Ed, he's upstairs," she said, closing the door behind him.

"Died and gone to heaven," said Calvino.

"It ain't heaven," said McPhail smiling down at him from the mezzanine level. "But Lek is definitely an angel. Aren't you, honey?"

Calvino walked through the ground floor, past framed pictures of actors, directors and a couple of movie posters. A highly polished writing desk stood at one spot, and old film cameras were scattered around as decoration. In the corner was a replica of Doctor Who's time-traveling police box, the door ajar as if the Doctor would soon appear from another time or dimension.

McPhail leaned over the railing at the edge of the second-floor mezzanine, watching as Calvino took a good look at the police box.

"I went inside. I tried to go back ten years to the Lonesome Hawk. But the damn thing isn't plugged in. Hey, Lek, honey, could you bring me another gin and tonic?"

Calvino looked up again at McPhail, who saluted him with an empty glass, and glanced at the waitress.

"You must be Lek."

"Yes, sir," she said.

"I'll have a Laphroaig," said Calvino. "Neat, no ice."

From the mezzanine McPhail belched out a loud croak.

"Lek, cancel my gin and tonic and bring me a double Laphroaig, no ice."

There was no sign of food. Single-malt was Scotland's way of rescuing a hungry man from his need to eat. Substituting liquor for lunch and dinner had been the diet that killed off over half of the old Washington Square crowd. As Calvino climbed the narrow spiral staircase to the mezzanine, he tried to remember if he'd ever heard anyone at the Lonesome Hawk order Laphroaig? He had no such memory.

"On the third floor they've set up a little cinema with nine cinema seats. I told 'em we'd stick to this floor," he said as Calvino emerged at the top of the stairs.

The open area looked like a Prince Street loft in Soho—polished wooden floor, a long gray sofa with white cushions at the end and a Persian carpet laid out in perfect alignment with the fake fireplace. McPhail sat on the sofa, his feet crossed on a long antique wooden box that functioned as a table, a pile of cinema magazines on one end. Above the fireplace was an LCD screen.

"In fifteen minutes *The Third Man* starts. It's a classic where nothing adds up—like the bar bill at Mama, Don't Call. Orson Welles plays Harry Lime and Joseph Cotten plays a pulp fiction writer named Holly Martins."

Calvino vaguely remembered the movie.

"Didn't Graham Greene write a book titled *The Third Man*?"

"He wrote the screenplay," said McPhail.

"*The Quiet American*, *The Third Man*... I guess he liked writing about secret agents. The Cold War."

McPhail looked impressed.

"He did. He novelized his screenplay of *The Third Man*. But he didn't write all of the lines in the movie. Orson Welles gave Harry Lime some of the best lines in the movie, like, 'You know what the fellow said—in Italy, for thirty years under the Borgias, they had warfare, terror, murder and bloodshed, but they produced Michelangelo, Leonardo da Vinci and the Renaissance. In Switzerland, they had brotherly love, they had five hundred years of democracy and peace—and what did that produce? The cuckoo clock.'"

The waitress brought a silver tray with two glasses and set it on the table.

"Honey, can you go out and buy me a pack of cigarettes?" said McPhail.

"Alden Pyle gets murdered in *The Quiet American*," said Calvino, "and Harry Lime fakes his murder in *The Third Man*. Greene believed there were two ways to go with an agent you want to get rid of. Kill him or have him create a situation that makes them think he's been killed."

Calvino's eyes closed, and in that moment of darkness he saw Ballard standing in front of the *Tabula Rogeriana, 1154* map, asking how much it would sell for. Would a man who is going to kill himself concern himself with the price? It occurred to Calvino for the first time that Ballard had left the copy of *The Quiet American* as a perfect piece of misdirection; it was the kind of thing that Harry Lime would have done. He lay back against the sofa.

"You okay, buddy?"

Calvino stayed silent, leaned forward and sipped on his whiskey.

"I don't think the old gang from the Lonesome Hawk will like this place."

He would try for his own misdirection.

"No more than they'd like the Happy Bar."

"Come on, they'd love the Happy Bar, only it's too far away. But I've got some good news, Vinny. The army released Noi from detention," said McPhail. "I talked to him. He said three soldiers, all of them officers, drove him back in a van to the Happy Bar and he bought them drinks."

"Did they give him the Borgia treatment with spiked drinks?"

"That didn't happen. One of officers became Noi's close friend and protector."

Calvino sipped the single-malt.

"Another Boston Red Sox fan?"

McPhail tipped his head and shook it.

"Not that I am aware of. Noi said they talked politics for about twenty minutes until he couldn't take it anymore, and then he emptied his soul about how the *katoeys* who worked for him had done him wrong. How he'd given them a job, lent them money that they never paid back, and when the money ran out, what did they do? They phoned the junta and said he was a troublemaker. They were told by whoever answered the hotline to rat out assholes who said bad things against the coup. They said that Noi was a Red activist. What other reason would he have for wearing a Red Sox baseball cap? That was a total lie. In fact, Noi told any of his customers who would listen that the coup was a homerun over the center-field fence, one that had cleared the bases.

Lucky for Noi, the main soldier in charge of interrogating him had a *katoey* in the family. His younger brother had saved up enough money dealing drugs to check into a hospital for the chop. The two of them spent hours talking about what it was like adjusting to a *katoey*'s way of thinking. The officer didn't want to let Noi go. Not because of his politics, but because here was a man who thought along the same lines as he did about the transgender mentality. After three days Noi convinced the officer to let him go so they could continue their discussion at the Happy Bar."

Calvino's mind was elsewhere, recalling what Ballard had said and what Pratt had said about Ballard being fished out of the river.

"Are you listening?" asked McPhail.

"Yeah, I was just thinking, did the army make Noi sign a release?"

McPhail nodded.

"He didn't give a shit about that. It was just a piece of paper to him. But when he returned to his perch at the Happy Bar, his heart nearly broke."

Calvino's mind was racing. Ballard had set up everything. Just as Osborne had said, he didn't work for anyone but himself.

"Vinny, I said it nearly broke Noi's heart."

"Another *katoey* story?"

McPhail shook his head and drank the Laphroaig like a man who needed an inch more of courage in the final stretch of a marathon.

"You remember that big fish in the tank at the Happy Bar? I went around to the bar. I saw the tank was empty. I asked Noi what happened to it, and guess what he said? That wasn't just any fish; it was a Banjar red Asian arowana. I'd never heard of that kind of fish. Noi said it was rare. When he returned to the bar, he found it floating belly up and smelly. No one had fed it. Mr. Banjar Red Asian Arowana died of starvation. That broke his heart. Noi loved that fish—though I'm not certain how you can love a fish, but Noi did."

McPhail headed down the stairs for another Laphroaig. When he came back, he sat on the sofa.

"You should write a book and put in the history of the Happy Bar, including Ballard and Noi, and of course I'll be the star. You know that? Write about the *katoeys* who double-crossed Noi, too. What else? Yeah, Patterson and Glover are a couple of characters you could only find in Bangkok. You could call it *Another Kind of Man* or *A Fish Named Banjar Red Asian Arowana.*"

The third glass of Laphroaig had made McPhail lyrical, and he began humming the theme song from *The Third Man*.

"You tell me to write a book. Yoshi thinks I should draw a map. Osborne says I should take up bullfighting. Ratana's on a fashion binge. And spooks at the US embassy are rifling through my medical files."

"No money in map-making, and picking a fight with a bull isn't gonna bring you happiness."

"That's not the point. Everyone has advice."

"What do they say?"

"Get out of Bangkok."

" 'Forget it, Jake. It's Chinatown,' " said McPhail in a half-assed Jack Nicholson impression.

"Movies end, but life goes on," said Calvino.

"What do you want to do?"

"Find some answers to a couple of questions. What was Ballard really doing in Bangkok, and why did a body they say was Ballard's end up in the river? When will the army release Osborne's girlfriend? Is there a replacement for the old Lonesome Hawk, or are we wasting our time? After I have the answers to those questions, I plan to retire."

"You tried that."

"I want to do nothing. No drama, no looking into cases where someone has gone missing, no hitting the street to locate people who have disappeared and don't want to be found."

"What's Ballard to you?"

"Just another mystery man that life steered over the dividing line to smash into me. People don't accidentally crash into your life. I want to know why it happened. I get this uneasy feeling that I've been set up, like being photographed nude with Alan Turing's teddy bear."

"You shouldn't drink in the afternoon, Calvino. You start speaking in tongues."

"I don't like it, McPhail, and neither would you. I waited for Ballard for forty minutes at the restaurant. I phoned his hotel. He'd booked into the Oriental."

"You need big bucks to stay at the Oriental."

McPhail hiccupped, reached for the fresh pack of cigarettes, shook one out and lit it.

"First time I laid eyes on him, something told me that he was loaded," said McPhail. "Someone killed him for money. Why look any further?"

"It wasn't his money they were after. When I phoned the hotel, I was told he wasn't answering his room phone. His cell phone was switched off, too. I thought, why does a man skip an appointment, one he's insisted on making? There's a reason. There's always a reason, whether the reason is any good is the question."

McPhail slowly exhaled a cloud of smoke.

"The army officer said something like that when he asked Noi to explain why he'd hung a picture of Che Guevara on the wall of the Happy Bar, because that photograph didn't make him happy. You know what Noi told him?"

Calvino had no idea.

"That he liked his style. Che Guevara's beard and hat appealed to him. It had nothing to do with politics. It was a fashion statement. That explained the *katoeys* working the bar, too. More fashion. Just like the phase Ratana's going through."

"What are you saying, McPhail?"

"You and the junta are on the same wavelength. You're suspicious of the wrong people. You can't distinguish a rebel from a fashion hound."

He burst out laughing.

"I'm joking, Vinny. You're tuned to a station broadcasting from Alpha Centauri, and the aliens are listening."

McPhail had turned cosmic after his third Laphroaig.

"What are they hearing, Ed?"

"A lot of chatter from a sad bunch of people who are deceived by appearances."

THIRTY-TWO

"We never get accustomed to being less important to other people than they are to us."—Graham Greene, *The Third Man*

CALVINO WALKED TOWARD Pratt's office, escorted by Lieutenant Pim, who smelled of rose water, and another officer with a steel jaw like a bank vault door.

"We have to stop meeting like this, Lieutenant Pim. People might begin to talk."

"You are the General's friend," she said. "If not, you wouldn't be in this place."

"We could always meet at my place or your place."

"Next life," she said.

"That's something to look forward to. Or Saturday night, if you're free."

"Let's stay with next life."

He nodded.

"I wanted you to come around to my condo and show you my map collection. But I guess it'll have to wait."

He walked into General Pratt's office, rehearsing in his head how to explain the feeling that he'd been set up to take the fall for Ballard's death. Not only had he not killed Ballard, but the possibility was growing that maybe Ballard wasn't dead. It was someone else that they'd dragged out of the river, and they wanted people to believe it was

Ballard. They needed someone to pin the murder on, so they opened a file and went through the motions of an investigation.

Ballard had left *The Quiet American* behind as a calculated act of misdirection, and Calvino had bought it. So had Pratt. The Americans had their reasons. Or was it that Ballard, like Harry Lime, guarded his secrets about a crooked sideline and that was a good enough reason to disappear? Which of the two Graham Greene storylines fit his case? Or was it an entirely new genre?

Calvino said, "Who identified Ballard's body?"

"The American embassy sent a doctor and a lab specialist."

"Your forensic department didn't perform the autopsy?"

"They assisted the Americans. The embassy had their reasons. They asked for this privilege, and frankly with things the way they are, a decision was made to cut them some slack in the official protocol."

"And the big bosses thought the Americans would reciprocate," said Calvino.

"Welcome to the world of cold-blooded politics, Vincent."

"Okay, I've got that much. But why would they fret so much over the apparent suicide of a citizen? Americans die here all the time. Does the embassy send a crack team of doctors to take over the autopsy for them? Exactly. Why did it happen this time? We're told he was murdered in Thailand, then the Thai police turn over the autopsy to the Americans, and then the embassy send two agents who look like black-belt waterboarding certified goons to my office asking questions about Ballard's murder."

"Like I said, these are extraordinary times. Irregular things happen. There's been a coup. An American official dies. It raises eyebrows. There's not always an answer, and that is the most difficult of all things to accept. Unless you're saying that you do know. Is that what you're saying, Vincent?"

"Ballard wasn't playing out the role of Alden Pyle, he was playing Harry Lime, and he had some powerful people in Washington helping him."

General Pratt sat back in his chair.

"I don't know these *farang*. Playing parts? Who are these two foreigners?"

"Pyle and Lime are characters from two Graham Greene novels."

He'd spent the previous evening rereading both books.

The only Englishman worth reading in General Pratt's opinion was William Shakespeare. He dismissed this Graham Greene as another diversion that foreigners used to escape reality.

"You've been under a lot of stress, Vincent. It wouldn't hurt if you made an appointment with Dr. Apinya."

"Should I make the appointment under the name of Thomas Fowler or Holly Martins?"

"Your literary references again? Since when have you taken up reading?"

"Pratt, listen to what I'm saying. Ballard may not be dead."

"Then who was pulled out of the river with his ID and fitting his description?"

"I have no idea. Or why Ballard would want to fake his death. I'd like to see a picture of the body fished out of the river."

Turning around to face his computer, Pratt searched through a folder, and a photograph appeared on the screen. A man with his face eaten away lay on a gurney, the nose, mouth, cheeks, eyes a twisted gnarl of shredded flesh.

"That stiff could be anyone. Any race, any age."

"Why would the Americans tell us it was Ballard if they weren't sure?" asked Pratt.

"Why did Ballard leave behind a copy of *The Quiet American* in my condo guestroom? Why did he insist on dinner near the pier not far from where his body was found? Something just like that happened to Fowler."

"Who's this Fowler you keep talking about?"

"You've memorized all of Shakespeare, and you don't know Graham Greene? Thomas Fowler's a journalist in *The Quiet American*. Pyle takes his girl away, but he gets killed. In *The Third Man* Holly Martins, a pulp fiction writer, finds out that Harry Lime has faked his death."

"And you think that Ballard is Harry Lime?"

"Pratt, it's a reference to a book. I'm not crazy. But something isn't right about Ballard's death. None of it adds up."

"You're making a convincing case for being crazy. Didn't Kukrit Pramoj play the prime minister in *The Quiet American*?"

"That was *The Ugly American*, the movie starring Marlon Brando," said Calvino.

"*Ugly American*, *Quiet American* and *Crazy American*—the titles all have 'American' in them, and the first word is a blur."

Lieutenant Pim slipped into the office, her perfectly pressed, tight-fitting uniform showing off her small waist and long legs. She carried two cups of coffee on a tray that she set on a table beside Calvino. He turned in his chair and winked at her. She pretended not to notice his attempt to flirt. All long hair and full lips, Lieutenant Pim had the look of a serial heartbreaker. As she left, Calvino pulled out the printouts from Glover's website and placed them on Pratt's desk.

"Secretly, Lieutenant Pim is in love with me," Calvino said, picking up one of the mugs and handing it to Pratt. "But she keeps it out of the reports she files about you, so it doesn't compromise her."

"She's too busy to file reports other than the ones I assign to her. Of course, she talks about you all the time," said Pratt, drinking from the mug.

Calvino gestured for Pratt to read the printouts. Pratt glanced at one page, turned to the next and the next, before sitting back and cupping the coffee mug in his hands.

"There's more. Ballard sent the emails to a expat website called Farang Lost in Thailand."

Calvino drank from his mug of coffee. Pratt watched him.

"These are from one of the two novels, right?"

"No, it's not from the novels. They didn't have email when Graham Greene wrote books. I'm serious, Pratt. Ballard sent these emails that go out of their way to provide cover for a man who wants others to believe that he's ready to kill himself. It's not from a novel. It happened. Here, in Bangkok."

He clenched his jaw, looked agitated and sat erect, his hands gripping the edge of General Pratt's desk. He noticed something was missing. The plaque he'd given General Pratt as an office-warming gift was nowhere to be seen. Calvino had had the plaque engraved with a couple of lines from Othello: "The robbed that smiles steals something from the thief; He robs himself that spends a bootless grief."

Pratt waited, thinking that Calvino wanted to say something.

"Are you okay, Vincent?"

"They've stolen the truth and replaced it with a lie."

"Who is they?" asked General Pratt.

"Howard and Davenport. Before they left my office, I smiled at them. You can steal a wallet, a passport, a car, but you can't steal the truth, or a man's dignity. That's the unique thing that makes him. No one can rob it from you. That's the true meaning of being free. A knowing smile robs the thief."

"About the plaque..."

"It doesn't matter, Pratt. What matters is what Shakespeare wrote. Someone can take everything from you, but if you smile at them, they've failed to rob you. You've won. They haven't broken you. Your spirit isn't violated. They can't steal it. It belongs to you, and the smile says that what has true value can't be taken."

Calvino paused, looked at Pratt and smiled.

"Like friendship, Pratt."

General Pratt wondered if he should call Dr. Apinya and asks her opinion about signs of erratic behavior by one of her former patients. He remembered how Calvino had gone to her office every week for sessions to work through the post-traumatic stress after his missing person case had gone so terribly wrong in Rangoon. She had reported to Pratt on his progress. They had both been worried about his state of mind. The two men had been in Rangoon together when the wings of death had fluttered, brushing against Calvino's cheek. As with the agents attached to the US Embassy, he'd cut Calvino a lot of slack. But there was only so much slack, and then the rope was no longer a rope.

Pratt studied the text on his screen and scrolled through more photographs of the autopsy. It was highly unusual that the Americans had asked so few questions after reviewing the autopsy report. They'd confirmed to the Thai police that the body matched the DNA samples they had from Ballard.

"The embassy says murder, you have evidence that suggests suicide, and at the same time you think the evidence is a plant and that Ballard's still alive."

"Yes, I believe the body belongs to a John Doe."

Pratt tapped his fingers on his desk. He opened the bottom drawer and pulled out the plaque and put it facing Calvino.

"One should never hide a smile," he said, "especially a teaching smile from Shakespeare."

Calvino rose from his seat.

"I've taken enough of your time."

"I thought you were coming to see me about Osborne's girlfriend," said Pratt.

Calvino tried to read the General's face, and Pratt took some pleasure in letting Calvino run through the scenarios.

"And?"

"She's been released. Osborne didn't tell you?"

"When?"

"This morning. None the worse for wear. She's learnt her lesson, from the report I saw."

"What lesson is that, Pratt?"

"We live in irregular times, and rocking the boat is a good way to drown."

"Maybe Ballard was a boat rocker."

From his condo perch Calvino watched the sunlight burst into supernova brilliance through the great pillars of gray clouds hanging like a Greek temple roof over Lake Ratchada. He thought about how things had been left with Pratt two days earlier. At the door Pratt had said he'd talked to the US embassy. Lieutenant Pim had stood with the door open, waiting for Calvino to pass through. Calvino gave Pratt a two-finger salute, "Thanks, General."

He thought about Howard and Davenport, their smugness, their certainty and their relentless interrogation, as if they'd made up their minds that he'd killed Ballard.

That morning a report in the *Bangkok Post* had quoted a US embassy source confirming that Ballard's death had been a suicide. Would the source have been Howard or Davenport, he wondered, or their boss? It didn't matter. No one from the embassy would be coming to his office to say they were sorry for the accusations and threats. No one who worked for the government ever apologized. Men like those were numb to feelings of guilt. Calvino thought of them adjusting their ties and moving on to the next case, where they would strong-arm the next person on a list that had been printed out and handed to them. If you were on the list, then they'd move on to you; if the boss took you off the list, that was the boss's business, and they'd cross your name off and go bother the next person. Only now nothing was ever crossed out as in the old days; the name, like a stain, remained forever in the system. Complaining wasn't an option. Complainers were put on another list. You lived with your suspect status, and you moved on, too.

That was the grand bargain with evil. No wrong ever got righted, any more than a hangman's rope was ever unknotted and used as a child's swing. The true identity of the person they pulled out of the river no longer mattered. Switching DNA was child's play. The deception meant nothing in itself. The news report went on to say that Ballard's relatives asked that his remains be cremated and his ashes spread in the sea. No one would come to Bangkok to mourn his passing, and Ballard had been close to no one there. He'd told Calvino that he'd stopped in Bangkok to do some business and to visit him. That lie was the most far-fetched creative act of all and made Calvino smile.

Ballard's heartbroken email to Glover, the collapse of his business deals and his humiliation as Christina Tangier's Number 22 all provided evidence to support a verdict of suicide. *The Quiet American* ending had to play out. Calvino had delivered the evidence that sealed the case for suicide. Could it be nothing but a great cover to put Ballard back into the field under another identity, one not notorious as the subject of an art photograph?

In the end, it didn't much matter whether it was a case of suicide, murder or disappearance. Ballard's fate had been shaped by forces larger than him. Alden Pyle must also have suspected that it wouldn't end well for him. He had a pipe dream of returning to the States with the beautiful Phuong, who'd ditched Fowler for a new life in America. Ballard, like Christina Tangier, had his own crazy dreams of pulling a fast one on oligarchs. It turned out she was much better at it than he was. That must have stung him.

"But the boat in Phuket might be a good way to escape, if it comes to that," Ballard had argued. He wasn't brokering the deal for the yacht. He was buying it for himself and using it to disappear off the radar.

If Ballard was alive, he was proving what every inner-city cop learned on the early morning shift, after the sound of gunfire and sirens wailing on the way to the scene. The dead guy's story can only be told by the living. That's the price of dying. You no longer get to tell people what happened. Your story is passed on like your car, furniture, fridge and second-hand wardrobe, told by others who will write their own script of what happened to suit their own needs. The story of Ballard's disappearance was left to the alphabet agencies' storytellers.

Calvino turned away from the sunset and raised a glass to salute the ancient map on the wall, remembering how Ballard had stood at the same spot, his back turned to him. He'd watched Ballard for a minute or longer before letting him know he'd come back into the room. He'd run the same footage through his mind so many times before that he could no longer be certain what part of his memory was the original and what part had entered through his imagination. What was left, once a man doubted what he'd seen in his own living room? An ever-changing residue of images, sounds, smells and emotions, a collage of conflicting details supporting different versions of the same story.

Ballard was Pyle, Ballard was Martins, Ballard was... He fled in a yacht, a private plane flew him out of the country, he was dead, he was alive... He still worked for the agencies, he'd cut all ties with them, he'd set up Christina Tangier, she'd set him up... Each theory was plausible, seemed probable, even, until he considered the other side and found it equally likely. A plausible story, he thought, reconciled the facts, assembled them into a convincing pattern, one that created reasonable doubt, the kind that allowed a shooter on trial for murder to walk out of a courtroom a free man. In Ballard's case, Calvino couldn't help but think the plausible story of suicide may have allowed one man to assume the identity of another.

Calvino was a part of all those stories. Each story was plausible, but only one of them was true. One notable question remained: who was taking the time and trouble to hide the truth?

THIRTY-THREE

"All through the night, men looked at the sky and were saddened by the stars."—Joseph Heller, *Catch-22*

OSBORNE WAITED BY the pool, reading. A servant escorted Calvino into the garden and swimming pool secluded within a three-meter-high stone wall. Black iron spikes, heavy with ivy like a green blanket, ran along the top—a nice touch, thought Calvino, though it fell a couple of meters short of a medieval castle courtyard. He found Osborne, wearing dark glasses, stretched out on a chaise longue with yellow cushions and aquatic green pillows, his head shaded by a green umbrella. A table had been set beside a kidney-shaped swimming pool.

Osborne wetted his finger before turning the page of *The Economist*. Calvino walked along the edge of the pool and stopped at the foot of the chaise longue.

"Why does *The Economist* pick on Thailand? Why aren't they writing about North Korea or Somalia? What do you want to drink, Calvino?" he asked, without looking up from his reading.

"White wine."

"Let's have some Champagne."

As Osborne leaned forward, his belly extended like a pinkish shelf. He wore a white cotton shirt, unbuttoned, and a pair of blue swimming trunks. He balanced his magazine on his bony knees.

"Why Champagne?"

"To celebrate Sky's freedom."

He got up from the chaise longue and took a seat at a glass and chrome table with three settings.

Calvino saw Fah at the far end of the pool, ankles hooked, feet touching the water, her face hidden under a large-brimmed bamboo hat with a blue band and a fresh white orchid. She lazily waved at Calvino like an exhausted film star at the end of a publicity campaign, pushing back her hat. He raised his hand to acknowledge her.

"Sit down, Calvino. Get out of the sun."

Calvino sat across from Osborne. That left one setting. Fah made no gesture of joining them.

"Isn't Fah drinking Champagne?" he asked.

"You must tell me how you managed to free her. Was it your friend Pratt?"

"Pratt, the flutter of an Amazon butterfly, my charm or random, blind luck. Take your pick," said Calvino.

"Have some mango."

In the center of the table was a large plate of mango, banana and watermelon slices. A big pitcher of orange juice sweated tiny rivulets like trails left by a drunken downhill skier. Tucked in an ice bucket, a bottle of Pol Roger Sir Winston Churchill 1990 tilted to the side. Three crystal glasses, juice glasses, silverware and cloth napkins had been carefully laid out in front of two empty chairs.

Osborne reached for the open bottle of Champagne. As he filled Calvino's glass, he glanced over his shoulder at Fah.

"Sky's pissed off about the world. Apparently she can't control it."

"She doesn't look unhappy."

From his seat at the table Calvino watched her kick the water, her painted toenails striking the surface. In her hands she held an iPad. He could see her working the screen.

"Every morning the army sends three or four soldiers to ask her questions. She signed a paper inviting them to come around. I said, 'Why did you sign it if you didn't want them to come?' She said, 'You can't negotiate when someone holds a gun on you.' Of course she's right, but that's life. There's always someone with a gun pointing at your head. Get used to it. Grow up. And the officer sits down and asks her the same questions every day: How are you doing? Where have you been? Who have you seen and talked to? Are you happy? How is your term paper coming along? Have you rewritten it yet? When can I read it? The kind of questions a father asks a slow-witted six-year-old.

"I give them wine and mango and that shuts them up. I tell her not to take them seriously. They're doing a job. You know what they want to hear. Lie to them. They don't expect the truth. If they thought you were truthful, they wouldn't bother coming around. So what does Sky do? She sulks. The soldiers seem genuinely concerned about her mental health. After the wine and mango, I pour each of them a large scotch and ask them about their mothers. The Thais love talking about their mothers. After an hour they're a little drunk. By the time they head back to whatever military camp they come from, I doubt they're in any condition to write a report."

Calvino watched Fah splashing the water as Osborne spoke. He saw now that she looked bored and angry. Kicking the water appeared to relieve some of her frustration. Osborne sipped the Champagne.

"How do you like it? You have drunk Champagne before?"

"Do I look like a Champagne virgin?"

"Nothing about you looks virginal, Calvino."

"What's with the 'Sir Winston Churchill' on the label?"

Osborne smiled, picking up the bottle and admiring the label before placing it back in the ice bucket.

"Sir Winston loved Pol Roger. If it hadn't been for that Champagne, we might have lost the war against the Huns. The Germans would still be sending around soldiers every morning to ask us questions, not unlike Sky's interrogators, but for Sir Winston and Pol Roger. He fell for Odette Pol-Roger at a British embassy party in 1944. She thought him special, too. He drained five hundred cases of Pol Roger in between his eighty-first and ninety-first birthdays. My goal is to beat Sir Winston's record."

"I thought you were dying."

Osborne's orange hair caught a ray of sun. The effect of the light fell short of a halo and was actually more like the backlight illuminating a suspect in a police lineup.

"We're all dying, Calvino, some of us faster than others, that's all. But being a bit slow in the dying racket is nothing to gloat over."

"You said there was something you wanted to tell me."

"There is. You Americans are always in such a hurry. Relax, enjoy the Champagne," said Osborne, holding the wine up and finding a ray of sun to strike the glass. "Such purity is marvelous to behold. And yes, there is something. I wanted to say goodbye."

Fah toweled her ankles as she sat down in the chair across from Calvino.

"Are you talking about me?"

"My dear, we talk of nothing else," said Osborne.

"Where are you going?" asked Calvino, as Fah poured orange juice into her glass.

"Madagascar."

Osborne had organized a little farewell party to celebrate their planned trip to Madagascar. Calvino was the only guest. Osborne said they had decided to get out of Thailand for a few months. He figured the daily visits from the army were themselves the real message, not just a medium for questions. The questions were an excuse. What they really wanted was for Fah to leave the country. Only then would the visits end. That suited Osborne, who longed to re-enter Madagascar's pre-Internet world. To him the island off the coast of Africa was like a fly trapped in a fifty-million-year-old piece of amber.

Osborne looked over the top of his eyeglasses as Fah ate an apple, her eyes focused on the screen of her iPad. The fruit crunched in her teeth.

"Look at her," said Osborne. "She's not even said hello."

Fah looked up, crinkled her nose.

"Hi, Khun Vincent."

"That's all?"

She shrugged and took another bite out of the apple before losing herself again in Twitter.

"Even when she eats, she's on the Internet. She doesn't know what the world was like before it. People have forgotten the joy of simply eating an apple. The taste, the color, the texture of the apple meet you, and you pay attention when you eat it. Now people who eat apples can Google for information about apple planting, annual production in western Canada, GDP tables comparing apple crops in growing countries, the market price for apple futures, but they're missing the experience of eating an apple. They know everything ever said or written about an apple but nothing about the experience of enjoying one."

Fah's face lit up. She let out a squeal of joy and raised her hand in a three-finger salute.

"Christina Tangier is about the coolest artist who ever lived," she said, not looking up from her screen.

"She's added speech to the conversation. Thank you, darling," said Osborne.

Calvino sensed something more was going on than idle talk.

"What's up with Christina Tangier?" he asked.

Fah glanced up and turned her iPad around. A teddy bear filled the screen.

"It's a teddy bear," said Osborne in a derisive tone.

"The same teddy bear she used in the famous photos?" asked Calvino.

"She's uploaded a new podcast. She reveals the mystery of the teddy bear. It was the Turing teddy bear. She'd been hired as an art intern at Bletchley Park to create the museum's Turing room. A private donor who admired Turing got her the job and gave her the idea—why not switch the Turing teddy bear with a lookalike? Who would be able to tell the difference? That's what she did. Christina used Alan Turing's teddy bear in all of the Elite John photos."

"Why would someone go to such trouble? asked Osborne.

"It's an enigma," said Calvino.

Osborne shot him an amused glance.

"Calvino, in all the years I've known you, that is the wittiest thing you've ever said. Shakespeare and monkeys typing come to mind. Still, you must come to visit us in Madagascar."

"Christina's clever. She makes a brilliant revenge," said Fah. "She does it with art. Christina knew exactly what she was doing. I love her! Wait, Christina says she gives the teddy back to the museum."

"She's feeling remorse?"

"Do you know how many people have seen this YouTube video? Over a million in forty-eight hours."

"We'll invite her to Madagascar, darling," said Osborne. "She can make videos about lemurs."

"As if she would ever go there."

"Be positive. You will love Madagascar," said Osborne. "I am in favor of this coup. It shows the powerful people aren't giving in. Fah and her generation are patiently waiting for us to die off, but we aren't giving in."

He smiled that cunning, knowing smile.

"Our child will be born in Madagascar. I've always wanted an African baby. One who grows up in the bush, searching the trees for lemurs rather than sitting in a room searching the Internet for porno and war games."

Fah reached over and grabbed Calvino's phone from the table.

"Do you mind if I use this?" she asked. "They took mine away."

"Who are you calling, darling?" asked Osborne.

"Munny. He's a friend," she said.

"He's the Khao San Road tattoo guy who also made your street art," said Calvino.

"Lucian Freud was once a tattoo artist. So what?" she countered.

"I told you she was clever," said Osborne.

"How do you know about Munny?" Fah asked Calvino.

"Never underestimate a man with a typewriter. That's the first rule."

"What's the second rule?"

"Secrecy is no longer an option."

"You think the army knows?"

"The third rule is the army is the last to know."

Calvino looked at the angle of her arm and hand. Grabbing a cell phone from a pregnant woman was never a good option. Instead he put his hand in front of the phone.

"Before you make that call, tell your husband about Munny."

"Munny helped us with the graphic art. I'm worried about him. I want to tell him he can go back home. It's over. Finished."

Calvino slowly withdrew his hand.

"Were you having an affair with him?" asked Osborne.

She laughed.

"With Munny? Are you crazy?"

"But you said it was over. Finished."

"Our protest project is shut down. I'm leaving the country. Oak is going to Cambodia. Palm is in Japan. Oak wants to meet him." She glanced at Calvino, who'd been following the conversation, and he nodded that he understood what she wanted.

"That leaves her to rewrite their university paper," said Osborne. "They fled the country to avoid homework."

"Well, can I phone him?"

Fah's request seemed, on the surface, reasonable enough. Osborne and Calvino nodded their approval to make the call. Osborne couldn't follow the phone conversation with Munny that ensued as Fah spoke Thai. Osborne tugged on Calvino's wrist and asked him to translate.

"Munny's got a problem. He needs money to get himself, a one-legged man and the man's kid to Cambodia. Fah told him that she'll have me deliver twenty thousand baht to him."

"You're not," said Osborne to Fah the moment she handed the phone back to Calvino.

"Not what?"

"Giving him twenty thousand baht. And you said that you didn't have sex with him. Why else would you give him a small fortune from my money?"

"It's my money."

Calvino cleared his throat.

"Just stop."

They both fell silent. Osborne poured more Champagne. Fah returned to her iPad screen to open Facebook. Tiny dog breeds, bowls of soup, tropical beaches, Jimmy Carter and Woody Guthrie scrolled past. Calvino started to get up from the table, dropping his crumpled napkin on the plate.

"I've got to go. Have a good trip to Madagascar."

"Sit down, Calvino. You'll miss the smoked salmon. And we won't have another chance to talk. You mentioned something you wanted to ask me about Ballard. Don't go rushing off just because Sky is acting out one of her little public fits of rebellion. She's young. The young define themselves through open revolt. Isn't that right, darling?"

"I'm the one who wanted you to come today," Fah said, looking up from chair. "Isn't that right, darling?"

"You were a large influence," said Osborne.

"That's his way of saying yes," said Fah. "I will give you the money. Phone him, please. If you don't want to go to him, he'll come to you."

Calvino's phone signaled that he'd received a text message. He picked up the phone and read: "Munny here. Meet me at building here. 9 p.m.?" Calvino clicked onto the link for the building location. It was in the triple-digit *soi* numbers on Sukhumvit Road. Calvino put down the phone. He looked worried as he glanced over at Fah.

"This is how drug deals are done," said Calvino. "Are you sure this is something I should know about?"

Fah turned to Osborne.

"I swear, Munny is the real thing. Without him we would have failed. He didn't let us down. He could have run, but he stayed. We all owe him. Think how it turned out—we were his audience. Aren't you the one who always said loyalty is the most important of all virtues?"

Osborne squirmed in his chair. He grabbed the Champagne bottle and refilled his glass.

"Haven't you already paid this Munny?"

"Can you ever repay loyalty?" she asked.

Calvino had loaded her iPhone with up-to-date tracking and surveillance apps. He'd known everything about her and her friends, from her playlist on iTunes to the names in her Line directory. He had read through her SMS texts and reviewed the graphic art snapshots taken inside the clandestine meeting space above the barbershop. He had records of her location at the times of each email or phone call. There had been no need to follow her. The iPhone apps had done the legwork, and everything that he'd collected in this mass of data suggested she was telling the truth. She owed Munny. And Oak and Palm. All three of them were in his debt.

"She's right, Osborne."

Calvino's reaction brought him a peck on the cheek from Fah.

"Thank you, Khun Vincent."

Osborne sighed and shook his head.

"Okay, gang up on an old man. What can I do? Let's give him the fucking money," said Osborne, peeling twenty thousand-baht notes off a thick wedge of bills. "Now leave us to talk," he said to his wife.

Fah pushed back her chair, adjusted her hat and with her iPad in hand walked back to the main house, her high heels clicking on the tiles like the click-clack of a typewriter.

"You didn't come here to say goodbye, Calvino. You came because you wanted to ask me about Ballard."

Calvino liked Osborne's brutal honesty.

"I had US embassy staff coming around asking me questions about him."

"I thought he killed himself. That's what the papers say."

"I have some doubt that he's dead."

"They have a body, Calvino. Someone died."

"Maybe someone other than Ballard."

Osborne studied the man across the table.

"I never thought of you as one of those conspiracy nutcases."

"Fah talked about loyalty. Does that extend to your relationship with Ballard?"

Osborne smiled and sipped his Champagne, making the sort of face Winston Churchill might have made on hearing that Hitler had killed himself in the Berlin bunker.

"Ballard was a slippery one. I presume the authorities are doing their job."

"Today's *Bangkok Post* says the autopsy report shows it was a suicide. Rocks in his pockets," said Calvino.

"That's how Virginia Woolf killed herself."

"I didn't figure Ballard for the literary type," said Calvino. "I think I misjudged him."

Osborne sipped more Champagne and smacked his lips.

"Ballard had more of a pulp fiction kind of mind," said Osborne. "Keeping it inside the mind is enough for most men; they see no point in writing anything down. Your life is the ink that writes the story. However Ballard died, why do you care? Were you close to him?"

Calvino swallowed a mouthful of Champagne, imagining Churchill running World War II knocking back glass after glass.

"At first I thought his old outfit wanted to pin a murder on me," Calvino said, smacking his lips. "Then I realized I had no idea what outfit, new or old, Ballard worked for. DEA? DARPA? NSA? CIA? I wonder if Ballard himself could keep straight who had jurisdiction over what he was doing. "

"And?"

"Maybe he pulled a Snowden?" asked Calvino.

"He mentioned a Snowden in a novel called *Catch-22*."

"This is a different Snowden," said Calvino.

Calvino scratched the stubble on his chin. There was something going on inside Ballard's life and head, and they could spin speculations all day long, but the fact remained that they were only guessing.

"Someone inside the chain of alphabet soup might have changed their mind," said Calvino. "Or they used me as cover to show they'd investigated the death. It doesn't matter what their intention was. A verdict of suicide clears me. What I've been thinking is maybe the body they pulled out of the river wasn't Ballard's. His death was faked. And it wasn't some agency that did it. It was Ballard."

"Why would he do that?"

"Like you said, he only works for himself. You spent a few days drinking with him in Madagascar. He must've opened up after a few drinks, said something he should have kept to himself but needed to get off his chest to someone."

"Hold on. You said he wasn't literary. That's not entirely true. He talked about *Catch-22*. I don't read American writers, but I believe it was made into a movie once. He was very American. He needed a Bible."

"I know the book," said Calvino.

"I thought you might. Ballard loved to talk about a character named Orr. It's very American to use a fictional character as a role model as real-life Americans are such a bore. Really a quite dismal lot."

Orr managed to get shot down during each flight, and that gave him practice in sea landings with all members of the crew surviving. Orr was a pilot and had planned a cover story as an escape from the insanity of war. Had Orr's scheme been drawn from Harry Lime's sleight of hand, to create the illusion of his own death?

"You never asked Ballard why he saw Orr as a role model?"

"Don't be ridiculous, Calvino. We were both drunk. Asking a serious question when you're drunk is like reciting lines from Monty Python's *Life of Brian* when you're fucking. It's terribly distracting to your mission."

"What was your mission?"

"Oblivion," he said as if that were his idea of the golden ticket.

The unfinished business from Rob's death in Rangoon a couple of years earlier had accelerated Osborne's desire for oblivion. His quest for reproduction was the other side of the unfair coin he used to wager bets with himself.

THIRTY-FOUR

"But it's just because the chances are all against you, just because there is so little hope, that life is sweet over here."—Henry Miller, *Tropic of Cancer*

THERE WAS A reason that the self-proclaimed "World's Most Famous Big Burger" van was parked on the site of the demolished Washington Square.

McPhail's big idea had come to him in the middle of a heavy drinking session, when he'd gone outside to have a smoke. A large black van was parked in front of a mom and pop shop across the street, with the driver's side door open. He watched as the driver bought fruit from an old lady who weighed the goods on an old-fashioned balance scale, adding and taking away weights like an opium dealer. She then bagged the fruit and passed it to the driver. McPhail ran across the road, dodging motorcycles, taxis and cars, waving his arms and shouting for the van driver to wait.

The driver's nickname was Gop—Frog, in English. Gop chewed on a piece of pineapple as he explained to McPhail that he couldn't just open his van and make him a hamburger parked where he was, in front of the greengrocer's. The cops would be on him in five minutes, hauling his ass to some military camp to cook for the troops until either democracy was restored or non-vegetarians launched a counter-coup. Gop said he had a family to feed, and getting locked up wasn't the way to feed them. McPhail explained that ordering a burger there and then wasn't exactly what he had in mind. He wanted to organize a party. He'd invite friends. He'd show the world that he, Ed McPhail, hadn't given up and had found a way to bring back the magic of the Square, if only for one lunch. He guaranteed that Gop would sell a mountain of burgers. Would Gop help him make this miracle happen?

The next day, around eleven-thirty a.m., Gop's mobile burger café, with the name Road Kill and a menu painted on both side panels, pulled into the old Soi 22, Sukhumvit Road entrance. The driver, a slim Thai in his mid-twenties, dressed in cut-off jeans and a polo shirt, sat behind the wheel. The Road Kill food van slipped into the Square like a hearse into a cemetery, moving slowly under McPhail's guidance into a small green, flat zone in the overgrown parkland of what had once been Washington Square. McPhail did his best to mimic an airport ground crew worker guiding a 747 to dock with the jetway as the accordion neck slithered out for a coupling. McPhail walked backward until the van had stopped behind a pile of rubble—broken tiles, bricks, window frames—his hands raised, palms out.

The driver scratched his head as he switched off the engine and climbed out. He'd never seen anything like the beginnings of a jungle in the middle of Bangkok, only a hundred meters from Soi 22. Two men and a boy hopped out of the back of the van as the driver climbed down from the cabin.

"Gop, you can put the tables over here," said McPhail, pointing to small patch of the old road that circled the square. Gop and his crew worked to set up five tables with three folding chairs tucked into each one. The late morning sun bore down, and by the time they'd finished, the workers dripped with sweat.

Glover was the first to show up and survey the setting. Gop opened the serving window, and the smell of cooking burgers drifted across the space between the van and the tables. Glover, hands on his hips, stood near the van, reading the menu. He ordered a Monster Hawaiian Burger with double fries. Gop nodded with a smile. He was in business. Glover, a camera slung around his neck, sat down at McPhail's table, where a bucket of ice, two glasses and a bottle of Jack Daniel's sat waiting.

"I thought of death when I first saw the van," said Glover.

McPhail poured Glover a drink.

"I don't see the connection. Drink this."

Glover gulped from his glass, rattling the ice against the side.

"One of my readers wrote a long letter about Chinese death vans. The authorities have equipped vans that look just like this one. They use them as mobile execution chambers."

"Get out of here!" said McPhail.

"I checked it out. It's true. They look like regular police vans on the outside, but inside is a different story. They've been outfitted with a mini-operating room. Video cameras roll as the poor sedated sod they've got strapped to a gurney meets up with a couple of doctors. Those are the last faces he sees. They inject him with a dose of sodium thiopental to knock him out, next comes a jab with pancuronium bromide, which cuts out his breathing, and to finish him off, the needle finds a vein to dump a large dose of potassium chloride. That stops the heart.

"Vans filled with death-inducing chemicals. Three shots of the right mix and ten minutes later you're stone dead. The Chinese papers report that Mr. Wong was vanized last night after consuming his last meal of a bowl of red rice."

"Or they could force feed him a couple of Gop's burgers," said McPhail.

After Glover had run the Chinese death van letter on his website, rumors had circulated that the Thai army had asked for a friendship price from the Chinese for a hundred of the vans. Glover had soon deleted all anti-military comments. There was no percentage in pissing off the very people who might or might not have placed an order for a fleet of death vans. Why take a chance? Why get yourself on the beta group list for a test run? As Glover waited for his burger, it made him think about how a man could go for years and never think much about the diverse functionality of vans but then one day realize that vans had expanded into all kinds of new niches: food trucks, execution chambers, massage parlors, campers, bookstores, clothing shops, beauty clinics—an infinite list of possibilities.

Glover snapped a picture of McPhail drinking. He had many such photographs. They lived in a time when life (and death) moved around on wheels, and few ever stopped to ask some basic questions. Glover was snapping more pictures of Road Kill when their orders arrived.

"You might want to hold off on eating your Monster Hawaiian Burger until they invent a way to grow new hearts," said McPhail.

"If I clutch my chest, you'll help me out?"

"Kiss of life? Fat chance."

"Don't be hostile."

McPhail lifted the top half of the bun off his burger.

"Pass the mustard."

"Where's Calvino?"

McPhail watched as the first of the old Washington Square regulars drifted in and sat at the tables.

"I invited him, but he went to see Osborne."

"The bar mogul," said Glover. "Is he still alive?"

"Ex-bar mogul. He's alive."

"There are miracles."

"By the way, there's no such word as 'vanized,' " said McPhail. "That's a fact. Vandalized, yes. Vanized, no."

"There should be," said Glover. "After my column it will go viral."

"Some years ago you invented 'herpesized.' How did that go, Glover?"

After a few bites from his meal, Glover got up from the table with his camera ready.

"Got to get back to work."

Three or four of the old-timers drifted into the grounds of Washington Square, their sagging jaws dropping as they looked around at the jungle that had reclaimed the area. Taffy's, Moonshine, the Happy Bar were nothing more than weed patches and old piss marks on the concrete slabs. The massage parlor where their tired old bones had gone for loosening up was now a tangle thick with the kinds of tropical trees that grow like weeds. The Bourbon Street restaurant and bar had left no trace amid the undergrowth. In the far distance a thick canopy marked where the Lonesome Hawk had once stood. Like carrier pigeons after a nuclear blast, the old regulars were returning to circle a roost that no longer existed.

McPhail strolled over and shook hands.

"No rules against smoking in this restaurant."

He held up his cigarette and laughed.

"You've got to go to the window and order your food."

"What? No waitress?" asked Jack, whose freshly pressed safari suit had large sweat marks under the arms.

"Where's the music?" asked Arnie, hair growing out of his nose and ears as fast as the jungle around him. "And where's Calvino? You said he was coming."

McPhail didn't want to tell them that Calvino was sitting around Osborne's pool drinking Champagne, and that he was missing what might be the last reunion of the old hands from Washington Square. It wasn't turning out to be the happy gathering he'd hoped for. The old-timers moaned, complained, demanded and cursed—and then he remembered that they'd carried on the same way with Old George at the Lonesome Hawk. It was just the way they were.

"You know in China they use these vans to execute prisoners?"

That calmed them down.

"What are you saying, McPhail?"

"Count your blessings. This one is bringing the best burgers in Bangkok, and all you have to do is get off your sorry asses and walk over to the hatch and tell Gop how you want them cooked. If this was China, you'd be in the back getting injections in those sorry asses to put you out of your misery."

Jack began a roll call of the old regulars who'd died, as Arnie strolled with McPhail over to the van and began reading the menu painted on the side. McPhail turned and walked back to his table to find Glover lost somewhere in cyberspace, trailing after someone on his cell phone screen.

"Let me tell you about my brother Chuck," said McPhail.

"What about him?" asked Glover.

It was a big mistake to give McPhail an open-ended invitation to talk about his brother.

"You got time?"

Whenever a *farang* said that, Glover had to resist the impulse to run.

"Sure," said Glover.

He liked McPhail.

"My brother lives in California. He's retired from a desk job at the state pension fund. He worked there for thirty-three years, so he had everything he ever wanted—house, car, wife and a couple of kids he put through college. He's sixty-six years old now and still married to the same wife. He has two grandkids. A couple of years ago, when I was back in California, we took a long walk by the sea. He was looking back in time and trying to make sense of his life. He went through all his successes and said they didn't add up to much. It hit him.

"He stopped walking, looked out to sea, tears in his eyes. He'd had one of those moments. He realized there was so much in life but it was too late for him. He told me that everyone in the family thought I was crazy. Going off to Asia, taking nothing but a small backpack, traveling to strange places, getting lost in raging rivers, blue-ridged mountains and tropical jungles, and settling in the most exotic and indecipherable, crazy, unmanageably noir cities in the world.

"He'd been fighting something, he told me. Something he couldn't quite acknowledge for a long time. You know what that was?"

Glover shook his head, biting into his Monster Hawaiian Burger with grease, mustard and ketchup oozing through his fingers like the special effects in a contagion movie.

"What'd he say?"

"Chuck wished he could wave a magic wand and trade his life for mine."

"He said that? He'd like to be eating out of a food truck called Road Kill in the middle of a reforested demolition site?"

McPhail drank his Jack Daniel's and said, "Maybe not every detail."

"Life's in the details, but that's where we also find the devil. Remember?"

"Let me finish," said McPhail. "Man, I'm opening up my heart here, and you want to talk about the devil."

"Sorry, what else did your brother say?"

"That he'd have given anything to have had my life. He'd never lived any life other than his own, and it had been on a narrow-gauge track that only went a few miles in either direction. He wished he'd built tracks to the outer world and taken them.

"After that walk on the beach, we didn't talk about it again. He left the conversation as something he'd said when he'd been drinking and feeling the blues. I could tell he was glad I didn't bring it up again. For the rest of the visit I never asked him about his life. I understood. I floated into their world as a mystery, and floated back out with them no more the wiser. But that's not the end of it."

McPhail watched Jack carry a plate with a Montana Mountain Man's Burger and onion rings back to the table. Arnie had already ordered his burger, and Jerry, leaning on a cane, still hadn't made up his mind.

"You've done good, Ed," said Glover. "Look at them. They're having the time of their lives."

"It's all in the attitude," said McPhail. "A year ago my brother began posting on Facebook stories about winning cups and medals in the sixty-five to seventy age group for marathons. He put up dozens of photographs of himself at the starting line or the finishing line, accepting a medal and smiling like he'd eaten the whole cookie jar. In the senior iron-man marathon, he's ranked third overall in the whole country. It's long-distance running, ten kilometers on a bike, ten kilometers swimming, then another five kilometers to the finish line."

"How old is he?"

"Sixty-seven in a few months," said McPhail. "He's found a new self. I was happy for him because the old self that he lost on retirement had nearly killed him. Now he's back, as a track and field champion. It's enough for him. That'll take him to the end. I don't think he wants to change places with me now. Of course, he never gets laid. He runs instead."

"Did you tell him that?"

"What do you think? You can't tell anyone in the States there's a sex life after forty, but you gotta get off your ass and go to those other places. They'd lynch you. You're going back there soon. You'll find out. Hopefully you'll be lucky like Chuck and find something that makes you feel like you're alive, a reason to get out of bed in the morning."

"I've got no choice, Ed. I've been threatened. I could be arrested."

McPhail's second Johnny Cash Burger came with a large dill pickle and hammer-sized French fries. He dipped one of the fries into a bowl of ketchup and took a bite. He chewed and sighed.

"Great fries. I have to tell a friend who runs the Happy Bar to add French fries to the menu. I told you about Noi?"

"Only that he was arrested."

"Calvino and me watched as soldiers dragged him off to a camp for some attitude adjustment. He'd had a pack of *katoeys* working for him, and they'd turned on him. One of the officers who interrogated him had a younger brother who'd had the chop. The officer had some personal issues about dealing with his *katoey* brother. The officer and Noi talked for hours, trying to figure out what made a man decide he wanted to be a woman. There were no more questions about Noi's politics, whether he supported the Junta, whether he was against the coup.

"After they took Noi back to the Happy Bar, the officer's *katoey* brother—or his new sister, or whatever she or he is—rounded up her *katoey* friends and pitched in to help Noi reopen the bar. When the old gang of *katoeys* found out from the bamboo telegraph that Noi had totally replaced them and reopened, they were truly pissed off and returned like a bad case of diarrhea, spitting, shouting, clawing and screaming. Silly bitches, they never bothered to ask who these new *katoeys* were connected to. Talk about a career-crashing mistake. The *katoey* with the army captain brother phones him, and a black, unmarked van with a half-dozen combat-ready soldiers pulls up. The old gang cheers, thinking history is about to repeat itself and Noi is going back for more adjustments to his mindset. Instead the soldiers handcuff and march the old gang into the back of the van and haul them off for an attitude adjustment of their own. Your readers might be interested in the story."

"I avoid politics," said Glover.

"It's about *katoeys*, for fuck's sake," said McPhail.

Jack, standing near the van, pulled off his reading glasses and turned his back to talk to McPhail.

"McPhail, did you read this?"

"What's that, Jack?"

Jack pointed at a separate menu beside the food menu painted on the side of the van.

"It says they offer tattoos. Inquire inside."

A moment later two Australians scampered out of the back of the Road Kill van, smiling and laughing. Munny stood in the door counting money, looking out at the Aussies, McPhail, Glover and the other old-timers. Next to him was a young dark-skinned boy with a large head and an Angkor Wat-style nose, who McPhail figured was around seven or eight years old.

"This man is a tattoo *artist*," said Roger. "A fucking genius."

Jack blinked and put on his regular glasses.

"I don't see any tattoo."

Roger turned and dropped his pants. Beneath the map were Ned Kelly's last words—Such is life.

"That's England in her full glory," said Jack.

The Lonesome Hawk regulars leaned forward for a closer look. It certainly looked like England. But none of them had ever been to that country, so they had to take Roger's word for it about the genius.

"Too bad Old George wasn't here to see this," one of them said.

A steady stream of backpackers had been walking in. The queue in front of the Road Kill van now stretched out to Soi 22.

"I didn't tell this many people," said McPhail. "How did they find out?"

Glover shook his head. McPhail hadn't concentrated on Glover's cell phone work during the time he was talking about his brother.

"While you were taking a walk down memory lane, I posted a few photos," said Glover. "The Montana Mountain Man Burger went viral. And the Road Kill truck has—hold on—on Facebook, 312 'likes' and on Twitter... Right, 73 favorites, and 456 retweets in an hour. Too bad Calvino missed a classic Bangkok moment."

"He can always relive it online," said McPhail, as he picked up his bottle and went over to the old-timers' table to pour each of them a shot.

The old men raised their glasses to departed friends and gazed about them at what looked more and more like a cemetery.

THIRTY-FIVE

"If we cannot live entirely like human beings, at least let us do everything in our power not to live entirely like animals."—José Saramago, *Blindness*

WHEN MUNNY HAD wandered along Khao San Road searching for his friend, he'd been looking in the wrong place. It turned out that Gop wasn't in a tattoo parlor. He'd moved into a converted van, selling hamburgers to foreigners. The name, Road Kill, painted on the side of the van, had come from an American customer from Missouri who had a striped tiger tattooed on his chest. Gop found out that the tiger was a sports mascot, and road kill was what happened after people got drunk and ran over wildlife on the road after a game. Gop liked the look and the sound of the words "road" and "kill" together. Gop had searched "hot and cool tattoos" and stumbled upon a photo of a hot young thing with "Road Kill" in blue ink tattooed on the small of her back.

He told Munny that he'd decided it made a lot of sense to buy a secondhand van, even though it needed some engine work. Since the curfews, crackdowns and squads of soldiers and police were freaking out the tourists in the usual areas, it was a good idea to be mobile. Gop saw no future in tattoos, preferring the food business, but brick-and-mortar restaurants were a problem, too. The thing was to be able to move quickly. Come trouble, you could drive away. If your business was set in concrete, it was a sitting target for the police and their street informants, who had only to walk through the door, sit down and ask for a bag of money.

Gop's old boss had given Munny his phone number, and Munny had given the man a hundred baht in return. Munny had phoned Gop and asked the hundred-baht question straight out: did he have any work for him? Gop had always had something for Munny when he needed help. Munny was counting on the coup increasing Gop's need for a talented tattoo artist. He hadn't thought much about the details.

Gop wasn't surprised to hear from him.

"Sure, I have a job. Always have work for you, Munny. When can you start?"

No questions about what Munny was still doing in Thailand. Gop didn't much care for "why" questions.

Munny served a three-day probation period of working in the food van—flipping burgers, washing dishes, setting up and clearing tables. Even the boy served drinks with the understanding that he could pocket the tips. After his probation period, as Gop called it, Munny was allowed to use the tattoo equipment and inks in the back of the van, and they split the tattoo money seventy-thirty with Munny on the short end. It was a shitty deal but a temporary solution to his problem, so Munny agreed.

Munny had told the Aussies he'd need three days before he could tattoo the map of England on Clive's buttock. He suggested they go to Koh Samet for that period, lie on the beach, get a good tan, chase women and come back to Bangkok for the artwork. Three days later the Aussies showed up again and said that Roger still wanted the tattoo. The next afternoon they climbed into the back of the van in Washington Square, and Clive emerged with a brilliant ink-work that would have made any Englishman proud.

Only Roger wasn't English; he was an Aussie who wanted to moon the English. It was a distinction that Munny took for one of those differences that really wasn't a difference at all.

Other than Roger, no one had ever phoned Munny on Fah's old iPhone. No one, as far as he knew, had the number. The only reason he had Roger's number was that he had used Munny's phone to call his own phone, and then he'd saved the number. That's why Munny was surprised when the phone rang and the voice on the other side didn't belong to Roger and didn't sound Australian. It was a woman, and she spoke Thai.

"You did good, Munny. Thanks," Fah said.

He felt in his bones that his luck had changed, breaking the spell of bad luck over the last couple of weeks. Like a flat-lined brainwave of a dead man, Munny's luck was spiking, making him feel alive with the world and himself. He asked if she could pay him the last of the money she'd promised.

"That's why I'm calling. I want to get you the money. You got a pen?"

"Hold on," he said.

Munny felt his knees buckle from excitement as he slipped into the kitchen section of the van, wiping down a spot on the counter and out of the corner of his eye catching Gop flipping a burger. He pulled out a piece of paper and a cheap ballpoint pen. Fah gave him the details about Vincent Calvino and said goodbye.

Leaning over, Munny's lips moved as he wrote out a new number and multiplied it, added another number, and multiplied again.

Gop's curiosity got the best of him as he watched him writing. He didn't know that Munny could write.

"What are you writing on that paper, Munny?"

"Some numbers."

Munny looked up and saw that he had Gop where he wanted him.

"What kind of numbers? You thinking of buying a lottery ticket?"

Gop smiled. He had bought lottery tickets every week following the tradition set by his father, who had a food stall and then a restaurant in Yaowarat Road.

"It's not a lottery ticket I'm thinking about."

"What are you thinking about, Munny?"

"How to make you some money."

Gop wiped the grease off his hands and stepped closer to Munny.

"I like that kind of thinking. Tell me more."

"We can make money at the border. It's only a six-hour drive."

Gop's smile vanished, his eyes narrowed.

"You're fucking crazy. The border's full of refugees. They got no money. Besides, they don't eat hamburgers."

"I've done the numbers. Don't you want to hear about the money?"

Gop's father, Wang Tao, who had immigrated from Yunnan, had taught him to always listen to a man who wants to tell you how he's going to make you rich and then throw him out. But listen first. It could be a lottery win, but the odds were very poor.

"The money's in Bangkok," said Gop.

"The money's wherever there are customers. You see any customers on Khao San Road?" asked Munny. "Look out the window. Who do you see? A few old men, and you won't get rich feeding them. You know what your problem is, Gop?"

"What's my problem?"

"Competition. You're not the only one looking to get rich. How many restaurants and other food vans are there? Thousands of owners just like you, Gop, all waiting for the same customers. Like Bangkok taxi drivers chasing the same five customers. You gotta think different. On the border you'd have the only burger joint for a hundred kilometers. No competition. That's how you get rich."

"Where's the money to make the trip?"

Munny put an arm around Gop's shoulder.

"I'll advance you eight thousand baht for the meat and buns," said Munny.

He guessed Gop would demand a higher price, but he'd found in the past that Thais always started negotiations with a low but not too insulting amount.

"Cut the shit, Munny," Gop said, taking Munny's arm off his shoulder. "You want me to drive you to Cambodia, right?"

Munny looked sheepishly at his hands.

"Seeing as I'd be at the border, sure I'd go on home. But only after we sold out the burgers."

"Twenty thousand baht," said Gop with fire in his eyes.

That was an insulting amount. The upside was it meant all that remained was coming to a negotiated price.

"You saw those *farang* backpackers who crowded around the van? They bought out all the food. It got me thinking. There are hundreds of foreigners coming in and out of the country through Aranyaprathet. They all want a decent burger, but there's no place to buy one. Stock up on ground meat and plan on selling two hundred burgers a day. That's thirty thousand baht from food. That's not counting the drink sales. What do you say? The boy and me work for you until you make twenty thousand baht, you pay me back the loan and we call it square. It's fair, Gop. After we're gone, I can see you making fifty thousand baht a day. How many days driving around Bangkok to make that kind of money?"

Gop stared at the paper. The figures looked solid. Something in the back of Gop's mind, though, told him that Munny wasn't doing this for Gop; he was doing this for Munny.

"What do you say, Gop?"

Gop scratched his head, wondering how a Khmer was so quick with numbers, playing the angles and giving him exactly what he'd asked for and thought he'd never get. There it was, just in a slightly different package than he'd expected, but twenty big ones was all that mattered. Munny was right, Gop thought. There would be huge numbers of *farangs* at the border. He saw them lining up at Washington Square.

"Only I don't pay back the float. You got that, Munny? As far as I'm concerned, I'm driving you home and that's it."

"Deal," said Munny.

"When do you want to leave?" said Gop.

THIRTY-SIX

"No price is too high to pay for the privilege of owning yourself."—Friedrich Nietzsche

IT WAS NEARLY nine at night when Gop and Munny finished shopping and loading up on supplies. They'd gone to a market in Chinatown, and Gop had executed the shopping spree with the efficiency and confidence of a serial killer in an armored suit. Wang Tao, Gop's old man, was a local celebrity among the merchants and vendors—a Chinese street vendor who had broken into the big time. They'd known Gop since he was a boy. Gop walked from stall to stall, *waiing* and shaking hands like the son of a famous politician, while Munny and the boy trailed behind as his entourage.

They bought nearly a hundred kilos of ground beef and packed it in ice chests. Four workers loaded it into the Road Kill van. They pushed the meat lockers next to a wall of stacked packages of hamburger buns and Styrofoam ice chests. Gop paid for five cases of Singha beer, five cases of Coke, two cases of mixers and ten bottles of whiskey, and put it on his father's running tab. After all, Gop's old man was good for it; he'd pay him back. Later.

That reminded Gop of his unfinished business with Munny. He turned to him and asked, "Munny where's my money? Don't look all surprised on me. It was your idea. Hand it over."

Munny smiled. He knew Gop had transferred all of his expenses to his old man and figured they way Gop burnt through money that he would soon be demanding the cash Munny had promised. He nearly raised the obvious point that Gop had plenty of capital from the lunch take. Why the huge rush to get more money? Just to walk around with it in his trousers?

"I don't walk around with that kind of cash," Munny finally said, eyeing Gop and wondering how he'd respond.

"Where is it?"

Gop had delivered the question Munny had been hoping for.

"The cash is at the place where the boy's father lives."

"Munny, if you're lying, I'm going to hurt you bad, and then I'm turning what's left of you in to the police."

"I'm telling you the truth, Gop. You'll get what I promised. No need to lie about it. I need you to take me where the cash is, or how can I give it to you?"

Gop eyed him long and hard. Two hundred customers ready to buy were already a certainty in his mind. He might stay a week. That would be three hundred and fifty thousand baht. A month would put it over 1.4 million baht, and he could kick back for a year. Gop had caught the money-making bug and was running a high fever.

"There's one other thing," said Munny. "When we pick up the money, we pick up the boy's father, too."

Gop looked at the back of the van.

"We're short of room."

"He's small. He won't take up much space. And he can help with washing dishes and cleaning up. With all of those customers, we need someone washing up. Besides, he's holding your money. So we don't have much choice, if you want to get paid."

Free labor was always an appealing prospect. Gop's father had taught him that lesson. And the Khmer and the Burmese begged for work.

"How much will this cost me?"

"He'll work for free. Same as me and the boy."

"I don't know," said Gop.

He'd inherited Wang Tao's doubt about doing something he hadn't thought of first. Doing something thought of by someone else almost always ended in disaster. Munny was Cambodian, and that doubled up the odds of some non-obvious double-cross.

"The boy needs his father. And it's right on the way. We pick up the money I owe you, and the father comes along. Tell you what... What if I throw in another five hundred baht for your trouble?"

"A thousand baht."

"Once we get there you can help me."

"Help you what?"

"Bring him down to the van."

"Why would I do that?"

"He has a disability."

"What's that mean?"

"He stepped on a landmine sixteen years ago and lost a leg."

"How's he going to wash dishes?"

"He doesn't need two legs for that. He's got both hands and arms, and that's all the job calls for."

"A thousand, right?"

Calvino waited in his car, the window rolled up, air-conditioning on, watching Fah's Twitter timeline—"I'm going on a long trip & won't be back soon. Bye." He'd parked twenty meters away from the dark, derelict building, from which the smell of fish diffused through the night. After dark the Aquarium looked like any other abandoned, half-constructed building, all shadows and concrete, with shafts of moonlight spilling through the cracks in the walls and open floors. From the street, other than some patches of flickering light, there was nothing to see, no movement on the lower levels and only the noise of traffic in the distance. He glanced in the rear-view mirror as another driver killed the headlights nearby.

The Road Kill van had pulled to the curb, and Gop cut the engine and looked up and down the street.

"Where in the fuck are we, Munny?"

Munny and the kid climbed out of the back and walked around to the driver's side.

"The money's inside."

Munny tapped his knuckles on the window frame.

"Let's go."

Gop was overtaken by fear. Strange neighborhood. No one ventured out on the street. No police, no soldiers. None of that stillness seemed right or normal, and Gop froze, hands locked on the steering wheel, knuckles white from the tightness of his grip.

"I'll wait here," he said.

"It's only going to take a few minutes, Gop. I'm counting on you."

The driver's door finally opened wide and Gop climbed out. He bent over, grabbed his knees and took a deep breath.

"I don't like this, Munny."

"Nothing not to like. We're stopping for the cash."

With Thais, Munny found that "cash" was the magic word that opened doors.

Gop stared at the kid in the dark, trying to make out his features. He hadn't said much all day. He stood close to Munny and let him do the talking.

"Okay, let's do it," said Gop.

Munny wasn't only an artist; he had that rare mind that comes from a hardscrabble upbringing, where planning an escape became second nature, like brushing one's teeth. Like Tom Sawyer, he'd convinced someone else to paint the fence.

Calvino waited until they were all out of the van and then climbed out of his car and called after them. He wore a blue Brioni suit, tailored to fit without the shoulder hostler showing. He'd once had worn a Brioni suit when he'd had to kill two men. It was a killer suit. With the light blue shirt, dark tie, jacket unbuttoned, he looked like in the half shadows like one of Ballard's yacht buyers who had ended up lost.

"Munny, I'm Fah's friend."

Both Munny and Gop turned around and looked down the *soi* as Calvino approached.

"Who's that?" said Gop.

Gop's heart was in his throat, and he looked like he might throw up.

The boy squeezed Gop's hand and told him, "You'll be okay, Mr. Gop."

"It's okay, he's my friend," said Munny.

"He's a *farang*," said Gop, stating what was obvious even in the dark.

Gop climbed back inside the van and locked the doors. At first Munny thought he might drive off. But with all that meat and buns in the back, where was he going to go?

Munny walked ahead, putting some distance between himself and Gop. In the dark, a few meters from the van and shrouded in the shadows, Calvino made a smooth hand-off, and Munny palmed the money in his hand. Gop, from that distance, had no idea about the amount of money. He couldn't even be certain it was money the *farang* had given him. Munny had already stuffed whatever it was in his jeans pocket as Gop powered down the window to talk.

"Is there something you want to tell me, Munny?"

Munny appreciated that Gop had the power of the van. Munny didn't want an ugly fight on his hands.

"Just got some good news," said Munny.

"What's that?"

"Not many roadblocks on the highway."

Calvino stared at Gop through the open van window.

"You with Munny?"

"Munny's with me," said Gop.

"This is Khun Vincent," said Munny in Thai.

A few seconds passed. No traffic came into the dead end. Calvino saw from Munny's body language, and the way he'd dealt with Fah's twenty thousand baht, that things were complicated.

Calvino turned back to Munny.

"Fah said you were an artist."

"I'm good at tattoos."

Munny's modesty made Calvino smile.

"I've seen your work."

"I really don't have time to talk. My friend's waiting, and he doesn't like to wait."

"Where are you heading?"

"We're picking up another friend." Gesturing at the dark building, he added, "He's waiting inside."

"What is this place?"

"The locals call it the Aquarium. I used to live here with my family."

"But not anymore?"

Munny shook his head.

"That's right. The coup changes things. I gotta go," Munny said, standing straight, hands in front of him.

Calvino looked him directly in the eye.

"You and your friend look nervous," said Calvino. "Are you expecting trouble?"

"No, sir, but trouble might expect me. It often does."

In the end, it was the uncertainty of a small detail that changed everything, like going into a squatter's building at night with a stranger—three strangers, counting the boy. The casual way Munny expressed his acceptance of whatever waited for him inside caused Calvino to close his car door and point the remote control to lock it.

"I can come along," said Calvino.

"No need to take on another man's troubles."

Calvino had made a living doing precisely that and hadn't run across many people who weren't willing to unload their troubles on a willing stranger.

"You're quite the artist," said Calvino. "My great-grandfather was an artist. A hundred years ago he painted scenes in Bangkok."

"That's something," said Munny. "I'm no painter."

"I've seen your art. You're more than a tattoo guy. You're more like Lucian Freud," said Calvino.

"Why do you think like that?"

"Fah."

Munny cocked his head to the side, wondering how Calvino was going to play it. Fah had told him about Lucian Freud, the great English painter who had a history as a tattoo artist during the war. Standing before him in the half shadows was a foreigner telling him the same thing. Such praise could go to a man's head.

"Let's go get your friend," said Calvino.

"What did your great-grandfather paint?"

"A Chinese man running."

"Where was he running to?"

"Good question, Munny."

With a long sigh, Gop climbed out of the van again.

"Are we getting your friend, or what?" said Gop.

Calvino gestured for Munny to follow him. He opened the trunk of his car and a light came on. Munny looked inside.

"In Brooklyn, my cousin Nero and me once got in some trouble. Nero's father, my father's brother, took us aside and said a man only needs three tools to solve ninety-nine percent of his problems."

Munny looked over Calvino's shoulder as he leaned forward into the trunk.

"A Brooklyn type of problem requires either a bolt cutter, a baseball bat or a .38."

Calvino lifted the bolt cutter and looked at Munny and Gop, who had joined them. He shook his head, and put it back.

"No bolts to cut, sir," said Munny.

"That's not the right tool," said Calvino, and he put it back into the trunk and picked up the baseball bat and a baseball. "My uncle said, Vinny, if you get yourself into a situation where none of these tools solve the problem, move to another neighborhood. Start over."

"We can't do that," said Munny.

Calvino saw him looking at the baseball bat.

"I thought that might be the case."

Calvino flipped Munny the baseball and he caught it with one hand.

"Nero always chose the baseball bat when we were kids."

Munny ran his fingers over the stitches on the ball's surface, smiling. Catching a ball in the dark isn't something anyone can do, thought Calvino.

"You ever swing a baseball bat?"

Calvino pulled out a Louisville slugger from the trunk. He handed it to Munny, handle out.

Munny shook his head.

"No, sir, I've never held one."

He took the bat and twisted the smooth wood handle around in his hands.

"Thanks, sir."

Calvino closed the lid of the trunk and leaned against his car.

"Do you know what kind of wood that is?"

Munny shook his head.

"Ash."

Munny repeated the word, smiling.

"It's a hard wood."

"I sometimes wondered when I was a kid whether the guy running in my great-grandfather's painting had hit a home run or a sacrifice fly ball to right field. I'm not certain he knew. Let's go in the building and see if the bases are loaded."

As Munny turned, the boy broke free and took off running.

"He misses his father," Munny said.

"I don't like the feel of this place," said Gop.

"Who are you?" asked Calvino.

He'd asked him before and was still waiting for an answer.

"Munny's boss."

"That's good, and if you came to help him, even better."

That made Munny smile.

"Let's just get your friend into the van," said Gop. "I've got a long drive ahead."

"Thanks, boss," said Munny. "We'll be in and out in five minutes. That's all the time we need to bring Heng down to the van. I told you, he's only got one leg. He can't make it on his own."

"You told me he was holding the money. That was a lie. The *farang* gave you the money. Now you tell me your friend doesn't have a wooden leg. Is that another lie, Munny?"

"He did have one, but some people took it away."

"Why?"

"Because they could."

Helping a friend was something Munny had a history of doing. In Munny's universe that's what friends were for, to give you help when everyone else had left you behind.

"You coming, boss?"

Gop stood in the road, half of him wanting to climb back into the Road Kill van and get the hell out of the area, and half of him not wanting to look scared in front of Munny and the stranger.

"Okay, okay, five minutes."

Munny guided by moonlight started up the entrance stairs and then turned and stopped. Dark shadows swallowed the small pools of light at each turn.

"I'm worried about someone coming in after us," he said to Calvino. "If you could stop that from happening, I'd be grateful."

"I'll stay," said Gop. "It's too dark. How can you see anything?"

"Boss, you come inside with me. We'll be okay. Because this *farang* is gonna stick out inside, and we don't want people noticing too much. You and me are gonna blend right in."

The more Calvino heard the results of Munny's planning, the more he saw that this was a man who thought two steps ahead. Survivors need luck, he knew, but they also need to anticipate the weak points of any plan. Munny was right. A *farang* in this place at night would create suspicion.

"I'll stay out of sight," said Calvino.

Munny nodded and continued up the staircase, a route he knew like a path through minefields.

"Vichet, where are you?" Munny called out.

"I'm up here," he heard from inside.

"Gop and me are coming. Stay where you are. Wait for us."

Munny waited for a reply, but the silence was broken by the splash of fish in the water in the basement below.

On the first-floor landing, Kiri waited until Gop had cleared the staircase before stepping out of the shadows behind him.

"Munny, you said you were coming back to work on the generator. You lied."

Munny turned around, concealing the bat. If Kiri hadn't been drinking, he would have seen it.

"It's not easy moving around with soldiers and roadblocks," said Munny.

"That's not my problem. It's your problem," said Kiri.

Munny flicked the flywheel on a cheap lighter, and a narrow yellow flame outlined Kiri's large head. He wasn't that old, but in the light of the flame he looked it. His eyes sank back in his skull, he had a fleck of spittle on his upper lip, and he hadn't shaved in several days. The cumulative effect was to add another twenty years to his appearance.

The full blast of the fetid air, rising from the stagnant water, hit Gop with the rank odor of a small ocean of fish, some dying, some dead and the others roiling, splashing in the water, making a racket.

"What's that stench?" asked Gop. "I can't breathe."

"There's water and fish all cooped up in the basement," said Munny, looking over the edge and into the void of darkness.

Kiri wasn't going to tolerate disrespect any time of day from someone like Munny, and he yelled at him, "You're not paying attention, Munny! Your business is with me and Nimol."

A slant of light across his red-eyed face showed Kiri had been drinking. A pressurized anger, bottled up too long, was threatening to come uncorked. Kiri was about to enter what the Thais called the *a-rom chua-woop* phase, when they didn't care about dying and all that lack of care went into hurting someone else real bad.

"Where's Nimol?"

"Over here, Munny."

Nimol stepped forward with Vichet, point a gun at his head.

Gop hyperventilated and bowed his head, his hands trembling as he clutched his knees. He tried to catch his breath to keep out the stink from the water below. If Gop could have mustered the strength, he'd have run down the stairs and out of the building. Fuck the Khmer who'd talked him into some crazy shit. He rose up and turned to leave.

"Stay where you are," said Kiri. "You wouldn't make three steps before I cut you open like a catfish."

Gop sat down on the floor, crossed his legs and closed his eyes. Kiri stepped in front of him.

"Go up and get Heng," Kiri said. "Sixth floor. Tell him Vichet and Munny are down here waiting for him."

"That's a good idea, Kiri," said Nimol. "Get this Thai to do the heavy lifting, so you and I can make a party of it. Munny, you can start thinking about the compensation you're going to give us for that lie you told about fixing the generator."

Gop looked over the situation, heading up the stairs alone didn't seem like a good idea but staying where he stood was even a more dismal one.

"If you were a real man, Kiri," said Munny, "you wouldn't be hiding behind a boy. You'd come after me. But you know you don't have the balls. Your style is beating up a man without a leg, or a seven-year-old kid.

Kiri pushed the boy hard and Nimol caught him as he stumbled.

"Time to teach Munny a lesson," said Nimol.

In the dark Kiri hadn't noticed the baseball bat, which Munny had kept in the shadow and behind his right leg. The instant Kiri glimpsed the moving Louisville Slugger, it was already too late. Teeth shards, bits of skin with flesh attached and a thick arc of blood fanned out like a cone of light from a supernova. The momentum carried Kiri's body across the cement floor.

First time at bat, and Munny had hit a home run. But now he wondered if he'd killed him. Only gurgling noises were coming out of Kiri's throat and nose.

"I didn't mean..." said Munny, dropping down on one knee beside the man.

The baseball bat fell from his hands onto the floor. He rolled Kiri's body over on its back, and blood and brains spooled down the sides of the shattered face.

"I'm so sorry, Kiri," said Munny, slowly shaking his head.

Calvino pressed his cell phone against his ear outside the building, like a baseball fan listening to a game on the radio. He'd heard the loud crack of the bat on Kiri's skull, the bat clattering on the concrete floor and then Munny's sorrowful voice. Calvino took the steps two at a time as he ran into the building. He drew his .38 Police Special from its holster beneath his jacket, half-crouching in and out of the shadows as he moved ahead. He heard the voices as he neared the top of the stairs. Ahead in the near dark he saw Kiri's body on the floor and Nimol's right arm stretched out with a gun. His left arm held the boy as a shield. Calvino couldn't get a clean shot.

"I'm going to blow your brains out, Munny," said Nimol.

Gop sobbed as he slowly made his way down the stairs with Heng's arm wrapped around his shoulder.

"Let my boy go!" pleaded Heng.

"Shut up!" said Nimol. "It's time to settle things that should have been settled a long time ago."

"You're right, there," said Heng. "You can start by giving me my artificial leg."

"Give me the money you owe me."

"I don't have the money."

Nimol's foot nudged a wooden leg on the floor of the landing.

"No money?"

He glanced over his shoulder to where the landing dropped off to the basement. He kicked the artificial leg. The force lifted it past Munny, and it arced over the edge of the landing and down into the water below.

"Why did you go and do that, Nimol?" said Heng.

"You don't pay, you don't walk. That's the Eight-Niners' rule."

No more than five feet from Nimol, Munny stood facing Nimol in the open space. Nimol applied his second hand to the handgun, letting the boy run to his father. Nimol slowly knelt down beside Kiri, who now lay still. He looked at Kiri's body, shaking his head as he examined the smashed face.

"Why'd you hit him, Munny? You've killed a man. And you shouldn't have done that."

"I didn't want to, Nimol. But he came at me wanting to hurt me bad. You let us go."

"Or you'll do what, Munny? I've got a gun. You've got a busted bat. How do you think that's going to work out?"

"I wouldn't do that," said Gop.

He had lowered Heng to the floor and now held a gun that he'd found the courage to pull from the waistband concealed under his shirt.

Calvino stooped low, leaning forward near the top of the stairs. Nimol stood in a pool of light reflected from the water in the basement. The distant sound of a thousand of fish breaking the surface of the water echoed. Nimol stood with his back turned toward Calvino, who now had a clear head shot. Calvino watched as Gop's hands held the gun unsteadily. Nimol ignored Gop and raised his gun toward Munny, concentrating on the Khmer and the half of a bat he'd snatched from the floor with one hand. Gop's position was slightly behind Munny, who stood two feet ahead.

Calvino quickly ran the scene's possible outcomes through his mind, pointing the gun at Nimol's midsection. Should he just shoot him? Nimol had crossed that threshold where killing him was the only choice. The possibilities ran through his mind in a maze of outcomes. Calvino asked himself if he should take a chance on Gop. It was the most dangerous of moments, the judgment of whether to leave room for another man to find his courage.

Time stopped. A hypnotic trance filled the space. In an upstairs room of a mansion in Rangoon, the closed door guarded, the Black Cat pointed a gun at the head of a sobbing Thai woman kneeling on the floor as Calvino had watched helplessly. That moment had burnt deep in his memory, a scene that had repeated itself over and over again in his sleep. This time it was playing out among two Khmer and a Thai in an abandoned building in Bangkok. The runner in Chini's Chinese New Year flashed across the darkness, a phantom suspended between Heng and Nimol. The boy had broken from his father and run forward, rushing and screaming at Nimol. A wild shot from Nimol's gun missed the boy. Munny reached down and scooped him up from the floor, shielding him with his body. Time restarted, and the surge of the fatal instant filled the space. All these events that passed before Calvino's eyes and through his mind were no more than small change that added up to a second. Then the sound of Gop's 9mm cracked like a whip. A 9mm round blew a ten baht coin-sized hole through Nimol's head above the right eye. His legs crumpled and he fell back; his body, in a free fall, after a couple of seconds slammed into the water below. Nimol's life ended without him ever reaching terminal velocity.

Gop lowered his gun and looked at Munny, who let go of Vichet.

"Go back to your father."

Heng, sitting on the floor, wrapped his arms around the boy's neck and hugged him. Out of the darkness a dozen or so of the remaining squatters appeared, coming down the stairs, forming a circle around the scene. They were free.

One of the women looked over at Gop.

"Thank you, sir," she said.

Gop stood, the gun hanging limp at his side.

"You did good," whispered Munny. "We can go."

Kiri's body, his head shattered like a pumpkin after Halloween, lay with his legs bent at strange angles. Calvino holstered his gun as he climbed the last two steps. He gently removed Gop's gun from his hand. Gop blinked away tears and wiped his face with his forearm.

"What are we going to do?" asked Gop, looking at Kiri's corpse on the concrete floor. Nimol's body floated in the water a few feet away.

Several of the squatters came up and touched Munny as if his good luck would rub off on them. He nodded and walked to the edge of the unfinished floor and looked down at the dark void, hearing the fish flop.

"Give me a hand."

Shards of concrete block soon appeared out of the dark. Several of the squatters worked to tie the shards to the arms and legs of Kiri's corpse. Two more men descended the stairs to the basement and used a long pole to guide Nimol's body to the side, where they weighted it down with bricks slipped into his clothes. Two of the squatters moved forward with a couple of pieces of rebar. They were construction workers and worked fast, fastening four ten-kilo jumbo steel bars with rope until they were secure against the chest and legs of Nimol's body. After slipping Nimol's body back into the murky water, they watched it sink. The remaining rebar was hiked up the stairs and tied around Kiri's body.

Gop struggled to pick up Kiri's body by the ankles as Munny held him under his armpits, getting blood all over his shirt. At the edge Gop dropped his end of the load. Munny stopped a moment as Gop stared at the body. Then he shoved it over the edge. Heng, sitting with his back against the wall, sheltering his boy, gently guided his head away so he wouldn't witness this moment. The body made a loud thud as it hit one of the main half-rusted girders on the way down. Vichet peeked out from under his father's arm but quickly turned away. He didn't really want to witness the way two men that he had known had gone from being alive to being dead and dumped in watery grave. He could hear the fish splashing in a frenzy, tails hitting the water's surface on the way back down.

Munny looked at the blood on his hands.

"The money!" he said. "Nimol had it."

"Why'd you give it to him?" Gop asked.

"He had a gun."

Gop nodded. Yeah, he'd remembered the gun, and he also remembered that it was his money they were talking about.

"I'm going to get it," said Munny.

The flight of stairs from the ground floor to the basement ended halfway down. The bodies had both sunk to the bottom. Munny stripped off his shirt and jeans and stepped out of his sandals. He dove into the water. Gop and half a dozen squatters watched as bubbles rose and fish jumped. A moment later Munny's head broke the surface. He spit out water and wiped it out of his eyes.

"Did you find it?" asked Gop.

Munny took a deep breath and disappeared again under the surface. He was gone nearly two minutes before his hand broke the surface and then his head. In his clenched hand was Heng's wooden leg—one of those crude limbs with no cosmetic cover, made with a jigsaw, a drill press and a grinder. He'd tucked the envelope into the knee hinge before swimming to the surface. Munny had a big grin on his face as he swam toward the concrete floor. Gop squatted at the edge, reaching out to Munny. Two other men helped him pull Munny up onto the concrete. His chest heaving in and out, Munny lay there for a moment, clutching the wooden leg, looking up at the faces staring down at him.

Munny put on his shirt and jeans, stuffing the envelope in his back pocket. He dried his hands on the sides of his jeans. One of the squatters handed him the busted baseball bat.

"You can go home now. No one's gonna stop you," said Munny. "You're free."

"We thought you'd never come up," said Gop.

Munny held up the wooden leg like a trophy.

"Without this, there was no way I could have pried back the rebar and rope. You tied him up good."

Heng had managed to hobble down, and the squatters stood back, letting him in close to Munny. Munny handed him the leg.

"I broke your leg, Heng. The foot got caught on the rebar."

"It was worn out anyway," Heng said.

"Get someone to fetch your things," said Munny.

Munny sat back on the stairs next to Gop. He counted out eight wet thousand baht notes and handed them to the Thai.

"That's the float."

Gop looked at the rest of money, and then at all the squatters looking at the money and at him, and decided these were Munny's people and it wasn't a good time to ask Munny for more. After all, the basement water was deep, and Munny had dived to the bottom and fished it out of Nimol's pocket.

They climbed the stairs back to the first-floor landing, where a couple of the squatters had brought down two old boxes with Heng's worldly possessions and set them on the floor.

Calvino said, "Someone will have heard the gun shot. Let's go."

Munny walked over and picked up the head of the broken baseball bat. He looked around for the bat's bottom half.

"Mr. Vincent, did you see the handle, sir?"

Calvino walked over and picked it up.

"Call me Vinny. You don't want to be leaving these behind. Leave the bat with me. I'll take care of it."

"Thanks, Mr. Vinny."

He handed Calvino the bloodied piece of bat.

Calvino and Munny then carried Heng down to the street.

"I'm sorry I broke your wooden leg," Munny said to Heng. "I've got money to buy a new one when you get back."

That was how Munny planned to spend the money—ten grand to Gop for transportation and ten grand to Heng for an artificial leg. That left nothing for Munny, but that didn't seem to bother him. Munny was free in a way most men never were. He'd stopped caring about money.

Munny and Calvino eased Heng into the back of the van. Gop switched on the Road Kill engine, as Calvino watched Heng stretch out on the floor of the van.

"I told you trouble had a way of finding me," said Munny.

"Maybe it's time for trouble to take a holiday and visit some other people."

"Yeah," said Munny, "I'd like that. It's been hanging around me too long."

"See you around, Munny," said Calvino.

"Thanks."

"My secretary's got a boy about your son's age," said Calvino. "May be one they will meet."

Munny smiled. "That would be a fine day."

The Aquarium squatters hadn't needed any help settling their score. Letting go of being the hero, allowing someone else to save the situation, had given Calvino the feeling he'd found something he'd been searching for over many years. Munny had no cash he could call his own, but he'd found the gold in his life.

Gop swung the van around, and Calvino watched the taillights disappear around a corner. He walked back to his car and eased himself into the driver's seat, hands on the wheel at ten and two o'clock. Beyoncé's "End of Time" played as he drove away.

The money delivery hadn't been a drug deal or some other setup with him as bait. He'd decided to do it for Fah based on his gut instinct that she wasn't just another of Osborne's women. He'd seen her life unfold, the one she shared only with her friends, and she was the real thing. She was too good for Osborne, and Osborne knew it too. Not that it mattered. They were on their way to Madagascar, and what had happened at the Aquarium was already as inaccessible to them as if it had happened on another planet. New boundaries that would shape their lives had begun to form. Munny was going home, crossing his own boundary. Calvino wasn't planning to cross any border. He was going to stay and see things through.

Gop drove fifty kilometers, eyes straight ahead on the road, before he said a word to the passengers. Munny sat beside him in the passenger seat, and the boy and his father sat in the back, clutching each other. Gop tried to process what had happened back at the Aquarium. It had been only a few minutes. But it hadn't seemed like minutes. Time had elongated, stopped. Only now did it seem to resume at a normal beat.

Munny had experienced the same disassociation from normal time. The pendulum had paused as Munny swung the baseball bat. The swing of the bat had seemed to measure tiny units of time like a fastball pitch hurled toward the batter. In baseball, the scale of time and the speed of a motion are calculated by a hitter's internal clock. Munny had that clock; he was a natural-born slugger. Not that it mattered much. A Khmer hunted in martial-law times wasn't going to be playing any sport. He was playing a different kind of game.

Munny reached into his pocket and pulled out the baseball Calvino had given him. He tossed it to Vichet.

"You can keep it," he said. "It's a baseball."

"I shot him," Gop said with a tremor in is voice.

It was as if he'd only just realized that he'd killed a man.

"Nimol had a lot of enemies," said Munny. "He hurt a lot of people, too. You saw how you were a hero to the people living there."

"You killed the other one, Munny."

"As sure as if I'd shot him," said Munny.

"You think someone will find the bodies?"

Gop had been worrying about what would happen if the police got involved.

"No one's going to find them. They're staying on the bottom, and I can't think of anyone who will miss them or report them as gone. Don't worry about them, boss. Two men like that will be forgotten by the world by the time we reach the border."

Munny watched Vichet turn the baseball over in his hand. He leaned his head back against the headrest. It felt good to be alive. The whole world, real but strange, felt sweet and free. He glanced over at Gop, who sat silently again, lost among the demons haunting his thoughts. He was driving in the middle lane, passing a convoy of army trucks. Munny managed a smile as Gop moved into the fast lane and accelerated.

"Who was the *farang*?" asked Gop.

"I don't know. Doesn't much matter. He was looking out for us," Munny said.

"Why would he do that?"

Munny shrugged his shoulders.

"Don't know. But it's a first. How about you, Gop? Anyone ever looked out for you?"

"My friends," he said in an uncertain voice.

"You're lucky, then. It's good to have friends. Like tonight."

"I did okay?"

"You were a superhero, Gop. Like Batman."

Munny had tattooed Batman on Gop's back almost one year earlier. If he could let himself believe what Gop and his friends had said, it was one of the better Batman tattoos that anyone had ever seen.

"We're going to sell two hundred burgers tomorrow," Munny said.

Gop wasn't listening to the boast about burger sales.

"I never shot a man before, Munny."

"Let's hope that Nimol is the last one."

"He shot at the boy. Something snapped in me."

"I know, Gop. You saved his life."

Munny shifted around for a good look at Heng and the boy in the back. Vichet slept against his father's shoulder. Kids could sleep almost anywhere. He missed Sovann, his own son, but was glad he'd been spared the experience of that night.

"Batman?" Gop asked, repeating his hero's name.

"Just like Batman."

Even a frog inside a coconut shell could lift his eyes over the edge in time to be a hero.

THIRTY-SEVEN

"Thought's a luxury. Do you think the peasant sits and thinks of God and Democracy when he gets inside his mud hut at night?"—Graham Greene, *The Quiet American*

ON ONE SIDE of his office desk, a Selectric typewriter idled in front of Calvino, making that low-grade buzz like a hornets' nest deep inside a wall. A sheet of A4 paper half-filled with text sat in the carriage. Calvino turned away. He worked the wireless mouse in front of his iMac. Swimming across the twenty-seven-inch screen were fish. He'd found a YouTube video recorded by an underwater camera adventurer who'd hunted until he'd found a school of snakehead fish attacking a pig in Brazil. The blue lake water churned with blood, the frantic squeals of the pig fading to the sound of splashing water.

The voiceover, in a godlike tone reminiscent of Morgan Freeman, told the story of how the snakeheads could grow up to one meter in length. The snakehead was no ordinary fish; it was a meat-eating machine. It could live for days out of the water, and for months buried in the mud. They were thoroughly tough bastards. He wasn't surprised to find that some species of the snakehead were native to Asia. Tough guys like eating tough guys.

Over time snakeheads had been added to the basement aquarium. Some said it was the Eight-Niners who had brought them in to terrify the squatters. Others said the Chinese owner had released them to make merit and to terrify the Eight-Niners, who had begun to get a little too independent. The sunlight didn't reach that depth, and the fish could feed unseen, undisturbed. Over a long enough stretch of time, all traces of the bodies would disappear.

McPhail stormed into Calvino's office, a lit cigarette hanging from the side of his mouth, and planted on Ratana's desk a bunch of orchids he'd bought at Villa Market.

"Good morning, Ratana. How's John-John doing in school?"

"Top of his class," she said.

"Is Vinny's grooming him to be an investigator or what?"

"It's more likely not an investigator," she said.

"Smart. Is the private eye open for visitors?" His voice was loud enough to carry into Calvino's office. McPhail laughed at his own joke. He went into Calvino's office, closed the door behind him and sat down in a chair.

"My brother won the California iron man triathlon. He did it, Vinny."

Calvino could see the pride in McPhail's face.

"He found what he was looking for," said Calvino. "But would you trade places with him?"

McPhail shook his head.

"Are you crazy? On Facebook he's holding up a trophy. Is that what's it's all about, showing the world you won a race?"

"Depends on the race you want to run in."

"But he did win, Vinny."

"No one ever wins," said Calvino. "When a man realizes there's no finish line, no tape to break with your chest, no audience on their feet cheering you, that's when his life starts to make sense."

"Okay, I get it. Enough about my brother. I have more news."

He waited for Calvino to ask him. Calvino knew the ploy and allowed the silence to lengthen.

"Have you seen Glover's blog this week?" McPhail finally asked. "He took down the black wreath. He's back in business." A broad smile crossed McPhail's face as if to say 'I told you so.'

"Wasn't he on his way out of Thailand?"

"He's not gone yet. Maybe he'll change his mind. He wrote a whole blog about Road Kill, with pictures of the old gang. I'm the one who introduced him to that crazy Thai who made Montana Mountain Burgers. You missed Road Kill at Washington Square."

McPhail waited for a moment for the importance of that information to register with Calvino.

"Aren't you going to open his website and look?"

McPhail leaned over the office desk, staring at the screen.

"Fucking fish. Go to Glover's site."

A few clicks later, the screen filled with images of the Road Kill van. There were pictures of Gop, the boy, Munny, McPhail and the old gang. McPhail was captured flashing the very same victory smile his brother had shown as he held up the trophy.

"What a fucking day that was, Vinny. You're looking at people who know how to make a real hamburger."

"They have that look."

"You're jealous because you missed it. It happened on the day you disappeared. The Lonesome Hawk crowd, or what was left of them, kept asking, 'Where's Calvino?' And I said, 'Drinking Champagne beside a swimming pool.' "

"I was tied up with Osborne."

"Fuck Osborne. He made you miss a piece of history, man."

"Ed, my goal is to live as far outside of history as possible. History is a territory where mostly bad things happen to good people."

"Glover's story took off like crazy. It's everywhere now. Road Kill has gone across the world. Right along with the madness of banning beer after midnight and warning labels on a bottle of beer. How fucked is that? No more beer girls. Kiss Mr. Tourist's ass *adios*. *Hasta luego*. Because he ain't comin' here. Even Road Kill has left the building, just like Elvis. Everyone is asking what happened to it. When is it coming back to the Square, the old-timers keep asking me. Those burgers gave them something to look forward to. Now, like the Square, it's gone. Vanished like Amelia Earhart or D.B. Cooper. What a mystery!"

"Road Kill is on the Cambodian border," said Calvino.

"Who'd you hear that one from?"

"McPhail, rumors in Thailand don't have fathers or mothers. They're orphans of loan sharks, con men, streetwalkers and fortune tellers. No one claims them until they become legitimate."

"In that case, I've heard Road Kill is still in Bangkok hiding out from the cops and military. They've gone underground. Glover's had hundreds of emails from his readers claiming they've found it and bought a burger."

"Any photos to support this?"

"They've said there's a code of silence. *Farangs* who find it swear an oath of secrecy to protect Road Kill."

Calvino nodded, smiling.

"I know that look, Calvino. But it's not bullshit. What if your rumor is bullshit, isn't that a good possibility, Mr. Selectric typewriter writer?"

Ratana came into the office in tight jeans, high heels and a scalloped-neck blue blouse with long sleeves, holding a printout.

"I couldn't help but overhear you talking about Road Kill," she said, handing the printout to McPhail. "I've seen a couple of posts on my timeline. One had some photos I thought you might want to see."

The photos showed the Road Kill van with a long line of *farangs* in shorts, T-shirts and flip-flops, smiling and giving the victory sign. Behind the van was an arch with a replica of the iconic temple of Angkor Wat and a sign reading "Welcome to the Kingdom of Cambodia."

McPhail looked up from the photo.

"Jesus, Road Kill right on the border!"

He handed the picture to Calvino.

"Business looks good," said Calvino.

"You wouldn't have a drink hiding in your bottom drawer, would you?" said McPhail. "Or is that just a rumor?"

Calvino leaned forward and gestured to McPhail to move in closer.

"Tell her she looks good in the jeans," Calvino whispered.

"Tell who?"

"Ratana, you moron."

McPhail leaned back and cleared his throat.

"Hey, Ratana, you look hot in those jeans."

"Thank you, Ed. At least someone in this office notices what a woman wears."

Calvino sucked in a couple of cubic feet of air to stop himself from replying. Instead he opened the bottom drawer of his desk and pulled out a bottle of Johnnie Walker Black.

"McPhail, you need a drink."

Ratana went to the cabinet and removed three glasses,

setting them on the desk. Calvino poured two stiff shots for McPhail and one shot for himself. He raised his glass and McPhail raised his.

"Here's to happiness."

"You forgot someone," said McPhail.

Calvino poured a neat shot into Ratana's glass. He raised his glass and McPhail and Ratana followed.

"Welcome to the deep end of the pool, where the non-swimmers are dropped," said Calvino.

McPhail shivered and flicked his ash before taking a long, steady pull on the whiskey.

"Man, this is going to break the hearts of the old gang. It's like, you thought she was your wife, and it was just another short-time boom-boom with a thick slab of meat packaged between two buns. Then a moment later she's at the door, not letting it hit her ass on the way out. Sorry, Ratana!"

McPhail looked up at her, but she'd already gone. Then his eyes found her empty glass.

"She's heard it all before," said Calvino.

McPhail leaned forward and whispered, "She's not only hot, she knows how to drink. You've been overlooking what's on your doorstep."

Then he smiled, took the bottle and poured himself a refill.

"You said there was something you wanted to tell me."

"How would you like to take a little trip across the border?" said Calvino.

McPhail lit a cigarette.

"When?"

"Next week."

"What do you have in mind?"

"I heard through a friend that Road Kill is franchising into Cambodia."

"You're kidding."

"A Cambodian needs financing. It could be a good investment."

"Calvino, you've become a capitalist pig. You and Osborne are always sniffing the money trail."

"I figure we'll spend three, four days looking around. All expenses paid."

McPhail finished the whiskey and poured another refill from Calvino's office bottle.

"This wouldn't be a cover for a relocation?"

"McPhail, when you've got skin in the game, you see it through."

"I can't wait to tell Glover about Road Kill going to Cambodia."

"The border, anyway."

"But Sarah Palin can see Cambodia from there while she eats a Monster Hawaiian Burger."

It was what the Internet and globalization had brought to the world—chasing a food van across borders in Southeast Asia. Calvino wanted to say something more but stopped himself. Cambodia was a place where a lot of families had died. The country was littered with villages of ghosts and fields of unmarked graves packed with bones. The old homes had long ago disappeared along with their occupants. Only the minefields remained. Many of the new generation, men like Munny, had taken their families to Thailand. But everything had changed for them there in just a few days, much as it had in the Khmer Rouge days. He'd gone back with nothing but the clothes on his back, a one-legged man and a boy who wasn't even his own. He was the kind of asset worth investing in.

THIRTY-EIGHT

"Innocence always calls mutely for protection when we would be so much wiser to guard ourselves against it: innocence is like a dumb leper who has lost his bell, wandering the world, meaning no harm."
—Graham Greene, *The Quiet American*

PRATT WAS OUT of uniform, sitting alone on a bench in Lumpini Park, the sun to his back, holding a book. He'd come a half hour early for the solitude and a chance to read. He looked beyond the garden to the lake, where a young Thai couple passed by on a paddleboat, pedaling and laughing as if the world they were living in were a friendly, ordinary place for lovers. He looked up from a well-thumbed collection of plays by William Shakespeare. Pulling out the bookmark, he studied a stylized drawing of the Bard.

How could one man have been so wise, he asked himself. As he waited for Vincent Calvino, he'd been passing the time reading Othello:

Good name in man and woman, dear my lord,
Is the immediate jewel of their souls.
Who steals my purse steals trash; 'tis something, nothing.
'Twas mine, 'tis his, and has been slave to thousands.

But he that filches from me my good name
Robs me of that which not enriches him,
And makes me poor indeed.

"Where's your lovely shadow? Or is the fair Lieutenant Pim hiding behind a tree?" asked Calvino, as he sat down beside Pratt on the bench.

"She's gone on to a new assignment."

Calvino nodded, looking at the water.

"A woman with high ambitions."

Pratt placed the bookmark into the volume and closed it.

"It's a long play. The script is still being written. New characters, new plots, new motives," he said.

"I should have seen the Ballard thing coming," said Calvino. "Him showing up in Bali was no chance meeting. He was on assignment, and we were his business. Think of it from their perspective. We were in Rangoon together. You had a thing with the wrong woman, someone with a connection to a big-time drug dealer."

"I cleared that inside the department a long time ago."

Calvino raised an eyebrow as if to ask whether Pratt really believed it was cleared as opposed to kicked down the road.

"Ballard and some other people had other ideas."

"But there was nothing to find," said Pratt.

"That hardly matters. Once people make up their minds there is something, they keep on looking even after it's clear they're chasing their own tails."

"You still don't believe it was Ballard they pulled out of the river?"

Calvino shrugged, leaned forward and stared at the lake.

"Ballard made a big play that his problems started with an art exhibition in London. His photograph was all over the Internet. Whether he set it up that way or was a victim, there's no way he could go back in the field. He needed a new identity, but first he had to die."

"He needed help to make the arrangements," Pratt suggested. "Finding an unclaimed body from the morgue."

"That works," said Calvino. "The Alphabets must have had a senior guy in your department. Otherwise there would be too many loose ends. Any idea who that might have been?"

"His name doesn't matter. He's been removed."

"Removed? Or transferred to an inactive post?"

"Let's call him General Sor. He was removed. Peace, order and work efficiency were the official reasons. There's more. A criminal investigation has started into his links with trafficking in the South. And according to Manee, his wife has left him. She would know. His wife was on the fountain restoration committee."

"Who burned him?" asked Calvino.

Pratt shrugged.

"I don't know. There were no fingerprints. He no longer served their interests. You were getting too close to the truth. That likely explains why they backed off."

"General Sor did his best to set me up for a murder charge."

"People like him don't play nice, but don't take it personally. He tried to set me up, too," said Pratt. "What matters is he's gone. He won't be coming back."

"The day Davenport and Howard came to my office, Davenport asked me why I had high-level encryption on my cell phone and office computers. I asked him how he had that information. He just looked at me, that dead-eyed stare. Howard said, 'How does some second-rate private dick from Brooklyn who's nothing more than a glorified skip chaser have access to encryption that even the NSA doesn't have?' From his tone of voice, I got the impression it was something he'd thought about. People who use highly specialized systems must be hiding something. They keep their information private, and that's the ultimate crime to the likes of Howard. Loyal citizens don't worry about who's reading their emails because they have nothing to hide. They should share improvements to encrypted programs so the good guys can stay a couple of steps ahead of the bad guys. They believe Marley is secretive, and they want to know her secrets. That's what they hate about her and about me, too. 'Whatever she's got on you, it's not worth betraying your country'—those were Davenport's words. Davenport wasn't the kind of guy who could string together more than three or four words without running out of gas, and there he was making a little speech to let me know they've failed to crack my contacts or read my email, and they're taking it personally."

"Marley's encryption program was a red flag to them," said Pratt.

"Howard and Davenport aren't important. They're just the face."

"Whose face, Vincent?"

"The face of the deep state, the double state, the one that runs like an operating system in the background. They work out of the embassy in Bangkok. They work with their counterparts here. People like you and me, if we're not useful, are just things that get in their way. A coup brings them into the spotlight. They were there all along. We just didn't see them."

"You are innocent, Vincent. It's always been a big part of your charm."

"Like the dumb leper who lost the bell around his neck years ago but no one had the heart to tell him."

"That sounds like Graham Greene," said Pratt. "Once a leper, always a leper. The bell no longer matters."

"I was making it easy for them. Someone working inside the deep state in Thailand or in Washington saw an opportunity. Real politics happens in that dark place where the light doesn't shine. That's where you find the people who make all the workarounds. With the system broken, workarounds are all we've got now."

"You want something, Vincent?"

"General Sor's real name."

"What use would that information be to you?"

"He was someone who hated the idea you returned and received a promotion. My leper's bell is ringing, telling me your guy was someone who trained with the FBI and then became an asset. Was Ballard his handler, or Howard? It doesn't matter who he ran errands for, does it? Someone decided—one stone, two birds. A body is fished out of the Chao Phraya River. They say it's Ballard and try to pin a murder rap on me. Only Ballard isn't dead. He's disappeared into a new identity. And General Pratt, my close personal friend, is implicated in covering up the murder. The scandal is leaked. You're forced out of the department again, only this time for good, and I'm frog-marched between a couple of US marshals back to the States on a murder charge."

"It nearly worked," said Pratt. "Only it wasn't me who discovered the link between the General, Ballard and the two agents stationed at the embassy. Ballard met him when they trained at Quantico."

Calvino exhaled, shaking his head.

"Marley."

"She had their cell phone conversations. She had something more powerful, too. She had taped their meeting where they planned the operation."

"And Howard and Davenport?"

"She had all of it. I couldn't protect you, but she did."

"All of this over a couple of jazz festivals that made them suspicious," said Calvino. "They're paranoid, and what do people like that do? They build a plausible story of conspiracy to prove they're right. It didn't matter that none of it was true. It was plausible. They thought you were hiding behind the saxophone and festivals while masterminding a drug cartel. They invented a story linking Rangoon, Jakarta, Bali and Bangkok. They'd written you down as the drug kingpin who had expanded your connections with a Rohingya smuggling group. With my encryption software, I was making the calls they couldn't trace or tap. You were forced into retirement because your own department wouldn't believe you. Then came the coup and your friends in the department found a way to bring you back. But someone inside convinced someone at the embassy that you used dirty money to buy your way back. Your enemy inside the department got them to believe that you'd bought your way back into the department.

"Pratt, this guy did everything in his power to bury you. Davenport was his shovel. Once they restarted that huge machine of a backdoor investigation, no evidence or facts could stop it from acquiring resources, people or an updated operational plan. The assembly belt kept getting longer and longer, and the engine running it speeded up. Ballard wanted out. It didn't have to make any logical sense; it just had to feed the original premise: that you and I were up to no good. Even if that weren't true, why risk the chance it was true?"

"Why would Ballard have left *The Quiet American* behind for you, and the note?" asked Pratt. "What was his game?"

"I've thought about that. Osborne said Ballard had questioned him about me."

"Osborne as a character reference. I'll try to digest that one."

"He told Ballard that I was an okay guy, and that he liked me. That I played fair."

"The book was his way to give you a sporting chance."

"Maybe he didn't like being used. He knew I was clean and so were you. But everything was being driven by politics.

From what Osborne said, Ballard didn't think much of DEA political types who had other alphabet agencies working with them. Ballard didn't have any choice. He couldn't stop them, but he could warn me."

Pratt looked at his watch.

"I applied for a leave of absence."

"So that's why you're out of uniform."

Pratt shook his head.

"The application was denied."

"You've left the department?"

"They don't really need me. It was a mistake on both sides."

"Why are you looking at your watch, Pratt?"

Pratt opened his briefcase and removed Calvino's office-warming gift, the plaque with the Shakespeare quote from *Othello*:

The robbed that smiles steals something from the thief;
He robs himself that spends a bootless grief.

"When I cleared out my desk, I found this in a drawer. It should have been on top of my desk from day one. The fact that I hid it gives me grief."

He handed to Calvino.

"Keep it for the beach house, Pratt."

Pratt took in a deep breath and glanced up at the sky.

"If I were a betting man, I'd wager that Marley isn't finished. She'll dox everyone linked to the Rohingya smuggling network. General Sor was the first. It won't take much to turn it into a full-scale purge. A lot of people are running scared."

Calvino grinned. The year before she'd released the names of girlfriends, *giks*, minor wives and escorts associated with ranking officers.

"Yeah, I bet people are afraid," Calvino said, "and they should be. If General Sor couldn't stop her with his connections, who's gonna be their papa?"

"She'll target them one by one, until not one of them involved in the Rohingya trafficking is left."

A chilling coolness in Pratt's voice conveyed the inevitability of what would happen. Pratt had painted himself out of the picture. When he'd returned to the department, he had seen what was coming, and that the pressure would be on him to stop her. The best way to stop Marley had been through Calvino. General Sor had run to the Americans for protection, but they couldn't help him, or wouldn't. The gamble hadn't paid off and no one could stop an excavation into a buried mountain of bones. Already a team had begun assembling the skeletons.

"You can't be sure it's Marley," said Calvino.

"With Marley no one can be sure, but let me ask you: do you believe for a moment that she's not behind this purge? No one can stop her. Not me, not you, not the Americans. She uncovered the detailed information about the Rohingya trafficking. She knows who was involved."

Calvino had discovered over the years that most people gathered information by using either the pig or the oyster technique. The smart pig had an uncanny ability to find truffles. The pig's attention focused on locating where the truffles were buried. Marley found General Sor's role in the trafficking, like a truffle, unearthed his involvement and displayed it for all to see. The second model, the oyster, was just as effective—it only required a single grain of sand clutched inside a wet, soft surface, and over time, with the right chemical reactions and tidal forces, layer after layer would wrap around the grain until a pearl formed. She must have gone through oceans of big data, wrapping her grain of sand, until General Sor jumped out as a fully formed pearl.

Marley's genius had been to evolve hundreds of pigs and oysters into algorithms and send them digging and layering, finding truffles and producing pearls, until the buckets overflowed. No one had ever seen so many truffles and pearls in one place. No one knew what to make of such a bounty or how to process all the corrupt officials swimming among the pigs and oysters.

"You're leaving the department because you can see how this is going to end."

"There's a line from King Claudius in *Hamlet*: 'Revenge should have no bounds.' "

"She's discovered new frontiers beyond the old revenge map," said Calvino.

Pratt smiled.

"Remember on the beach you said the department and I were like mismatched socks? You were right. I pretended we matched, and they did their part, too. But reality caught up with us. I feel like a fool. I should have seen this coming. It was a mistake for me to have left the beach house. I'm much better at growing orchids. I do well within those boundaries.

"I'm meeting Manee for lunch. Later we're driving back to Banglamung. Why don't you plan to come visit us this weekend? Bring Ratana along with you. You must hear Manee tell her story about the Generals' Wives Committee and the fish in the fountain. And I'll show you the latest orchid project I have in mind."

Calvino returned the smile and let it fade as he thought about Shakespeare's idea of revenge.

"Pratt, let me ask you something."

Pratt was still smiling.

"Do you believe in evil?"

"What do you mean?"

"Do you believe revenge can expel evil from the world? Did Shakespeare? That it was something a man could crush or cage?"

"What about you, Vincent?"

Pratt flashed a lawyer like smile.

"Answering a question with a question—I know that trick," said Calvino. "I don't think that evil can ever be eradicated. The seed is in all of us. You rip it out by killing some people. The revenge feels good, but it doesn't change anything. The seed grows somewhere else, changes shape, shift locations, like the tiny grain of sand that a black pearl grows from. Marley believes in the necessity of doing battle with evil. She knows no battle is decisive but still believes that not putting up a fight is a mistake. That's why she tried to help the Rohingyas."

"How did that work out?"

"Not so well."

Calvino looked at his watch and brought their discussion to an end.

"It's time for a drink."

THIRTY-NINE

"With relief, with humiliation, with terror, he understood that he too was a mere appearance, dreamt by another."—Jorge Luis Borges, *Labyrinths: Selected Stories and Other Writings*

"A fool tries to look different: a clever man looks the same and is different."
—John Buchan, *The Thirty-Nine Steps*

THE LOFT SPREAD out like a minor principality, curving elegantly, covering a territory of more than four hundred square meters. Gallery lighting, temperature control, air-conditioning compressors out of sight, and Bach's Sonata No. 2 filling the space from a system of hidden speakers. The open area, divided by temporary walls, had a strange arrangement of geometric spaces that only a mathematician could calculate, with angles leading to dead ends like wrong turns in a maze.

"Is this a museum?"

Yoshi smiled at Calvino.

"More like a private gallery. Museums suggest dead things. You'll discover everything you encounter here is very much alive."

Yoshi's guided tour started just inside the door. The unit occupied the entire twenty-second floor, and only a special key allowed the lift to stop there. He pointed his iPhone at one panel to activate the lights. Colors formed waterfalls of reds, blues, greens and yellows on the walls. The ceiling coned into a dome with concentric green and jasmine circular lines, changing places, jumping one over the other.

"Let me show you a series of walls you may find of interest."

The first wall had ancient maps hung beside digital maps that constantly updated in real time: for instance, a map of the world's current, growing population next to a map from the fifteenth century. Maps of the analog and digital worlds were hung side by side—one side fixed, static, permanent, the other side in constant flux, the borders, features and numbers continually changing. The walls had many themes such as political space, social space, economic space, technology, metals, mountains, rivers and climate.

Big-screen digital maps projected the Milky Way galaxy, our local system, nearby galaxies and the rest of the universe. Other walls featured regional maps: Europe, Africa, South America, North America and Asia. Yoshi showed Calvino the Southeast Asia wall. The wall displayed dozens of maps—some depicting political borderlines, others languages or ethnic populations, as they evolved through time. Ancient maps, maps from three hundred years ago, from colonial times and post-World War II.

"It's difficult to know where to start," said Yoshi. "But there is one map in particular I want to show you. I think you'll like it."

A digital map of Thai rivers, each river represented by a wiggly blue line registering motion shifts—the Mekong, Chao Phraya, Pong, Ramphan, Prachin, Nan, Salween, Pa Sak, Sakae Krang, Wang, Dom Noi, Ping, Tarang, Wa, Yai, Ing, Pao, Tha Chin and Tron. Yoshi explained to Calvino that the tributaries and rivers on the map shared a common destiny, one that carried them home either to the Gulf of Thailand or the Andaman Sea.

"If you want to understand the true nature of a people, read a map of their river system," said Yoshi. "Water is the story of life. The major rivers, from the Amazon to the Nile to the Mississippi waterways, add up to a library of human history. You can't know the story of change until you study a river system. We struggle to control the rivers. We dam them, divert them, build locks and canals. None of these attempts are new. Each generation learns that rivers are free to choose, and we can be carried along or we can resist and fight the current. The river, in the end, wins.

"The political river system looks like it is about to jump channels. Looking for new boundaries. That's what makes this a dangerous age. The old boundaries no longer hold people as before. They are porous and weak."

Calvino looked around, and in every direction were digital panels, holograms and virtual reality alcoves.

"This room is finite," he noted, "but the panels in it seem to go on forever."

Yoshi moved ahead to the next panel, featuring a neurological map, a DNA map and a human capillary map.

"The infinite within the finite. What we see is a small percentage of one percent of what has been mapped, measured, bounded, contained. What you see is a beginning."

Calvino followed Yoshi about twenty feet and entered a space different from the others, with old-fashioned tables and chairs and display cases. It was a perfect replica of a room at Bletchley Park Museum—rotary Bakelite telephone, desk and chair, a teddy bear dressed in bib overalls inside a glass case, a statue of Alan Turing seated at a table, his hands gripping a decoding machine. Hanging from the walls were duplicates of all twenty-nine of the Elite John photographs. As Calvino walked into the room, a chair turned around and there was Marley, sitting cross-legged, smiling, her blue eyes filled with life. Calvino had known women whose face radiated life; Marley had gone a step further, entered another level of being.

"It's a hologram, right?"

He turned to look at Yoshi, but Yoshi had already moved to Marley's side. The two exchanged a look.

"Vincent wants to know if you're real."

Ever since the coup, what was and was not real had become a political controversy.

"You're asking if I'm real? Is this place real?"

"Is it?"

"Marley," said Yoshi, "you've assembled this exhibition. You should explain it to Vincent."

"My dear curator, you are unusually modest," said Marley.

"You were Christina Tangier's patron," said Calvino.

"I gave her an idea," said Marley. "I thought it right to add *Crackdown: Teddy Occupies the 1%* to Alan Turing's room at Bletchley Park. What do you think, Vincent?"

Calvino moved among the exhibits and the photos, Marley watching him as he stood before each one. He turned to her.

"Marley, what are you doing here? I get it that you're famous and complicated, and I like complicated women, but this..."

"This is for you."

He turned around with his hands stretched out, palms up.

"You've been generous. The rare map, the Hong Kong Harbor show. You uploaded an encryption so powerful that the best minds at NSA couldn't crack it. And now you bring me to this place. I've been thinking about all these gifts, your interventions like a fairy godmother—not a lover, but a protector—and asking why. Then I figured it out. Why you stayed in the background. Unnoticed. Paying attention but remaining invisible. It was your way of showing love, in the only way you knew how. To make yourself a part of not just my life, but the way I thought about life and about myself."

"You taught me something about myself, Vincent."

"What could I possibility have taught you?"

"When a man really loves a woman, he gives her the space to cultivate her garden, even when it takes her far away. You let me go. That was the greatest gift of all because if you'd asked me to stay, I would have."

"You should have left me to handle Osborne and Ballard," he said.

"Solving a murder requires better tools than those used by the murderers."

Marley's fingers danced over a control panel in the arm of the chair, and a map lowered from the ceiling. It bore the legend "Ballard Map Co-ordinates."

"It's his digital history: schools, friends, family, teachers, coaches, employers, wives, girlfriends, banks, insurance, medical, dental, preferences, likes, address book, fingerprints, literary tastes, associations, links and connections to on-the-record and off-the-record agencies, and their connections to each other. A person's life is like a river flowing into the sea. All the small streams that feed into canals and rivers show the direction of a life, where it overflowed the banks and when it went parched and dry, on its rush to meet the sea."

"How did you get this information?"

"NSA files are less secure than you'd expect. They have millions of files, and a forest of trees to patrol, prune, cut, replant and modify. Trees of generals, admirals, prime ministers, dictators, moguls, inventors, politicians, writers, scientists, intellectuals, academics and the wealthy. Think of Google Maps but with thousands of times more detail and resolution, all of it automatically updated every second with every phone call, email, Internet search, tweet, Facebook comment, 'like' and retweet."

"Have you seen yours?" he asked.

She smiled.

"They have the tree, and I've let them grow it."

The screen filled with the tree of information on Pratt.

"You'll recognize your friend's tree. You'll see yourself, Ratana and Manee in the structure. And here's the one for Ballard."

Ballard's tree had a gnarled root structure, jumbled, overlapping and tapering into nothingness, and above the ground, hundreds of branches created the body of a huge tree. It looked like the Bodhi Tree near Marley's seafront house in Chon Buri—the tree the locals called the Marriage Tree, where wedding dresses were hung for the spiritual union of a dead young girl with her pop-singer suitor. Monks performed the ceremony of marriage, and Marley had placed a dress for her own unborn daughter in that place.

"It looks like a Bodhi Tree."

Marley tilted her head.

"His personal Bodhi Tree."

"Are you going to show me mine?"

"And if I did, what would you choose to see? How the tree is also a river emptying into the sea?"

"You mean dying?"

"Rivers don't die, Vincent. The old saying is you can never step into the same river twice. The water moves; it's never still. Water enters the system and finds its way to the ocean. We are those streams and rivers."

She rose from the chair, walked over and kissed him on the lips.

"Hi, Vinny," she said. "Let me show you something else."

She stopped in front of Ballard's mental map.

"This one is difficult to decode without knowing what shaped the mind."

"Is Ballard alive or dead? And don't give me some uncertainty-principle mumbo jumbo for an answer. He's not a cat."

Marley responded with a laugh.

"A practical man who avoids ambiguity. That surprises me, but why should it? I'll give you an answer but not now. The probability is that Ballard is alive and on a remote island off the coast of Africa."

"Madagascar?"

Osborne had met him there. Osborne had been the middleman in an aborted yacht deal involving Ballard and another foreigner, only the deal had collapsed after the coup. Osborne had flown his young bride to Madagascar.

"You're visualizing new branches growing on Ballard's Bodhi Tree, Vinny."

She had him dead to rights. He wasn't going to lie and deny it. He felt himself inside not so much a room but a mind space, and it seemed to generate an infinite number of maps in forms and shapes that never stayed stable. To examine one was to change some feature or detail, zooming in or out, as his attention followed a river, a fjord or a chain of mountains. Yoshi, hands unfolded, worked the electronic panel on the vacated chair, and Ballard's literary preferences appeared on the screen.

"When Ballard decided he wanted to escape, he turned to what he knew from a book he'd read in college, *Catch-22*," said Yoshi.

"Orr kept getting himself shot down over water so he could learn to escape."

Yoshi nodded.

"Orr was that exceptional mind who saw a way from the sea back to the river. He looked for a way to reverse his destiny. Everyone thought he was unlucky or crazy or both, but Orr was smarter than all of them. He'd found a way to avoid death. He came up with an escape plan that didn't look like one. He played the unlucky man well. Sound familiar?"

"Does it sound like Ballard?" asked Marley.

"So he pulled it off," said Calvino. "He found a way to tunnel out of the deep state, out of the forest. That was what he was running away from. Not the exhibition in New York. He was running from this grotesque forest like a fire warden who's seen an out-of-control blaze on the horizon."

"Letting the trees burn to save the forest is an old idea," said Marley. "Ballard wanted out."

"Before I thank you for getting the two agents from the embassy off my back, Marley, I have a question," said Calvino. "Did you know that they were setting me up? Ballard and I weren't exactly close. I hardly knew the guy. He showed up, disappeared, was dead, then wasn't dead. If he's alive in Madagascar and drinking Champagne with Osborne, it means I was set up to get sucker-punched from the day he walked into my condo."

"I couldn't be sure, Vinny. Ballard's path accidentally crossed mine when Christina Tangier photographed him. I found out who he really was, and he certainly wasn't one of the 'one percent.' I asked Christina to include him after I found and read his field reports about meeting you and Pratt in Bali. You have to trust me that I was doing what I thought was the right thing. I had no idea he'd come to Bangkok later."

It was the sort of defining moment with another person when one is called upon either to trust them or to double up on the arsenal of doubt and suspicion to defend oneself against attack.

"Okay, you didn't know," said Calvino. "Ballard isn't the first person to disappoint me, and he probably won't be the last. It's happened before and will happen again, unless I decide to stay out of the ring."

"The ring is an interesting metaphor. There's another map I'd like to show you before you decide whether you will be in or out of the ring."

Marley curled a long finger at Calvino.

"Follow me."

She didn't wait for an answer and walked ahead, weaving through one maze of temporary walls after another until they were deep into the interior of the room. When they arrived, Yoshi was already there, waiting. Calvino shook his head. He couldn't explain how the pair of them coordinated their appearances and disappearances. A mathematical shortcut; it had to be, thought Calvino.

On the screen was a map of the world with two sets of lines—one Oxford blue and one blood red—connecting cities, big and small, famous and obscure: New York, Big Sur, London, Barcelona, Madrid, Paris, Rangoon, Motihari, Mandalay, Berlin, Moscow and Rome. Bangkok, off in a bottom corner of the digital map, had neither a blue nor red connecting line. The map legend showed Henry Miller's picture wearing a hat cocked to the side, staring out. The red line was his—New York, Paris, Cyprus and Big Sur. George Orwell's blue line connected cities in Europe and Asia.

"In Rangoon, you had a crisis," said Yoshi.

"I admit, I lost something," said Calvino. "I've been trying to find my way back ever since to figure out what went missing there."

"Nothing went missing. You woke up in Rangoon, Vinny," said Marley. "And I believe you still haven't realized what that means."

After the Rangoon murders something had shifted inside Calvino's consciousness. The direction and force and depth of the violent deaths had stripped him of his certainty about how he understood the world and himself. It was as if a stranger had taken up residence in his mind. If life really was a river, as Yoshi said, then his river had lost any hope of reaching the sea. When he'd first met Yoshi and Marley, he was still struggling with it. It was his most vulnerable time, and these two new figures in his life had found something in him they thought worth salvaging. They had rallied in his corner of the ring and given him the strength to finish the fight, and they were still rallying around him.

"You are walking knee deep in a political river," Yoshi said, "and the current is swift, carrying people away. And you're wondering…"

"Am I going under?" asked Calvino.

"How will I survive? How can I escape?" asked Marley. "Those are reasonable questions to ask. And when you sleep, the questions find you again, when your defenses are down."

"Henry Miller questions," said Calvino.

"When Henry Miller set off for France," said Yoshi, "he felt an emotional release. Call it freedom. Miller thought that he'd disconnected from all of the ties that bound him to America. You know that moment, Vincent. All expats experience it. When you learn that the truth of life isn't exactly what you thought it to be.

"He also realized at the end of his Paris days that he'd traded one set of boundaries for another. Falling in love with another culture and place is like finding a new woman after a messy divorce. At first she seems unbounded in her love and purity, but after a few years the traveler realizes that all relationships, at the end of the day, pretty much end up the same. Henry Miller returned to America. One of Miller's Paris friends once wrote that Miller never looked back on his Paris days."

"He went home. But I've never left Bangkok," said Calvino.

"Have you ever wondered whether the exchange of New York boundaries for Thai ones was a fair trade?" said Yoshi.

"You don't move forward looking in the rearview mirror."

"Or maybe you're closer to Orwell, the most famous of literary boundary crossers in fiction and non-fiction. He emptied his elephant gun. When the smoke cleared, Orwell saw that people always long for a man in uniform to raise his gun and fire a deadly round to show his power. The deep state has flourished because the mob wants it."

"Orwell was a political man," said Marley. "Only a political man would think it was possible to wean the mob from their tyrants. What do you believe, Vinny?"

" 'Forget it, Jake. It's Orwell,' " said Calvino.

"Orwell is Chinatown," said Marley. "Always has been the guide to how powerlessness feels and fear works."

"It's 'Forget it, Jake. It's Henry Miller's world and his world was definitely not Chinatown.' "

Marley nodded.

"No, nothing evil ever happens in Miller's world."

"The Black Cat would be alive if she'd followed Henry Miller," said Calvino. "All she had to do was accept that the deep state is also inside each of us, and no matter how we try, it can never be defeated. The deep state is always underneath. We only detect it from the endless cycles of violence and injustice that follow power plays. We only catch a glimpse of it as it runs between the shadows."

"If the choice is between the American Henry Miller, an escape artist, hustler, and sensualist, or the Englishman George Orwell, a Barcelona street fighter, champion of the underdog and British colonial official, who would you choose?" said Marley.

"I want to be both," said Calvino.

"You can't be the Irrawaddy and the Mekong rivers at

the same time," said Marley. "And what if both Miller and Orwell were mapmakers who are now sixty years out of date," she asked, "and they've missed rivers we've discovered since then, and uncharted rivers, too?"

Yoshi smiled patiently as Calvino drifted into thought.

"What Marley means is we are always moving to a place that can't be mapped," he said.

"What's the name of this place? What are these uncharted rivers?" asked Calvino. "Are they guarded by dragons?"

"It's a place that isn't a place. A river that is all rivers."

"We don't live in that world," said Calvino.

"That's where you're wrong. We are part of that world, even though we don't understand it. It connects to us and we connect to it."

"Vincent, do you remember Anaïs Nin?" said Marley. "She helped Miller understand the mental neighborhoods of Paris. She gave him a magical passkey to open the mystery of its ways to him. What more love can a woman show to a man than to give him that gift? George Orwell had no Anaïs Nin in his life. Political men don't need such a woman. But a sensual man needs an Anaïs Nin or he'll be lost in confused thoughts, sitting at the end of the bar."

"And that's why you brought me here? To let me know that you've appointed yourself my Anaïs Nin?"

"Henry Miller would never have been Henry Miller without her," Marley said. "He needed a partner, even though he never acknowledged her as one."

"Anaïs Nin gave Miller a choice," Calvino said.

"You have the free will to send me away."

Calvino looked around, wondering how to respond. He had no idea how the three of them had got to this panel or even the direction of the door they had entered from. Whatever elements made up freedom, he wasn't feeling them inside this space.

"I need to get back."

Yoshi and Marley smiled, and Marley leaned over and hugged Calvino.

"That's the point of this room. We all want to find our way back. To decode our lives as we live them. That's why I've brought you to Bletchley Park: to understand that Turing's work was never finished."

"You've decided to finish it?"

"To make a contribution," she said.

"Where do I come in, Marley?"

Marley slipped her hand into his.

"In your great-grandfather's painting, where is the man running to? Was he running toward something or away from someone? The New Year celebration had started. What was his hurry, when everyone else was standing still as if waiting? He left us with those questions. Maybe there is no answer, and we can only imagine what was inside the runner's mind."

"Have you ever gone to a racetrack?" Calvino asked. "Stood in the stands and watched the horses before a race? You watch the horses prancing in front of the starting gate, each one filled with spirit, adrenaline pumping through their veins. You feel the tension working through their muscles and guts. They're gonna run the way they're gonna run. No one goes to the racetrack just to watch. You place a bet on the winner. How they run and how you bet on them are two different things that a lot of people confuse in their minds. You've put a bet on the runner and on me. So if you don't mind my asking, what's your take on the runner?"

"That he's free of the illusion. He understands there's no finish line to cross. He's not watching from the stands. He's in the race. He's saying, catch me if you can. The painting is a prophecy about freedom. You can choose your race, but you can never know how it will run."

"You like betting on long shots?" asked Calvino.

She nodded.

"As with your great-grandfather, Galileo Chini, it's a race you've been running your entire life. I'm betting you'll never stop. How many more times do you need to experience it before the message sinks in?"

Calvino ran. His chest pounded as he skirted around the partitions, through the manifold colored screens, the ancient paintings and the concentric circles on the ceiling dome changing overhead. The smell of cordite, dank water and death mixed into a suffocating brew. He stopped to catch his breath, leaning against a chair, his hands pressed against the headrest. He looked around. Neither Marley nor Yoshi had followed. He circled through the maze for what seemed like hours and never found the entrance. Somewhere there had to be a map of maps, a map of this room. He ran from partition to partition until he was exhausted. When he could go no farther, he cried out, "I'm lost!"

There was no answer. Calvino shouted Marley's name. He saw the face of every man he'd ever killed, the eyes of every woman he'd ever loved, and heard the voice of every friend who'd ever called his name. When he turned around, he saw the door he'd come through with Yoshi. He pulled it open and it was a clear, bright day outside, the sky blue, the grass green, and there was Munny holding the baseball. He tossed it to Calvino, who caught it with one hand.

"It's good to be free," Munny said.

When Calvino opened his eyes, he sat up in his bed. Outside his window the sunrays touched the surface of Lake Ratchada. Early morning joggers were tiny figures on the track around the lake. He rolled out of bed and walked into the sitting area, breathing naturally, slowly, and looking at the framed map that Marley had given him.

He looked at it through Ballard's eyes. Then he saw it through Fah's eyes, and those of Osborne and Yoshi and Marley. He ran through the roll call—Rob Osborne, the Black Cat, Munny, McPhail, Pratt, Ratana and Manee, each one embedded as a different mystery inside the same enclosed territory. Through all of those eyes, he stared at the map as if seeing it the first time. Marley's gift, a kind of Bodhi Tree, alive and growing in his sitting room.

One thing Davenport had said still troubled him. He'd said Philip Marlowe wouldn't have lasted a day working in Bangkok today. That time was over. He knew that if it hadn't been for Dr. Marley Solberg watching his back, he'd have been caught in the ropes of life by now and pulled under. They'd tried to break him from Marley. It hadn't worked. She remained, despite their efforts, a daily presence in his life. What had been the bond? He'd been a fool not to see how she'd done it. Only then did it come to Calvino. It was the map. He'd caught Ballard staring at it, asking questions. Maybe he knew something he wasn't at liberty to discuss. Maybe he was a quiet American.

Calvino pulled the frame from the wall. He crossed the room, opened a drawer, then another drawer until he found a box cutter. He returned to the frame, flipped it over and used the box cutter to carefully slice through the back fabric. He removed it, exposing the back mat. It wasn't made from the usual wood pulp. He tapped it with his knuckle. Silicon. Next he slowly removed the map, set it on the table and turned to extracting the mat board that had fit flush against the glazing. Like the back mat, the mat board was constructed from layers of silicon.

He took it to the balcony and held it up to catch the sunlight, illuminating an infinite number of pinpricks across the surface. When he placed the back mat and mat board together, he saw how they'd been connected by a series of sensors the size of a nail head. The tiny transponder nodes had remotely relayed real-time information. But it was more than a relay; it had gone deep into his sleeping mind. Marley had constructed a sky bridge to his dream state. She'd designed an Alan Turing Enigma machine, one equipped to decode his thoughts in wakefulness and sleep. A mind hack, a direct feed, a communication technology so skillfully conceived, designed and implanted that it was undetectable. DARPA had wanted that network. No matter how many rabbit holes they went down looking for Marley, she was always someplace else. From a dozen other places she watched them poking about like slow children in their confusion, anger and need. They would never find her.

Whose company had he been keeping? Calvino wondered. He smiled as he realized that the ones who had come to his dreams had been wise. The old Thai saying about thugs and wise men had its exception, which went like this: wise men sometimes fail. In other words, no one could guarantee that the wise would succeed, even if the thugs were sidelined.

Calvino agreed with what Munny had said just as he woke up from his dream, that it was good to feel free. But to be awake in a world of tracking apps, sensors, databases, algorithms, nanotechnology and super-intelligent enhancements was to enter another kind of dream, one where being free to choose, like the certainty of the wise man's judgment, lost its core meaning. For Calvino, freedom, like wisdom, had only been a feeling, an illusion that coiled around what appeared to be real, and in the cold light of day he'd been revealed to be no more than any other river on its way to the sea.

The struggle was less about free will versus choice than a lesson in resilience to the hardships of the journey. Getting up after falling down—that took courage. Accepting that the best of us can fail—that took wisdom. It was hard to admit that the world's most experienced runners were still learning to walk, taking baby steps while pretending to be sprinters. Calvino had stayed on as their audience. Like Turing's teddy bear, he had once been a wise person's exclusive audience.

The teddy bear's journey from private wise man's quarters to a museum to the conceptual art world had delivered a personal message—the best of all runners never had enough time or ability to explore anything more than a fraction of the hidden rivers and mountains. They always came up short of a finished map. It took a teddy bear to tell that story, to teach that lesson. Calvino stood on his balcony looking out at the city. When he glanced down at the white Chinese slippers with red dragons on his feet, Calvino smiled. Dragonflies, he thought. Even after a hundred years the Bangkok skyline was still lit once a year by Chinese fireworks, and it was forever New Year on the runner's personal map of the world. And Calvino, a one-man audience, breathed in the hot tropical air and began a new day.

ACKNOWLEDGMENTS

Over the many drafts of *Crackdown*, a number of people have provided me with useful and insightful comments and suggestions: Michaela Striewski, Mike Herrin, Charles McHugh, and Chad Evans. They dedicated many hours reading an earlier draft and their contribution assisted me greatly.

Colin Cotterill created the memorable artistic illusions that are included in the book. His vision has channeled the Banksy-like street art vision where imagination and creativity meet the rotary blade of politics.

My wife, Busakorn Suriyasarn, read with patience and care, and as usual provided her advice on how best to mine the hidden mysteries of Thai culture and language, making certain the Thai aspects of the story were authentic.

I have dedicated this book to Steven A. Samuels who, along with his team at FilmNation, has been dedicated into making the Vincent Calvino series into a feature film or TV series.

SPIRIT HOUSE
First in the series
Heaven Lake Press (2004) ISBN 974-92389-3-1

The Bangkok police already have a confession by a nineteen-year-old drug addict who has admitted to the murder of a British computer wizard, Ben Hoadly. From the bruises on his face shown at the press conference, it is clear that the young suspect had some help from the police in the making of his confession. The case is wrapped up. Only there are some loose ends that the police and just about everyone else are happy to overlook.

The search for the killer of Ben Hoadley plunges Calvino into the dark side of Bangkok, where professional hit men have orders to stop him. From the world of thinner addicts, dope dealers, fortunetellers, and high-class call girls, Calvino peels away the mystery surrounding the death of the English ex-public schoolboy who had a lot of dubious friends.

"Well-written, tough and bloody."
—Bernard Knight, *Tangled Web* (UK)

"A thinking man's Philip Marlowe, Calvino is a cynic on the surface but a romantic at heart. Calvino ... found himself in Bangkok—the end of the world—for a whole host of bizarre foreigners unwilling, unable, or uninterested in going home."—*The Daily Yomiuri*

"Good, that there are still real crime writers. Christopher G. Moore's [*Spirit House*] is colorful and crafty."
—*Hessischer Rundfunk* (Germany)

ASIA HAND
Second in the series
Heaven Lake Press (2000) ISBN 974-87171-2-7
Winner of 2011 Shamus Award
for Best Original Paperback

Bangkok—the Year of the Monkey. Calvino's Chinese New Year celebration is interrupted by a call to Lumpini Park Lake, where Thai cops have just fished the body of a farang cameraman. CNN is running dramatic footage of several Burmese soldiers on the Thai border executing students.

Calvino follows the trail of the dead man to a feature film crew where he hits the wall of silence. On the other side of that wall, Calvino and Colonel Pratt discover and elite film unit of old Asia Hands with connections to influential people in Southeast Asia. They find themselves matched against a set of farangs conditioned for urban survival and willing to go for a knock-out punch.

"Highly recommended to readers of hard-boiled detective fiction"—*Booklist*

"Asia Hand is the kind of novel that grabs you and never lets go."—*The Times of India*

"Moore's stylish second Bangkok thriller ... explores the dark side of both Bangkok and the human heart. Felicitous prose speeds the action along."—*Publishers Weekly*

"Fast moving and hypnotic, this was a great read."
—*Crime Spree Magazine*

ZERO HOUR IN PHNOM PENH
Third in the series
Heaven Lake Press (2005) ISBN 974-93035-9-8
Winner of 2004 German Critics Award for Crime Fiction (Deutscher Krimi Preis) for best international crime fiction and 2007 Premier Special Director's Award Semana Negra (Spain)

In the early 1990s, at the end of the devastating civil war UN peacekeeping forces try to keep the lid on the violence. Gunfire can still be heard nightly in Phnom Penh, where Vietnamese prostitutes try to hook UN peacekeepers from the balcony of the Lido Bar.

Calvino traces leads on a missing farang from Bangkok to war-torn Cambodia, through the Russian market, hospitals, nightclubs, news briefings, and UNTAC headquarters. Calvino's buddy, Colonel Pratt, knows something that Calvino does not: the missing man is connected with the jewels stolen from the Saudi royal family. Calvino quickly finds out that he is not the only one looking for the missing farang.

"Political, courageous and perhaps Moore's most important work."—*CrimiCouch.de*

"An excellent whodunnit hardboiled, a noir novel with a solitary, disillusioned but tempting detective, an interesting historical and social context (of post-Pol Pot Cambodia), and a very thorough psychology of the characters."
—*La culture se partage*

"A bursting, high adventure ... Extremely gripping ... A morality portrait with no illusion."
—Ulrich Noller, *Westdeutscher Rundfunk*

COMFORT ZONE
Fourth in the series
Heaven Lake Press (2001) ISBN 974-87754-9-6

Twenty years after the end of the Vietnam War, Vietnam is opening to the outside world. There is a smell of fast money in the air and poverty in the streets. Business is booming and in austere Ho Chi Minh City a new generation of foreigners have arrived to make money and not war. Against the backdrop of Vietnam's economic miracle, *Comfort Zone* reveals a taut, compelling story of a divided people still not reconciled with their past and unsure of their future.

Calvino is hired by an ex-special forces veteran, whose younger brother uncovers corruption and fraud in the emerging business world in which his clients are dealing. But before Calvino even leaves Bangkok, there have already been two murders, one in Saigon and one in Bangkok.

"Calvino digs, discovering layers of intrigue. He's stalked by hired killers and falls in love with a Hanoi girl. Can he trust her? The reader is hooked."
—*NTUC Lifestyle* (Singapore)

"Moore hits home with more of everything in *Comfort Zone*. There is a balanced mix of story-line, narrative, wisdom, knowledge as well as love, sex, and murder."
—*Thailand Times*

"Like a Japanese gardener who captures the land and the sky and recreates it in the backyard, Moore's genius is in portraying the Southeast Asian heartscape behind the tourist industry hotel gloss."—*The Daily Yomiuri*

THE BIG WEIRD
Fifth in the series
Heaven Lake Press (2008) ISBN 978-974-8418-42-1

A beautiful American blond is found dead with a large bullet hole in her head in the house of her ex-boyfriend. A famous Hollywood screenwriter hires Calvino to investigate her death. Everyone except Calvino's client believes Samantha McNeal has committed suicide.

In the early days of the Internet, Sam ran with a young and wild expat crowd in Bangkok: a Net-savvy pornographer, a Thai hooker plotting to hit it big in cyberspace, an angry feminist with an agenda, a starving writer-cum-scam artist, a Hollywoord legend with a severe case of The Sickness. As Calvino slides into a world where people are dead serious about sex, money and fame, he unearths a hedonistic community where the ritual of death is the ultimate high.

"An excellent read, charming, amusing, insightful, complex, localized yet startlingly universal in its themes."
—*Guide of Bangkok*

"Highly entertaining."—*Bangkok Post*

"A good read, fast-paced and laced with so many of the locales so familiar to the expat denizens of Bangkok."
—*Art of Living* (Thailand)

"Like a noisy, late-night Thai restaurant, Moore serves up tongue-burning spices that swallow up the literature of Generation X and cyberpsace as if they were merely sticky rice."—*The Daily Yomiuri*

COLD HIT
Sixth in the series
Heaven Lake Press (2004) ISBN 974-920104-1-7

Five foreigners have died in Bangkok. Were they drug overdose victims or victims of a serial killer? Calvino believes the evidence points to a serial killer who stalks tourists in Bangkok. The Thai police, including Calvino's best friend and buddy Colonel Pratt, don't buy his theory.

Calvino teams up with an LAPD officer on a bodyguard assignment. Hidden forces pull them through swank shopping malls, rundown hotels, Klong Toey slum, and the Bangkok bars as they try to keep their man and themselves alive. As Calvino learns more about the bodies being shipped back to America, the secret of the serial killer is revealed.

"The story is plausible and riveting to the end."
—*The Japan Times*

"Tight, intricate plotting, wickedly astute ... *Cold Hit* will have you variously gasping, chuckling, nodding, tut-tutting, ohyesing, and grinding your teeth throughout its 330 pages."—*Guide of Bangkok*

"The plot is equally tricky, brilliantly devised, and clear. One of the best crime fiction in the first half of the year."
—*Ultimo Biedlefeld* (Germany)

"Moore depicts the city from below. He shows its dirt, its inner conflicts, its cruelty, its devotion. Hard, cruel, comical and good."—*Readme.de*

MINOR WIFE
Seventh in the series
Heaven Lake Press (2004) ISBN 974-92126-5-7

A contemporary murder set in Bangkok—a neighbor and friend, a young ex-hooker turned artist, is found dead by an American millionaire's minor wife. Her rich expat husband hires Calvino to investigate. While searching for the killer in exclusive clubs and not-so-exclusive bars of Bangkok, Calvino discovers that a minor wife—mia noi—has everything to do with a woman's status. From illegal cock fighting matches to elite Bangkok golf clubs, Calvino finds himself caught in the crossfire as he closes in on the murderer.

"The thriller moves in those convoluted circles within which Thai life and society takes place. Moore's knowledge of these gives insights into many aspects of the cultural mores ... unknown to the expat population. Great writing, great story and a great read."—*Pattaya Mail*

"What distinguishes Christopher G. Moore from other foreign authors setting their stories in the Land of Smiles is how much more he understands its mystique, the psyche of its populace and the futility of its round residents trying to fit into its square holes."—*Bangkok Post*

"Moore pursues in even greater detail in *Minor Wife* the changing social roles of Thai women (changing, but not always quickly or for the better) and their relations among themselves and across class lines and other barriers."
—*Vancouver Sun*

PATTAYA 24/7
Eighth in the series
Heaven Lake Press (2008) ISBN 978-974-8418-41-4

Inside a secluded, lush estate located on the edge of Pattaya, an eccentric Englishman's gardener is found hanged. Calvino has been hired to investigate. He finds himself pulled deep into the shadows of the war against drugs, into the empire of a local warlord with the trail leading to a terrorist who has caused Code Orange alerts to flash across the screen of American intelligence.

In a story packed with twists and turns, Calvino traces the links from the gardener's past to the door of men with power and influence who have everything to lose if the mystery of the gardener's death is solved.

"Original, provocative, and rich with details and insights into the underworld of Thai police, provincial gangsters, hit squads, and terrorists."
—Pieke Bierman, award-wining author of *Violetta*

"Intelligent and articulate, Moore offers a rich, passionate and original take on the private-eye game, fans of the genre should definitely investigate, and fans of foreign intrigue will definitely enjoy."—Kevin Burton Smith, *January Magazine*

"A cast of memorably eccentric figures in an exotic Southeast Asian backdrop."—*The Japan Times*

"The best in the Calvino series ...The story is compelling."
—*Bangkok Post*

THE RISK OF INFIDELITY INDEX
Ninth in the series
Heaven Lake Press (2007) ISBN 974-88168-7-6

Major political demonstrations are rocking Bangkok. Chaos and fear sweep through the Thai and expatriate communities. Calvino steps into the political firestorm as he investigates a drug piracy operation. The piracy is traced to a powerful business interest protected by important political connections.

A nineteen-year-old Thai woman and a middle-age lawyer end up dead on the same evening. Both are connected to Calvino's investigation. The dead lawyer's law firm denies any knowledge of the case. Calvino is left in the cold. Approached by a group of expat housewives—rattled by *The Risk of Infidelity Index* that ranks Bangkok number one for available sexual temptations—to investigate their husbands, Calvino discovers the alliance of forces blocking his effort to disclose the secret pirate drug investigation.

"A hard-boiled, street-smart, often hilarious pursuit of a double murderer."—*San Francisco Chronicle*

"There's plenty of violent action ... Memorable low-life characters ... The real star of the book is Bangkok."
—*Telegraph* (London)

"Taut, spooky, intelligent, and beautifully written."
—T. Jefferson Parker

"A complex, intelligent novel."—*Publishers' Weekly*

"The darkly raffish Bangkok milieu is a treat."
—*Kirkus Review*

PAYING BACK JACK
Tenth in the series
Heaven Lake Press (2009) ISBN 978-974-312-920-9

In *Paying Back Jack*, Calvino agrees to follow the 'minor wife' of a Thai politician and report on her movements. His client is Rick Casey, a shady American whose life has been darkened by the unsolved murder of his idealistic son. It seems to be a simple surveillance job, but soon Calvino is entangled in a dangerous web of political allegiance and a reckless quest for revenge.

And, unknown to our man in Bangkok, in an anonymous tower in the center of the city, a two-man sniper team awaits its shot, a shot that will change everything. *Paying Back Jack* is classic Christopher G. Moore: densely-woven, eye-opening, and riveting.

"Crisp, atmospheric ... Calvino's cynical humour oils the wheels nicely, while the cubist plotting keeps us guessing."
—*The Guardian*

"The best Calvino yet ... There are many wheels within wheels turning in this excellent thriller."
—*The Globe and Mail*

"[*Paying Back Jack*] might be Moore's finest novel yet. A gripping tale of human trafficking, mercenaries, missing interrogation videos, international conspiracies, and revenge, all set against the lovely and sordid backstreets of Bangkok that Moore knows better than anyone."
—Barry Eisler, author of *Fault Line*

"Moore clearly has no fear that his gloriously corrupt Bangkok will ever run dry."—*Kirkus Review*

THE CORRUPTIONIST
Eleventh in the series
Heaven Lake Press (2010) ISBN 978-616-90393-3-4

Set during the recent turbulent times in Thailand, the 11th novel in the Calvino series centers around the street demonstrations and occupations of Government House in Bangkok. Hired by an American businessman, Calvino finds himself caught in the middle of a family conflict over a Chinese corporate takeover. This is no ordinary deal. Calvino and his client are up against powerful forces set to seize much more than a family business.

As the bodies accumulate while he navigates Thailand's business-political landmines, Calvino becomes increasingly entangled in a secret deal made by men who will stop at nothing—and no one—standing in their way but Calvino refuses to step aside. *The Corruptionist* captures with precision the undercurrents enveloping Bangkok, revealing multiple layers of betrayal and deception.

"Politics has a role in the series, more so now than earlier ... Thought-provoking columnists don't do it better."
—*Bangkok Post*

"Moore's understanding of the dynamics of Thai society has always impressed, but considering current events, the timing of his latest [*The Corruptionist*] is absolutely amazing."
—*The Japan Times*

"Entertaining and devilishly informative."
—Tom Plate, *Pacific Perspective*

"Very believable ... A brave book."—*Pattaya Mail*

9 GOLD BULLETS
Twelfth in the series
Heaven Lake Press (2011) ISBN 978-616-90393-7-2

A priceless collection of 9 gold bullet coins issued during the Reign of Rama V has gone missing along with a Thai coin collector. Local police find a link between the missing Thai coins and Calvino's childhood friend, Josh Stein, who happens to be in Bangkok on an errand for his new Russian client. This old friend and his personal and business entanglements with the Russian underworld take Calvino back to New York, along with Pratt.

The gritty, dark vision of *9 Gold Bullets* is tracked through the eyes of a Thai cop operating on a foreign turf, and a private eye expatriated long enough to find himself a stranger in his hometown. As the intrigue behind the missing coins moves between New York and Bangkok, and the levels of deception increase, Calvino discovers the true nature of friendship and where he belongs.

"Moore consistently manages to entertain without having to resort to melodramatics. The most compelling feature of his ongoing Calvino saga, in my view, is the symbiotic relationship between the American protagonist and his Thai friends, who have evolved with the series. The friendships are sometimes strained along cultural stress lines, but they endure, and the Thai characters' supporting roles are very effective in helping keep the narratives interesting and plausible."—*The Japan Times*

"Moore is a master at leading the reader on to what 'should' be the finale, but then you find it isn't...Worth waiting for... However, do not start reading until you have a few hours to spare."—*Pattaya Mail*

MISSING IN RANGOON
Thirteenth in the series
Heaven Lake Press (2013) ISBN 978-616-7503-17-2

As foreigners rush into Myanmar with briefcases stuffed with plans and cash for hotels, shopping malls and high rises, they discover the old ways die hard. Vincent Calvino's case is to find a young British-Thai man gone missing in Myanmar, while his best friend and protector Colonel Pratt of the Royal Thai Police has an order to cut off the supply of cold pills from Myanmar used for the methamphetamine trade in Thailand.

As one of the most noir novels in the Vincent Calvino series, Missing in Rangoon plays out beneath the moving shadows of the cross-border drug barons. Pratt and Calvino's lives are entangled with the invisible forces inside the old regime and their allies who continue to play by their own set of rules.

"[Moore's] descriptions of Rangoon are excellent. In particular, he excels at describing the human and social fallout that occurs when a poor, isolated country suddenly opens its borders to the world.... *Missing in Rangoon* is a satisfying read, a mixture of hard-boiled crime fiction and acute social observation set in a little known part of Asia."
—Andrew Nette, *Crime Fiction Lover*

"The story is delicious. Calvino gets a missing person's case that takes him to Myanmar (Burma), drugs are involved, and the plot takes several wonderful twists that keep the reader mesmerized... It's Moore at his best... Reading a book like *Missing in Rangoon* will open up a whole new world of knowledge that will help the reader to understand the element in the story that the newspaper—and reporter—dared not reveal." —*WoWasis Travelblog*

THE MARRIAGE TREE
Fourteenth in the series
Heaven Lake Press (2014) ISBN 978-616-7503-23-3

It's okay for Thais to believe in ghosts—it's their birthright. But why is Vincent Calvino seeing ghosts, and why are they so angry? Calvino is haunted by a series of deaths in Rangoon and Bangkok, when he stumbles onto a new murder case—but is it a new case, or an old one returned from the dead? A murder investigation leads Calvino inside an underworld network smuggling Rohingya out of illegal camps and detention centers. Calvino looks for the killer in the mystical Thai world of sword and marriage trees.

"[*The Marriage Tree*] will keep the reader up at night, though, as the action is fast-paced and full of enough twists to foment insomnia. For readers who loved Missing in Rangoon, this follow-on book provides something of a final resolution."
—wowais.com

"The plight of the Rohingya refugees has been documented many times, but never dramatised like this.... [W]hen a novelist brings his powers of description and sense of empathy to bear on such a subject, the wholehearted tragedy of these crimes against humanity hits home in a powerful way. The opening is riveting ... The plotting is taut and the pacing sharp."
—Jim Algie, The Nation

"*The Marriage Tree* is a top tier crime novel set in a top tier city, Bangkok, to be enjoyed by crime fiction readers everywhere."
—Kevin Cummings, *Chiang Mai City News*

Christopher G. Moore is a Canadian novelist and essayist who lives in Bangkok. He has written 26 novels, including the award-winning Vincent Calvino series and the Land of Smiles Trilogy. The German edition of his third Vincent Calvino novel, *Zero Hour in Phnom Penh*, won the German Critics Award (Deutsche Krimi Preis) for International Crime Fiction in 2004 and the Spanish edition of the same novel won the Premier Special Director's Book Award Semana Negra (Spain) in 2007. The second Calvino novel, *Asia Hand,* won the Shamus Award for Best Original Paperback in 2011.

CPSIA information can be obtained at www.ICGtesting.com
Printed in the USA
BVOW08s1312010615

402693BV00010B/26/P